It was all Jesse's fault.

Jesse and that damned hot mouth of his.

And now Tania's life was being shaken up. Shaken up for the first time since she'd consciously pulled her emotions out of the game, sealing them away.

She'd never lost herself before—lost the ability to think clearly. To function. For more than just a split second when Jesse kissed her at the door, her mind had gone blank and her body had grown hot. As for the longing...

Well, she just didn't do that. Didn't long for anyone. And yet...

Jesse had made her long.

Made her want...

Dear Reader,

Welcome back for the fourth installment of THE DOCTORS PULASKI. I cannot begin to tell you the memories working on this series brings back for me. I grew up in New York City—Queens specifically—and worked in a building that looked out on Radio City Music Hall. At lunchtime, I would walk the very streets I'm writing about now. And while the hospital where my dedicated doctors work is fictional, the Diamond District in the first chapter is very, very real.

Many a lunch hour was spent looking into windows along that route and sighing. The engagement ring my now-husband bought me came from one of those shops. After the purchase, he brought the ring right over because he was afraid of losing it, which is how I came to be engaged on the twenty-second floor of what was then The Equitable Building. You'll soon see why all this brings back fond memories for me.

In reading about Tatiana and Jesse, I hope their story sparks you into creating fond memories of your own.

As always, I thank you for reading and with all my heart, I wish you someone to love who loves you back.

Marie Ferrarella

MARIE FERRARELLA

A Doctor's Secret

Silhouette®
Romantic
SUSPENSE

SILHOUETTE BOOKS

ISBN-13: 978-0-373-27573-1
ISBN-10: 0-373-27573-0

A DOCTOR'S SECRET

MARIE FERRARELLA

This *USA TODAY* bestselling and RITA® Award-winning author has written more than 150 novels for Silhouette Books, some under the name Marie Nicole. Her romances are beloved by fans worldwide. Readers can visit her Web site at www.marieferrarella.com.

To Misiu and Marek, and growing up in New York City.
Love, Marysia

Chapter 1

"Stop, thief!"

When he looked back at it later, Jesse Steele would have to say those words had ultimately changed his life. Had he not heard them, he probably would have never met her.

It was an overcast Manhattan late spring morning and he was worried about rain. That, and making the meeting on time.

One moment he was taking a shortcut through New York's famous Diamond District. He had to hurry because New York's more famous traffic was making it impossible for him to get back to his office in time for the one o'clock meeting with the senior partners of the architectural firm of Bryce, Newcomb and Tuttle. The next moment he was breaking into a run, charging down the crowded sidewalk and then tackling a rather upscale but guilty-looking man running from the scene.

The rather elderly distinguished man who had uttered the cry stood in the narrow doorway that led to his small, exclusive shop on the second floor. Dressed in dark slacks, a white suit and a black vest, the unique ties of a prayer shawl peeked out from beneath the bottom of the vest. A black, hand-sewn yarmulke completed the picture.

The blood from the cut on the old man's cheek was a startling contrast to his somber clothing. He swayed slightly as he clutched at the doorjamb, but the anger on his face was fierce.

All this Jesse had taken in within half a heartbeat. While heads turned toward the man in the doorway and several women yelled a protest as the object of the old man's cries barreled down the long city block, Jesse sprang into action. Using the prowess that had gotten him a football scholarship and seen him handily through his four years at NYU, he flew after the thief.

Throwing his weight forward, Jesse grabbed the man by the waist. They both went down on the concrete less than a foot shy of the gutter.

Frantic to get away, the robber fought and kicked with a fierce determination that only made Jesse angrier. Nothing got to him as quickly as someone trying to take advantage of someone else. The robber was young, strong and well-built. The man in the doorway looked as if he could easily blow away in a stiff breeze.

"Let go of me, you bastard!" the thief shouted, his arms flailing wildly as he tried to beat Jesse off.

Still struggling, the thief cracked him across the side of his head with what turned out to be a toy gun. He'd used it to intimidate the store owner. Jesse's grip on the man tightened and he brought the thief down, straddling him to keep him in place.

The bag the thief clutched when he fled the store flew out of his hand and spilled. Diamonds appeared on the concrete, creating their own rainbows in the sparse available light.

Suddenly the people in the immediate area came to life, converging on the two struggling men, their attention collectively focused on the brilliant booty displayed for them to see.

Jesse was on his feet instantly, holding on to the thief's arm and jerking him up in his wake.

"Don't even think about it," Jesse ordered one man who was close to him. The latter was bending to scoop up some of the bounty.

Jesse's harsh voice, added to his six-two stature, succeeded in keeping the man honest and the rest of the crowd at bay.

The man in the doorway took out a handkerchief to dab at his wound as he hurried over to Jesse. Shock and surprise registered on his bewhiskered face.

"Thank you, young man. Thank you," he called even before he reached Jesse. "My name is Isaac Epstein and you have done me a great service."

The thief was squirming next to Jesse, doing his best to get out of his grasp.

"Let me go!" the man ordered. When Jesse merely glared at him, the thief's indignation retreated. He became supplicant and meek. "Look, this was all a big mistake. A big, stupid mistake. I won't—"

Jesse had no desire to listen to anything the man had

to say. Anyone who would try to rob an old man was worthless—worse than dirt in his opinion.

"Shut your mouth," he advised evenly. "You'll get a chance to explain your side of it to the police."

The man's eyes widened even more, bulging like marbles. "The police?" he echoed. "But I—"

The sound of approaching sirens abruptly halted the thief's protest. But not his attempts to get away. He tugged mightily, getting nowhere rather quickly.

Jesse's smile was as steely as his last name. His fingers tighten around the thief's arm, squeezing it as he continued to hold the man in place.

"You're not going anywhere," he told the thief coldly. Jesse looked down at his light gray suit. There was a tear at the knee and what looked to be an oil stain across the other leg, sustained when they'd wrestled on the ground next to the subway grating. *Damn it.* Jesse swallowed a curse. "But when this is over, you are going to buy me a new suit."

What the would-be thief said in response was enough to offend several of the people watching the minidrama.

Jesse jerked him up, squeezing even harder as he held his arm. The man yelped.

"You say anything like that again," Jesse growled, "and I guarantee that you'll be picking up your teeth from the sidewalk."

If there was a retort coming, it disappeared as the sirens grew louder. Two squad cars and an ambulance arrived almost at the same time, one practically tailing the other.

The thief whimpered.

* * *

Tatania Pulaski loved being a doctor, or more accurately, loved being a resident. Tania was in her fourth year, that much closer to being able to hang up a shingle if she so desired. She loved everything about her duties, even the grosser aspects of it. Very little of what she dealt with at Patience Memorial Hospital fazed her.

Even so, she took nothing about her journey or her ultimate goal for granted. She, like her three older sisters and her one younger one, had paid her dues and was acutely aware of every inch of the long, hard, bumpy road it had taken to get here. She knew the sacrifices her parents had made and the contributions each of her older sisters had made. It was an unspoken rule: the older always helped the younger. It was just the way things were.

Although her heart was focused on becoming a spinal surgeon, there was no task Tania wasn't willing to do if the occasion came up. The only thing she didn't like were the rare moments that other doctors lived for.

A lull in the activity.

She didn't like lulls. Lulls caused her to think and, eventually, to remember. To remember no matter how hard she tried not to, no matter how often she forced herself to count her blessings first.

She had a great many of those and counting always took a while. She had a supportive family, parents and sisters who cared about her. Even her brother-in-law and the two men who, very shortly, were going to become part of the family were all nice guys.

On top of that, she was becoming what she'd always dreamed of being ever since Sasha, her oldest sister, had announced she was going to be a doctor. The revelation gladdened the heart of her father and, most of all, her mother.

All Tania had to do was to take in the scene that that long-ago afternoon and that made up her mind for her. She was going to be a doctor. She, too, was going to save the world one patient at a time. The fact that Natalya and Kady followed in Sasha's footsteps only made her resolve that much stronger that she was going to be a doctor, too.

There'd only been one dark incident to cast a stain on her life, one in comparison to the multitude of blessings, and yet the shadow of that one stain managed to cast itself over everything, blackening her life like a bottle of ink marring a pristine white sheet.

One stain had caused all the happiness to slip into abeyance.

She tried, more for her family's sake than her own, to put it behind her. To forget. But forgetting for more than a few minutes at a time was next to impossible. The incident lived with her every day, shadowing her. The memory of it found her when she was at ease and assaulted her mind, making her remember. Making her suffer through it.

Especially in her dreams.

Trying to block it out of her mind was the reason why she'd eagerly volunteered to work in the emergency room every time the area was shorthanded. Ninety-nine times out of a hundred, the E.R. was crowded with patients, all seeking immediate help. The atmosphere was nothing short of frantic and hectic. And nothing made her happier than being there. She was forced to concentrate on procedures, on patients who needed her help,

And while she concentrated on that, the cold, hard

reality of what had happened to her that one horrible evening was pushed into the background.

For the time being.

This particular morning the bedlam that was called the E.R. seemed especially acute. A trauma bay was no sooner emptied than someone else was brought in to fill it. She'd been on duty for close to twelve hours, on her second "second wind" and had cleared over thirty-one cases before she stopped counting.

Tania felt dead on her feet and there were still several hours to go until her second shift was finally over.

Be careful what you wish for.

It wasn't an old Polish saying, like the ones her mother was so fond of quoting, but it certainly did fit the occasion.

She was just erasing the newest case she'd discharged, which meant she was up for the next patient, when another fourth-year resident, Debbie Dominguez, tugged on the sleeve of her lab coat.

When Tania glanced in her direction, the dark-haired woman pointed to the rear doors that just sprang open. The look in Debbie's eyes was envious.

"Boy, some people have all the luck." She referred to the fact that Tania was up for the patient being brought in by two ambulance attendants.

Strapped to the gurney was a tall, muscular man in what appeared to be a disheveled, gray suit. The patient's hair was several shades darker than her own blond hair and he didn't exactly look happy to be there.

Behind him were two more gurneys, one with an older, somber-dressed man and the second with a rather vocal patient. The latter had a police escort in addition to the two attendants bringing him in.

"I don't need a doctor," the man in the gray suit on the first gurney protested. "Really, all I need is just to get cleaned up."

The older man on the second gurney seemed noticeably concerned. "Please, young man, you need stitches. I know these things. I will take care of everything. The hospital, everything," he promised with zeal. "But you need to have medical attention."

The head ambulance attendant began rattling off the first man's vitals. Tania listened with one ear while giving the man on the first gurney a swift once-over. As far as patients went, they didn't usually come this exceptionally good-looking. While distancing herself, Tania could still see why Debbie had been so interested. Any more interested and the woman would have been salivating.

When her patient struggled to get off the gurney, Tania placed her hand on his shoulder.

"Listen to the man," she advised, nodding toward the second gurney. "He's right. Besides, if you put on another suit, you're just going to wind up getting blood on it unless I stitch you up."

Turning his head in her direction, Jesse's protest died in his throat. His eyes swept over her and he had to admit he did like what he saw.

"You're my doctor?"

Rounding the corner to the trauma bays, feeling as if she was at the head of a wagon train, Tania grinned in response to the appreciative note in the man's voice. "I'm your doctor."

Jesse settled back against the gurney. "I guess maybe I'll take those stitches."

"Good choice." She looked at the attendants still guiding the gurney. "Put him in trauma bay one."

"I thought you said—" Jesse craned his neck to keep sight of her.

"Be right there," she promised.

Moving to the second gurney, she nodded at the older man. "Looks like you'll be getting the group rate for stitches," she commented, examining the gash on the man's cheek.

Isaac shrugged, as if this was nothing new to him. "Never mind me, young lady, make sure that he's all right." Wrapping his long, thin fingers around a black bag he was clutching, with his other hand he pointed in the general direction that Jesse had gone in. "He's a hero, you know."

Tania glanced over her shoulder even though by now the gurney had been tucked away into the trauma bay.

"No, I didn't know." She smiled at the man. "So that's what one looks like," she murmured, playing along with the older man. She took a step back, getting out of the gurney's way, then pointed toward another area. "Put this one in trauma bay three," she instructed the attendants.

"Treat him well, Doctor," Isaac called to her as he was wheeled away. "Anything he needs, I will take care of."

"He'll have the best of care," she promised before she turned her attention to the last gurney. The attendant closest to her gave her the patient's particulars. The latter looked far from happy, but it was a toss-up as to who was more disgruntled, the patient or his police escort.

The man on the last gurney struggled against his restraints. "It's a mistake, I tell you. The old guy must've slipped the bag in my pocket when I was leaving his store."

"Now why would he do that?" she asked. She'd come across all kinds in the E.R. and this was just another odd case to add to the list.

"I don't know. Maybe he wanted to pull some insurance scam. Who knows? Do I look like a thief to you?" he demanded hotly, indicating his clothing. Tania had to admit, except for the tear in the jacket, it looked like a high-end suit. "I'm going to sue that ape in the gray suit for battery and if you don't want to be included, you'd better uncuff me!" he growled, yanking at the handcuff that tethered him to the gurney's railing. "You hear me?" he demanded. "I want out of here."

"No more than we want you gone, I'm sure," Tania replied evenly. "But we can't have you bleeding all over the place now, can we?" she asked sweetly. Glancing at the board over the front desk to see which room had been cleared, she saw a recent erasure. "Put him in trauma bay number four." She pointed in the general direction, since she didn't recognize these attendants. Tania spared the third patient one last glance. "Someone'll be along to talk to you in a minute."

"Not soon enough for us," one of the patrolmen complained. He shook his head wearily as he followed in his partner's wake. "It's the heat," he confided to Tania as he walked by. "It makes the crazies come out."

She smiled. "So does the rain." Tania signaled over toward the nurses' station. "Elaine, take the gentleman's information in trauma bay three."

"What about one?"

"I'll handle that myself."

Elaine nodded, a knowing smile on her lips. "I thought you might." Picking up a clipboard, she walked into trauma bay three.

Armed with a fresh clipboard and the appropriate forms, Tania went to trauma room one.

The moment she walked in, she could feel the man's restlessness. Not the patient type, she thought, amused. Well, they had that in common.

While waiting for someone to come in, Jesse had taken off his jacket in an effort not to get it any more wrinkled than it already was. He wasn't altogether sure why he did that. There was no saving the pants and without the pants, the jacket was just an extraneous piece of clothing.

Habit was responsible for that, he supposed. Habit ingrained in him since childhood, when every dime counted and no amount was allowed to be frivolously squandered or misspent. Stretching money had been close to a religion for his parents. They'd taken a small amount and somehow managed to create a life for themselves and for him.

He twisted around when he heard someone enter the room.

And smiled when he saw who it was.

"Hi." She extended her hand to him. "I'm Dr. Pulaski. And you are…?"

"Jesse Steele."

Succinct, powerful. It fit him, she thought, trying not to notice how his muscles strained against his light blue shirt.

"Well, Jesse Steele, I'm afraid there's some paperwork waiting for you at the nurses' station, but first, let's see the extent of your injuries."

"It's nothing, really," he protested. The woman was drop-dead gorgeous and in another time and place, he would have liked to have lingered. But hospitals made him uneasy and, in any event, he definitely had somewhere else he needed to be.

"The blood on the side of your head says differently," she replied cheerfully. With swift, competent fingers, she did her exam. "I need you to take off your watch. I think you have a cut there."

"It's just a scratch."

"Potato, po-ta-to, I still have to see it." He took off his watch and set it aside on the nearby counter, then held his wrist up for her to see. "Okay, that's a scratch," she asserted. "You win that round. However—" she indicated his head "—that definitely needs attending to. Which means I get to play doctor."

She smiled brightly as she crossed toward the sink. "So—" she turned on the faucet and quickly washed her hands "—I hear that you're a hero."

"Not really," he answered with a mild shrug. Heroes were people who laid their lives on the line every day. Cops, firefighters, soldiers. Not him. "I was just in the right place at the right time. Or…" His lips gave way to a hint of a smile. "Taking it from the thief's point of view, in the wrong place at the wrong time."

"Do you always do that?" she asked, looking at him as she slipped on a pair of plastic gloves. "Look at everything from both sides?"

Crossing back to him, she gingerly examined the gash at his temple more closely.

He tried not to wince. She could feel him tensing ever so slightly despite her light touch.

"Occupational habit," he replied through clenched teeth.

Taking a cotton swab, she disinfected the wound. He took in a bracing breath. "You're a psychiatrist? By the way, you can breathe now."

He exhaled, then laughed at her guess. "No, I'm an architect. I'm used to looking at everything from *every* side," he added before she could ask for more of an explanation.

"Never thought of it that way," she confessed.

It was good to keep a patient distracted, especially when she was about to run a needle and suture through his scalp. The best way to do that was to keep him talking about something else.

A quick examination showed her that the bruises were superficial, but the gash at his temple was definitely going to require a few stitches.

"Well, aside from a couple of tender spots that are going to turn into blacks and blues—and purples—before the end of the day," she warned him, "you do have a gash on your right temple. I'm afraid I'm going to have to take a couple of stitches." He looked as if he was going to demur, so she quickly added, "But don't worry, they won't be noticeable. You'll be just as handsome as ever once it heals."

"I don't need stitches, it's just a cut." He shrugged it off. "So, I guess that's it," he said, beginning to get off the examination table.

She put her hands on his upper torso to keep him from going any farther. For a little thing, he noted, she possessed an awful lot of strength.

"No, it's *not* a cut. That thing on the inside of your

wrist is a cut. That—" she pointed to his temple "—is a full-fledged gash that needs help in closing up. That's where I come in," she added cheerfully. "You're not worried about a little needle, are you?"

"No, I'm worried about a big meeting." He blew out a breath, annoyed now. If he'd stayed in the taxi, he wouldn't have gotten into this altercation. But then, he reminded himself, the old man would have lost his sack of diamonds. "The one I was going to when this happened."

"Important?" Tania pulled over the suture tray and, taking a stool on rollers, made herself comfortable beside the gurney. "The meeting," she added in case he'd lost the thread of the conversation.

Right now, her patient was eyeing the surgical tray like a person who would have preferred to have been miles away from where he was.

"To me." He watched as she prepared to sew him up. From where he sat, the needle and suture was one and the same entity. He'd never been fond of needles. Jesse sat perfectly still as she numbed the area. "I was supposed to do a presentation. That was why I was cutting across the Diamond District," he added. Then explained, "Because the traffic wasn't moving and I needed to be there in a hurry."

She nodded, her eyes on her work. "Lucky for that man that you did." When he stopped talking, Tania momentarily raised her eyes to his face. Amusement curved her mouth. "I could write you a note, say you were saving a nice old man from a big bully," she teased. "It'd be on the hospital letterhead if that helps."

"No, I already called them to say I'd be late. They weren't happy about it, but they understood."

Her eyes were back on the gash just beneath his hairline. He had nice hair, Tania caught herself thinking. Something stirred within her and she banked it down. There'd be no more wild rides, she told herself sternly. They always led nowhere.

"Sound like nice bosses."

"They are. For the most part," he qualified in case she thought he had it too easy. Nothing could have been further from the truth. "What they are is fair."

"So," she said in a soothing voice, taking the first tiny stitch, "tell me exactly what you did to become a hero."

Chapter 2

Tania heard the man on the gurney draw in his breath as she pierced the skin just above his temple. He sat as rigid as a soldier in formation.

Not bad, she thought. She'd had big, brawny patients who had passed out the very moment she'd brought needle to skin.

"It's nothing, really," Jesse said in response to her question as she slowly drew the needle through. He was aware of a vague pinching sensation and knew he was in for a much bigger headache later, when the topical anesthetic wore off.

Tania smiled to herself. Modesty was always a nice quality. It was also very rare in men who looked as good as Jesse Steele did. There was something about women throwing themselves at their feet that gave handsome men heads that barely fit through regulation-size doorways.

She kept her eyes on her work. "The man in trauma room three seems to think you're the closest thing he'd seen to a guardian angel. And the man in trauma bay four thinks you're the devil incarnate, so my guess is that you must have done something."

He was probably going to have to give a statement and maybe show up in court, as well, if it came to that. No good deed went unpunished, Jesse thought.

Still, he did feel good about having saved the old man's diamonds. "I tackled him."

The doctor arched an eyebrow. He found it very sexy. "Excuse me?"

"The guy with the police escort," he clarified. "I tackled him."

"Why?" she asked.

His response had been immediate. There hadn't been even a moment's hesitation. "Because the old man yelled 'stop thief,'" he told her and then, before she asked, he added, "and the guy in the suit was the only one running away from him."

She could see why the old man had sounded so grateful. "That was pretty brave of you," she acknowledged. "Most people would have looked the other way or pretended not to hear."

He couldn't do that, couldn't look away or count the cracks in the sidewalk when someone needed help. He hadn't been raised that way, wouldn't have been able to live with himself if he'd just walked on. "I don't like thieves."

"Most of us don't," she agreed, humor curving her lips. And then she paused for a second to scrutinize him. There was more to this man than just looks, she decided. "Sounds like it's personal." Because her father had been and her new brother-in-law still was involved with the police force, she guessed, "Is someone in your family in law enforcement?"

He had meant to stop with just the first word, but somehow the rest just slipped out. She was extremely easy to talk to. "No. Someone in my family was robbed."

Something about the way her patient said it made her look at him again, her needle poised for a third tiny stitch. "Who?"

"My parents."

Tania felt her heart tighten in empathy. "What happened?"

Her patient blew out a breath and was quiet for so long, she thought he'd decided not to answer. Which was his right. She was prying.

But just as she completed the last stitch, he said, "My parents ran a small mom-and-pop-type grocery store in Brooklyn. We lived right above it. One night some thug came in and robbed them. When he tried to steal my mother's wedding ring, my father pushed him away. The thug shot him point-blank and ran. My mother got to keep her wedding ring, the thug got seventy-three dollars in cash, and my father died." His voice was stony. He could still remember hearing the shot and wondering what it was. He was home that night, struggling with his math homework and planning on asking his father for help. He never did do his math homework that night.

Tania cut the black thread and felt numb. When he mentioned his parents, she could envision her own, Magda and Josef, being in that situation. Granted, her father was a retired police detective, but, judging from the way Jesse's jaw had tightened, the underlying emotional ties were the same.

She lightly placed her hand on his arm. "I'm very sorry."

He nodded, trying to put distance between himself and the memory of that night. The memory of flying down the stairs and bursting into the store, only to see his father on the floor, not breathing, blood everywhere. His mother sobbing. Funny how it still cut so deep, even after all these years.

Jesse cleared his throat. He could feel the passage growing smaller, threatening to choke him. "Yeah, well, that happened a long time ago. I was thirteen at the time."

Sympathy filled her. "Must have been rough, growing up without a father."

She didn't know what she would have done without hers. Especially after the incident. It was her father who'd broken through the stone wall she'd built up around herself rock by rock. Her father who'd held her hand throughout the ordeal and who'd given her the courage to stand up for herself. Without him gently, firmly urging her on, trying mightily to control his own anger, she didn't know if she would have pressed charges, much less been willing to go to court to tell her story yet one more time. Each time she recited it, it got worse for her, not better.

But the latter never turned out to be necessary. She was spared the courtroom ordeal. Jeff Downey confessed at the last minute and the case was settled out of court with a plea bargain. He was sent upstate and got ten years. Less with good behavior. He was paroled six months ago. Which meant he was out there somewhere. She tried very hard not to think about that.

She'd always suspected that her father had had something to do with Jeff's confession and his accepting the plea bargain, that somehow, Josef had managed to put pressure on the boy she'd once thought was the answer to her prayers instead of being the source of recurring nightmares. Her father had denied doing anything out of the ordinary when she asked.

But she knew her father, knew how he felt about all of them. How he felt about her being violated. There was nothing more important to Josef Pulaski than his wife and his daughters.

Although logically, she knew that not everyone had parents like hers, in her heart she always envisioned her parents whenever people mentioned their own. It was always sad to find out the opposite was true. Those were the times when she felt really lucky.

"It was," Jesse agreed. His father had been a stern man, but fair. They were just beginning to get along when Jason Steele was murdered. "But I got through it."

Interested, Tania asked, "What about your mom? How did she handle it?"

"She sold the store, bought a flower shop instead. Most people don't rob flower shops." He remembered how he begged her not to buy another store and how she'd tried to reassure him with statistics about flower shops. He still went there every day after school —to guard his mother until she closed up. "And she managed." He paused, wondering how the blond-haired doctor with the killer legs and the sweet smile had so effortlessly gotten so much information out of him. "Is this part of the treatment?"

"Sorry, my attending always says I get too close to my patients." Which wasn't strictly true, Tania added silently. She asked questions, but she didn't get close. Getting close involved vulnerability. She hadn't gotten close to anyone since the incident. Not even to the men she'd gone out with since then. She didn't know how.

He eyed her for a second, as if he was trying to make up his mind about something. "Do you?" he asked. "Get too close?"

She didn't answer him directly. She gave him a reply she felt worked in this case.

"I find patients trust you more if you take an interest in them. And I am interested in them," she assured him. "If I wasn't, I wouldn't be in this field." Smiling, she mentioned the first job she could think of that had to do with solitude. One she'd actually considered, except that solitude meant that she would be alone with her thoughts, and that she couldn't do. "I'd be a forest ranger."

"A forest ranger," he repeated, amused. "That would have been the medical world's loss."

Tania laughed softly. "Well, I see your encounter with the thief didn't knock the charm out of you." Pushing back the surgical tray, she stripped off the rubber gloves and deposited them into the trash bin. "We're done here," she announced, then took a prescription pad out of her lab coat pocket and hastily wrote something down.

"There might be pain," she warned him, tearing off the paper. "You can get this filled at your local pharmacy, or use the hospital's pharmacy." She gave him directions since he was probably unfamiliar with it. "It's down in the basement, to right of the elevator bank when you get off."

Jesse took the prescription she held out to him and glanced at it. His eyebrows drew together in consternation. He was looking at scribble. "You sure it says something?"

Tania grinned. Her mother, she-of-the-perfect-hand-writing, used to get on her case all the time. "It does look like someone dipped a chicken in ink and had it walk across the paper, doesn't it? That was my first inkling that I was going to be a doctor. I have awful handwriting."

Jesse folded the paper and put it into his wallet. "Not awful…" he said with less than total conviction, letting his voice trail off.

Before she could say anything, someone behind her asked in a jovial voice, "So, how is the hero?"

They both looked over to the trauma room's entrance. The man whose diamonds he'd recovered stood in the doorway, beaming at him. There was a butterfly bandage on his cheek but other than that, he seemed none the worse for wear.

Tania pushed her stool back, then rose to her feet. "Good as new," she declared, then turned back to Jesse. "Now comes the really hard part." Her mouth quirked. "Filling out the insurance forms." She turned to lead the way out. "You can do that at the outpatient desk."

Isaac stepped into the room. He raised both hands, as if to beat the notion back. "No need. It's on me. I'll pay it," he told Jesse eagerly.

Jesse slid off the table, picking up his jacket. "That's all right," he told the older man. "My company has health insurance. They'll take care of it."

Isaac gave him a once-over, taking in the torn trouser leg and the stains. "Then a new suit," he declared with feeling. "I owe you a new suit."

For just a second, there was a mental tug of war. But in the end, pride prevented Jesse from taking the man up on his offer. The suit he had on had set him back a good five hundred dollars because he knew appearances were everything.

But he was his own man. He always had been. That meant he paid his own way and was indebted to no one.

"No," he assured the old man, "you really don't owe me anything."

This could go on all afternoon, Tania thought. She gently placed a hand to each man's arm and motioned them out of the room. "I'm afraid that you two need to settle this outside." She smiled brightly at Isaac. "We need the room."

Isaac began backing out immediately. "Of course, of course." He took both of her hands into his, his gratitude overflowing and genuine. "Thank you for all that you did."

Jesse debated slipping on his jacket, then decided to leave it slung over his arm. A dull ache started in his shoulder. He was going to feel like hell by tomorrow morning, he thought, remembering his days on the gridiron.

"What about you?" he asked the old man as they walked out of the room. "How's your face?"

Isaac touched the bandage, then dropped his hand. Even the slightest contact sent a wave of pain right through his teeth.

"If Myra, my wife, was alive today, she would say 'as ugly as ever.'" He shrugged philosophically. "When you are not a good-looking man, a blow to the face is not that big a tragedy." And then he smiled, nodding at his Good Samaritan. "Not like with you." He stood for a moment, cocking his head like wizened old owl, studying the doctor's handiwork. "Nice work. My brother Leon would approve. Leon is a tailor," he explained. And then his eyes lit up. "Of course. I'll send you to Leon." The thought pleased the jeweler greatly. "He will make you such a suit. And I will pay him."

How did he get the old man to understand that he didn't owe him anything? That successfully coming to the jeweler's rescue was enough for him. "No, really, I don't—"

But Jesse got no further in his protest. Isaac pursed his lips beneath his neatly trimmed moustache and beard. "Pride is a foolish thing, young man." He wagged his finger to make his point. "It kept the Emperor without any clothes." His voice lowered. "Please, it'll make me feel better."

Tania passed the two men on her way to get the chart for her next patient. "I'd give in if I were you," she advised Jesse. "It doesn't sound as if he's about to give up." And then she winked at the old man, as if they shared a secret. "Trust me," she told Jesse, thinking of her father, "I'm familiar with the type."

And with that, she hurried off to a curtained section just beyond the nurses' station.

Isaac watched her walk away. There was appreciation in the man's sky-blue eyes when he turned them back to Jesse. "Nice girl, that one." And then he asked innocently, "Are you married?"

"What? No." Was the man matchmaking? Trying to line up a customer for a ring? Well, he wasn't in the market for something like that right now. Maybe later, but not for a couple of years or so. "And not looking for anyone right now, either," Jesse emphasized.

His words beaded off Isaac's back like water off a duck.

"Sometimes we find when we don't look. And should you find," Isaac said, digging into his pocket, "you come to me." Producing a business card, he tucked it into Jesse's hand. "I will take good care of you. I'll match you up with the finest engagement ring you've ever seen." And then he added the final touch. "On the house."

Jesse nodded, pocketing the card, fairly certain that this was an empty promise the old man felt he had to make. Once there was a little distance from the events of today, Jesse was confident the man would feel completely differently. He had no intentions of holding a man to a promise made in the heat of the moment.

Besides, the last thing he needed right now was an engagement ring.

"And you, do you have a card?" Isaac asked him curiously, his bright blue eyes shifting to Jesse's pants' pocket.

Just by coincidence, he'd been given his first batch of cards yesterday afternoon. He hadn't had a chance to hand any out yet. "Yes."

Isaac waited for a moment. When nothing materialized, he coaxed, "May I have it? So that I can have your phone number," he explained. A gurney was being ushered by. Jesse and Isaac stepped to the side, out of the way. "Not to bother you, of course, but to see how you are doing and to find out when you are available for that suit."

Maybe saving this man's diamonds hadn't been such a good thing, after all, Jesse mused. Then again, maybe he was being a little paranoid. After all, the man was justifiably grateful. But after what he'd been through recently with Ellen, well, it had him still looking over his shoulder at times.

"Believe me, it's really not necessary."

Isaac fixed him with a long, serious look. "Neither was coming to my rescue, young man, but you did. Isaac Epstein does not forget a kindness. You are a very rare young man." So Jesse dug into his pocket and handed the man his card. "Jesse Steele," Isaac read, then glanced at what followed. "You are an architect?"

It had been a long road to that label. He still felt no small pride whenever he heard it applied to him. "Yes, I am."

"You know—" Isaac leaned his head in as if he was about to impart a dark secret "—my house could use expanding…"

Jesse couldn't help laughing. Isaac was harmless and well-meaning, if pushy. He put his arm across the older man's shoulders, leading him out of the area and to the outpatient station so they could both get on with their lives—especially him.

"I think we need to get out of everyone's way, Mr. Epstein." The police had indicated that he could come in later and give his statement, for which he was extremely grateful. "And I need to get to my office."

They weren't going to hold the meeting for him forever, he thought. He had a change of clothing at the firm, in case he had to take a sudden flight out on business. The suit might be wrinkled, but anything was better than what he was currently wearing.

"Let me make a call," Isaac offered. "My cousin's son, John, he owns a limousine service. You can arrive to your office in style."

"I can arrive on the bus," Jesse countered as he walked down the hallway with the older man.

Isaac released a sigh that was twice as large as he was. "I never thought I would meet anyone more stubborn than my Myra."

Jesse tried to keep a straight face as he said, "Life is full of surprises, Mr. Epstein."

"Isaac, please," the man corrected him as they turned a corner.

A little more than two hours later the flow of patients temporarily became a trickle. It was then that Shelly Fontaine, a full-figured nurse with lively eyes and a quick, infectious smile, came up to her, dangling a watch in the air in front of her.

"What would you like me to do with this, Dr. Ski?" The name was one Tania had suggested after Shelly's tongue had tripped her up several times while trying to pronounce her actual surname.

Glancing up from the computer where she was inputting last-minute notes, Tania hardly saw the object in question.

"Have Emilio take it down to Lost and Found where everything goes," she murmured. And then her mind did a double take. "Hold it," she called to Shelly who moved rather fast when she wanted to. "Let me see that again." She held her hand out for the watch. Upon closer examination, she recognized it. The timepiece was old-fashioned with a wind-up stem. And, if she wasn't mistaken, it had come off Jesse Steele's wrist. She had assumed he'd put it back on after she'd examined the scratch beneath the band. Obviously not.

But just to be on the sure side, she asked, "Where did you get this?"

"Trauma bay one." Shelly nodded back toward the room where, even now, another patient was being wheeled in on a gurney. It looked as if the flow was picking up again. "You were taking care of that hunk in there." Shelly's mouth widened in a huge, wistful grin. "I thought you might know where to find him. Assuming this is his and not some patient who was there before him."

"No, this is his," Tania said with certainty. "I recognize it."

It would be too much of a coincidence for there to be two watches like this worn by patients occupying the same room on the same day. Rather than give the watch back to the nurse, Tania slipped the watch into her pocket. Hitting several more keys, she saved what she'd input and rose from the desk.

"His address has to be on file," she said, thinking out loud. She knew for a fact that she'd seen it written on the information form the nurse had taken before she'd come in to treat the man. "I'll look it up and have someone mail it to him."

Shelly sighed soulfully as she followed her away from the desk. "I'd like to mail me to him."

"Shelly, you're married," Tania pointed out.

"I'm married, I'm not blind. I can look. And maybe lust," the older woman added mischievously. "It's not like Raymond doesn't look every woman over the age of eighteen up and down when he passes them."

Obviously not every marriage was made in heaven, Tania thought.

"Hey, you ready?" Kady called, coming around the corner like a runaway steamroller.

Tania made a show of looking at the watch on her wrist. "For lunch or dinner?" It was a blatant reference to the fact that her older sister was more than half an hour late.

"Sorry, it's been crazy today. I had to perform an emergency cardiac ablation. This man had an attack of atrial fibrillation that just wouldn't stop. I know I should have called, but there wasn't any time—"

"Save your apologies." Tania grabbed her purse from the drawer beneath the nurse's desk. "You lucked out. It's been hectic here all morning, too."

"Did it have anything to do with the camera crews outside?" Kady wanted to know.

She hadn't seen the light of day since she'd walked in yesterday. Armageddon could have swept the street of Manhattan and she wouldn't have known about it. "Camera crews?"

"Yeah, outside the E.R." Only extremely tight security, instituted right after the serial killings that had rocked the hospital last January, had kept the pushiest of the crew members out. "Something about a hero saving a dealer's diamonds. Security kept them out, but I heard that the media swarmed all over the guy when he finally left the hospital."

Tania shook her head. "Poor man probably never got to go to his meeting."

Kady stopped walking and looked at her sister, confused. "Meeting? What meeting?" And then the answer dawned on her. "Did you treat him?"

Stopping by the elevator, Tania pressed for the basement where the cafeteria was located. "I sewed up his scalp wound."

Kady sighed. "Some girls have all the luck," she teased. Tania looked at her and for one moment Kady could have bitten off her tongue. Because for one unguarded moment, Tania had allowed the pain to come through and register in her eyes.

But the next, Tania was flashing the wide smile she'd always been known for and nodding her head in agreement. "Yeah, we do. Your turn to buy lunch, by the way."

Kady was relieved that the moment had passed. "I distinctly remember that it was your turn."

"Maybe you should be marrying a neurosurgeon instead of a bodyguard. There's something going wrong with your memory."

The elevator arrived and the doors opened. Kady put her arm around Tania's shoulders and guided her in. "Not today, little sister, not today."

Chapter 3

She'd just wanted to make sure he was all right.

She'd been a safe distance away, trailing discreetly behind him—far enough away not to be noticed, close enough to see—when Jesse had stopped that thief.

Her breath had caught in her throat as she'd watched the two grapple on the ground. And it had taken everything she'd had not to run up to Jesse when she'd seen the blood trickling along the side of his head. She'd wanted to clean the wound with her handkerchief and make it better with her kisses.

In all probability, she *would* have run up to him to do just that, but the ambulance had arrived in the blink of an eye. When it had, rather than step forward she'd melted back in with the crowd. That was when she'd read the logo on the side of the vehicle. It had been dispensed from Patience Memorial Hospital.

She knew where that was.

Several months ago they'd treated her there when her wrists had had an unfortunate meeting with a shard of glass. The police had brought her there, summoned by her nosy superintendent who'd come about the overdue rent and had illegally let himself in when she hadn't answered the door. The police had wanted to label it a suicide attempt. She'd talked them out of it, saying it was just an accident. A glass had broken when she was washing dishes and she hadn't realized it until the jagged edges had scraped against both of her wrists and she'd felt faint.

They didn't look like they believed her, but she'd convinced them. She was good at convincing people when she set her mind to it.

Except for Jesse.

But then, Jesse was different. Special. He always had been. She'd known that from the moment she'd first seen him walk through the doors of the firm she worked for. Used to work for, she corrected herself. They'd fired her. Didn't matter. Nothing mattered. Except for Jesse. He was special.

Special. And hers.

He was so brave, so selfless. So willing to put everyone else first. That's why she loved him. Or at least that was one of the reasons. There were so many. She'd need a lifetime to count them. A lifetime that they would spend together.

Once she knew where the ambulance was going, she took off, availing herself of shortcuts in order to get there before the vehicle arrived. She succeeded, beating out the ambulance by a couple of minutes. Even using the siren, it had been slow going. The streets were clogged with lunchtime traffic and there was nowhere for the cars to pull over.

She'd counted on that, on the ambulance arriving at the rear E.R. entrance just as she had. She was in time to see Jesse being taken in.

Because there was so much activity in the immediate area, what with two other ambulances arriving on the heels of the first and the usual general commotion that occurred around an emergency room at midday, she managed to slip in without even being noticed.

She'd gotten very good at slipping in without being noticed.

Just like a little fly on the wall, she thought, her lips framing a smile that didn't quite move into her soul.

When the fluffy looking blonde in the lab coat approached Jesse, she'd felt a sharp flare of temper, a surge of red-hot jealousy, but she banked it down. Her anger could be kept in abeyance as long as she thought that the woman was there to help Jesse. Jesse's well-being came first. Always. Besides, he didn't like shallow types like the blonde. He liked women like her.

He liked her.

Loved her, she silently corrected.

As the minutes ticked away, she finally managed to pass by the room where Jesse was being treated, peering in through the window. He wasn't looking in her direction, so he didn't see her. Which was good. But it was so hard to resist the temptation to rush in, to throw her arms around him and tell him that she would take care of him. That she was so proud of him for saving that old man's property but that he must never, never do that again. He could have been killed. What if that horrible man he'd brought down had had a gun?

She couldn't bring herself to think about it, it was just too awful.

She hated that man. Hated him for bruising Jesse's beautiful skin, for making Jesse hurt his head. If she could have, she would have made the thief pay for what he did. She would have stabbed him, then laughed as she watched the life dribble out of him. Someone like that didn't deserve anything better.

But those stupid policemen kept hanging around. They'd probably arrest her if she punished that man and gave him what he so richly deserved, what he had coming to him.

Jesse had almost seen her when he left the hospital, but she was too fast for him. She was certain that if he had seen her, he would have recognized her even though she wore a disguise.

The heart sees what the eyes don't.

And he loved her, she knew that. He was just a little confused, that's all.

He'd loved her once and you just don't stop loving someone. You don't.

She'd slipped out of the hospital close behind him when he'd left, but she'd managed to mix in with all the cameramen and reporters outside. She'd been tempted to shove one or two of the women. Women with their perfect hair and their pretty makeup, all trying to get close to Jesse. But she didn't. She'd kept her cool. Jesse would have been proud of her had he known.

He'd know soon.

Walking back to her apartment, she clenched and

unclenched the hands that were thrust deep in her pockets. She had to be patient. She'd make her move soon, but not yet.

Not yet.

It was oh so hard being patient. But it was a small price to pay for forever.

She was sure Jesse would agree.

Tania chewed on the inside of her lower lip, staring at the watch sitting on the desk in front of her. She'd almost forgotten about it until she'd shoved her hands into her pockets as she'd walked out of yet another trauma room and her fingers had come in contact with the leather band.

Jesse's watch.

In all the commotion this morning and his hurry to get to his meeting, had he just forgotten it? Or had he left it behind on purpose, left it behind so that he'd have an excuse to see her again?

Tania sighed. She had to stop being so paranoid. Sometimes an oversight was just an oversight, nothing more.

Even if Jesse *had* orchestrated this, the man had no way of knowing that a) she'd be the one to find the watch, which she actually wasn't, and b) that she'd opt to deliver his watch back to him in person. The most logical way to get this back to Jesse was just to have someone ship it out, the way she'd already mentioned to Shelly when the nurse had brought the watch to her.

But then, she wasn't the type to make someone do things for her that were not in some way directly related to hospital procedures. And even then, she had a tendency to try to do everything herself. Her sisters teased

her and called her an overachiever. On occasion, Sasha
had bandied about the word "controlling," trying, she
knew, to make her come around and relax.

She supposed that "controlling" was actually more
on target as far as assessing her behavior. She'd always
been an overachiever, they all were in her family. But
controlling, well, that was a later development. One designed to make her feel more secure.

If you controlled everything around you, or at least
as much as possible, then you never had anything unexpected happening to you. You stayed safe. She had made
a vow at seventeen never to be at the mercy of circumstances—and especially not at the mercy of any person.

She eyed the watch again, then made up her mind.
Her endless shift was just about to finally come to an
end. It would be no great hardship for her to drop this
off on her way home—provided that the man didn't
live in Connecticut, she mused.

Tania laughed softly to herself. If he did, this was definitely going into the mail. She was not about to go out
of her way for any man, even if that man happen to be
drop-dead gorgeous. That sort of thing no longer carried
any weight with her.

Just the opposite was true.

Rising from the desk and dropping the watch back
in her pocket, she went to outpatient registration to get
Jesse Steele's home address.

He didn't live in Connecticut, or any of the other out-
lining states, either. As it turned out, when Sally Rich-
mond "conveniently" turned away from the computer
screen to let her look without actually saying she could,

Tania discovered that Jesse Steele lived right here in Manhattan, just the way she and her sisters did. Jotting the address down on an index card, she whispered, "Thank you" to Sally and slipped away from the outpatient registration area.

Hanging up her lab coat in her locker and resuming her civilian life, Tania took the crosstown bus to the address she'd written down. She'd taken care to write it in big block letters because she had just as much trouble reading her own handwriting as everyone else did. And given the choice of winding up in the wrong part of town or not, she'd choose "not."

It wasn't that much of a ride. Had she had more energy, she would have walked and probably gotten there faster, but by the end of her second shift, she was more or less drained. It had been a hell of a grueling sixteen hours.

So what are you doing playing messenger girl?

She had no answer for that.

After getting off the bus, Tania walked one block over until she reached the address on the card. She and her sisters had grown up in Queens, but they'd all made the trip into Manhattan, to take in the sights and wander the streets every chance they got. She knew the city like the back of her hand. Better.

While on the bus, she'd made up her mind to leave the watch with the doorman if there was one.

There wasn't.

The wide glass door leading into the modern highrise was unattended.

Doormen were swiftly going the way of the elevator operators of the last century. Into the mist.

As luck would have it, someone was just entering the building. Not wanting to ring bells at random, Tania slipped in behind the woman before the door closed again.

There was a bank of mailboxes along the far wall. Crossing to them, she scanned the names and apartments until she found "Jesse Steele, 10E." His was the only name listed. He lived alone.

Or maybe with someone who hadn't put up her name yet.

That made no difference to her, she insisted silently.

Tania pressed for the elevator. It must have been on the floor above because it arrived almost immediately.

She'd just leave his watch on his doorstep, she decided. Just before she'd left P-M, she'd taken an envelope with the hospital logo on it and placed the watch inside. Taking the envelope out of her purse, she sealed it as she rode up the elevator. There was no harm in leaving the watch on his doorstep. It'd be safe until he got home—provided he was out. The building was in the better part of town and it looked very respectable.

Stepping off the elevator, she began reading the numbers on the doors. The floor was tastefully done in subdued blues and grays, with paintings of flowers scattered through spring meadows hanging every few feet. It made for a pleasant, soothing atmosphere.

Apartment 10E was at the end of the hall.

Since she was just going to leave the watch on the floor directly in front of the door, Tania really couldn't explain what made her ring the doorbell at the last moment.

Even as she pressed the button, she turned away and started to retrace her steps to the elevator.

As it turned out, Jesse must have been on his way out,

because she'd only managed to take three steps before the door to his apartment swung open.

Jesse had trained himself to look through the peephole before opening the door. It wasn't his way, but better to be safe than sorry. Technically, he no longer had to be on his guard like this. The restraining order was in force and would continue to be for some time. And there hadn't been any incidents for a while now, not since he'd moved. For a while there, though, he'd found out firsthand exactly what a buck had to feel like during hunting season. And, granted there hadn't been any incident since the restraining order had been taken out, but he still wasn't a hundred percent at his ease. Someday, he hoped, he could reclaim his life and go back to being laid back, or at least not feel edgy every time he heard the doorbell ring.

But for now, he had to remain vigilant.

And surprised.

The woman's back was to him and she wasn't wearing a lab coat, but he recognized the soft sway of her hips immediately. It was part of what had caught his attention to begin with.

"Dr. Pulaski?"

Tania turned around, forcing a bemused expression to take over her features. She made a point of appearing nonchalant, so much so that no one except her family would have even remotely guessed at the tension she lived with every waking moment.

To the untrained eye, the smile was warm, perhaps even a little inviting. "Hi."

What was she doing here? Not that he minded, of course. This spared him the chore of coming up with a reason for going back to the hospital to try to see her again before he was scheduled to have his stitches rechecked.

"I thought house calls had gone the way of the dinosaur—or is there a problem with my insurance?" he joked.

She'd been on his mind, off and on, since he'd fought his way past the camera crew, shielding the jeweler while he was at it. The people he worked with were far more interested in having him retell the events of what had happened than they were in his contributions to the meeting he'd ultimately wound up missing. And then he'd had to stop at the precinct to give his statement. All the while, his thoughts kept straying to the woman who had tended to his wounds, vacillating between wondering if he'd ever see her again to *wanting* to see her again.

"No, no problem that I know of," she qualified. "But you did leave without your watch," she told him. She indicated the envelope on the floor.

"My watch." A look of astonishment slipped over his face as he looked at his wrist. Running behind all day, he'd chosen not to look at his watch, confirming just how late he was. If he had, he would have realized that it was missing.

And remembered where he'd last seen it.

Now *that* would have been a legitimate excuse to see her again.

"I didn't even know it was gone," he confessed, opening the envelope. "I'm so used to it being there, I thought it was. What do they call that, phantom something or other?"

"I think you're trying for 'phantom pain' and that only involves amputated limbs, not missing wristwatches." She didn't bother suppressing an amused smile.

He put the watch back on, then looked at it, relieved and satisfied all at the same time. "You have no idea how much this means to me."

"Obviously a lot." Which made her glad she'd gone out of her way to bring it back to him.

"It belonged to my father," he told her.

She'd already figured out that it was old. "That would explain the winding stem," Tania commented.

"My mother gave it to me when I graduated high school, said she knew he'd want me to have it." Not ordinarily an emotional person, he remembered fighting tears when he'd opened his gift and seen the watch. "It belonged to my grandfather before him."

"So passing it on is a family tradition."

The thought made her smile, not in amusement but with a feeling of empathy. Despite the fact that they had come to this country from their native Poland with hardly anything more than the clothes on their backs, her parents were very big on family tradition.

She needed to get going. She'd promised Kady to help her decide on wedding invitations. "Well, I'm glad I could reunite the two of you."

Tania paused for a moment longer. Everything told her she had to leave, but there was something about him, something warm and inviting that had her lingering just a second more.

To keep from looking like some kind of idiot who said one thing but did another, she asked, "By the way, how's your head?"

She looked even better without her lab coat. And probably excellent with less on than that. Jesse squelched the thought.

"It hurts," he admitted.

"That's what the prescription for the painkillers is for," she reminded him. Had he forgotten to get it filled?

But Jesse slowly shook his head, the way someone would if they were afraid their head would fall off. "I'd rather not take them if I can help it."

Oh, another one of those, she thought. "Macho, huh? I have a father like that. Do yourself a favor, take the pills." She second-guessed his reasons for doing without. "A few doses aren't going to make you slavishly dependent on them."

His best friend in high school had succumbed to addiction. And then just succumbed. Life was long and he intended to enjoy it. Unencumbered. But he had no desire to get into that now. So Jesse merely shrugged it off.

"I know, but it's really not that bad," he told her. Realizing that he was still standing in the doorway, he opened it a little wider and stepped back. "Can you come in for a minute?"

It was Tania's turn to shake her head. For all intents and purposes, he seemed nice. But no one knew where she'd gone and there was no way she was about to walk into his domain.

Come into my parlor, said the spider to the fly.

Jesse Steele didn't come across like a spider, but then, neither had Jeff. There was absolutely no way she was ever going to be anyone's fly again, anyone's victim. Everything was always going to be on her terms, or not at all.

"I can't," she answered. "I need to get home," she added. "I just thought you might miss your watch and I wanted to drop it off."

He seemed disappointed, but didn't push. "I would

like to pay you back for going out of your way," he told her. "Dinner?"

"Not tonight," she began.

He'd already assumed that. "Tomorrow?" he queried, then asked, "The day after?" when she didn't answer.

Despite her efforts to the contrary, she was amused. "If I say no, are you going to keep going?"

He nodded, crossing his arms before him. "Pretty much."

"What if I have a jealous husband?" she asked with a straight face. Did a little thing like marriage make a difference to him? Or was he accustomed to getting his way whenever he wanted something?

She saw him looking at her left hand, then raise his eyes again. "Do you?"

It was the perfect excuse, the perfect out. All she had to do was say yes and walk away. Something inside of her played devil's advocate and kept her from cloaking herself in the lie.

It was almost as if she was daring herself, seeing how far she would go. To see how far she would inch along the plank before it would bend beneath her weight, threatening to make her fall into the water. It was her usual modus operandi. She'd always scramble back to safety, but it seemed that each time she pushed herself a little harder, a little further.

Someday, she was going to hit that water.

No, she wasn't, she thought with confidence just before she answered his question.

"No, I don't."

"Good, then I'll just keep going." He thought a moment. "I think I was up to Thursday. Thursday night?" he asked.

She tried not to laugh. "I—"

Jesse just kept going. "Friday, then. Or Saturday. Saturday work for you?"

She gave up and laughed, shaking her head. "Okay, okay, dinner. Wednesday evening. You pick the place, I'll meet you there."

"I could pick you up," he offered.

"You could meet me there," she countered.

He looked at her for a long moment. "Are you sure there's no husband?"

"Just two nosy sisters."

He was an only child who had grown up longing for siblings. "You have two sisters?"

"Four, actually," she corrected. "Three older, one younger." And then she added with the same touch of pride that everyone in her family felt, especially her parents. "All doctors at Patience Memorial."

Now that was unusual, he thought, not to mention impressive. "Sounds like a really nice family."

Had he planned it, he couldn't have said anything better to her. Her family was everything to her. "It is. So, which restaurant?" He gave her the name of one and she nodded. "Expensive. Dinner there will probably cost more than that watch did when it was new."

"Some things," he told her, "you can't put a price on."

It was the sincerity in his voice that finally won her over. Part of Tania still felt that she might be making a mistake, since she really knew nothing about him except what he'd told her, but then, a man who comes to the aid of a stranger couldn't be all bad.

Right?

Chapter 4

Tania found herself looking at Kady as the latter threw open the door to the apartment she, Kady and Natalya shared.

"Well, it's about time. I was all set to fill out a missing person's report on you," Kady told her, one hand on her hip in a gesture that fairly shouted Mama. Apparently her older sister had flown to the door the second Kady'd heard her putting her key in the lock.

"Not me," Marja offered carelessly.

She came walking in from the kitchen after having foraged through her sisters' refrigerator. Her search had yielded a half-empty carton of chicken lo mein and she was well on her way to making it a completely empty carton.

Marja paused to render a wide, wistful smile. "I was all set to put my stuff in your room and move in."

"Antsy to get out from underneath Mama and Daddy's protective eye, are we?" Natalya laughed.

They'd all been there, all but smothered in genuine affection and concern. Not a one of them would have traded either of their parents in for any amount of riches. They all knew how very rare a couple Magda and Josef Pulaski were. Selfless, willing to work twenty hours a day if necessary to put them all through college and medical school.

Her father had said more than once that education was a blessing, which made it a family affair.

But right now, Marja was apparently focusing on the downside and she rolled her eyes in response to Natalya's teasing question.

"God, yes." The words were accompanied by a dramatic sigh. The drama she got from her mother. "I love them both to pieces, but they still think of me as a child," she wailed.

"No," Sasha corrected, keeping a straight face, "they think of you as the baby. The last little bird to fly out of the nest." She felt for her sister, but at the same time, she couldn't help teasing her. Lifetime habits were hard to break. "I'm not sure they're ready to acknowledge your flight plan, Marysia."

Marja preferred answering to her nickname, but she only allowed her family to use it. Didn't even mention it to anyone else. They had enough trouble with Marja. For the outsider, "Marysia" became nothing short of an unrewarding, gabled tongue-twister.

"Well, whether or not they acknowledge it, I'm out of there the second Natalya says 'I do' to Mike. I'm not even going to stick around for the reception," she said loftily, licking her fork to get the last of the lo mein, "just hitching the U-Haul to Sasha's car and bringing my stuff over."

Finished, she crossed back to the kitchen to throw the empty container out and toss the fork into the sink.

Natalya and Kady exchanged glances, shaking their heads. Marja might have graduated at the top of her graduating class, but she still had a bit of growing up to do.

Sasha grinned. As if leaving the house where she was born were that easy. One by one, they had moved out of the house in Queens, to be closer to the hospital where they all ultimately worked. Her parents had gone through the experience four times already. The fifth and last time was definitely not going to be a piece of cake, not if she knew Mama. Or Daddy, who was more versed than most about the kind of lowlife that was known to sometimes walk the streets of New York.

"Daddy will probably want to supervise," she told Marja. "You know how he is."

Marja sighed, planting herself beside Sasha on the love seat. "Yes, I do, God love 'im." It wasn't that she didn't have the utmost admiration and respect for her parents, and she did love them to death. She just wanted the opportunity to miss them once in a while. And to leave the house occasionally without verbally leaving a detailed itinerary in her wake. Whenever she tried, her father made it a point of telling her that he was asking because, just in case she went missing, they'd know where to start looking for her.

"Girls, they are going missing all the time," he told her with feeling. "You, we will not have missing. So, where is it you are going?"

Marja knew the dialogue by heart—and wanted to put

some distance between it and herself until such time as she could hear it without having it set her teeth on edge.

She glanced from one sister to another, looking for support. It wasn't as if this was something new, a phase their parents were going through. This was everyday life at the Pulaski residence.

"I just *really* need some time away from them. A vacation," she added because it sounded less harsh.

Natalya nodded, feigning sympathy. "Yeah, I know how it is. Hot meals, clean sheets, no rent to worry about, laundry done." She sighed loudly, shaking her head. "Must be hell."

"Oh, like you didn't leave the first chance you got," Marja reminded her.

"I had to. Sasha was lonely." She glanced toward her older sister. "Weren't you, Sasha?"

"I was too busy to be lonely," Sasha deadpanned.

"It's not that I'm not appreciative," Marja persisted. "It's just that I want them to stop looking at me as if I was their little girl." The others might not have thought so, but it really was no picnic, being the youngest.

"News flash." Perched on the arm of the love seat, Tania leaned over and pretended to knock on Marja's head. "You'll *always* be their little girl."

"We all will," Sasha interjected. "Even when we're in our nineties."

Marja shivered at the very thought. "Well, we need to fix that."

Sasha curved her hand protectively over her abdomen that was just beginning to swell. "Can't. It's a fact of life, Marysia. I'm already beginning to feel extremely protective and the baby's not even here yet."

Marja leaned over her older sister's stomach, cupping her hand to her mouth as she addressed the tiny swell. "Run, kid, run for your life. This is your aunt Marysia speaking. I know what I'm talking about."

"Idiot." Sasha laughed, thumping her youngest sister in the head affectionately.

If she didn't move this along, they'd never get to the reason they were all here. Kady looked at the last arrival. "I thought you said you were coming straight home to fall into bed." She'd all but had to twist Tania's arm to get her to agree to this get-together. It was called at the last minute because all five of them were very rarely off at the same time and she wanted everyone's input.

Tania's mouth curved in an enigmatic smile. She'd almost forgotten about that. "I was."

"Last-minute emergency?" Though their areas of expertise were all different—Sasha was an ob-gyn, Natalya, a pediatrician, Kady a cardiovascular surgeon, Tania was leaning toward spinal surgery while Marja thought about being an internist—they all knew how that was. One moment they could be walking out the door, the next they were being paged or button-holed to work on a patient who'd just been escorted in with flashing lights and sirens.

She wouldn't say that Jesse Steele constituted an emergency, but in some people's opinion—women people—he might be seen as a five-alarm fire. Still, she inclined her head and murmured, "Not exactly."

"Then what 'exactly'?" Natalya asked, exasperated.

Kady leaned forward on the sofa, her eyes narrowing as she carefully peered at Tania's face. "Wait, I know that face."

Tania drew back. "You should. I've had the room down the hall from you for—"

But Kady wasn't about to get distracted by an avalanche of rhetoric. She waved her hand for Tania to stop talking. "That's your I'm-going-out-with-a-new-guy face."

Intrigued, Natalya moved Kady out of the way and took her turn studying Tania's face. "You're right, it is." She looked properly impressed as she glanced back at Kady. "Boy, you're good."

Tania was on her feet. She wasn't in the mood to be teased. "You're all crazy. I expect this kind of thing from Mama, not you," she complained, slanting a glance to Kady and then Natalya.

As she began to turn away, Kady put herself directly in Tania's face. Of the five of them, Kady and Tania were the ones who looked most like one another. They all looked different. Their father was fond of saying that it was as if someone had given him a rose garden with five very different roses. Sasha had hair the color of midnight, Natalya was a vibrant redhead, while Marja's hair was golden-brown with red highlights shot through it. Natalya and Tania were both honey blondes.

"I'm afraid it's hereditary," Kady said with as straight a face as she could manage. "Something that's passed on from mother to daughter—"

"Like nagging?" Tania countered.

Natalya shook her head. "Uh-uh, don't let Mama hear you say that she nags. You will *never* hear the end of it."

"Which constitutes nagging," Tania declared. She spread her hands. "I rest my case."

"The hell with your case. Spill it," Natalya ordered.

"Who is it this time? You dumped poor Eddie less than three weeks ago." Eddie Richards was a fifth-year resident in pediatrics. "His body's not even cold."

"No," Tania agreed with a smile that Sasha had often called inscrutable, "but then, his body never was." And then she shrugged, as if tossing aside that part of her life. "But it was time to move on."

Like her parents and her sisters, Sasha worried about Tania, about the fact that Tania had had more boyfriends than the rest of them put together. There were times when Sasha felt that Tania acted more like a moving target than someone looking for a meaningful relationship, something that had, up to this point, never been part of her life. They all knew why and they gave Tania her space, but that didn't mean they weren't concerned.

If she wasn't careful, Sasha thought, Tania could very easily wind up on a self-destructive path. "You don't move on, you move around, like someone who—"

Tania shot Sasha a warning look. "Don't start, Sash. I'm too tired to go ten rounds with you, okay?" And then she looked at Kady. "I thought we were supposed to get together to hold your hand and help you make decisions about your wedding. I think we should do it quick before your groom comes to his senses and decides to head for the hills."

"Nobody's running anywhere," Sasha said in a quiet voice, purposely looking at Tania. "Running was never a solution." She let her words sink in before defusing any protest Tania might offer by saying, "I should know."

Sasha was referring to the way she was after her fiancé was killed right in front of her. Before Detective Tony Santini came into her life and they healed one another.

Well, things had worked out for Sasha, but that didn't mean that they worked out for everyone, Tania thought with a sigh. "If we're going to get serious, I'll drag out the tissues."

"Why isn't Mama here?" Natalya asked suddenly, realizing they were short one very vocal participant. "She likes to be in on these plans."

That would be her fault, Kady thought. "I just want to have a few things in place before Mama takes everything over."

"Mama doesn't always take over," Sasha said, defending the woman they all adored. Their mother meant well, she just was accustomed to doing things faster than waiting for someone else to do the task. She tended to be a little overzealous.

Tania laughed, shaking her head. "Right, and Napoleon ran a day-care center because he was so easygoing."

Just then, the doorbell rang. The five sisters all exchanged glances.

"Are you expecting anyone?" Tania asked Kady, but her question was meant for the others, as well.

"No," Kady answered.

"Not me," Marja chimed in, getting up again for another go at the refrigerator.

"You owe me dinner," Tania told her.

"Bill me," Marja said cheerfully, rummaging around again.

Natalya was on her way to answer the door. "Well, since none of us has X-ray vision, maybe someone should answer the door."

"Since you're on your feet anyway…" Tania let her voice trail off as she waved her older sister on.

"No respect for your elders," Natalya lamented, pulling the door opened.

"My thoughts exactly," Magda Pulaski agreed, walking in. As she passed her second child, Magda gently placed two fingers beneath Natalya's chin and pushed upward. "Close your mouth, dear. You are catching flies." She looked about at her other daughters. No one could tell if she was hurt, angry or just taking advantage of the moment and the element of surprise. "Why are you all leaving me out? Have I done something to offend you? Have I been a bad mother?" she asked. "Sasha, were you not happy with the wedding I helped you make?"

"It was a wonderful wedding, Mama." In truth, Sasha would have been satisfied exchanging her vows in whispers in the middle of the New York public library as long as her family was there and Tony was by her side.

"And you, you are not happy with the plans for your wedding?" she asked Natalya.

"Super plans, Mama," Natalya responded. It had taken about eight go-rounds, but now they were pretty super.

Kady slipped her arm around her mother's shoulder, stooping just a little because Magda was so short. "We're not leaving you out, Mama, we thought we'd do some of the preliminary work before taking up some of your valuable time and asking you for your opinion."

Magda frowned. She was versed to a greater or lesser degree in a dozen languages, but there were words in her adopted country that still eluded her. "I do not know what this 'preliminary' is, but if there is work to be done—" The look she gave Kady made her meaning clear. She meant to roll up her sleeves and pitch in from the very beginning.

Tania bit the side of her lower lip. A sign that she was uneasy. "We thought you'd be bored after planning two weddings."

"Bored?" Magda eyed her incredulously. "Bored is sitting at home, listening to your father tell the same stories over and over again." Sasha slipped behind her and handed her a glass of merlot, her mother's favorite variety of wine. Magda took it without skipping a beat, nodding at her oldest daughter. "I love that man, I really do. But he can be boring." She sighed. "So boring." And then she beamed. "Planning weddings for my girls is not boring, it is heaven."

Something wasn't adding up for Kady. Only the five of them knew that they were getting together. She'd gone out of her way to make sure the word didn't spread. "How did you find out we were having a meeting here this afternoon?"

Tania was on the receiving end of a beatific smile, as mysterious as it was amused. "I am a mother. Mothers always know when their children are up to something."

"And this all-seeing thing hits when?" Marja asked. "Right after the water breaks?"

Magda merely smiled. "I will let you find that out for yourself, Marysia," she promised. She sat on the sofa, taking a spot beside Kady. "All right, what have I missed?"

"Not a thing, apparently," Marja murmured under her breath.

Magda turned to look at her youngest, her line of vision straying toward Tania, as well. Rather than respond to what her youngest had commented, Magda's gentle hazel eyes widened.

"Oh, Tania, another one?" she asked. Surprise, dismay and sadness all mingled in her voice. "You are seeing someone new?" It wasn't really a question so much as a request for confirmation—or better yet, denial.

Stunned, Tania threw up her hands as she looked at her sisters for an answer. "How does she *do* that?" she cried helplessly.

The only answer she received was the concerned expression on her mother's thin and still remarkably unlined face.

The next moment, the previous moment was quickly swallowed up by chatter as catalogs were produced and questions and comments about the upcoming wedding flew back and forth across the room.

Magda Pulaski didn't believe in wasting time.

The next evening, when her shift was over, found Tania staring into the contents of her closet, looking over her clothing options. Her mind was elsewhere.

The ritual was always the same. An internal argument tantamount to an emotional tug-of-war would ensue every time she was about to go out with someone.

Every single time.

It didn't matter if it was the first date or the tenth—it had never gone beyond that number and rarely, if ever, even came close to it—she went through the same motions, the same wavering, undecided whether or not to go forward. If she canceled on the date, decided not to go through the hassles involved, then ultimately it meant that Jeff had won. Won because his presence, his memory, intimidated her.

Won because he made her afraid to live.

So, to "show" him, Tania would usually go ahead with her plans for the evening. Because she was so attractive and so seemingly outgoing, she wound up going out with a great many different men. Never becoming serious about any of them.

She'd laugh, perhaps even have a good time. But she was always split about things. So split internally that she never could fully experience anything that was happening. If she went to bed with a man, if her desire to negate Jeff's hold on her took her that route, it was only her body that was there. Emotionally, she always slipped away, too afraid of what the consequences of her actions might entail.

And her mental game of Ping-Pong always began here, in the bedroom, as she pondered the sanity of what she was undertaking while she moved hangers about in her closet, trying to pick out something to wear.

Just as she took out a dark blue sheath, she cursed under her breath.

No, damn it, she wasn't going to keep doing this. Jesse Steele was a nice guy, gave off nice-guy vibes, and it was just dinner, anyway. The man didn't even know where she lived and as long as she went to a crowded place, she'd be fine. They'd meet, eat, talk and then, for tonight, go their separate ways.

And then she would think about her options.

Nothing to worry about, she told herself sternly as she slid the zipper up the back of the sheath.

She didn't set out to like him.
Wasn't prepared to like him.
Didn't *want* to like him.

Liking someone only complicated things. You didn't have to like the person you were physically attracted to. Liking them got in the way of the sex and, when she came right down to it, that was as far as she ever planned things. To cap off the evening with sex. Sex that would—maybe this time—somehow disintegrate the memory of that other time. That time that had smashed her soul into tiny pieces.

But all that would come—if it came at all—later. She never, ever allowed herself to be coaxed into bed on the first date. She might be lost, but she wasn't easy. And things were done according to her plans, not anyone else's. She made the terms, she called the shots. She only allowed the man to think he was the aggressor. He wasn't. She was. And as the aggressor, she had the right to end it whenever she wished.

Still, Jesse made her laugh. More, he made her smile. Not just one of those fleeting smiles where the corners of her mouth quirked, but one of those deep, penetrating smiles that went clear down to the bone and made you glad to be alive.

In her case, it made her glad that she had decided to meet him for dinner instead of bowing out at the last minute, using her old standby excuse: I'm on call—and they called.

Half an hour into dinner, Tania caught herself actually thinking about shutting off her cell phone and wishing that she could. As far as she could remember, it was the first time that had happened.

"I read about you in the paper," she said as the waiter cleared away the few crumbs that were all that was left of a sinfully delicious appetizer.

Jesse winced at the mention of the coverage. "Please, the less said about that, the better."

His response aroused her curiosity. In her experience, most people tried to get into the limelight, not avoid it.

"Why?" She nodded a silent thanks to the waiter who now began to serve the main course. "I thought everyone liked getting their fifteen minutes of fame."

"Not me," Jesse said with feeling. The less attention he had drawn to him, the better. He'd already been the recipient of enough attention to last him a lifetime. More. "I'm perfectly satisfied to donate my fifteen minutes to someone else. As far as I'm concerned, they can have thirty."

Despite her best efforts not to, Tania found herself intrigued. Jesse looked as if he really meant what he said.

Chapter 5

Tania waited until the waiter retreated again before asking her question. "Are you just shy, or is it that you're harboring the soul of a hermit?"

"Neither." He turned his attention to the main course, discovering that he was pretty hungry. "I'd just rather not have the attention."

The signs were posted, she mused. This was where she was supposed to back off, to artfully change the subject to something light. Knowing things about other people eroded the barriers, theirs and hers.

But he'd made her curious. And besides, for the time being she had no desire to lapse into inane statements that fell in the category of "How 'bout those Yankees?"

So, even as she picked up her knife and fork, she fixed Jesse with her most penetrating, interested gaze and prodded a little.

"But why?" she asked him. "There has to be a reason why—" She added what she thought of as the clincher, "And you might want to get it off your chest."

No doubt she was thinking about confession being good for the soul. "It's nothing like that."

"Like what?" she asked innocently, silently urging him on.

To confess, he had to have done something wrong, and he hadn't, Jesse thought. Except pay attention to the wrong woman. It had made him gun-shy for a while. Until yesterday.

She was waiting, so he elaborated. "I'm not someone who jumped bail in another state, or a delinquent dad who's fallen so far behind in his child support payments that there's a warrant out for his arrest."

"Good to know." She didn't bother to add that he didn't seem like the type. She wasn't all that great a judge of character. Tania took a sip of her Long Island Iced Tea and then placed it back on the table. "You're also not shy because shy people don't spring into action. They hope someone else will do the springing so their conscience won't haunt them." Tania paused, waiting. But Jesse didn't take the bait.

She leaned in a little closer, creating a small, private world for the two of them. "Now you have me really curious. C'mon, get it off your chest. They say it's good to face your fears." She parroted what the therapist had said to her during her first—and only—session. The therapist was a friend of Natalya's and had a very gentle, soothing manner. But gentle, soothing manner or not, she just didn't have the desire to bare her soul to a stranger.

But Jesse didn't need to know that.

"True," he agreed. "But only if voicing them leads to conquering them. In my case, I could stand on a rooftop and conduct a thirty-minute monologue, it still wouldn't change the situation." He appeared rather complacent about the matter when he said, "I've already done everything that I could."

She couldn't make the pieces fit, couldn't second-guess what he was referring to.

"Okay, you're not leaving here until you spill your insides to me, Jesse Steele. I was just teasing before, but if there's one thing I can't stand," she told him honestly, "it's not knowing the outcome of something." She'd been like that as far back as she could remember. "That's why I finish every mystery I start reading, watch every horrible movie to its conclusion. I need to know things, even things of no interest, and I thrive on answers. You now have one of those in your possession." Her eyes teased him. "So give."

He laughed, not quite knowing if she was serious or not. "You're really making more out of it than it deserves."

"I'm not," Tania countered as bits of her salmon fillet continued to disappear from her plate, making their way into her mouth, "you are." She paused to level her gaze at him, issuing a royal decree. "So talk."

He was within his rights to tell her it was none of her business, because it wasn't. But he didn't want to say something like that to her. *Didn't* want to shut her out. So he took a long sip of his drink and began. "I made the mistake of dating a woman who worked for the same firm that I did."

The information was vaguely disturbing. There was no reason why it should be. After all, someone who looked like Steele wasn't destined to live life as a monk. And yet it bothered her, which made no sense to her.

Of course the man dated women before he asked you out. What did you expect? That he lived in a monastery before he was brought in strapped to that gurney? Monks just do not have muscles like that.

She deliberately kept her thoughts from registering on her face. Tania raised her glass to her lips before she nonchalantly asked, "A fellow architect?"

Jesse shook his head. "She is—was," he corrected himself, the very action giving him discomfort because despite everything, he did feel bad that she'd lost her job, "an administrative assistant."

Tania picked up on the one telling, all-important word. "'Was'?"

Jesse nodded. His appetite was slipping away. He forced himself to eat a little more. He wasn't the type to take home leftovers wrapped in aluminum that had taken on the shape of a swan. "The company let her go after certain behavior came to light."

He didn't look comfortable, Tania thought. Was that because he retained his position while the woman he was talking about had lost hers? Empathy engulfed her, coming out of nowhere.

She tried to lighten the moment. "They didn't approve of her making love with you in the supply closet?"

That was the ironic part, he'd never made love to Ellen at all. She'd spun her fantasies out of air and imagination, nothing more. "That wasn't the behavior they disapproved of."

Tania's eyes widened. "So she did make love in the supply closet with you. I'd thought it was understood that quick trysts in small, windowless enclosures were the sole domain of hospitals."

Not that she ever had done that, but she'd accidentally walked in on one of the nurses in more than a simple amorous clinch with an attending. Not hers, thank God, because that might have been the end of her career. Attendings didn't like being laughed at and she still wasn't able to look at the man without picturing him with his scrubs and his underwear around his ankles.

It would have been difficult taking orders from a man like that.

"No closets," he assured her. The topic, because it considered him, made Jesse uncomfortable. But there was no getting away from it now. He'd started it, he had to finish it. "Just a difference of opinion."

She wasn't sure she followed this. Tania looked at him quizzically. How did a difference of opinion lead to an employee being fired?

"About?"

He studied the last few drops in his glass. Amber, they caught the light and shimmered beneath it. "Whether or not there was a relationship between us. She thought there was one, I didn't."

"I take it she didn't like your version of things."

The laugh that escaped his lips had no humor in it. "Not in the least."

Well, now he had her hooked. "So what happened?" She wanted to know. "Did you find a rabbit in one of your pots?"

He counted himself lucky that it hadn't gone that route. But for a while there, he'd held his breath. "No, but I would come home to find her cooking dinner for me." It happened twice before he lost his patience and put an end to it.

Tania stared at him. "You gave her the key to your apartment?"

There had to have been some sort of relationship for that to have happened, she thought. Maybe he wasn't as innocent of blame as he seemed. Maybe he had led the woman on.

But his next answer negated that line of thinking. "No. Apparently she picked the lock."

"Resourceful."

Jesse frowned. "That makes her sound like a Girl Scout. Believe me, she wasn't." She was mentally damaged. Incapable of taking no for an answer. He sincerely hoped that she was getting the treatment she so badly needed.

His response begged for a question. "What was she?"

"As near as I can figure, a sociopath." There was no other label he could apply. Other than crazy. "I tried to make her understand that it just wouldn't work out between us, but it was like my words were just bouncing off her head and disappearing into the atmosphere. She acted as if everything was just fine. As if she belonged in my apartment. It took me forever to make her leave. The second time I found her there, she refused to go, said we belonged together for all eternity.

"When I tried to physically put her outside my apartment, she started screaming at me, pinching, kicking, biting. The neighbors called the police—" his mouth curved in an ironic smile "—who promptly proceeded to arrest me for abusing her. Ellen cheered them on. But when one of the policemen started to put handcuffs on me, she suddenly had an about-face and flew into a rage. She started pummeling the guy with her fists." His mouth curved a little more. "That was when they realized that maybe I wasn't the one at fault here."

"You think?"

Tania's sarcastic remark momentarily hung in the air between them. She felt as if she'd just crossed over a bridge and while she wasn't exactly close to Jesse, she was at least a little closer than she had been a moment ago. They'd both endured things at the hands of another that they shouldn't have.

Although the damage that she'd sustained as opposed to him were worlds apart, at least Jesse understood what it meant to be at the mercy of someone else.

"So then what happened?" she asked.

"They arrested her for assaulting an officer. I had no trouble taking out a restraining order against her. I don't know how—" because this was something he hadn't shared "—but someone at the firm got wind of the restraining order and what had caused me to take one out in the first place. Ellen was summarily dismissed before the end of the workday."

He'd felt genuinely bad about that. Ellen had told him she hadn't had much in the way of savings. Because he felt responsible, he'd been tempted to send her money to help tide her over. But when he mentioned it in a conversation with one of the senior partners, Alfred Bryce, the man immediately read him the riot act, warning him that Ellen would only misconstrue the gesture, thinking he'd committed to her, after all.

In his heart, Jesse knew that Bryce was right, but his conscience still bothered him.

"Ellen," Tania echoed, plucking the woman's name out of the array of information.

He nodded. He hadn't said her name out loud for six months now. That was how long he hadn't seen her. It was beginning to look as if he was finally home free, that Ellen seemed to have moved on. "That was her name. Ellen Sederholm."

The name made her envision someone petite and mousy, but that was probably unfair, Tania thought. "And where is 'Ellen Sederholm' these days?"

He'd heard via the grapevine that she'd moved, but he wasn't about to attempt to find out if she had. He could only hope that it was out of state.

"Not within five hundred feet of me is all I know or care about," he told her.

And then it all suddenly came together for her. "And that's why you didn't want your face on the five o'clock news—because you're afraid that it might set Ellen off again."

The way she said it, it didn't sound like a question but an assumption. He answered it anyway, even though it sounded a little egotistical.

"Something like that." Jesse's lips twisted into a small smile. "My mother taught me not to take foolish risks."

Obviously the man only reflected on that when it served his purposes. "And your tackling a fleeing, armed robber was, what, a smart risk?" She laughed, then added, in case he was about to claim that it hadn't really been that risky, "I saw the video someone got of you in action on their cell phone." There was no such thing as privacy left in the world, she thought. Someone was always filming you, invading your life in hopes of being able to sell what they captured to the news media and the highest bidder. "Looked pretty risky to me."

At the time he hadn't paused to weigh his options, he'd just reacted. Still, he shrugged. "Calculated risks are okay."

Tania just wasn't buying it. Mr. Epstein had been right. Jesse was a hero, the kind her father had always approved of. "And you had time for these calculations—when?"

She had him there, Jesse thought. "Are you sure you're a doctor and not a lawyer?"

Tania pressed her lips together, suppressing a laugh. He had no idea how funny his suggestion was. Her father would have gone into anaphylactic shock if she'd told him that she wanted to become a lawyer.

"I'm sure. My father would have never let me become a lawyer," she said with a fond laugh. She could just hear her father's voice, enumerating the many faults of lawyers. "Depending on the time of day you ask him, he thinks they're just a little above or a little below snakes on the food chain."

"Sounds like a man who has opinions," Jesse commented diplomatically as the waiter returned to discreetly refill his glass. "You take after him?" It was a question he already felt he knew the answer to.

"To an extent." Tania played with the stem of her own glass. The waiter raised one eyebrow in a silent query, but she shook her head. One was her limit. Never again was she going to relinquish her control to a hazy world just because she liked the taste of a particular drink. "Not that he would admit it. He thinks I'm stubborn and he's just being steadfast."

In truth, she and her father had had few arguments. Josef liked to indulge his girls. Mama, on the other hand, had been known to lock horns with everyone but Sasha. Sasha was too easygoing to be drawn into an argument.

Amused, Jesse asked, "And what is it that you're stubborn about?"

"Not always taking his advice."

Her father had wanted her to all but become a nun after the incident. He hadn't actually said so in so many words, but every time she went out, his face became a mass of concern. And then there was always an endless barrage of questions.

Granted, he was worried about her, and she was, too. But determination trumped worry and she was determined not to let Jeff's actions brand her.

At least, not any more than they already had.

She refused to become a hermit. But then, on every outing, fear always turned up somewhere within the course of the evening and shut her down. More than anything, she wanted to break the cycle. She wanted to be whole again.

"Tell me more about your father," Jesse coaxed.

She wondered if he was just making conversation or if he was hungry to picture a father, any father, because his own had been taken from him at a young age.

So she gave him details. "He was born in Poland. Warsaw," she added. "That's where he met my mother. And where he married her. They decided to come to this country when she became pregnant with Sasha. They both wanted their children to have the opportunities they hadn't had.

"They settled in Queens and Dad became a cop. That was where my sisters and I grew up. My parents still live in the first house they ever owned."

It was hard to miss the fondness in her voice when

she spoke about her parents, Jesse thought. It was clear that she loved her family.

"Marja, my younger sister, still hasn't flown the coop. But it'll probably happen anyday now."

"And your sisters are all doctors," he marveled, thinking that was an incredible feat.

Tania nodded. "Every last one."

"Your parents must be exceptionally well-off."

Tania laughed. "Not hardly. At least, not in the way you mean. As far as money goes, they both worked their fingers to the bone, putting us through school. And it was understood that the second each of us graduated, we were to help the next in line."

Finished, he moved back his plate. "That's an interesting take on the domino theory."

"My parents are interesting people," she responded. Tania paused to take a sip from her water glass to clear her palate.

Jesse wondered what it was like, being part of such a seemingly harmonious unit. What it felt like to have people to count on, people to turn to. "I'd like to meet them sometime."

Tania studied him for a moment. That had more than just a transient sound to it. But then, men said all sorts of things while they were orchestrating scenarios that hopefully guaranteed that they'd be in someone else's bed by evening's end.

She inclined her head. "Maybe you will—sometime," she qualified. She glanced at her plate and realized that she'd finished eating. "My God, I had no idea I was that hungry."

"You certainly did justice to it." He liked seeing a

woman who wasn't afraid to eat, who didn't feel compelled to pick at her food as if she were dissecting something toxic for a science project. "Would you like some dessert?"

She had a sweet tooth that demanded tribute whenever it could, so she nodded. "There's still a little room just under my rib cage," she decided. "The perfect space for ice cream."

"Ice cream it is," he promised. Jesse had only to raise his hand.

The next moment the waiter was hovering over their table again, ready to bring in dessert.

After dessert was savored and he had paid the check, they left the restaurant. When he began to hail a cab, she stopped him.

"It's such a nice night, let's just walk. It's not far," she reminded him.

"All right."

In a disarming gesture, she slipped her arm through his. "I like the city at night. It's subdued, elegant. The pulse isn't quite so frantic and people don't seem to be in as much of a hurry at night as they do in the daytime."

There was a reason for that. "That's because everyone only has thirty-eight minutes for lunch," he pointed out. "And a list of errands to run at least the length of their arm."

She laughed. "You have a point."

The warmth that seeped into her via the contact was subtle. It took a moment before she was even aware of it. She released his arm and then promptly felt awkward. Not that she'd taken his arm in such a familiar way but that she'd let it go in the next heartbeat.

If he noticed anything strange, Jesse gave no indication.

"I don't live far from here," she told him, forcing a cheerful note into her voice.

"I'm not afraid of walking," he assured her. "Sometimes the only exercise I get is walking."

She turned her head to look at him. "And other times?"

It was a loaded, leaded question. She waited to hear his response.

"And other times I get it from the gym. One of those thirty-day, free-trial deals. If I'm not satisfied with the results by then, I can get my money back."

Her eyes swept over him and she smiled. She'd seen him without his shirt on and could honestly say that he had a body other men would kill for. "I don't think you'll be getting your money back anytime soon."

He grinned. "Why, thank you."

She could feel the effects of his smile going straight through her gut. "Wasn't a compliment, just an observation," she pointed out.

Her building was just up ahead. How had they gotten here so soon? It was as if the minutes had just melted into one another, melting away faster than snowflakes landing on a radiator.

Taking a long breath, she stopped walking right by the building's doorway. "Well, we're here."

"Not yet," he contradicted. "We're not officially 'here' until I bring you to your door."

Where was this panic coming from? It had been going so well, too. But there it was, with sharp, pointy little cleats, making holes in her. She tried not to sound as if she was nervous. "That's not necessary."

His smile was reassuring. Some of the nervous flutter left her stomach.

"That all depends on which side of the testosterone you're on." Holding the door open for her, he followed her inside. The elevator was to the right and it was waiting for them. He pressed the button and the doors opened. "See, it's an omen. I was supposed to take you to your floor."

She made no reply. Instead she pressed the button for the fifth floor. When he glanced at her, there was a new expression in her eyes. Wariness? Why? He did what he could to make her comfortable.

"Don't worry, I won't ask to come in," he assured her softly.

"I wasn't worried," she said a bit too quickly. The doors opened and they got out. Shoulders slightly stiff, she led the way to her apartment.

It was a lie, Jesse thought. A concerned look had crossed her face. She seemed slightly distracted. Had someone forced himself on her? Pushed his way in at the end of a date and that made her leery of everyone who came in the guy's wake?

He wanted to ask, but knew that would only make her more tense.

"Good to know," he murmured as they stopped before a door he assumed was hers.

There was that smile again, she thought, watching it unfurl on his lips.

Feeling it unfurl within her, as well.

Chapter 6

One moment his smile was affecting her insides, turning them upside down. The next moment it touched her on the outside as Jesse brought his mouth down on hers.

Tania was conscious of everything within the immediate vicinity. Conscious of the roots of her hair all the way down to the tips of her toes, which were curling within her shoes. Warmth spread out from their point of contact to all parts of her, threatening an immediate meltdown. She felt his hands as, still kissing her, he gently framed her face.

Felt her own heart slip into double-time as the kiss deepened.

She struggled not to be swept away.

Ordinarily she was the one who set the pace, she was the one who knew when a kiss was coming, or when anything physical was going to transpire, because she initiated it. She was the one who called the shots. Always. But this time, she had barely gotten to the starting point before the gun was fired and the race had begun. She wasn't ready.

Deeply ingrained survival instincts pleaded for her to pull away, to stop this until it could transpire on her terms. But something else, something even stronger, something lost and needy, whispered, "Continue."

She didn't like the way she felt.

She loved the way she felt.

Her head spinning, she was both dizzy and exhilarated. The upshot being that she was hopelessly confused. So confused that rather than follow her instincts, instincts that had kept her safe for more than ten years now, Tania wove her arms around Jesse's neck. And continued.

She told herself she could handle this as she sank further into a kiss that offered no escape hatch, no way out, only a path further down into a fiery, all-consuming furnace.

Her lips moved over his, taking him with her into the inferno. If she was going to be incinerated right here on her own doorstep, she damn well intended to leave an impression on him.

Jesse couldn't catch his breath.

He was right. There was chemistry here. Enough chemistry to blow up an entire building if he wasn't careful. She numbed his mind and made him fervently wish he hadn't told her that he wouldn't ask to come into her apartment. Because he wanted to come inside her apartment, wanted to make love with her slowly, with feeling. Wanted to have his hands slip along a body he knew in his gut was soft and firm and inviting.

Desires collided with reason. Something told him that he needed to go slowly with this woman who could set him on fire simply with the sweet taste of her mouth. Not because Ellen had spooked him when it came to women, but because this lady doctor seemed to want to take it one measured step at a time.

She would be worth the wait.

The ringing noise intruded, cramming its way into his consciousness until he realized what it was. Taking a deep breath, Jesse reluctantly moved his head back and looked at her.

"You're ringing," he said, his mouth still so close that, as he smiled, she could almost feel the movement of his lips. "I'd take it as a compliment, except that I think it's your cell phone."

Her brain felt as scrambled as a hot pan filled with stir-fried ingredients. Dazed, she tried desperately to focus, to understand what he was saying. The ringing abruptly ceased.

"My phone?" Tania murmured, looking up at him. The trap she'd tried to set for Jesse had snapped shut around her instead. She wanted to go on kissing him, wanted to continue basking in the sensations he created for her.

And then Tania's brain finally engaged. "Oh, my phone."

Taking another long breath, Tania fumbled at her waist, searching for the cell phone she kept clipped there. Just as her fingers closed over it, about to remove the now silent phone so she could see who'd called, the door to her apartment opened.

The movement had Jesse looking in that direction. A redhead with green eyes stood in the doorway, the doorjamb framing her. If she was surprised, she hid it rather well. Amusement entered her eyes and when she smiled, her mouth moved in exactly the same way that Tania's did.

Her voice was almost melodic. "Tania, you brought home takeout."

And she took a closer look at him. Jesse knew recognition when he saw it. It wasn't his most comfortable moment, but then, it was something he told himself he was going to have to put up with for a while longer, until some other New Yorker did something print-worthy and took his place.

"You look very familiar," the redhead said. "Do I know you?"

Tania took the opportunity to pull herself together. When Jesse didn't answer immediately, she glanced at him. He seemed a little uncomfortable, as if he might think it presumptuous to say that Natalya recognized him from the newspaper or from a sound byte that had aired on TV.

He *was* shy, Tania thought. Somehow, that made her feel better, although for the life of her, she couldn't have explained why. "This is Jesse Steele, Natalya—" Tania got no further.

Her green eyes widened with admiration and pleasure. "The guy who tackled the jewelry store thief, right? My sister sewed you up. You must like her work." And then, before he could comment, Natalya grew serious for a second. She glanced over her shoulder into the apartment. Even as she did so, there was a murmur of voices. "Um, Tania, if you'd like him to come in, I can move everyone into my room."

Tania's eyebrows drew together. "Everyone?" she echoed. "Who's everyone?"

"That's all right," Jesse cut in. "I've got to be going. I was just saying good-night."

Natalya's amusement returned in spades. Her eyes washed over him appreciatively. "Yes, I noticed." She flashed Tania a smile. "It's up to you. I can—"

Tania knew better than to let her sister talk. There was nothing any of her sisters liked more than to playfully embarrass one another and this was perfect fodder for Natalya.

"He was just leaving," Tania said firmly, even though inside she caught herself wishing that he wasn't. That it was her sister and whoever comprised "everyone" who were leaving.

"A pity," Natalya said, giving Jesse one last once-over. "Well, it was nice meeting you, Jesse." She put her hand out to shake his. Her eyes darted from Tania back to him. "Don't be a stranger, now. There isn't always a three-ring circus taking place in the living room," she promised.

As if to negate her words, two more young women had come up behind Tania's sister. They both had Tania's eyes if not her coloring, Jesse noted.

He inclined his head toward Tania and said, "I'll call you," before backing away. The next moment he'd turned on his heel, intent on going back to the elevator.

Kady watched the man disappear while Marja craned her neck to get a better view.

"Nice," Kady commented wickedly, then glanced at Tania. "Who was that?"

"Nobody," Tania said before Natalya had a chance to tell them.

"'Nobody' has a really nice walk-away," Marja interjected. She turned around to look at Tania. "If you don't want him, I don't mind taking some of your castoffs…" Her voice trailed off with a hopeful note.

"He's not a castoff," Tania informed her.

Marja pretended to look disappointed. "Then you're keeping him?"

Tania closed her eyes, searching for patience. "He's not mine to keep or give," she insisted.

"Really?" Natalya looked completely unconvinced. "From where I was standing, you two looked pretty hermetically sealed."

Marja waved her hand at the so-called evidence. "This is Tania you're talking about, have lips, will travel. She's an equal opportunity kisser. Her hobby is breaking hearts, remember?"

Tania ignored her younger sister and changed the subject. She directed her question to Natalya. "So what's this about a three-ring circus in the living room? What's up?"

Natalya slipped her arm around Tania's shoulders and gave her a small squeeze, a show of unity in case Tania felt put upon.

"We're holding an impromptu meeting." And then Natalya inclined her head so that neither Marja nor Kady, walking ahead of them, could hear. "Go easy on this one, Tania. He looks like a keeper." Tania shot her a warning look. She wasn't in the mood to be teased. "Someone's, if not yours," Natalya added.

Tania merely shrugged at the unsolicited advice. Her sisters all knew that she was not in the market to do anything beyond being diverted.

"If you say so," she said dismissively, then looked around the living room. All four of her sisters, Sasha's husband and Natalya's fiancé, as well as Kady's, were there. This was apparently big, whatever it was. Had something happened to one of her parents? Ever since the incident, Tania did her best to present a happy face to her family, but her thoughts always veered to the dark side. "What is going on?" She wanted to know.

The first thing out of Natalya's mouth set her at ease.

"We're brainstorming," her sister told her.

A sense of relief swept over Tania. Nat wouldn't have said that if something was really wrong. Whatever was going on, it wasn't life-threatening.

Her mouth curved as she glanced at the three men. "And, look, you brought in extra brains."

Tony Santini, perched on the arm of the sofa where his wife sat, held up his hands in silent disclaimer. "I'm just the driver, nothing more."

"Here for moral support," Mike DiPalma, Natalya's fiancé, chimed in.

"Same here," Byron Kennedy, Kady's fiancé, told her.

"And why is there a need for moral support?" Tania wanted to know, looking from one sister to another. "What is it that you're all brainstorming about?"

Since it was her problem, Sasha spoke up. "Mama's going a little overboard about this baby. Ever since she found out I was pregnant, she's been hovering and trying to get me to cut back my office hours." Sasha sighed. "Cut back my life, really. I think she's about to surround me with bubble wrap and I'm not even showing yet." The irony of the situation made her laugh. "You'd think that I wasn't an ob-gyn." Tony took her hand in his in a silent show of support. "There's nothing about giving birth that I don't know."

"Except how to handle Mama," Kady interjected with a sympathetic grin.

Sasha sighed and nodded her head. "Except how to handle Mama."

"Seems to me that Daddy should be in on this, don't you think?" Tania suggested, looking from Sasha to Natalya. "After all, he's the one who's survived with her all these years. That should give him a little insight into the matter."

Natalya looked at her as if she should know better. "Daddy's insight can be summed up by two little words. 'Yes, Magda.' He dotes on Mama and he's learned to placate her."

Sasha shook her head. "You'd think that having two weddings to help plan would be more than enough to keep Mama busy."

Tania laughed. Their mother was nothing if not a whirlwind. "You know Mama. Multitasking should have been called 'Magda-tasking' in her honor since she practically invented it."

As Kady began to put in her own two cents, Tania's cell phone went off again. The sound reminded her of the call she'd ignored earlier on her doorstep. She angled her cell phone's LCD screen to see who was calling her even as her sisters checked to see if it was their phones that were ringing.

"Mine," Tania declared with a note of resignation. "It's the hospital." So much for spending the rest of the evening at home. Taking the phone off the clip, she held off opening it for a second. "My advice is to get Mama entrenched in the idea that she's been toying with off and on for the last five years—her own catering business." She looked at Sasha. "That *plus* the two weddings should keep even Mama too busy to make you crazy."

Mama seemed to be tireless and to never need any sleep. Sasha had her doubts that even if they could convince her to finally turn her dream into a reality, that Mama would back off—even a little.

"If only," Sasha sighed.

As Tania turned away, placing the cell phone to her ear, Natalya took up the suggestion. "You know, Tania just might have something there. Mama loves to cook and she's really good at it." Her tone indicated that they had nothing to lose by championing the idea and bringing it to their mother's attention as a unit. "Hey, it's worth a shot."

Tania moved away from the others. One hand to her ear to block out the noise, she held the cell phone to her other ear. "Dr. Pulaski."

"Are you up to taking on another shift?" the voice on the other end of the line asked. She didn't have to ask who it was. She recognized Mark Howell's crisp, precise enunciation. The chief attending's speech was as neat as his work in the E.R. He also didn't wait for an answer before adding, "Two doctors called in sick."

Of course they did, Tania thought. To be fair, there was a particularly strong strain of flu making the rounds. "When do you want me?"

"Now would be good." His tone indicated that the conversation was a formality and that he expected her to comply.

Tania longed for the day when she was finally at the

top of the heap and her own boss. She began to doubt it would ever come. Biting back the sigh, she told Howell, "I'm on my way."

"I'll expect you." The line went dead.

Out of the corner of her eye, she saw Sasha looking in her direction. The moment she closed her phone, Sasha crossed to her. "I know you're indestructible, but shouldn't you get *some* rest?"

Yes, Tania thought, that had a nice sound to it, but she was the one who'd put her name down as backup for any no-shows in the E.R. So she forced a smile to her lips and said, "I take after Mama."

Sasha didn't back off. "That's when it comes to multitasking, not doing an imitation of some deranged mechanical bunny that never stops going. In case you don't remember, you don't run on batteries—and you just came off another one of your famous double shifts before you went out for dinner."

She knew Sasha meant well, but there were times when she felt everyone was looking over her shoulder, critiquing her life. "How would you know?" she asked. "You don't even live here anymore."

Sasha smiled as she unconsciously slipped her hand over her stomach. "I'm studying to be a mother, remember? Omniscient powers come with the territory. It's a package deal."

"Well, don't practice on me, okay?" And then, because she did know that Sasha was only looking out for her, Tania added, "Don't worry, if I get too tired, I'll take a cat nap."

"Just don't do it while you're sewing someone up," Kady deadpanned.

"Hey, she might do a better job that way," Marja pointed out.

Tania gave her a look before she went to her room. "That's enough out of you, Marja. You need to respect your elders."

"You're only my elder by thirteen months," Marja protested.

"And every second counts," Tania called back.

In her room, Tania went to her closet to get a change of clothing. Unlike her quandary while getting ready for Jesse, she pulled out the first two items that she came to, a navy-blue skirt and a light gray pullover. Less than ten minutes later, she was ready.

"Want to take the car?" Kady asked as Tania crossed the living room to the front door. "The car" was the one they all shared now that Sasha had moved out, taking hers with her.

Like the rest of her sisters, Tania had a driver's license. Unlike them, she was never completely comfortable behind the wheel. Her mind, so disciplined in the E.R., wandered too much when there was so much to look at. And besides, she grew impatient with the traffic that, at best, moved like petroleum jelly on a cold day.

So she shook her head in response to Kady's question. "It's a nice night, I think I'll just walk to the hospital."

Mike, Tony and Byron all exchanged glances and rose to their feet, propelled by the same thought. Tony and Byron put it into the exact same words almost simultaneously. "The hell you will."

Mike, the easier going of the three, grinned and jerked a thumb at the other two. "What they said, except maybe not so gruffly." He looked at Natalya. "You stay here with everyone. I'll be right back," he told his fiancée.

Natalya appreciated Mike's thoughtfulness. It wasn't something she'd take for granted anytime soon. "Looks like we've picked out good men," she said, addressing Kady and Sasha.

"Then hang on to them," Tania advised. She tried to beg off as politely as she could. "Really—" as she talked, she made her way to the door "—I just want to stretch my legs, maybe do a little thinking."

But Mike wasn't about to stay behind. The Pulaski women were all headstrong, but he'd been raised with sisters and he was not about to be talked out of what he knew was right.

"I won't interfere with your thoughts," Mike promised her, following her out the door. "But I'm not taking no for an answer, either."

Mike walked her to the elevator.

"You know, I am a big girl now," Tania told him as they rode down together to the first floor. "Been crossing the street by myself and everything ever since I was five years old."

He put his hand out to keep the doors open as he waited for her to walk out first. A second later he fell into step beside her.

"Knowing your mother, it was probably closer to eight, not five," Mike guessed, his voice easygoing. "You remind me a lot of one of my sisters," he continued. "Everyone else would say white, Gina would say 'black' just to stir things up and be different."

Where was this edginess coming from? she demanded of herself. He was just trying to be nice to her.

She should be grateful that Natalya was marrying such a good guy, not sulking because she couldn't be alone. Alone wasn't a good thing, she reminded herself. When she was alone, thoughts would come crowding into her head. Memories she didn't want, blocking out the myriad memories that were good.

"I'm not trying to be different. Or difficult," she added, guessing what might be crossing his mind. "I'm just trying not to inconvenience anyone."

In the basement, he led her toward where he had left his car in guest parking. Mike spread his hands wide. "Do I look inconvenienced?"

No, he didn't. He also wasn't quite as easygoing as he pretended, she thought. Her sister's marriage was going to be an interesting one.

"You look like a man who's going to spend a lot of time locking horns with Natalya. You know—" she waited for him to unlock her side "—Nat's not as easygoing as she might have led you to believe."

"Believe me, 'easygoing' was never a word I would have associated with your sister." He grinned. "Besides—" he put his key into the ignition and turned it "—a little bit of friction is what makes life interesting."

She glanced behind her as he pulled the car out of the parking spot. She thought she saw a movement out of the corner of her eye. Someone running. But when she looked, there was no one there. Maybe she *was* too tired, like Sasha said.

"Maybe not," she agreed absently. "But you know, you really don't have to go out of your way like this."

"The sooner I drop you off at the hospital, the sooner I'll be back," he pointed out.

She nodded. "I guess I can't argue with that."

He laughed, guiding the car out into the street. "That would be a first in your family."

Chapter 7

The light at the corner turned green. Tania went with the flow, working her way across the busy street. Even at seven-thirty in the morning, the streets and sidewalks were crammed with traffic, both vehicular and human.

She couldn't shake the feeling that she was being watched.

As she walked, she looked around. No one stood out, no one made eye contact. Just the opposite, if anything. The feeling refused to go away. Tania told herself that it was just her old paranoia revisiting her. She could feel the hairs standing up at the back of her neck.

Maybe she was just going crazy.

Granted, Jeff had been paroled recently and there was a part of her that worried he might try to make contact with her, might want to avenge himself because of the years she'd supposedly cost him.

But that would only put him back in jail. As part of his parole, he was supposed to stay far away from her. Her father had seen to that. And Jeff had sounded sincere at his allocution years ago, rendered just before he'd gone to prison. He'd apologized for the anguish and bodily harm he'd caused her. He'd blamed it on alcohol consumption, saying that none of it would have happened if he hadn't gotten drunk.

Of course, that had all been part of the bargain for a reduced sentence, his allocution and the fact that she didn't have to go through the gut-wrenching ordeal of a trial where she would have had to tell and retell her story before a courtroom full of strangers.

Jeff had been out for several months. Why was this uneasiness descending over her now?

Because her life was being shaken up, she thought. Shaken up for the first time since she'd consciously pulled her emotions out of the game, sealing them away. It was all Jesse's fault. Jesse and that damned hot mouth of his.

She enjoyed physical contact up to a point, but not to the degree where she'd lose herself, lose the ability to think clearly and function. For more than just a split second, when Jesse'd kissed her at her door, her mind had gone blank and her body had grown hot. As for the longing—well, she just didn't do that, didn't "long" for lovemaking.

And yet...

He'd made her long, made her want.

No wonder she was paranoid, Tania thought, annoyed. Jesse had thrown a huge monkey wrench into her life. She couldn't allow that to happen. From now on, she just needed to concentrate on her work and *nothing else.* God knew that was more than enough to keep any two people occupied.

Coming to the end of another block, Tania waited for the light to turn green and the Walk sign to beckon her forward.

She was walking to work, not exactly by choice but necessity. The bus she normally took when one of her sisters wasn't driving in at the same time she was due at the hospital had broken down and the one sent in to take its place, the driver had informed them, was running late. There'd all but been a mutiny as all the passengers got off the grounded bus.

Instead of waiting for another bus, Tania opted to walk off some of her nervous energy. The hospital really wasn't all that far. The sky above her was ominous with dark gray, pregnant clouds. She could almost smell the rain, but for now the air was heavy with oppressive humidity that seeped its way into everything. Running late, Tania had left the apartment without taking an umbrella.

Mentally she crossed her fingers that she'd reach Patience Memorial before the rain finally began to come down.

Waiting at yet another corner, Tania glanced to her right and thought she saw a long-range camera lens emerging from the driver's side of a car stopped at the light. The car had tinted windows so she couldn't look in to see the driver. Just the camera.

Her heart jumped. The camera was pointed in her direction.

It's a tourist, idiot, she upbraided herself. Probably some native from a tiny town in Montana whose entire population could fit on any New York street corner with room to spare.

The city could be overwhelming to people unaccustomed to the street's crowds at any given time of day or night.

So why did it feel as if the damn lens was focused on her?

Because you're overwrought and tired and your imagination is running away with you, she silently insisted. Just as it had the other day when someone had accidentally bumped into her, sending her off the curb and into the path of an oncoming bus. If someone else hadn't quickly grabbed her arm and pulled her back, she had no doubt that she would have found herself spending time in the hospital on the other side of the guardrail.

Tania picked up her pace. Even as she did, a fat raindrop fell directly on her head.

Terrific.

The car with the camera lens kept pace with her.

Drawing some of the oppressive air into her lungs, Tania wove her way through the crowd, moving faster. Four more long city blocks to go.

All the while, out of the corner of her eye, she continued to watch the car.

To her relief, the car disappeared at the end of the next block.

See? You're worried about nothing.

Her nervous feeling refused to retreat into the shadows.

Tania stripped off her surgical mask and took a deep breath. What a difference a few hours made.

She'd arrived at the hospital wet — it had rained for

the last block—with her nerves close to the surface. And then her current attending, Dr. Thomas Benedict, had asked her if she wanted to assist in what he whimsically referred to as a "simple procedure." It was a kyphoplasty. Her very first.

In essence the operation was a cousin to an angioplasty, except that it concerned itself with the spine rather than the heart. It entailed making a cut in the groin and snaking a wire up to the spinal area where, in this case, two balloons were inserted, one in each section where the patient had a minor spinal fracture. The balloons moved the spine back to its original position and then bone cement was squeezed into the newly created spaces to make the restoration permanent.

Under Benedict's watchful eye, Tania had inserted the cement, as well as closed up the initial incision. She left the operating room feeling as if she walked on air. The power to help, to heal, was an exceedingly heady sensation. It was like nothing else she'd ever experienced.

If, at dark times, she doubted herself, doubted the wisdom of her choices, being in the operating room lay those doubts to rest.

Surgery gave her a purpose, an identity.

Walking through the operating room's swinging doors, she leaned against the wall and savored the feeling.

One of the surgical nurses came out behind her. The woman raised her eyes as the P.A. system went off. She glanced at Tania. "Are you going to answer that?"

Tania blinked, realizing that she'd temporarily slipped into her own little world. She straightened, standing away from the wall. "Excuse me?"

The older woman pointed up in the general direction of the loudspeaker. "You're being paged."

Tania focused, listening. The woman over the P.A. said her name and asked her to pick up the nearest phone.

"Oh, right, I am. Thanks." She flashed a grin at the nurse and hurried over to the first interhospital wall phone she could find. "This is Dr. Tania Pulaski. You paged me?"

"You have a call," the operator told her. "Would you like me to put it through?"

"Sure, go ahead." She noticed a few of the hospital staff glancing in her direction as they went toward the elevator bank. Probably because she couldn't stop smiling, Tania thought.

"Go ahead, please," the operator said. Whether it was to her or whoever was on the other end of the line, Tania didn't know.

"This is Dr. Tania Pulaski," she repeated, turning to face the wall. It gave her the illusion of privacy.

"Finally," she heard the deep male voice on the other end say.

Tania felt an immediate, involuntary reaction. Her pulse accelerated. "Jesse?"

"You recognize my voice. I'm flattered."

She hadn't heard from him in three days and had begun to think that she wouldn't. "I'll call you" was such a throwaway line. Her smile widened. "Why are you calling me at the hospital?"

"Because your home number's unlisted and you never gave me your cell number."

She realized he was right. Self-preservation? "I didn't, did I?"

"You know," he told her, his voice deliberately lofty,

"if I wasn't as secure as I am, I'd say you were trying to avoid me."

Tania felt her mouth curving and told herself she was just still riding high from her OR experience. "Good thing you're so secure," she agreed.

"Listen, this hero thing has a few perks attached to it. The theater manager at the Schubert is somehow related to Mr. Epstein, the jewelry store owner. A nephew or second cousin, twice removed, something like that. Anyway, he called to tell me that there would be theater tickets waiting for me at the box office if I wanted to use them."

Tania's eyes widened. "For *Colors of the Rainbow?*"

The theater wasn't his thing and he wasn't sure if she had the right name. "I think that's the name of the play he mentioned."

She'd tried unsuccessfully to buy a pair of tickets for her parents. "That's the hottest musical in town," she told him. "The show is sold out for the next nine months."

"Since you know that, I take it that you like musicals."

She could hear his smile over the phone. "It's my guilty pleasure," she freely admitted. Her father had taken her to her first Broadway musical when she was ten. It was a Wednesday matinee on a two-fer ticket. He'd called in sick in order to take her to the play. She'd fallen in love that afternoon and had adored musicals ever since.

"Then would you like to go with me? It's for a week from Thursday night." He paused as he realized that he really didn't know her hours. "Unless you're on duty."

She was scheduled for the night shift on Thursdays until the end of the month, but that didn't daunt her.

"I can find someone to switch with." She said it as if it were a done deal. She'd put in so much extra time covering for other people, Tania was fairly certain that she could get someone to take her shift. If need be, she'd bribe someone.

"Great. I'll pick you up at your place at five-thirty."

That sounded pretty early. "Doesn't the show start at seven-thirty?"

"Yes," he answered. "But I thought I'd wine and dine you first."

What was the harm in that? she thought. As long as she knew what was ahead, she was prepared and could call the shots. And she *did* want to see the play. "You do know how to show a girl a good time."

"I do my best."

Tania could almost feel his words traveling along her skin and it took effort for her not to let herself drift with the sound of his voice. She abruptly changed the subject.

"Say, what's this I hear about you turning down an interview on *The Today Show?*"

"Not my thing, remember?"

Because she liked to fill the apartment with sound when she was alone, Tania always turned on the TV set in the living room. She'd caught part of the local heroes segment before she hurried out the door this morning. "Maybe you should have made an exception this time. They had Mr. Epstein on in your place and to hear him tell it, Joshua storming the walls of Jericho was a wimp in comparison to you. I think he just drummed up another fifteen minutes of fame for you."

She heard Jesse sigh. "I keep hoping this'll all blow over."

"It will." Everything always did. "But in the meantime," she reminded him, "you do have those tickets to the hottest show in town."

She heard him laugh softly and the sound went straight to her stomach despite her efforts to block it. "Yes, I do. Which allows me to take out the hottest woman in town. See you next Thursday."

Tania ran her tongue along her extradry lips. "See you."

Hanging up the receiver, Tania stood where she was for a second, trapped in the excited moment.

"I heard you just assisted in your very first kyphoplasty. Congratulations." Coming to, Tania turned to see Sasha approaching. "By the way, did that candy striper ever find you?"

Tania forced herself to focus. Was it her imagination or was Sasha looking thinner these days? "What candy striper?"

"I guess she didn't, then," Sasha surmised. "Just some candy striper who wanted to know where to find you earlier. I said you were in surgery."

Tania shook her head. She couldn't imagine why one of the volunteers would be searching for her. Maybe whoever it was had her confused with one of her sisters. That seemed the more likely scenario.

"Did she say what she wanted?"

"Not to me, although I did tell her you were my sister so I'd pass any message along if she wanted me to. But she said that was okay."

Mildly curious, Tania asked, "Did she give you a name?"

"No, but she had 'Carol' sewn on her blouse." Sasha

began to walk toward the elevator banks. Tania fell into step with her. "Funny thing, though, when I called her that, she didn't respond right away."

Tania didn't see anything unusual in that. "Okay, so Patience Memorial doesn't attract rocket scientists as volunteers." She shrugged. "I guess whatever she wanted to tell me couldn't have been all that important, otherwise she would have left a message in my in-box."

Sasha nodded as she pressed for the up elevator. "How long are you going to keep grinning?"

Tania thought of the operation she'd just assisted with—and the phone call from Jesse. Her grin grew. "Not sure. A while. Why, does it bother you?"

Sasha's eyes crinkled as she smiled back at her little sister. "No, just reminds me how much I miss seeing you look like that. Happy."

Just like Mama, Tania thought. "I'm happy, Sasha."

An elevator dinged, then opened, but it was going down to the basement. Sasha pressed the up button again. "It wouldn't have anything to do with that guy you were kissing the other evening, would it?"

"Kissed, not kissing," Tania corrected. Sasha had been the only one who hadn't come to the door the other night. "'Kissing' implies something that was ongoing. He just kissed me good-night."

Sasha shook her head. "Not to hear Nat tell it. She said the two of you were so sealed together, not even air could have slipped in between you."

Tania sighed. Privacy was not a viable word in her family. "Natalya exaggerates."

"If you say so, kid." Sasha's tone indicated that she was more inclined to believe Natalya over her protest.

The up elevator finally arrived. "Well, I have a baby to usher into the world. I'll see you tonight at Mom and Dad's," she said, stepping into the car.

"Oh, dinner." Tania caught her lower lip in her teeth. "I forgot."

The doors began to close and Sasha put her hand in the way, causing them to spring back. "I kinda thought you might. This is the push to get Mama to start up her own business—and back away a little from ours."

"I'll be there with bells on," Tania promised as the doors closed again.

Josef Pulaski sat at the head of the dining-room table, hands placed on either side of his plate, his eyes all but disappearing as he smiled broadly in deep, nostalgic satisfaction. All five of his daughters were present, along with his son-in-law, his two sons-in-law-to-be, as well as his much beloved wife. If there was any man who was more fortunate than he was, Josef wanted to meet him.

"Ah, all five of my girls sitting at my table at the same time. It is making me remember when they were all young," he said to Byron who sat closest to him.

"We still are young, Daddy," Natalya corrected. "The word you're looking for is 'younger.'"

"No." Josef sighed dramatically—years with Magda had rubbed off on him. "The word is old. I am getting old. Old, and my babies are getting married, getting babies, too."

"Baby," Kady interjected with feeling. She'd made it clear she wanted children, but not immediately. "There's only one in the immediate future."

"But there will be more babies, yes?" Josef looked hopefully at all three of the men seated around him at the table.

Mike laughed. "Hey, if it were up to me, you'd have a houseful—and soon."

"Houseful, huh?" Natalya's eyes went from Mike to Byron to Tony and then back to the culprit. "And you men can take care of them."

Josef took the words at face value and beamed. "Now that is what I want to be hearing. I will be watching them for all of you," he promised.

Sitting at the other end of the table, Magda made a small, dismissive sound as she waved away her husband's words. "Like you watched Marja when she put all those fuzzy plants into her nose?"

Marja cringed. "The pussy willow story again."

Josef rolled his eyes and looked at the three men at the table for empathy. "One time." He held up his index finger. "One time I am looking away, watching baseball game, and this one—" he waved a hand at Marja "—is breaking my record as a good father."

"Can we move on, please?" Marja pleaded.

"All right," her mother allowed magnanimously. "Tony, have some more of my dessert," she urged her son-in-law. It was a golden bundt cake made with wine and drizzled with melted powdered sugar and more wine. As Sasha reached for one of the sliced pieces herself, Magda drew the dessert back. "Not you, Sasha. You do not want the baby to get too much wine."

"Alcohol evaporates when you bake," Sasha reminded her mother, and then she exchanged looks with Kady and Natalya. It was time.

Natalya rose to the occasion. "Mama, we've been thinking you need a hobby."

Magda looked put off. "What 'hobby'? I have your father. I have all of you—and the baby. I have no time for this 'hobby.'"

Undaunted, Kady put in her two cents' worth. "We were thinking of a catering company."

Magda frowned. They had danced this dance before once or twice. She loved to cook, but to charge for that cooking was another matter. "That is not a hobby, that is a business."

"Wouldn't you want your own business?" Sasha asked, trying to sound supportive.

"I have my own business," Magda insisted. She gestured around the table. "Family—this is my business."

"We're going around in circles," Tania pointed out to her sisters.

"Yes, we are," Magda agreed. "So, we step out of that circle," she declared, then turned intent hazel eyes on Tania. "How is that new young man?"

Josef looked from his wife to Tania and then back again. He was obviously not happy about being out of the loop. "What new young man? There is a new young man?"

"No," Tania said firmly.

"Yes," Magda contradicted. "The hero," she informed her husband. "The one who stopped that thief. In the paper," she said with exasperation when Josef continued to eye her blankly. "I showed you."

Josef's eyebrows drew together to form one wavy, gray line. "She is seeing a hero? Why am I not knowing about this?"

"You are knowing about it now, Josef," Magda said, slipping another piece of cake on his plate.

It was going to be a very long night, Tania thought, bracing herself.

Chapter 8

"You know, maybe I'll just elope," Natalya muttered as she stood outside the rear E.R. doors beside Tania.

She'd sought out her younger sister a few minutes ago, opting to take Tania's break with her before going back up to her own office. The sigh that followed sounded as if it came from her very toes.

"All these plans, all these choices, it's just driving me crazy. I've been so busy, I haven't seen Mike in three days, not since dinner at Mom and Dad's. But somehow, whether I want to or not, I've managed to see Mama every day. She keeps popping up like toast." Natalya flashed a semicontrite smile that was gone the next instant. "Not that I don't love her, but—"

Tania didn't need to hear the disclaimer. They all loved Mama, but they all knew she could be a bit much at times. However, there was no getting away from a few simple facts. Tania pinned her sister with a look.

"You elope and Mama's going to have heart failure. And you *know* you'll have that on your conscience for the rest of your natural life."

"I'll tell her with Kady around." Kady was the heart specialist in the family. "If anyone can bring Mama back from the dead, it's Kady." And then she surrendered with another deep sigh. "Don't give me that look. I know, I'm only talking. I'll go through with this three-ring circus." Natalya shoved her hands deep into the pockets of her crisp lab coat. "I just think it's too much of a fuss. Who cares what kind of flowers are used as the centerpieces?"

"Mama does," Tania replied simply. She ran her hands along her arms and glanced up at the less than blue sky. More rain was coming. "What does Mike think about all this?"

Natalya smiled at the mention of her fiancé's name. "Mike comes from a large Italian family. He's used to mothers fussing over nonsense."

Tania thought someday Natalya was going to look back at all this organized chaos and laugh. But probably not anytime soon. For a second she found herself envying her older sister for having found someone so understanding. She really liked the police detective who was joining the family. "Lucky for you."

"Yeah," Natalya agreed, echoing the sentiment. "Lucky for me."

"You have that goofy grin on again," Tania teased.

"It is *not* a goofy grin," Natalya said defensively, then relented just a little. "Wait'll you fall in love, Tania. You'll see."

As far as Tania was concerned, it was a promise without foundation.

"Maybe," Tania said carelessly.

She sincerely doubted she would ever be in that position, ever find anyone she wanted to love. And even if she did, even if she met someone absolutely perfect in every way—and what chance was there of that?—opening up to someone wouldn't be easy for her, if not impossible. A part of her was completely blocked off inside, unreachable.

But there was no point in discussing it. So Tania humored her sister and agreed. She winced as she heard the squeal of brakes in the distance. But it wasn't followed by the sound of metal meeting metal and the tension left her shoulders.

Tania glanced at her watch. "Looks like my break's over." She turned toward the rear doors. "Time to get back to work."

Natalya stopped leaning against the wall. "Yeah, me, too." She hurried inside and turned left, heading toward the back elevators. "See you later."

"Think honeymoon," Tania called after her.

"It's the only thing keeping me sane," Natalya assured her as she walked quickly to the elevator bank.

The moment she walked back into the E.R. area, one of the nurses handed Tania a file. There was a broad grin on her face as she did so.

Tania raised an inquiring eyebrow.

"Mr. Wonderful is back," the young woman told her. There was a hint of a sigh attached to the statement.

"Excuse me?" Tania glanced at the file for some edification.

The nurse gave Tania the answer before she had a chance to read the name neatly typed across the tab. "That hunk that made the newspapers. By the way, he asked for you." There was envy in the nurse's brown eyes. "Room five," she added, needlessly nodding in the trauma room's direction.

File in hand, Tania quickly made her way to the last trauma room.

She didn't like the way her pulse quickened for a second, wasn't happy that anticipation suddenly surged in her chest. And certainly wasn't thrilled by the way her heart all but leaped up when she pushed open the door and Jesse looked in her direction, their eyes meeting.

She wasn't supposed to feel any of these things. Wasn't supposed to feel, period.

"Been tackling another thief?" she asked, coming closer and opening the file.

It wasn't his imagination, Jesse thought. She *was* gorgeous. Even more than he remembered. "No."

She placed the folder on the side counter. "Then to what do we owe the pleasure of your company?"

My God, that sounded as if it had come out of a grade-B movie straight out of the seventies, Tania berated herself. What the hell was the matter with her? She didn't talk like that.

A smattering of confusion brought his eyebrows together. "You told me to come, remember? Follow-up care," he prompted when she gave no indication that she knew what he was talking about.

Embarrassment kissed her cheeks, giving them a very inviting, pink hue. He caught himself wanting to rub his thumb along her cheek, to lightly trace the path of the color as it made its way up her skin.

"I can come back if you're too busy," he offered.

"No, there's no point in that. We're always busy," she said quickly.

God, but she felt like an idiot, forgetting those very basic instructions. Seeing him had knocked all logic out of her head. For a split second, she'd thought that maybe he'd come just to see her.

Why should that even matter?

It didn't, she insisted silently.

Doing her best to seem all business, she paused to slip on a pair of gloves. "How have you been doing?" she asked. "Any headaches, blurred vision—" she drew closer to him "—dizziness?"

As she leaned forward to examine a bruise, he took in a deep breath, letting the scent of her perfume filter into his senses.

"Maybe a little dizziness," he allowed.

Tania drew back to look at him, concerned. "When?"

His smile hit her right in the pit of her stomach, causing a minor tidal wave. "Whenever I'm around you," he told her innocently.

"Oh, that kind of dizziness." She gave him a knowing look. "The flirting kind." She lightly touched another, larger bruise at the side of his neck. "I'm talking about the serious kind."

"Then no, no dizziness." She stepped away for a moment and he twisted around to watch her. "You know, I don't really do this sort of thing."

"Flirt?" Her mouth curved with amusement. "I find that hard to believe."

"No, go to a doctor, especially for something like 'follow-up care.'" He'd grown up without any health care of any kind and learned to tough things out for the most part.

She paused a moment, her eyes meeting his. He was just too damn good-looking. How she tried vainly to maintain proper boundaries. "Then why did you?"

Jesse had a feeling that honesty was the best way to go with her. "Because I wanted to see you again and a follow-up seemed like a good excuse. You know," he pointed out, "if you were a gnarled old man, I wouldn't be here right now."

Tania couldn't help smiling. "So this is all my fault."

He nodded solemnly, but his eyes gave him away. "That's the way I see it."

She took a disinfectant out of the overhead cabinet, just in case. "But you are going to see me again," she reminded him. "The play next Thursday." She stopped as the thought occurred to her. "Or is that off?"

"No, that's very much on." He barely felt her fingers as she gently examined the area around his stitches. "Listen, can you get away for a cup of coffee? I told them at the firm that I wouldn't be back until after lunch, sometime around one. That gives me a least an hour to kill."

"And you want to kill some time with me?"

She sounded amused, he thought, grateful that she hadn't taken his statement the wrong way. "That didn't come out right, did it?"

He heard her laugh. "At least I know you're not the type who hands out lines. Unless this tripping-over-your-own-tongue is really just a bit."

Her lab coat brushed against his face as she examined another scrape. "Not very trusting, are you?"

No, she thought, trust was forfeited more than ten years ago. She finished and gazed down at him. "I'm a New Yorker, remember?"

Jesse studied her for a long moment. "No, I think it might be something more than that."

That he could see past the surface made her uncomfortable. "I thought you said you were an architect, not a psychiatrist." Stepping back, she removed the rubber gloves and then tossed them into the wastebasket. "Well, you look fine. The stitches are coming along nicely. No sign of infection. You won't be needing any more follow-up care," she told him. "Unless there's a problem."

This had gone much too quickly and he wasn't willing to give up her presence just yet. "Well, my first problem is that you won't have coffee with me."

She made a notation in his chart. An enigmatic smile played on her lips. "I didn't say I wouldn't."

"Then it's yes?"

Done with the chart, she flipped it closed. He was relieved to see humor in her eyes. "I didn't say that, either. I don't like being second-guessed."

He kept it light. "The question is, do you like coffee?"

What was it about this man that made her want to smile? She remembered Natalya's words about the goofy smile and waiting until it was her turn.

Just proved that her sister didn't know everything, Tania thought stubbornly. If she had a goofy smile, it had nothing to do with being in love, just being tickled and amused, that's all.

"Yes," she told him, "I like coffee."

"Then would you be willing to have a cup with me now?" he asked.

He was asking, not assuming. They were making progress.

"Better," she commented with a nod of her head. "But the answer's still no. I just had my break," she explained. "And we're full up here. So, Mr. Steele, if you don't have any further questions—"

Anticipating her departure, Jesse slid off the gurney to his feet. He grabbed the suit jacket he'd removed. "Oh, but I do. Lots of questions."

"Such as?"

Placing himself between her and the door, Jesse began to enumerate.

"What's your favorite color? Are you a morning person or an evening person? Do you prefer long walks on the beach or window-shopping on Fifth Avenue? What kind of movies do you prefer?" Jesse took in a breath. "Are you—"

"Wait, wait," she cried, laughing, raising her hands up to stop the torrent of words. "I meant questions about your condition."

He turned the word to his advantage. "This *is* about my condition," Jesse told her innocently. Taking one of her hands, he placed it across his chest. She could feel the beat of his heart beneath her fingertips. "My heart condition."

She rolled her eyes as she reclaimed her hand. "Oh, brother." Still laughing, she shook her head. "I take it back. You *do* have lines."

The grin on his lips slipped into a smile, a small, deep, heartfelt smile. "No, actually," he told her solemnly, "I don't. Nothing's tried and true here. I'm just saying what comes into my head." His eyes held hers. Something rippled inside her very core. "There's something going on here, Tania. An attraction I haven't felt in a long, long time." Since the episode with Ellen, he hadn't really trusted any of the women he'd come across. The few he had gone out with in the last six months had been interchangeable. But this was different. He could feel it in his bones and he needed to explore it further. "I'm hoping it's not one-sided."

Why couldn't she lie? Other people lied without effort. But she couldn't.

"No," she admitted with more than a little reluctance. "It's not."

He'd heard project bids rejected with more joy. "You don't sound very happy about it."

"I don't trust attractions, Jesse." It felt strange saying his name, strange removing that small, artificial barrier between them where he called her by her title and she used his surname. This was getting way too personal way too fast.

Jesse was silent for a moment and then he asked, "Relationship go sour?"

Too close, too close, her mind cried, sounding an alarm. "I don't know you well enough to tell you that," she said stiffly.

She needed boundaries, he could live with that. For now. "I'm willing to wait."

It was going to be a *very* long wait. She shrugged. "Suit yourself."

Damn, but he wanted to kiss her, to break through her reserve and get her to trust him. But he knew he couldn't.

Slow and steady, his mother used to say. "You know, you're a lot more complicated than you seem."

She raised her chin, not happy that he had her pegged so easily so quickly. "Life is more complicated than we're led to believe," she countered.

He didn't quite see it that way. "Not the important things. They're still relatively simple." Because he could see that he hadn't convinced her, he enumerated, "Love, loyalty, family."

Tania laughed despite herself. And then she shook her head. And where had she heard *that* before? "My father would love you."

The ex-policeman, he recalled. "I'd like to meet him."

Oh, no, she wasn't about to bring him around. She hadn't brought anyone around in ten years and it was staying that way. Her family was precious, this was just a diversion, albeit a good-looking one, but just a diversion, nothing more.

"You're getting ahead of yourself," she told him quietly.

He took no offense. Instead he agreed with her, in an effort to catch her off guard.

"I have that tendency," he admitted. "Part of my go-getter personality." And then he became serious again, just for a moment. "I won't hurt you, Tania."

Her response was glib. "I know." *Because I won't let you.*

He broke the tense moment with a laugh, dragging his hand through his hair, careful to avoid the area with the stitches. "Wow, this is a lot more serious than I intended to get." He slipped on his jacket and left it unbuttoned. "So, no coffee?"

He was tempting her more than she was happy about,

but she wasn't about to bend the rules over something as minor as an illegal break.

"No coffee."

Taking her answer in stride, he had a second request. "Walk me out?"

Did he never stop? "How long are you going to play the irresistible card?"

"As long as I can." In the corridor, he glanced around. To his left was the front of the hospital, to his right, the way he'd come in the first time, on a gurney. It was closer and far less busy. "Can I take the back way?"

Leaving was leaving. Tania shrugged. "Sure." And then, since everyone went out the front, curiosity got the better of her. "Why?"

"Because it's shorter and it gives me a shot at asking you to walk with me a little longer."

He *was* charming, she thought. And she needed to be on her guard. "I'm on duty."

He nodded, acknowledging her words with a solemn, straight face. "I know."

"That means I should be attending to other patients. *Real* patients," she emphasized in case he missed the obvious point.

"I am a real patient," he told her. "If you prick me, do I not bleed? If you kill me, do I not die?"

He was damn cute and he knew it. "Okay, okay, Shylock. I'll walk you—but just to the back exit." If he thought he could convince her to keep walking until they came to the coffee shop on the next block, he was in for a disappointment.

He spread his hands innocently, fighting the urge to slip an arm around her shoulder. "I'm not a demanding man."

"The hell you're not."

Tania walked beside him until they came to the rear doors. When they opened, she took a few steps outside. Going further than she knew she should. She was aware that they'd garnered more than a few glances as they passed some of the hospital staff.

Still his fifteen minutes of fame, she thought, amused.

"Okay, here we are, outside." She gestured about the opened area to underscore her point. "Now, off you go."

But he lingered. And the look in his eyes told her why. "One more thing."

"Of course there is." Resigned, she asked, "And that is?"

There was not a hint of a smile on his face as he said, "I'd like to kiss you. I normally don't believe in asking for permission, but with you, I have a feeling that I should."

A breeze of anxiety mingled with anticipation. This man was too damn intuitive for her own good, Tania thought. He was changing the rules and blurring the parameters. She desperately needed to be on top, to take charge.

So, instead of answering, Tania took his face in her hands, raised herself up on her toes and pressed her lips against his. The moment she did, the control she thought she'd just taken instantly slipped right through her fingers like water through a sieve.

Her head swirled.

It was just like the first time, except more. More exhilarating, more overwhelming, more exciting.

More.

Caught off guard, Tania leaned her body into his as the kiss continued to deepen. Her hands left his face and were now knotted around his neck, anchoring her because she was afraid of being swept out to sea.

Afraid of this kiss.

And more afraid of it ending.

The longing she'd felt the other night returned in spades, hot and demanding, and she was oh so grateful they were out here, in public, so that nothing could come of it. So that she couldn't give in to the urges that all but ravaged her.

There it was again, Jesse thought. The want. The need. Battering his body so that he could hardly stand it. He knew he had to break contact before he broke into a million little pieces.

Breathing heavily, he leaned his cheek against the top of her head, just holding her for a moment. Waiting for the fever to pass.

"I'm glad I asked," he finally said softly.

"Me, too," she murmured before she could stop herself. She was giving too much away, damn it.

He stepped back to look at her, reluctantly releasing her from his arms. "I'll see you next Thursday."

And with that, he turned on his heel and walked away. Quickly.

Aroused, shaken, confused, Tania stood to the side of the electronic E.R. doors, watching him go. Her insides were so jumbled, she didn't know where to begin to try to sort them out.

At the very least, she needed her heart to stop doing double-time.

Closing her eyes, she took a deep breath and let it out very slowly. When she opened her eyes again, she realized that she was experiencing that odd sensation again. The one that had her thinking someone was watching her.

She looked around, but there was no one there, no one visible.

Get a grip, she ordered herself.

Turning, she walked back through the electronic doors. A candy striper quickly moved out of her way.

"Sorry," the woman apologized.

Preoccupied, Tania merely nodded. "My fault," she murmured as she hurried back to the central desk.

Chapter 9

The state-of-the-art printer hummed loudly as the color ink-jets within it rhythmically passed back and forth over the four-by-six glossy paper being fed through its carriage.

Slowly the paper inched its way out of the mouth of the printer, displaying an image of two people kissing.

The moment the process was finished, she snatched the paper from the printer, tossing the newly minted photograph on top of the other photographs she'd just printed. The captured images formed an untidy little pile, all of which had been locked within the tiny, thin body of a memory stick.

Now those images were multiplying, emerging on paper and sealing themselves into the computer's hard drive where they would remain forever more.

Until rage or its kin made her delete them.

It wasn't that she was storing and producing the images for sentiment's sake.

Quite the opposite was true.

Sentiment had only been involved in the flattering photographs she'd taken of Jesse, the ones that made love to his face, to his body, or caught him in midaction, doing something noble, the way it had that day he'd come to the jeweler's aid.

There'd even been poetic images, thanks to the long-range lens she'd invested in. Images like the ones of Jesse being taken out of the ambulance and into the hospital. A hero in need of mending.

Those she'd printed up immediately. They joined the others, the hundreds of photographs both on her computer and in the score of albums she'd painstakingly put together. The albums that she'd sit and pore over, night after night. Looking and remembering.

And waiting.

But these photographs that the printer was now spitting out, the ones she planned to upload onto her hard drive, they served a different purpose.

They were to galvanize her into action, to make her remember that she couldn't become too complacent. To remind her that there was a threat and she had to be ready to deal with it.

Not some distant "someday," but soon.

Soon.

The printer finished producing yet another photograph. The one of Jesse kissing that slut outside the hospital. Her rage mounting to barely contained proportions, she reached for the photograph.

Soon.

* * *

It was a long time, years to be exact, since Tania had been governed by impulses. In the last ten, she'd become very didactic, very controlled when it came to her personal life away from the family.

So no one was more surprised than she when she heard herself saying yes to Jesse's impromptu invitation to dinner the next evening. Especially since the latter part of her evening wasn't free. She had things to do and promises to keep.

She was deviating from her normal pattern and it didn't make her happy. And yet the prospect of seeing Jesse, of sitting across from him at a table, with soft music in the background, made her pulse quicken and ushered in a feeling of anticipation.

Warning herself to be careful in no way tempered her reaction to him. She did what she could to put safeguards in place.

"This is going to have to be quick," she warned, vaguely aware that she was guilty of repeating herself. Nerves did that to her.

The restaurant turned out to be far from romantic. Located not far from her apartment and specializing in crepes, *Wraps* smiled upon families. The well-behaved kind. There were no children throwing tantrums or running in between the tables, but they were there nonetheless, displaying the true riches that life had to give.

"I know," Jesse replied mildly, "you told me." Being a gentleman, he didn't go on to say just how many times she had told him. He would have said that she really didn't want to be here, but that wasn't what her eyes were telling him.

Still, he sensed tension from her and wasn't sure what to make of it. But tension or not, he liked being around her. Each time he saw her, he became more and more aware of that.

"I promise not to tie you up and toss you into my car after dinner," he assured her, a smile playing on his lips. He raised his eyes from his dinner. "Would I be out of line if I asked why this has to be quick?"

He wasn't challenging her, Tania realized, he was being understanding and putting up with her various quirks.

Mama would have said to grab the man and run. But while involving scores of hardships, Mama's history did not come close to equaling the trauma that she had gone through. Mama's travails had not taken her young, trusting optimism and shattered it into a million pieces by having her suffer betrayal at the hands of someone she'd regarded as a friend.

Regarded as more than that.

With effort, Tania managed a smile, trying very hard to banish the darker feelings that kept trying to surface.

"Yes, you can ask." Amusement curved her mouth. "And I'll even answer you. I have to meet my sisters and mother at a bridal shop." She saw him raise an eyebrow in a silent query. "Two of my sisters are getting married. We were going to have two separate ceremonies, but now the idea of a double wedding is being bandied about." She remembered her father's response when the idea was broached. "Daddy calls it killing two crows with a rock." She grinned. "Daddy and the English language are not always all that compatible. But he does try."

"A double wedding is cost-efficient," Jesse allowed. Although, when it came to the big day, he wasn't sure if he would want to share the occasion with someone other than his bride-to-be.

She took a sip of the drink, thinking of the last spate of "disagreements" that had taken place over pending wedding plans. "Nerve efficient is more like it."

Her choice of words intrigued him. "You're going to have to explain that."

Tania looked at him for a long moment. "My mother," was all she said. All she felt she needed to say. She didn't want to sit here and spend her time complaining about the kindest, most loving woman in the world. Jesse didn't know her mother and he might get the wrong idea. However, Magda Pulaski was not perfect and there were times when her forceful personality did get under everyone's skin in one way or another.

Except for her husband.

Josef Pulaski was a saint when it came to tolerating his wife's various quirks. A marriage that had obviously been made in heaven. Too bad so many marriages were made here on earth instead.

Jesse nodded as if he knew exactly what she meant. "I hear a lot of mothers of the bride and the groom— terrific women normally—go off the deep end when a wedding's involved."

Yes, she thought, Mama would definitely love this man. "Mama never had anything fancy when she got married. A bouquet of flowers Daddy picked for her from the field. They said their vows before a priest and a couple of witnesses, that was all," Tania told him. "So I guess she's trying to make up for it with us." There was affection in her voice when she said, "I think she was planning weddings from the minute each of us was born." She grinned. "Natalya keeps threatening to run off to city hall and elope if Mama doesn't tone things down. It kind of helps rein Mama in." She saw the amused expression on his face. He leaned forward, as if trying to absorb every word she said. "What? Did I just say something funny?"

"No, I just like hearing you talk about your family, that's all." He drew himself back a little. "Sounds like you all really love each other."

"We do," she said simply. And then she remembered something he'd told her before. "That's right, you don't have any siblings." Despite the fact that there were occasions when she wanted to be alone, being an only child sounded awfully lonely. He had to have somebody. "How about cousins?"

He shook his head, his face impassive. "As far as I know, both my parents were only children."

She could almost *feel* the emptiness. Her heart went out to him before she could stop it. "Christmas must be very tame around your place."

"So tame that sometimes it goes completely unnoticed."

"Oh." There was a great deal of pain and compassion packed into the single, one-syllable word. So much so that it made him smile.

He shrugged carelessly. It had been a long time since this was of any consequence to him. "I've gotten used to it."

She shook her head. "That's not anything to get used to," she said firmly. And then suddenly, impulse took over before she could head it off at the pass. "You're invited to our place for Christmas—and by that, I mean my parents' house," she clarified. "It's where all of us celebrate the holidays. Wouldn't really seem right anywhere else," she confided. And then she realized how Jesse might interpret the invitation. As if she were making plans for the future. *Their* future. "I don't mean to imply that you and I will still be seeing each other by then—"

"Out of sheer curiosity," he interrupted her, his voice low, intrigued, "why wouldn't we?"

She evaded the question, offering only a vague answer. "I never plan my social life that far ahead—and most men I know don't, either," she added with feeling. "I didn't mean to give you the impression that I think of us as a couple." She was sinking badly. "I just don't want you to have to be alone during the holidays."

"That's very nice of you," he acknowledged and then, after mulling it over a beat, asked, "What do you think of us as?"

She'd decided it was safer to focus her attention for the remainder of the meal *on* her meal. Obviously he wasn't going to let her. "Excuse me?"

"You said that you didn't think of us as a couple, so I was just curious how you did think of us. Two ships passing in the night?" he suggested helpfully.

"Not passing. Not yet," she qualified, then added, "Maybe two ships docked at the same harbor for a stretch of time."

Finished with his meal, Jesse moved the plate aside. She felt as if he was peeling away barriers. "That's very antiseptic sounding. I don't feel very antiseptic when I'm around you," he told her quietly. "And you certainly don't kiss antiseptically." He paused for a moment, as if searching for something. She felt as if he was looking right through her. "What are you afraid of, Tania?"

Tania's chin shot up as she pulled her shoulders back. She looked like a soldier about to go into battle.

"Nothing," she retorted. "I'm afraid of nothing."

"Ah, fearless." He nodded, playing along.

His gut instincts told him that her answer had been triggered by some sort of defense mechanism. He intended to get her story, but knew that it wasn't just going to come pouring out. Certainly not here at the table. Probably not soon, either.

Jesse understood secrets, understood the self-preserving need to have them and the need, eventually, to share them. They weren't at that point yet—at least she wasn't, but something told him that they would be. Eventually. Just because he'd told her about Ellen the other day didn't necessarily mean that she was going to show him the skeletons in her closet.

But he knew she had them as surely as he knew his own name. "I find that very sexy in a woman—being fearless—as long as you don't try to catch bullets with your bare hands," he teased.

She felt uneasy, as if he could read her thoughts the moment that she formed them. It was a ridiculous notion and yet...

Tania changed the subject, turning the conversation around so that it was about him for a change and not her. She needed the respite.

"So, tell me about your work," she asked, her tone mild, coaxing. She knew how to play the dating game if she had to. "Would I have seen any of your buildings in the city?"

Jesse grinned. He could have lied to her if he wanted, make himself seem more important than he was, but he never saw the point in that. It took the edge off triumph when it finally did arrive.

"I haven't been in the game long enough to 'have a building,'" he told her. "However, bits and pieces of my contributing designs have turned up in a few edifices currently going up."

It seemed to Tania that the city was continuously under construction. It was hard to walk any distance in any direction within New York City, especially in Manhattan, without finding some building going up or being torn down so another could be put up in its place.

"Eventually," he was saying, "if the firm continues to be happy with me and likes my input, there may someday be a building I can point to and claim as mine."

Someday. Which was a time beyond Christmas. Beyond the scope of anything she intended to think about. It almost took her breath away. A kind of panic threatened to overtake her. There were no "somedays" for her, at least, not when it came to male companionship. There was only "now," only the present. Tomorrow wasn't something to be contemplated.

So why did what he had just said frighten and thrill her at the same time?

Her head began to ache. He confused her, scrambled her brain, and she didn't like it. Didn't like not having a clear head. This couldn't go on. She would have to come up with a better defense strategy, not just against him, but against herself, as well.

Because from where she stood, she was inching over to his side.

Just for the time being. Just for fun, nothing more.

Tania drew in a breath. Her plate was clean, her drink consumed, and the minutes were ticking away fast. She needed to get going in order to reach her mother's friend's shop on time. It was the same store where Sasha had bought her wedding dress. Mama's friend had promised to close the bridal shop this evening so that Natalya and Kady could take as much time as they needed to look around and make their decisions without interference.

Without interference. Well, for that to happen, she mused, Mama would have to be locked out.

Tania needed to get going. For more reasons than one.

Wiping her fingers, she tossed her napkin on top of her silverware and prepared to evacuate. Quickly, before reluctance got the better of her.

"I'm afraid I have to eat and run," she apologized, moving back her chair.

Leaning forward, he caught her wrist. She looked at him quizzically, debating whether or not she would need to make a scene.

"Well, you've eaten," he said, "but in all good conscience, I can't let you run."

Okay, here it comes, Tania thought, her own reluctance instantly disappearing. He was going to try to talk her into lingering. She knew he'd been too good to be true.

"I told you," she reminded him evenly, her free hand gathering her purse to her, "I have to meet my mother and sisters at the bridal shop."

"I know, I remember our conversation this afternoon." Still holding her by the wrist, Jesse raised his other hand to get the waiter's attention. The young man spotted him and smiled obligingly. Jesse mouthed, "Check, please."

With a nod of his head, the waiter went to get their meal's final tally.

"Then what is all this about your conscience?" she asked.

"My car's in the lot across the street," he reminded her. He'd driven them over from her apartment rather than use a taxi. "I'm not about to have you run, take the bus or the subway, to this shop. There's no point in my having a car in the city if I can't drive you where you have to go."

There was something flawed in that, but she couldn't put her finger on just what. She opened her mouth to argue the point and discovered that she really didn't want to. Moreover, the thought of more time with Jesse tempted her.

She wondered if twenty-nine was too young to be losing her mind.

Tania tried to appeal to his sense of logic, although a man who chased after a thief with a gun couldn't be the most logical resident in the building. "Are you sure you want to put up with city traffic at this time?"

In his opinion, anytime was a bad time for city traffic. "Whether I take you to the shop or go home, I still have to put up with the traffic," he pointed out. And then he smiled. "I might as well be doing a good deed."

There it was again, that disarming smile that sliced through everything like a rapier, leaving her damn near defenseless. She surrendered gracefully. "All right then, thank you."

He released her wrist and rose, as did she. For a split

second, their bodies almost collided. Jesse stepped back, giving her room.

"You're welcome."

The waiter arrived, their receipt poised in his hand. Jesse had had his credit card run through when he'd initially ordered drinks for them so it was merely a matter of signing the slip of paper after adding in the tip.

Rather than write an amount in, Jesse dug into his pocket for his wallet. He handed the waiter what came to a little more than twenty percent of their bill in cash. The young man stared at the windfall before stammering a thank-you and hurrying away.

Tania eyed the man beside her. "Why did you do that?" she asked as he held the outside door open for her.

Once she was across the threshold, he followed her out. "Do what?"

For once, the humidity seemed manageable. Thank God for small favors, she thought. "Give the waiter cash instead of adding the amount to the credit card slip?"

"This way, if things are very, very tight, he doesn't have to claim it."

She glanced at him, remembering times that had been "very, very tight" for her family. Her parents would have welcomed a helping hand like that. Still, she played it straight. "So you're advocating fraud?"

He couldn't tell by her expression if she was serious. He could only tell her the truth. "I'm advocating compassion and bending the rules a little. Besides, who's to say I didn't just give him a loan instead of a tip? That is possible, right?"

"Right." Tania couldn't hold back any longer. "You are a nice man, Jesse Steele."

"That's what I've been trying to tell you," he said solemnly, then grinned. "Okay, let's go. You can help me find my car."

He placed his hand to the small of her back as he escorted her across the street. If he noticed that she had stiffened the moment he'd touched her, he made no mention of it.

And he didn't notice the person in the silver sedan duck down just before he and Tania passed the car.

Nor did he pay attention when the same vehicle started up immediately after he exited the parking structure.

Chapter 10

On the lookout for any sign of her errant daughter, Magda Pulaski was out the bridal shop door and on the sidewalk like a shot before the vehicle even came to a full stop. Definitely before her daughter had a chance to open the car door and get out.

"Ah, finally," Magda declared, clapping her hands together as if in thanksgiving to God for answering her prayers. "Even Marysia is here and she is *always* late."

Hitching her purse onto her shoulder, Tania was already striding toward the shop.

"Sorry, Mama. I lost track of the time." It was a lie. The traffic had been the problem, but saying so would only prompt Mama to ask where she was coming from and so on. Giving Mama an inch usually had her constructing a condominium.

But Magda was not looking at her daughter. Approaching the car, she leaned over to look into its interior, specifically at the driver.

"Is this why you are not tracking time?" she asked, gesturing at Jesse.

Turning back around, Tania hooked onto her mother's arm. "Let's go in, Mama. It's not nice to keep your friend waiting like this," she urged, trying to tug her mother around toward the shop's entrance.

But Magda continued looking into the car. Directly at the lone occupant. "Why you are not getting out?" she asked Jesse.

Tania came to Jesse's defense. "This is a no parking zone," she said, pointing to the sign several feet away.

Magda seemed unimpressed by the information. "It is not parking if he is standing near the car," she argued with the conviction of someone married to a former member of the police force. "Come out," she urged Jesse. "I would like to see you."

"Ma-ma." Tania's voice vibrated with warning. She slanted a quick glance toward Jesse. "You don't have to listen—"

But Jesse was already getting out of his car. As he rounded the front of the vehicle, he extended his hand to the petite, dark-haired woman who was obviously Tania's mother.

"Hello, I'm Jesse Steele."

Magda nodded, slipping her small hand in his. It was obvious that she was pleased the young man had obeyed. She made no effort to hide the fact that he was being scrutinized, dissected and measured by those sharp hazel eyes.

"The hero. Yes, I have read about you," Magda told

him, removing her hand after a beat. "You look better in your skin."

Amused, Jesse grinned. "I'm hardly ever without it."

Tania stifled an exasperated sigh. "She means in person. You look better in person," Tania explained. "She gets her idioms confused."

"You do not have to talk for me," Magda told her, not bothering to turn her head to look at her daughter. She was too busy still assessing the young man who had driven Tania here. "He is understanding what I mean."

Tania rolled her eyes. "Nobody could talk for you, Mama." Again she tugged on her mother's arm, but for a small woman, Magda Pulaski could exude a great deal of strength when she wanted to. Her mother remained exactly where she was. Tania let her hand drop, but insisted, "They're waiting, Mama, remember?"

Magda waved her hand, every iota of her attention focused entirely on the tall, blond-haired, *handsome* man before her. She had questions.

"They were waiting before, they can be waiting a few more minutes." Her eyes pinned him. "You are seeing my daughter?"

"As much as I can," Jesse replied, his amusement growing. He slanted a quick glance in Tania's direction and saw that she was less than happy with her mother's version of the inquisition. "If she lets me."

Nodding, Magda told him confidently, "She will let you." Only then did she turn toward her daughter. "All right, Tatania, say goodbye to him."

Tania shook her head. She should have insisted on taking the bus and spared both of them from witnessing her mother's reenactment of a benevolent dictator.

"Goodbye," she said to Jesse, her teeth only slightly clenched.

Magda frowned. "Not like that. Like a woman says goodbye to a man she is going out with. I will wait in the store." She glanced toward Jesse. "I will not look," she informed with solemnity. Before leaving, she inclined her head toward Jesse. "It is nice to meet you."

Then, turning smartly on her heel, she walked back into the bridal shop. Visible through the large bay window, Magda came to a halt in the center and crossed her arms before her, her back deliberately to the street.

There were no words for this, Tania thought, but she tried. "I'm sorry about that."

"Why? Your mother obviously cares about you. It's nice having people care about you," he added with feeling.

He had a point, of course, but there were times she could have done with a little less "caring."

Tania glanced over her shoulder. She'd thought as much.

"She's watching," she told Jesse.

Jesse looked again at the figure in the bay window. Was he missing something? "Her back is to the window," he pointed out.

Her mother, the illusionist. "The shop has mirrors everywhere," she told him. "Her back might be to the window, but her eyes are fixed on the mirror in the corner. Gives her a perfect view."

Tania saw his mouth curve. A wicked gleam flared in his eyes. "Then let's not disappoint her."

Before she could demur, Tania found herself not just in his arms, but dipped back as if the last note of a passionate tango had just resounded. She was at a forty-five-degree angle.

Her eyes went wide. "What are you doing?"

His grin grew. "Giving your mother what she wants."

And then, there was no more time or space for questions. It was impossible to talk when his lips were sealed to hers. Just like that, her breath deserted her, while the rest of her swiftly turned to jelly. Mama, the bridal shop, the sidewalk, everything, just disappeared.

And just as her head began to spin out of control, Jesse drew his lips away from hers and straightened. His arm was still hooked about the small of her back, for which she was very grateful. Otherwise, she was certain that she would establish a close relationship with the sidewalk below.

Trying hard to breathe, Tania murmured, "Well, that should make her happy."

"She's not the only one," Jesse told her. His expression looked so serious, she wasn't sure if he was pulling her leg or not. "Doctor, you pack quite a punch."

So do you, Jesse.

But it was better for everyone if she kept that thought to herself.

"I better go," she said.

Jesse nodded. He would probably wind up burning the midnight oil—even if every second thought wasn't about her. And if it was, well, then, he knew he might as well prepare himself for an all-nighter.

"Me, too. There are blueprints on the desk at my apartment, waiting for me to make them magical." Damn, but he wanted to kiss her again. And again and again. "I'll see you soon."

She said nothing, merely nodded.

It was hard getting back his bearings. Making his legs function again. Initially he'd kissed Tania for fun, to give her mother a show. But then, once he'd started, he'd wound up giving himself something, as well. At the very least, a great deal to think about.

The only thing he knew for sure right now was that somehow, some way, they were going to make love. There was far too much going on between them for him to ignore or turn his back on out of some sort of half-baked attempt at self-preservation. Tania wasn't Ellen, nor was she like any other woman he'd ever known.

Tania was in a class by herself.

And while she kept putting up obstacles between them, he was certain that Tania felt this pull, this electricity for lack of a better word, between them, too.

He could taste it on her lips, feel it in his soul.

Jesse rounded the front of his car again and got in behind the steering wheel. He had to find a way to make that look of wariness disappear from her eyes.

"So, he knows how to kiss," Mama said with more than a smattering of satisfaction the second Tania entered the shop.

Thinking that discretion was the better part of valor, Tania said nothing.

Over in the corner, wearing one of the wedding gowns and pretending to look at herself from all angles, Natalya couldn't resist saying, "I could have told you that, Mama."

Magda turned and glanced at her second-born sharply. Her pleased look melted away faster than an ice cube in the oven. "Why? You have been kissing him, too?"

"No, Mama," Natalya answered patiently, "I love Mike, remember? But I did see Jesse kissing Tania at the front door of our apartment."

Magda exhaled a deep, no longer troubled breath. Her face softened as she took Tania's hands in hers. "Maybe you would like to look at some of the wedding dresses, too, while you are being here."

"No," Tania told her mother firmly. "No wedding-dress looking. I'm a bridesmaid. I need to find a bridesmaid dress. Two," she added as Kady came out from one of the rear dressing rooms wearing a particularly beautiful wedding gown. "Unless you're serious about a double wedding," she said to the two brides. "In which case, Sasha, Marysia and I will need only one."

"Sorry, two," Natalya told her, slowly giving herself the once-over again. "Otherwise, it'll turn into a competition." She turned toward Kady and fluttered her lashes. "And we all know that I'll be the more beautiful bride."

"Ha," Kady countered. "In your dreams, Nat, in your dreams."

Tania knew what her sisters were doing, bless them. They were creating a diversion so that Mama's attention would be directed toward them and not her. Mama would no doubt remember when she had to be the peacemaker when they were all growing up.

"No competition," Magda declared. "There will be two weddings."

"Guess that's that," Kady said, turning around and seeing how well the train moved behind her.

"Yes, Mama," Natalya responded obediently, "whatever you say."

"Two weddings," Magda repeated, then looked at Tania. "For now."

Tania picked up a light blue bridesmaid dress from the nearest rack. This was her cue to duck into a dressing room. She didn't feel up to taking on her mother right now.

"Dr. Pulaski, do you have a minute?" The question, directed to Tania, came from the attractive candy striper. She moved around the desk at the nurses' station, coming into the small, glass-walled alcove that comprised the main station in the E.R.

As happened every so often, just a little more frequently than a blue moon, there was a lull in patient traffic. Tania was hoping to use it to catch up on some of the files she'd left in less than stellar condition. Dr. Howell had been breathing down her neck to rectify her omission.

Even though she knew it was necessary, Tania hated this part of doctoring, hated having to sit and carefully make sense out of her own notes so that anyone could pick up the file and go forward from there. She regarded it much the way she had homework while in school—a necessary evil.

Happy to grasp any excuse, Tania looked up. The woman seemed familiar to her, but for the life of her, Tania couldn't place her.

"That all depends on what side of the paperwork you're on." An excellent surgeon and teacher, Dr. Howell was a stickler for crossing t's and dotting i's and her t's and i's were way overdue. Still, she argued silently, if someone needed medical attention, that came first.

"Why?" Tania glanced past the volunteer down the corridor. "Is there a patient?"

A sheepish expression came over the volunteer's heart-shaped face. "Kind of."

Tania closed the file she'd been working on and rose to her feet. "Where?"

"Here." The candy striper spread her hands to either side of her. Embarrassment colored her neck and cheeks. "Me."

At first glance, there appeared to be nothing wrong with the woman. Her color was good, she wasn't standing in a manner that indicated pain. But then, she could just have been a trooper.

"What's wrong?" Tania asked gamely.

The woman pressed her lips together, as if she loathed to take up a doctor's time. After a moment she said, "It's my back, Doctor—they told me that you're going to be a spinal surgeon," she added quickly.

Tania responded with a small, self-deprecating smile. "In about a hundred years." And some days, it actually felt as if her goal was that far away. Her comment, she noted, seemed to make the woman hesitate. "What about your back?" Tania coaxed.

Relaxing a little, the volunteer placed her hand to the small of her back, as if that helped her manage the pain. "It's been giving me a lot of trouble lately. I think I might have pulled something the other week," she confessed. Lowering her voice so as not to be overheard, she added, "They had me restocking the supply closet and some of the boxes were pretty heavy. I felt a strong twinge on my back when I put one of the boxes up on a high shelf—"

Tania frowned. "You should have asked one of the men to do it."

The volunteer nodded. "I know."

"Why didn't you?" Tania asked.

The question was met with a hapless shrug. "Pride, I guess." She sighed. "Not a very good excuse, I know, but I hate bothering people."

"Okay, you're forgiven," Tania told her. She looked back at the board. Several rooms were empty. "Trauma room three is free. Let's go have a look at that back."

The volunteer smiled broadly. "I appreciate this, Doctor." She stopped, as if realizing she had omitted something. "I'm Carol, by the way."

"Well, Carol-by-the-way—" Tania led the way to the trauma room "—let's see if we can do anything to make you feel better."

"It's all up to you," Carol said as she walked into the room.

That was an odd way to put it, Tania thought. "Why don't you get up on the exam table?" she suggested, crossing to the cabinet.

Opening the top set of doors, Tania took out the glove dispenser. Carol watched her every move. Probably afraid, Tania thought as she slipped on the gloves.

"I was hoping to catch you before you went out to lunch," Carol confided.

"No lunch plans today," Tania told her, approaching the table. "I need you to turn over on your stomach so I can examine your spine."

Carol did as told. "You mean, you're not going out with that guy for lunch?"

Watching Carol shift to her stomach, Tania frowned. "What guy?"

Carol's voice was partially muffled as her cheek was

pressed against the pillow on the table. Her answer came in bits and pieces. "The one who was in the paper. He stopped a robbery. Jason something."

"Jesse," Tania corrected.

"Right, Jesse." Carol raised her head slightly, trying to look at her. "You're not seeing him anymore?"

Tania carefully kneaded her fingers along Carol's spine. "I was never really seeing him."

"Huh." Carol lowered her head again. "I guess I was mistaken. I thought I saw you kissing him the other day. Outside the E.R. doors."

That was where she knew her from, Tania realized. She'd bumped into the woman on her way back into the E.R. that day. "I'm not sure what any of this really has to do with your back pain, Carol."

"Nothing," the young woman said quickly, retreating like a rabbit that had spotted a coyote. "I was just making conversation. I'm sorry, I shouldn't be asking personal questions like that."

She sounded so contrite, Tania felt guilty for being so frosty. "That's okay, I guess I'm a little touchy."

Carol tried to turn her head again. Tania gently pushed her back down. "How come?" And then Carol laughed, the sound rumbling against the exam table. "There I go again, asking more personal questions. My mother always said I was a chatterbox, always talking when I should be listening."

Tania made no comment. Instead she continued to work her fingers up and down the woman's spine. Nothing felt out of the ordinary and Carol had not reacted to her touch.

"Any of this hurt?" she finally asked.

As if on cue, or maybe by coincidence, Carol stiffened, sucking in her breath.

"There," she murmured breathlessly. "Right there. It feels like needles and pins are being pushed into the small of my back."

"You can sit up now," Tania told her. Standing back, Tania stripped off the gloves. She hadn't really needed them this time.

"What's the verdict?" Carol asked, seeming a little like a deer in the headlights.

"It's probably just a strain, but just to be sure, we'll need to take an X-ray. If that doesn't show anything— and a good deal of the time, it doesn't—we might need to take an MRI."

Carol looked intimidated. "An MRI? That's expensive, right?"

Some of them, depending on the number of views done, cost more than two thousand dollars. "Sadly, yes."

Carol shook her head. "I can't afford that," she confessed. She looked embarrassed when she said, "I don't have any health insurance."

Tania figured as much. The woman was a volunteer here, not an employee. If she worked anywhere else, that company might not offer any health insurance, either. "Let me worry about that. For the time being, let's get to the bottom of this pain of yours."

Carol looked hesitant. "I wouldn't want to do anything to get you fired."

"I won't get fired," Tania assured her. Taking the prescription pad out of her pocket, she wrote down a few words on the top sheet, instructions for the radiology department. "Take this to X-ray." Tearing the page off, she held it out to Carol. "You know where that is, right?"

Carol nodded, accepting the paper before getting off the table. "They gave the volunteers a tour of the hospital the first day."

"All right then. Tell them to send the X-rays to me when they're ready. If we don't find anything, then we'll tackle the MRI."

Carol had already crossed to the door. "You're one of a kind, Dr. Pulaski."

Tania smiled to herself. "Actually, I'm one of five," she said under her breath.

Walking out behind Carol, she watched the young woman go down the hall. Either the volunteer was a fledgling hypochondriac, or she was a very stoic soldier because, for someone who said she had back trouble, Carol was moving rather well.

Chapter 11

It seemed to Tania that the candy striper had no sooner turned the corner than the E.R. suddenly came alive again. The back doors sprang open, admitting several sets of paramedics.

Patients poured in, including four people involved in a car accident, each brought in by a separate ambulance. Caught up in the fast pace, Tania lost track of time. And of the candy striper.

It was only at the end of her shift, as she hurriedly went through her files for the day, anticipating the evening ahead of her, that Tania realized that Carol's X-rays had never reached her. They were missing.

And so was Carol.

Guilt and confusion came over her as Tania took a quick peek into the room where she'd initially examined Carol. As she'd suspected, the volunteer wasn't there.

In her place was a rather battered-looking skateboarder, looking none too happy about cooling his heels in the E.R. He had a broken wrist, which was being attended to by Ronald Morris, another one of the fourth-year residents on duty.

In the middle of applying a cast to the grumbling skateboarder's injured wrist, the doctor glanced over in her direction. "Can I help you with something, Dr. Pulaski?"

"Do you know what happened to the patient who was in here a while back?" Tania asked, trying vainly to pinpoint a time.

"They got better?" the doctor suggested whimsically.

"Maybe," Tania murmured, wondering if that was what actually happened. Had Carol felt better and decided not to have the X-rays done?

Tania withdrew from the room. Turning, she noted the head nurse heading toward the central station. She hurried after the woman. "Hey, Shelly, did you see Carol?"

The woman stopped and frowned. "Carol?"

According to Sasha, Shelly had been with the hospital forever and, in her opinion, the woman made it a point to know everyone on staff. "The candy striper." There was no sign of recognition on the older woman's face. "She was complaining about a bad back, so I sent her for X-rays. She was supposed to be in trauma room three."

Habit had Shelly glancing up at the patient board. "You've got a broken wrist in there now. Dr. Morris is treating him."

Tania looked at her watch. It was getting late. She needed to be on her way, but sense of order made her hate leaving things up in the air. "Yes, I know. I was just wondering what happened to Carol."

Shelly lifted her wide shoulders, letting them fall carelessly. "Maybe she changed her mind. Felt better. Happens." And then she looked at Tania over the top of her glasses. "Isn't your shift over, Doctor?"

"Yes, but—"

Shelly's expression told her she wasn't about to be swayed from her position. The chief attending might be at the head of the E.R., but everyone knew that it was Shelly who kept everything running smoothly.

"Go home, Doctor." Tania looked around the area, hoping to spot the missing volunteer. No such luck. Shelly moved her full figure in front of her. "I know it'll be tough but we'll soldier on without you." And then her voice softened. "You're not going to be any good to us if you don't start getting some rest."

Tania felt the corners of her mouth curving. "Since when did you become a doctor?"

Shelly appeared completely unfazed by the question. "I pick things up. Now go." The nurse waved her off to the rear doors.

Tania thought of the play she was seeing tonight. And the man taking her. One stray thought about Jesse and she could feel her anticipation grow. "Actually, I do have somewhere to be."

The woman nodded, turning her attention to the files that were on the desk. "As long as it's not here, that's all I care about."

"It's not," Tania assured her, already backing away, on the path to the lockers. "I'm seeing *Colors of the Rainbow* tonight."

Shelly spared her one long, envious glance. "Lucky dog."

The comment surprised Tania. "I didn't take you for a musical lover."

"I'll have to sing my rendition of *The Impossible Dream* for you someday," Shelly called after her, then chuckled.

It seemed rather appropriate to be seeing this particular play, Tania thought as she boarded the bus on the next corner some ten minutes later. The title actually reflected the way she felt. As if there were a rainbow just beginning inside of her, its collection of colors ready to shoot out of her at a second's notice.

If she were honest with herself, this happiness terrified her. She was afraid to feel this way.

Common sense told her to back away, to cancel tonight and any other "tonights" that might be in the offing. Because not to cancel was to become further involved and becoming further involved would only lead to disaster.

But a stubborn will to soar, to enjoy life, refused to let her cancel or retreat. Refused because there was supposed to be more to life than just going through the motions.

Pros and cons battled it out within her, even as she doggedly continued to move forward.

By the time Tania got off the bus and ran into her building, she had less than twenty minutes to get ready. The elevator seemed to take forever, even though she was the only one on it.

Dashing through the front door of her apartment, she locked it behind her and all but flew to her room.

This time, there was no indecisive hunting through her wardrobe. She knew exactly what she was wearing, a simple black dress that subtly adhered to her figure. That and matching heels. She'd had the foresight to pick it out last night just in case she was running late—which she usually was lately.

When the doorbell rang, she'd just barely finished putting on her makeup. She glanced at her watch. He was five minutes early. The man kept her on her toes.

"Coming," she called out, pausing to step into her shoes. Grabbing the string of pearls she wanted to wear, she flew to the front door, hoping she didn't look as rushed as she felt.

When she got to the door, Tania took a deep breath to center herself, then turned the doorknob to open it. She was still holding on to the necklace.

Jesse was standing on her doorstep, looking better than a man had a living right to.

She tried not to notice that her heart didn't so much skip a beat as jump up in her chest. Either she'd suddenly developed a case of atrial fibrillation, Tania thought, or something was definitely happening here. Something that could have more far-reaching consequences than the condition she'd just diagnosed and discarded.

"You look beautiful," Jesse told her.

So do you, she thought.

Out loud, she said, "Yeah, yeah, I bet you say that to everyone." Tania turned her back to him and held out the pearls while lifting her hair away from her neck. "Could you help me put this on?"

He frowned slightly, taking the pearls from her. He didn't want to help her put on her necklace. He wanted to press his lips against the smooth expanse of skin she'd exposed to him.

Jesse took a breath, reining in his thoughts. "I'm pretty much all thumbs," he confessed. It took him more than one try to hook the clasp. Relieved, he backed away before he wound up giving in to temptation. "Okay," he told her. "Done."

She turned around to face him again and he had this overwhelming desire to kiss her. He banked it down. He'd never been one to allow himself to be governed by impulses.

"And as for saying that to everyone," he commented drily as she grabbed her purse, "I'm pretty sure that this is the first time I'm saying it today." Jesse glanced around just as they were about to leave. "Where's the rest of your team tonight?"

"Elsewhere," she answered simply, fishing out the key to the apartment. "Why, you miss getting the third degree?"

He laughed, shaking his head as Tania locked the door behind them, then slipped her key into her clutch purse. "No, but I was getting used to it. Besides, they were just proving that they cared about you," he told her. "Nice having someone care about you."

"In small doses," she allowed.

He had the distinct feeling that the remark was somehow meant for him.

"Are you aware that you're humming the opening number?" he asked Tania nearly four hours later as she hunted for the key to her apartment door. She'd been humming off and on ever since they'd left the theater and the melodic sound, as well as her pure enjoyment of the play, made him smile. Her eyes were shining. He couldn't recall ever being with a woman whose eyes reflected her inner joy.

Tania stopped humming, but she wasn't embarrassed. It had been a wonderful show, a wonderful evening all around, and right at this moment, she felt incredibly content and happy.

Looking up from her purse, she nodded. "I know. The song was wonderful. The whole play was wonderful." Her eyes smiled at him as her fingers located her keys. "*Everything* was wonderful."

Including the time she'd shared with him. They'd gone to a five-star restaurant not too far from the theater. Then, because his car was parked in a structure, they decided to leave it there and walk to the theater. It was a warm, sultry night and they continued their conversation from the restaurant. There'd been no awkward pauses, no hunting for something to say. She discovered that they liked the same movies, the same authors, the same baseball team.

For the life of her, Tania couldn't remember when she'd enjoyed herself so much.

"No argument from me," Jesse assured her softly.

She could almost feel his eyes caressing her face. Could feel her heart start hammering even before his lips touched hers.

Tania threaded her arms around his neck and gave herself up to the moment, silently arguing that since it was for the moment, it was all right.

The keys slipped from her lax fingers as she lost herself in the kiss. But just as it felt as if it was going to continuing building, Jesse drew back.

"You dropped your keys," he told her, bending to pick them up for her.

"I guess my fingers went numb." Her eyes danced with

amusement. Taking the keys from him, she inserted one in the keyhole. And discovered that the door was unlocked. "That's weird," she murmured under her breath.

"What is?"

She pushed the door open slowly. "The door wasn't locked."

"Maybe one of your sisters came home and forgot to lock it." He'd done it himself once or twice when his mind was on other things.

But Tania shook her head. She was still standing on the threshold, peering in. He saw the uneasy look in her eyes. "My father was on the police force for twenty-seven years. He drummed that into our heads—always lock your door behind you, coming and going, even if you're only home for five minutes. It's just something we do."

"Maybe I'd better look around for you," he suggested.

Independence warred with common sense. Common sense won. "Sure."

Tania banked down the surge of nervousness that threatened to overwhelm her. She was grateful to him for volunteering rather than waiting to be asked. But she didn't want him to think she was one of those women who needed to check her closets and look under her bed before she went to sleep each night.

Still, the first thing that popped into her head was that somehow, after all this time had passed, Jeff had broken in.

That Jeff was waiting for her.

C'mon, Tania. Stop being an idiot. She forced a smile to her lips. "Miss being the hero?"

Jesse made his way through the living room. "I'm not a hero yet," he told her. "That's only if there's a bad guy hiding in one of your closets and I get to engage him in hand-to-hand combat." He noticed how quiet it was. If someone else was home, he was fairly certain that by now, they'd be out to investigate. "Your sisters still aren't home?"

"Apparently not," she murmured. Then, in an audible voice, said, "Doctors keep erratic hours."

Jesse slanted a smile in her direction. "I'm beginning to learn that. Why don't you stay by the door while I check the rest of the apartment out?" he suggested.

"The hell I will," was her answer.

She wasn't a shrinking violet. He had to admit he liked that about her. "Okay, then stay behind me, just in case."

Her breath caught in her throat even as she tried to brazen it out. "Why? Do you think that someone's still here?"

"Probably not. But it doesn't hurt to be cautious. I had a friend who walked in on a burglar once. Burglar was so scared, he almost trampled my friend trying to get out." Jesse looked at her meaningfully. "But some burglars *aren't* afraid."

"I know," she said quietly.

With Tania half a breath behind him, Jesse made his way from room to room. There was no one else in the apartment. When they walked into the last room, the kitchen, Jesse saw two notes posted on the refrigerator door, held in place by magnets, one shaped like a stethoscope, the other like a miniature Empire State Building.

Moving ahead of him, Tania read first one note, then the other. Natalya's note said she was at their parents' in Queens and would probably spend the night there, while Kady's note, which appeared to have been left first, said she was spending quality time with her fiancé.

"Quality time?" Jesse echoed. He'd only heard the term applied to parents and children.

Tania grinned. "That's code for spending the night," she told him. She saw his quizzical look and beat him to the obvious question. "We use code in case one of our parents stops by and sees the note."

"Your parents don't approve of Kady's fiancé?" He'd only met her briefly, but Magda Pulaski didn't strike him as a woman who would hold her tongue if she disapproved of something or someone.

Tania was quick to correct the misimpression. "Oh, no, they love him." She led the way back to the living room. "He saved Kady's life."

A knowing smile curved his mouth. "Then it's your sister sleeping with him before they're married that's the problem?" he guessed.

It sounded so unforgiving when he said it and her parents were warm, caring people with huge hearts.

"My parents aren't prudes." She wanted him to know that. The next moment she asked herself why that was important. "They just don't want it stuck in their faces."

He nodded. Sexuality was a difficult thing for one generation to accept about another—and it worked both ways, he thought. He never wanted to think about the possibility of his mother dating after his father was killed.

Jesse glanced toward the door. He knew it was time to leave, even if he didn't want to.

"Well, I guess it looks like one of your sisters did forgot to close the door when she left. There's no one here but us," he added needlessly, looking down into her face. "I guess I'd better get going."

Tania caught the bottom of her lip between her teeth, debating. In a minute she'd be home free. Despite that, she heard herself saying, "Since you're already inside, would you like to stay awhile? I could make some coffee—or maybe you'd rather have a drink?" As she asked, she made her way over to the small liquor cabinet against the far wall.

"Sounds good," he acknowledged, right behind her. He glanced into the cabinet as she opened the double doors. "What do you have?"

Tania stepped back and turned around to give him a better view. Which was her mistake. Her body brushed against his. Instantly her pulse quickened. Breath caught in her throat, she turned her face up to his.

Jesse didn't need more of an invitation. Ever so lightly, he framed her face with his hands and brought his mouth down to hers again.

Something exploded inside of her. Something fierce and overpowering.

Her breath came in quick snatches as her head began to spin. One thought throbbed in her brain. Quickly, this had to be done quickly.

Before she could think.

Before she could remember.

Her mouth still sealed to his, Tania urgently pushed his jacket from his shoulders, tugging the sleeves down his arms. She needed to hurry, to go as fast as she could in order to outrace instincts bent on stopping her. On protecting her from the very thing she found herself craving and wanting.

Without any warning, Jesse felt as if he suddenly had a whirlwind in his arms. His blood heated and it was all he could do not to follow her lead, not to drag her dress from her body. But if he did, if he kept pace with Tania, then their lovemaking would be over with almost before it began. It wasn't his way and even if it were, he sensed that there was far too much going on here for him to race to the finish line like that.

So when her eager fingers began to fumble with the clasp on his belt, Jesse caught them in both his hands, stilling them even though desire all but slammed into him with the force of a Mack truck.

"Hey, hey, hey," he chided softly. Still holding her hands in one of his, he caressed her cheek with the other. There was something in her eyes that he couldn't place. Fear? "What's your hurry, Tania? Got a plane to catch?"

Her hands trembled within his. "No," she breathed.

Please, please, please, don't stop me, don't let me think. Please don't let me remember.

Jesse brought his lips down to the side of her neck, skimming the delicate skin there. Excitement soared through his veins.

"Then let's take this nice and slow," he whispered coaxingly. Taking her by the hand, he asked, "Which was your room?"

"The second one," she answered breathlessly. She moved ahead of him, striding down the hall as if the devil was after her.

Because, in a way, he was.

The second she was inside her room, Tania pushed the door closed with the flat of her hand. "All right," she managed to get out.

Whether it was a question or a statement, he didn't know. He was only aware that she'd all but glued herself to him. The rush was incredible and he nearly lost his bearings right there. It took superhuman control not to give in to the urges that threatened to tear him apart.

They tumbled onto the bed, clothes leaving their bodies in unsyncopated rhythm until they were both nude, pressed against one another.

Tania felt as if she was on fire. On fire and at the same time, in danger of being doused by a huge bucket of ice. Because the memory of *that* night was never that far out of reach. It was always ready to claim her.

Jesse kissed her over and over again, but it was already too late. Too late because fear had reared its head, freezing her body. She struggled to keep it at bay, to push the fear back so that she could lose herself in what was happening.

She won small victories, but the war was, for the most part, lost. Her body ceased heating as his touch, so gentle, brought back memories of another touch, far less gentle. A touch that was hard, grasping. Possessive.

It wasn't fair to him, Tania thought, fighting back tears. Not fair to Jesse. Not fair to her to feel like this, to be locked away from what she felt certain, in her heart, was wondrously pleasurable and good.

She did her best to seem eager, to keep up the illusion that they were on the same wavelength, all the while hoping against hope to somehow unlock the door to the cell that kept her a prisoner. The cell that kept her from him.

But in the end, as he murmured her name against her ear and entered her, Tania could only congratulate herself for putting on a believable act. She tried to mimic his movements, to make him think that they came to the crest together when all she wanted was to shrink back, to have it done with.

When his weight suddenly sank against her, she knew it was over.

The sadness that seized her heart was almost excruciating.

Pivoting on his elbows, Jesse drew his head back and looked down at her. She'd turned her head away from him, but he thought he saw a tear in the corner of her eye.

So he wasn't wrong in what he'd felt, Jesse thought, far from happy about being right. He withdrew and lay down beside her. He had no idea what to make of what had just happened here. Because it had never happened to him before.

Taking a breath, he slipped his arm around Tania and drew her closer to him. He felt Tania stiffen. Could almost feel her forcing herself to relax. This wasn't right.

With the tips of his fingers, he moved her hair away from her cheek. "Where were you?" he asked quietly.

Tania forced a smile to her lips. Reaching around for the comforter, she drew it up over herself to cover her nakedness. "I'm not that thin. I was right here." The solemn expression on his face made her nervous.

"Your body was," he agreed.

Holding on to the comforter tightly, she raised herself up to look at him. "Are you trying to tell me you were disappointed?"

"No—and yes," he told her honestly. Tania began to get up and he blocked her move. "We just made love, but you weren't there. You were literally MIA—missing in action." Jesse gently tapped her temple. Her eyes were huge, he thought. Was she afraid of him? He didn't understand. "Where were you?" he repeated.

Her breath was shaky as she released it. "I'm sorry if it wasn't good for you—"

"I didn't say that," he interrupted patiently. "If anything, maybe it wasn't good for you." She seemed surprised at his willingness to take the blame. "Because if it had been, you would have been there, just as wrapped up in it, as grateful to be part of it, as I was. But you weren't."

Tania felt torn and tortured. He was asking the right questions, the questions she didn't want to face, didn't want to answer. He deserved better. He deserved more than she could give him.

Fighting tears, she touched his face. "Don't get involved with me, Jesse."

The laugh that came from his lips had no humor to it. "I think it's too late for that warning. The question is, why won't you get involved with me?" He took her hand in his. "Is it something I've done?"

She closed her eyes, lost. Wishing she hadn't let it get this far. "Oh no, no, it's not you. Well, it is, but it's not. It is because you're on the unfortunate receiving end of this. It's not because you are damn near perfect."

That made absolutely no sense to him, but he played along. "Is that a flaw?" he asked. "Because if it is, I can be imperfect," he offered. "I could trip you before we make love again."

She stared at him, stunned. "You want to make love again?"

How could she even ask? "I want to make love with you for as many days as there are in a month. Every month."

This after she'd gone cold, Tania thought. How could anyone be this good? And how could she allow herself to jeopardize this? How could she break out of her prison? "Wow."

"That wasn't quite the answer that I expected—I was hoping for a 'me, too,'" he told her with a grin. "But I can work with 'wow.'"

"Why would you want to?" she asked. "Why would you want to make love with me again? Why would you want to stay?"

"Because if I do, then maybe you'll learn to trust me enough to let me in—or at least give me the name of the guy who did this to you so I could kill him."

His voice was so mild, uttering the words, she laughed despite herself. It had a sad, hollow sound. "You'd have to forfeit your Good Samaritan standing."

"I don't care," he told her, deadly serious. "It would be worth it."

Tania watched him for a long moment. He wasn't just mouthing what he thought she needed to hear. Jesse was serious.

She began to cry.

Chapter 12

Jesse never felt so helpless as when faced with a woman's tears. He vividly remembered the moment when his mother found out that his father hadn't survived the gunshot wound he'd sustained during the robbery of their grocery store. He'd given her the news and had been at a complete loss when she'd burst into tears.

At the time, no words could afford her any comfort. Little had changed over the years. No real words of comfort came to him now in the face of Tania's silent tears. All he could do was take her into his arms and hold her, give her the silent comfort of his arms and his presence.

Jesse let a few moments go by before he asked, "Do you want to tell me about it?"

Jesse's question scraped the depths of her soul. She didn't want to talk about it, hadn't said a word about the incident in years. Not since the assistant D.A. had told her that Jeff and his defense counsel were accepting a plea bargain. Back then, countless months after the rape, she'd been forced to sit in the closed courtroom, listening to Jeff own up to what he'd done. Listening to Jeff apologize and ask forgiveness for the unforgivable.

It had all felt so surreal then. She'd been the good little victim, she'd brought her rapist up on charges so that he wouldn't do to someone else what he'd done to her. And then, after it was over and the judge and the two opposing lawyers went back to their lives, she'd been left to deal with the black hole that Jeff's attack had created inside of her.

Her way of dealing with it was to try to fill the hole up any way she could, with work and by searching for someone who would make her forget, who could make her finally move on. But all she'd ever managed to do was find men who, by the very act of lovemaking, caused her to remember. And to regret.

Tania took in a long, ragged breath. Jesse was right. This had to come out. If nothing else, she owed him that. Owed herself that.

"I was seventeen years old, invincible, and as trusting as a puppy. And Jeff was the handsomest thing I'd ever seen. A college freshman. And my friend. Or so I thought." Tania pressed her lips together to keep back the sob that erupted in her throat.

"Take your time," Jesse said softly, his arms tightening ever so slightly around her. Close enough to protect, but not tight enough to cause her to feel trapped.

Tania shrugged helplessly, her cheek pressed against his chest, her eyes looking into the past. "It's the usual story. We were at a party, he had too much to drink. I drove him to his dorm. It was the beginning of spring break and it seemed like everyone was gone." How many times had she gone over this in her mind? If only she'd left him at the entrance of the building, things would have been different. *She* would have been different. If only… "So I helped him up to his room and suddenly, once we were inside, it somehow turned into a wrestling match."

She paused again. When she spoke, her voice was shaky. It cracked several times. "I always thought that, in a situation like that, I'd know what to do, how to get away. My father taught all of us self-defense, drilled us on how to take care of ourselves." Her mouth dry, she ran her tongue along her lips, trying to moisten them. Each word she uttered seemed to stick to the roof of her mouth. "I honestly thought I could talk Jeff out of it. I thought I could handle him—until I couldn't."

Tania closed her eyes, tears seeping through her lashes. Jesse could feel them against his chest as they slid down her cheek. He remained quiet, letting her tell him at her own pace.

"And then he was like somebody else, somebody I didn't know," she said heavily. "Had never known. He raped me and fell asleep. Like it was nothing," Tania whispered, her voice cracking again.

Jesse felt anger surging within him, explosive anger. It took effort to keep it from taking over. But there was no one in the room except for the two of them. No one to lash out at, to make pay for the crime committed against this woman.

He stroked her hair, silently telling her she could lean on him. "Did you tell anyone?"

She sat up then and wrapped her arms around her knees, drawing them into herself. The comforter pooled around her.

"I didn't have to. My father was waiting up. He took one look at me when I came in through the door and he knew. He *knew*. They were very good to me, my parents," she murmured. The tears continued to flow down her cheeks, mingling with the ends of her hair. "But my father wouldn't let me bury it. He told me that the rape would always haunt me until I brought Jeff to justice." She exhaled loudly. "So I did, and for the most part, my father was right." A touch of irony entered her voice. "They all think I'm okay, my sisters, my parents. And I am. Usually. Except when I freeze up inside." She turned her head, looking at him over her shoulder. "So you see, Jesse, it's really not you, it's me."

"No," he answered very gently, "it's him. That worthless piece of trash who raped you, *he's* keeping you from moving on. He robbed you of your trust, kept you from enjoying something very basic, very vital." Jesse ran the back of his knuckles gently along her cheek. "Don't let him do that to you."

Too late, she thought. She tried to smile and failed dismally. "You're being awfully nice."

"Haven't you heard?" he teased. "Heroes are supposed to take Nice 101 before they're allowed to rescue someone. Can't do a decent rescue without it."

Her smile was marked with sadness. "Is that what you're going to do? Rescue me?"

I'll do anything you want me to. The ease with which the thought came to him surprised Jesse. And it felt right. "Can't think of anyone I'd rather rescue than you."

He was being so good about this that she felt even guiltier. Tania shook her head. "I'm sorry I spoiled this for you."

"The only way you could have spoiled it for me is by not being here in the first place. Then, of course," he added with a teasing smile, "I'd be arrested for breaking and entering because I would have had no business being in your apartment."

Something stirred inside of Tania that she hadn't felt before. Not about someone outside her family. She'd only been on the brink of infatuation once and that had been with Jeff. And then he'd shattered her. Since then she'd never reacted to any male on anything but a physical level.

But this was something different, beyond the basic pull of attraction she'd felt. Something she couldn't—wouldn't—put a name to. At least not yet. Naming it would only jinx it.

She laughed at his protest. "You make me feel… safe," she confessed to Jesse after a beat.

He pretended to be disappointed. "And here I thought I had this bad-boy thing going."

The smile that curved her mouth was far less difficult to summon. And, miraculously, some of the sadness was gone.

Tania cleared her throat. She'd asked men out before, but this was different. Harder.

"If you want to give it another try…" Her voice trailed off.

Jesse cupped her cheek with his palm. "You already know the answer to that," he told her. "But only if you're ready and you want to."

She looked at him incredulously. "Otherwise, you'd wait?"

He nodded. "Otherwise, I'd wait." He brushed his fingertip along her cheek, capturing a precious bit of dampness. "You're crying again."

"Good tears," she told him, trying hard, and unsuccessfully, to stop. "Good tears."

"Good tears, bad tears." Jesse shook his head, mystified. "I don't understand how you can cry when you're happy," he told her honestly. "But I'll take your word for it."

Tilting her chin up, Jesse gently brushed his lips against hers. And then again. And again, each time a little deeper than the last, a little longer than the last.

One arm around her, he moved her closer against him. His free hand delved beneath the comforter and, very slowly, he caressed her, lightly tracing the outline of her hip.

His movements were languid, as if she were a wild mare that had wandered onto his property and he was afraid of spooking her, of driving her away.

Even as the urges multiplied within him, Jesse kept himself in check. Like a man inching his way across a tightrope stretched over the Grand Canyon, where any misstep could be his last, Jesse made love to every part of her. Slowly, one movement building on another.

He took his cues from her, listening to her intake of breath, feeling her heart hammering against his. Ever on the alert for her shrinking back because that would mean that he needed to back off a little before he could move forward.

It was all about her and because he succeeded in

arousing her, because he heard her moan with pleasure, he experienced triumph upon triumph.

No part of her was left untouched, uncaressed, unkissed, until he felt her movements accelerate, not as if she were in some sort of race to finish quickly, but because she was in the midst of a fever pitch.

Drawing the length of his body over hers, Jesse joined his hands with Tania's, threading his fingers through hers and making them one before the actual physical act reinforced that.

"Are you all right?" he whispered in her ear.

She didn't answer. Instead she moved her legs apart and let him enter. Rather than stiffen the way she had last time, the way she had every time since she'd been attacked, Tania arched her hips, a silent invitation. The heat and desire traveling through her body moved everything else into the background.

This time she actually felt the rhythm overtake her rather than her struggling to mimic the movement of his hips.

And then, for the first time in her life, she let this incredible sensation vibrate through her, making her scramble toward the feeling, wanting more even as she savored its essence. It seemed to her like an explosion that kept on going.

Enthralled, Tania grasped hold of his shoulders, arching higher, seeking to prolong the moment. And then, when it was over, she sank into this soft, welcoming cloud. Her pulse slowly decelerated.

What had just happened here? She felt like such a novice.

Tania opened her eyes and saw him, still pivoted on

his elbows, looking down at her face. There was concern in his eyes.

"Are you all right?" he asked softly.

It took her a minute to find her tongue. Longer to locate her wits. Try as she might, she couldn't even begin to define what she was feeling, other than overwhelmed.

And powerful.

And free.

"So all right that they haven't even invented the word to cover how all right I am," she finally answered, her voice barely audible. She drew in two more deep breaths and then released them. Her odd euphoria was wondrous. "I think I might have just had an out-of-body experience."

Jesse did his best not to laugh. But he did smile. Broadly. Smiled and pressed a kiss to her temple. Getting off her, he moved to the side and tucked his arm around her again, once more drawing her to him. "Then I guess that my work here is done."

She turned her face into his. They were barely inches apart. So close that she could taste his breath. And found herself aroused again. "Is that what you call it? Work?"

"I call it ecstasy, personally," he confessed. And then Jesse kissed her again, softly, tenderly, not like a man who wanted to make love again, but like a man who loved.

She nodded at his response, curling into him. Thrilled beyond words that she wanted to, that she didn't want to bolt and run or hurl herself into an hour-long shower.

"Sounds like a good call to me," she murmured.

She splayed her hand along his chest, sinking further into a web of contentment. Resting her head against his shoulder, Tania was soon asleep.

Jesse lay there beside her, listening to her breathe, so moved by the simple act that he hardly recognized himself. It was a little scary, he mused, feeling all these different sensations.

He felt protective toward this woman. Protective and completely and unnervingly at her mercy.

There was an interpretation for all this and he knew it, but right now, he didn't want to explore what it meant. Tonight, he would bask in the triumph generated by all the walls that had been breached.

Jesse remained with her for a while longer. Her breathing remained steady. No nightmares assaulted her, no sudden fits and starts overtook her. Only sleep.

And then, very slowly, so as not to wake Tania up, Jesse retreated from her. When his arm was clear of her body, he sat up and then got off the bed.

It was late.

He was acutely aware that one or both of her sisters might come home anytime now despite the notes they'd left on the refrigerator. He had a feeling that Tania might not want to explain his presence to them.

To spare Tania the awkwardness, he decided to leave. Moreover, if she awoke to regret having trusted him with her secret, or her body, he didn't want to see all that reflected in her eyes. She had such expressive eyes.

Taking his clothes into her bathroom, Jesse got dressed quickly. And then, very quietly, carrying his shoes in his hand, Jesse left the apartment. He pulled the door closed behind him.

He heard the tumbler click as the lock fell into place.

After pausing at the door to put on his shoes, Jesse walked quickly to the elevator. He passed no one in the corridor, but he had the distinct, uneasy feeling that someone was there.

This was a bad time to be paranoid, he thought. It was all just in his head, he assured himself. Residue from when Ellen had stalked him, nothing more. Even so, he paused by the elevator, listening before he pressed the down button.

There was nothing to hear.

Jesse had walked all the way to the parking structure and was actually sitting in his car, his key in the ignition, about to turn the engine on, when he had a change of heart. Concern about Tania got the better of him.

He'd been thinking of himself when he left.

His unwillingness to see regret on Tania's face had prompted him to go. He hadn't really thought about it in terms of how *she* would feel if she woke up to find him gone. What if she didn't feel relief when she reached out only to find that space beside her empty?

What if the wrong message was sent by his absence from her bed? What if Tania felt abandoned? Or even used?

A lot of one-night stands slipped out in the middle of the night, leaving their partners to face the dawn alone. That wasn't what he wanted her to think. At the very least, he wanted her to know that this was not a one-night stand. Not to him.

What the hell had he been thinking, leaving like that? Jesse upbraided himself.

Exiting the vehicle, he paused only long enough to lock it again. And then he hurried back the long city block to her building.

Getting in the building's front door was no problem.

He rang a series of doorbells until someone's voice finally crackled over the intercom.

"Jake, is that you?" a husky woman's voice asked.

"Yeah," he rasped.

The woman cursed on the other end and, for a second, Jesse thought he would have to go on pressing buttons. But then the harsh sound of the buzzer filled the air. He lost no time pushing the heavy door open.

A great deal of pent-up energy coursed through his veins. It had been roughly about fifteen minutes or so since he'd left. Jesse crossed his fingers and hoped that Tania hadn't woken up in the interval.

Entering the lobby, he glanced at the dial above the closed elevator door. The car was on the fifth floor. Her floor. Too impatient to wait for the elevator car to make its way down to the first floor, Jesse decided to take the stairs instead.

He raced up all five flights and was breathing heavily when he threw open the door that led out onto her floor. He didn't pause to catch his breath. Instead he hurried over to her apartment. Knowing the outcome ahead of time, he tried the door anyway. It was locked, just the way he'd left it.

It wasn't a problem.

He'd had a lot of friends in his youth, not all with savory backgrounds that followed straight and narrow paths. One of his former friends was currently serving five to seven upstate for burglary. The same former friend who had once taught him how to pick any lock "in case of an emergency."

Jesse was determined to let himself in without waking Tania if he could. If possible, he didn't want her to even suspect that he had ever left.

Because it had been a very long time since he'd attempted to pick any lock—sheerly for practice—it took him several attempts and as many minutes to finally conquer the lock. Trying the doorknob, he felt it give beneath his hand. As quietly as possible, he turned the doorknob all the way and opened the door.

The second he walked into the apartment, he smelled it.

Gas.

Chapter 13

Jesse didn't even stop to think, he just reacted. Dashing into the apartment, he began throwing windows open as he made his way to Tania's bedroom.

He found her just the way he'd left her, in bed and sound asleep. The only difference was, when he shook her to wake her up, Tania remained unresponsive. The smell of gas began to get to him but he focused on what he had to do. Get Tania out of there as quickly as he could.

Throwing off the comforter, he wrapped her nude body in a sheet and picked her up. His throat felt scratchy and his head began to spin. Trying to breathe as little as possible, Jesse carried her out of the apartment and into the hall.

He leaned a still-unconscious Tania against the wall right next to the apartment door. As he squatted beside her, at a complete loss as to what to do, his mind raced.

He started rubbing her wrists, hoping that if he got her circulation going, he could make her come around.

He endured several very scary minutes, watching her face as he continued to rub. Just as he was about to call 9-1-1, her eyes fluttered open. She moaned and then began to cough as she put her hand to her head.

He sat back on his heels for a second, looking at her, so relieved he could barely catch his own breath. "Oh, thank God."

Tania stared at him, unseeing and disoriented, her head pounding like the inside of a bowling alley when all the lanes were in play. Taking a deep breath and blinking, she slowly looked around, trying to get her bearings. Trying to focus. Where was she? And then it came to her.

"Jesse, what are we doing out in the hallway?" As bits and pieces became clearer, she looked down at herself. And saw she had the top sheet from her bed wrapped around her like a blue flowing toga. What the hell was going on? "Am I still naked?" she asked him incredulously.

"You're still alive," he corrected. Suddenly feeling light-headed himself, Jesse shifted so that his back was against the wall, too. Leaning, he sank beside her. At the moment, his knees didn't quite feel as if they could support him.

She didn't understand what he was saying. "Why wouldn't I be?" she asked. "And *what* are we doing out here?"

Tania hoped he had some kind of plausible answer for this. Had she been wrong about him, after all? Had she let her barriers down just to allow some kind of weirdo closer to her?

Her nerves began to shift even as something inside her head whispered for her to withhold final judgment.

He wanted to take her into his arms, to hug her and hold her to him and just listen to her breathe. But right now, if he gauged the look in her eyes correctly, that would probably frighten her.

So instead he told her, "There's a gas leak in your apartment."

Holding the sheet to her, bracing one hand against the doorjamb, Tania rose shakily to her feet. He sprang to his, as if ready to catch her if she fell.

"That's not possible," she insisted. "Kady said we just had someone come through the other day, checking to make sure everything was up to code." And then her eyes widened slightly as she remembered. "The building's super even replaced the old gas stove with a new one."

Something just didn't make sense. Had a faulty stove been put in on purpose? Why? By who? He needed to look around. "Stay here," he ordered.

"Naked in the hall?" she demanded. Granted it was the middle of the night and probably no one would pass by, but she wasn't about to stay here to find out. "I don't think so."

But as she started to follow him, Tania suddenly swayed, her light-headedness getting the better of her.

Alert, Jesse moved back and caught her before she could sink to her knees. "Stay put," he told her firmly. Both hands on her shoulders, he pressed her back against the outside wall and then went inside the apartment.

The late evening air came in through all the windows he'd opened and began to cut into the overpowering smell of gas. But he could still smell it.

Walking into the kitchen, Jesse immediately saw that all four burners had been turned on. They were on, but not a single blue flame was visible. He looked at the knobs that ran along the side of the stovetop. Someone had deliberately turned on the gas jets while making sure that the flames had been extinguished.

Why?

"What did you find?"

Jesse swung around to see Tania in the kitchen doorway, looking pale but determined to be there. She held the sheet to her with one hand, while grasping the doorjamb with the other to keep herself steady.

He banked down a surge of anger. What did it take to make the woman stay put? "That you don't take instruction well."

Tania waved her hand at the comment, her attention on the stove. "We already knew that." Her eyes narrowed as she came forward. "Is the stove on?"

"Apparently." Taking a kitchen towel, Jesse held it against his fingers and turned all four jets back to "off" before she could do it herself.

"What are you doing?" she asked.

"Whoever turned the gas jets on probably left their fingerprints."

Whoever. That meant someone had come in and done this on purpose. That wouldn't have been the first thing she would have thought of. Tania's mouth curved slightly.

"You've been watching too much television." She had a more logical explanation. "Kady or Natalya probably just forgot to turn off the stove."

"Like they forgot to lock the door?" he asked pointedly.

Her head jerked up as her thought process leapfrogged. "Do you think something happened to one of them?"

She was agitated, so he spoke calmly, putting his hand on her arm to steady her. "No. And I don't think either one of them left unlit burners on, either. We would have smelled something earlier," he pointed out.

She nodded. That made sense. What didn't make sense was why the burners had been turned on in the first place. And by who?

Tania shook her head. The throbbing was getting worse. "This is just so strange. One weird thing after another," she murmured, more to herself than to him.

But she had his undivided attention. "What do you mean, one weird thing after another? What other weird thing are you talking about?"

She looked at him, debating. He was probably going to think she was a little crazy. Or maybe a lot. "I can't shake this feeling that someone is watching me. And the other day—" She paused, searching for a way to say this without sounding dramatic. "I was nearly hit by a bus."

He stared at her, stunned. Was she putting him on? "What?"

Tania shrugged, as if it was really nothing and she was sorry she'd mentioned it. "I was standing on the corner, waiting for the light to change, and I guess it was too crowded because suddenly it felt like someone pushed me from behind. I started to fall forward and if that guy hadn't grabbed my arm and pulled me back, I would have been road kill."

She was embarrassed by the revelation, he realized. She *wasn't* putting him on, but she was trying to downplay it. "Why didn't you say anything before?" he asked.

An awkwardness descended over her. She struggled against feeling like a victim. The way she'd struggled off and on all these years.

Again she shrugged, looking away. "Didn't see the point. There are eight million people in the city and sometimes two or more try to occupy the same space, especially on a street corner. Accidents are bound to happen."

One was an accident, two or more made for an unnerving pattern. He knew all about denial. He's used it as a tool when he was being stalked.

Jesse glared at the stove. "Maybe too many accidents." He didn't want to ask, but he came to the only logical conclusion he could. "Does this Jeff know where you live these days?"

Tania suddenly felt cold. Trying to bank down the feeling, she ran her hands over her arms. "You think this might be him?"

"I don't know. I'm not the police." He came over to stand beside her and slipped his arm around her shoulders. "I think we should call them."

She shook her head so hard, she nearly became dizzy again. "No. I don't want this getting back to my father. He has connections all over the force. He'll worry." She could see that Jesse wasn't about to back away. She hit on a compromise. "I'll call Sasha's husband. He won't say anything to my father."

She'd mentioned to him that Tony Santini was a homicide detective. Jesse nodded. "As long as you call someone," he told her. "How do you feel?"

Tania raised her chin and forced a smile to her lips. She was *not* going to be the object of pity, especially not his. "Like I have my own private hero."

He didn't reciprocate her smile. "I'm serious, Tania. I couldn't get you to wake up at first." He swept her hair back from her face. "Maybe you should go to the hospital and get checked out."

Tania stepped back and he instinctively knew he wasn't going to get her to listen unless he slung her over his shoulder and carried her to the hospital.

"I'm an E.R. doctor. I can check myself out as easily as any of them," she insisted. "Physician heal thyself and all that stuff."

"This isn't funny, Tania. If I hadn't come back—"

"Come back?" she echoed, surprised. "From where? When I fell asleep, you were right there." And then it suddenly dawned on her. He wasn't wearing a sheet, he had his clothes on. He wouldn't have stopped to get dressed before getting her out of the apartment. "Why are you dressed? When I fell asleep, you were naked."

He had wanted to avoid having her find out the truth, but there was no getting around it now. "I thought maybe one of your sisters might come home unexpectedly and I didn't want you to have to explain what I was doing there."

"I wouldn't have had to explain. They're both doctors. They both have a pretty good handle on the birds and the bees thing." She dropped her sarcastic tone and her voice was low, serious. "So what made you come back?"

There were a lot of ways to couch this, but he gave it to her as honestly as he could. "I realized that if you woke up in an empty bed, you might feel a little abandoned." His eyes met hers. "And I really didn't want that."

She took in a deep, fortifying breath. Her lungs still

ached and her head felt a little fuzzy. But not her heart. That felt just fine. "You didn't?"

"No, I didn't." He wasn't about to be sidetracked. Jesse took out his cell phone. Flipping it open, he placed the phone into her hand. "Now call your brother-in-law."

Tania closed the phone in a fluid movement and handed it back to him. "It's after one in the morning. I'll call him at a more decent hour."

Jesse didn't accept the phone. Instead he pressed it back into her hand. "He's a policeman, he's used to strange hours. Call him," he said firmly. "Or I'll call 9-1-1. Your choice."

She sighed, frowning at the phone. "So much for twisting you around my little finger."

"I wouldn't fit." Jesse nodded at the phone. "Which will it be?"

There was no real choice. "I'll call Tony. Can I at least get dressed?"

He smiled for the first time, his eyes sweeping over her frame. Remembering what she'd looked like, pliant and giving, in his arms. "For the sake of Sasha and Tony's marriage, I'd highly recommend it."

A little more than half an hour later, Tony, Sasha, Mike, who had been called to the scene by Tony, and Natalya arrived almost simultaneously at the apartment. Using Sasha's old key, Tony unlocked the door and came in first.

Jesse and Tania were on their feet instantly, meeting them in the foyer before they'd taken more than one step into the apartment.

Tony had been filled in about the gas leak over the

phone when Tania called him. His concern was evident, even if his expression remained stoic. "Are you all right?" he asked Tania. She nodded. Tony turned toward his wife. "She's all right." There was a strange finality about his voice, as if he had just proven a point. "Now will you go back home?" Without waiting for an answer, he turned toward his sister-in-law's fiancé. "Mike, can you take her—"

Moving forward, Sasha sniffed the air. "I don't smell any gas," she said, interrupting her husband. "No need to rush me out of here, Tony. The baby'll be fine," she assured him, then turned toward Tania. "My question is, are you sure you're all right?"

Tania nodded, feeling bad about having dragged not one but four members of her family out of bed. "This is all getting out of hand," she protested. "It was just a leak, nothing more."

"This wasn't a leak," Jesse insisted. "Leaks don't suddenly stop when you turn a knob on the stove." He looked from one detective to another, realizing that the men probably had no idea who he was. "Hi, I'm Jesse Steele. I'm the one who insisted she call you. Or the police," he tacked on.

"Same thing," Tony said, shaking Jesse's outstretched hand. "Tony Santini."

"Mike DiPalma." Mike took his turn shaking Jesse's hand. "And it's not the same thing," he corrected Tony. "It's better." He looked at his future sister-in-law. "All right, tell us what happened. From the beginning," he qualified.

"I was asleep," she explained, then turned toward Jesse. "You fill them in."

So Jesse did, as quickly and succinctly as he could.

Ending his story, he added that he'd just found out from Tania that she'd been pushed in the path of an oncoming bus and that for the last few weeks, she'd been trying to shake the feeling that she was being watched.

Mike nodded, jotting everything down in the small spiral pad he kept in his pocket. When Jesse was finished, Mike went on to ask the usual questions in cases like the one this seemed to be.

He looked at Tania. "Do you have any enemies? Is there anyone who might want to see you permanently out of the way?"

Sasha and Natalya exchanged looks, clearly horrified at the very suggestion, but Tania took the questions in stride.

"No," she answered firmly. "No to both."

Out of the corner of her eye, she caught Jesse watching her. She knew by the expression on his face what he was thinking. He was remembering what she'd told him earlier. A part of her wished she'd never opened up.

She closed her eyes for a second, letting out a long breath. And then she turned to Mike. "There might be someone."

"I'll check it out," Tony volunteered. "Who is it, Tania?"

Tania didn't answer immediately. Instead she looked at her sisters for a long moment. So close that they could read each other's minds at times. She was grateful that neither of them rushed to fill Tony in. That was up to her.

"Jeff Palmer," she finally said. Tony raised an eyebrow in silent query. "Because of me, he was sent to prison."

"No," Natalya cut in firmly. "Because of *him* he was sent to prison," she declared.

Tania waited a moment before clarifying. "He raped

me," she said as simply as possible, allowing none of the pain to come through. She could tell by their reaction that neither man knew about this. Her sisters had kept her secret. "And I went to the police about it. There was a plea bargain and Jeff was sent to jail. He's been out for a few months now," she concluded.

"Is that when you started feeling that someone was watching you?" Mike asked.

She shook her head. "Not immediately." She tried to pinpoint the first time. "Just in the last three weeks, I guess."

Mike had crossed over to the stove and gingerly examined it. He'd pulled a pair of latex gloves out of his pocket and put them on, careful not to smear any evidence.

He glanced at her over his shoulder. "You said all four were turned on?"

It was Jesse who answered. "Yes."

Mike nodded, as if absorbing what was said. "I'll have someone dust for prints." Pulling off the gloves, he crossed back to Tania. "Does anyone else have the key to this apartment?"

Everyone in this room had a key, she thought, except for Jesse. "Just family," Tania answered.

"And you," Natalya interjected, looking at Mike with a whimsical expression on her face.

He gave her a patient, fond look. "I believe you're my alibi."

Tania thought she saw a blush creeping up her sister's face.

"The door wasn't locked when she came home," Jesse suddenly recalled. The two couples turned to look at him, surprised by this new piece of information. "We went to the theater and when we came back, the door wasn't locked."

Natalya spread her hands in protest. "Don't look at me, I locked it when I left—and I left after Kady." The import of her words sank in. Her eyes shifted toward Sasha. "So, unless you dropped by in the interim…"

"Not me," Sasha told her. "I was at the hospital until an hour ago. Mrs. Cassidy *finally* gave birth after four false starts."

Some of the pieces were coming together and it was apparent that Tony didn't like the picture they were forming. "So whoever it was let themselves in to check out the place might have even been here when you came home."

Jesse was quick to set him straight. "I checked out every room, every closet. So unless it was a homicidal monkey hiding in the medicine cabinet, there was no one here when we came in."

"Then they came to get the lay of the land," Mike guessed. "And came back later to tamper with the stove." He turned to Natalya. "You're coming back home with me."

In union there is strength, Jesse thought as he addressed Tania. "That's exactly what I was going to say to you."

Tania gave him a wide-eyed, innocent look. "You want me to go home with Mike? Three's a crowd."

Natalya laughed sympathetically. "Personally, I don't know how you put up with that," she teased. "As for you," she addressed Mike, "since I'm here, I might as well stay here. I'm due at the hospital in less than seven hours and this is closer." She smiled at Tania. "I'll keep Tania company."

Mike seemed a little exasperated, but he knew that tone. There was no arguing with her.

"It's a stubborn family," Tony told him.

Mike sighed, shaking his head. "Tell me something I don't know." He was not about to leave Natalya in a place whose security had been compromised. "Looks like I'll be here for a while."

With that, he took out his cell phone to call someone in the crime scene unit who owed him a favor.

Chapter 14

Over the course of the next week and a half, Jesse saw Tania as often as their two schedules permitted. Because he was working against a deadline, he would bring his blueprints and sketches with him and spend evenings working at her apartment when he couldn't talk her into coming to his. In either situation, he made it a point to pick her up from the hospital no matter how late she got off.

Despite all her efforts to remain nonchalant, Tania quickly grew accustomed to seeing Jesse in the E.R. lobby, waiting for her.

"You know, you really don't have to play my bodyguard."

Sitting on a worn, creased brown vinyl sofa, with a rerun of some program droning on in the background, Jesse discovered to his embarrassment that he had dozed off. The sound of Tania's voice, low and breathy as she'd whispered in his ear, instantly roused him. And aroused him.

Jesse took a deep breath, pulling himself together as best he could. He saw her smile in amusement. "What do you mean 'play'?" he asked. "I thought I was doing a pretty good job of being the real thing."

Actually, he was. He was quickly becoming her knight in shining armor and everyone knew that knights in shining armor weren't real. They belonged in fairy tales. Thinking of him that way only set her up for a fall.

"You don't have to be the real thing, either," she said as he tucked his sketches away and closed his portfolio. "At this rate, you're going to wear out in a couple of days and then who am I going to ask to Natalya's wedding?"

Jesse rose to his feet, his eyebrows momentarily raised in surprise. He was aware of the wedding, but this was the first he'd heard of an invitation. More progress, he thought.

"I won't wear out," he promised, walking beside her to the front entrance. He stepped back, letting her out first. The electronic doors slid open and the night air, pregnant with unshed rain and oppressive humidity, instantly met them, providing a startling contrast to the air-conditioned interior. "You keep these hours and you haven't worn out yet," he pointed out.

"I keep these hours," she agreed, threading her arm through his as they walked to the hospital's parking structure, "but I don't moonlight as an architect." She paused for a moment to brush a kiss to his cheek, surprising him again. "In essence, you're almost juggling two careers. You shouldn't." She saw another protest rise to his lips. "I appreciate what you're doing, Jesse, but really, everything seems to be fine. No one's pushed me off the sidewalk into traffic lately and the stove's been behaving itself." They crossed into the structure and took the stairs down to the basement. "I think I was just being a little paranoid the other week, because I was kind of anxious."

The classic "which came first, the chicken or the egg" runaround, he mused. "That's kind of a catch-22 isn't it?"

"Maybe," she allowed with a casual shrug of her shoulders. Theirs were the only footsteps echoing in the structure on this level. She was secretly glad she wasn't alone. But then, if he weren't here, she'd be waiting for the bus out in the open. It was a trade-off. "If I was anxious about being followed. But that wasn't why I was anxious."

Arriving at his vehicle, Jesse took out his keys and unlocked the passenger side. He held the door open for her. "What was it, then?" he probed.

Tania got in. The moment her body met the seat, she realized how very tired she was—and how grateful she didn't have to wait for public transportation.

She tugged the seat belt into place. "Let's just say I could feel myself heading for a place I hadn't been before and I was afraid it would blow up in my face."

Jesse quickly rounded the rear of his car and got in on the driver's side. "But you don't feel that way anymore?"

That wasn't entirely true. "I've decided to take a wait-and-see stance."

He nodded. The woman was hard to pin down. "Interesting."

"That's one word for it." Jesse closed the door, but made no move to insert the key into the ignition. She eyed him quizzically. Was there something wrong with the car? "Aren't you going to start it?" she asked.

"In a minute."

Before she could ask him what he planned to do in that minute, Tania had her answer. Twisting in his seat, his seat belt still in the at-rest position, Jesse cupped her chin in his hands and kissed her.

Tania had already buckled herself in. Her lips occupied by his, she felt blindly around for the release button and pressed it. As the belt slid back from her body, she moved a breath closer to him. She could feel herself sinking further into the kiss. Without realizing it, she sighed, the outward sign of her vulnerability.

She felt his mouth curving in a smile a second before he drew his head back. "Now I'm ready to go," he told her. Shifting back around, he buckled up and then started the car.

"You certainly are," she murmured. Tania slid the seat belt back into the groove. "Bucket seats do leave something to be desired," she commented. "They sure weren't designed for romance."

He laughed, comically lowering and raising his eyebrows. "Well, there's always the backseat."

Tania did her best to look stern even as his suggestion aroused her. She pointed to the street up ahead. "Just drive," she told him.

"Yes, ma'am." Both hands on the wheel, Jesse guided the car passed the empty guard hut and out onto the street.

Neither one of them saw the figure hiding in the shadows, watching them.

Watching and silently cursing.

* * *

"So, it really wasn't Jeff?" Tania asked her brother-in-law.

Sitting on the arm of the chocolate-colored sofa in her living room, Tony shook his head. It was several days later and Tony, as well as Mike, had devoted as much time to the private investigation as they could. With frustrating results.

"Sorry." He was far from happy with the results. "The fingerprints didn't match. Palmer's are in the system. The prints that were lifted from the knobs on the stove aren't."

He'd had the CSU investigator take samples of all the sisters' prints, using those to pair up with partials that had been found on the knobs and the stove itself. One lone thumbprint did not match any of the sisters. That belonged to the perp, but without matching a set in the system, they were nowhere.

Tania made the best of it. "At least I can stop worrying that Jeff is stalking me." She tried to sound upbeat. This was, after all, an upbeat evening. Leaning forward, she placed her hand on top of his and gave it an appreciative squeeze. "Thanks for looking into that for me."

"We're not out of the woods yet," Tony reminded her. "Someone *did* turn on the gas jets, which means that someone did try to kill you."

She wanted to protest that it might have been one of her sisters that this mysterious "someone" was after, but neither one of them had been pushed into the path of an oncoming bus, nor had either one of them mentioned that they thought someone was following them.

Still, she wanted to release Tony from any sense of

obligation. "There's been nothing for over a week. Maybe whoever it was gave up. Or got hit by a bus," she said whimsically. "At any rate, I'm not going to have this spoil Natalya's wedding."

The doorbell rang and she went to answer it, aware that Tony had risen from the sofa. Ever vigilant, she thought, amused.

"It's just another cop," she announced, stepping away from the doorway and allowing Mike to enter. "She's almost ready," Tania told him as she walked back into the living room.

As if on cue, Natalya came out of her room and into the living room. She looked at her sisters instead of the man she was marrying tomorrow at ten.

"This is my last night as a single woman. Shouldn't I be doing something more decadent than going to the wedding rehearsal?" she asked innocently, struggling to keep a straight face.

"That can be arranged," Mike told her, slipping an arm around her waist and pulling her in close for a quick kiss.

"Not with you." She put her hand on his chest as if to fend him off. "I'm going to be decadent with you for the rest of my life. I was thinking of something else. Maybe a male strip club."

"Stop right there," Sasha warned. "Mama will kill you."

"That'll keep me on the straight and narrow," Natalya commented, nodding.

Sasha merely laughed in response. "First time for everything." Getting up from the sofa, she looked at Tania. "Can we give you a lift to the restaurant?"

Tania shook her head. Bringing a change of clothes with her, Kady was going to the restaurant straight from the hospital. Byron was meeting her there. Their youngest sister and the senior Pulaskis were probably already there. Daddy insisted on being on time, but for the most part, it was a losing battle.

"Jesse is coming by to pick me up in a few minutes." He was actually running a few minutes late, but she kept that to herself.

"We can wait with you," Natalya offered.

"I do not need to be babysat," Tania protested. She glanced at her watch. "Besides, if you don't get to the restaurant soon—" she turned to look at Mike "—Mama is going to think you came to your senses and ran for the hills. She'd come after you."

"Not a chance." Mike looked at Natalya, their own form of silent communication humming between them. "Besides, even if I did make a break for it, my mother would hunt me down before yours ever put on her track shoes."

Natalya laughed, clearly amused. "You obviously don't know my mother."

"Go," Tania urged, putting her hands to Natalya's back and pushing slightly. "All of you. Jesse'll be here in a few minutes and then I'll go."

"Technically," Sasha commented, "since he's not part of the wedding party or the family, Jesse doesn't have to be there." Sasha looked closer at her younger sister. "Unless, of course, he *is* going to become part of the family. Is he, Tania?"

In response, Tania appealed to her brother-in-law. "Tony, please, take your wife and go."

"We live to protect and serve," Tony replied good-naturedly. "Let's go, little mama." Putting his hand to the small of her back, he gently guided her out the door and into the hallway.

Mike was the last one out. Just before he left, he paused for a moment, looking at Tania. "You're sure you don't want one of us to—"

Hands to his arm, she pushed him out the door. Harder than she had her sister.

"I'm sure," she said firmly, then added, "And thank you. But really, Jesse will be here in a couple of minutes. I'll be fine. Really."

Quickly shutting the door behind the groom-to-be, Tania leaned against it for a second and smiled to herself. Natalya was getting a really nice guy. Just as Sasha had. And Kady. All three of her sisters had really lucked out.

Amazing odds in this day and age, she mused, crossing back to the living room.

And what about you? the reflection in the mirror on the wall above the liquor cabinet seemed to ask.

Tania supposed that, when she wasn't being fearful that she was allowing herself to be too trusting again, she just might have blindly stumbled onto something good, as well.

Or someone good.

Because, all things considered, Jesse Steele seemed almost to be too good to be true. She kept waiting for a fatal flaw to surface, for a shoe to drop. For something that would come and burst the bubble that, for now, continued to thrive.

Part of her still felt that maybe she should back away while she still could, before she was hopelessly ensnared and completely lost.

"Who are you kidding?" she asked the wide-eyed woman in the mirror. "There is no more 'before.' You *are* hopelessly ensnared. You *are* completely lost. If this thing ended tomorrow, you'd be devastated and you know it." She stared at her reflection for a long moment. "Face it, Tania," she whispered, "you're in love with the man. The only thing you can do now is hope that he doesn't crush you like a bug."

He didn't seem like the type. On the contrary, everything about him, from the moment she'd met him, fairly shouted "good guy." But even good guys had their dark side, she argued. She had learned that firsthand. Jeff had seemed like a good guy. He hadn't been someone she'd just met casually. She *knew* him.

Or thought she did.

Stop it, Tania ordered herself silently. *You're making yourself crazy.*

Just then, the doorbell rang. Thank God. Jesse. No more internal Ping-Pong matches. With a sense of relief flowing through her, Tania fairly dashed toward the front door, pausing only to slip into her shoes.

"Coming," she cried when the doorbell rang again. She was so focussed on Jesse's arrival, she didn't even look through the peephole the way she normally did. Throwing open the door, she chided, "You realize you're late, don't you?" and then stopped dead.

It wasn't Jesse.

"Not really," the woman in the doorway replied tranquilly. "The way I see it, I'm really just in time."

Tania stared at her, confused. It was the volunteer from the hospital. The one she'd attempted to treat for a bad back. She'd disappeared after being sent to the

X-ray department. Not for the day but ever since then. Tania had asked after her only to be told that the woman was no longer coming in to volunteer.

"Carol?" Tania stood just inside the apartment, blocking the way in. "What are you doing here?"

Slightly taller than Tania and a little wider, the woman entered as if she belonged there. Once inside, she pushed the door closed. "What I'm doing here is stopping you from making a horrible mistake."

"What mistake?" Tania could feel her stomach knotting. There was something wrong with this woman. Why hadn't she seen it before?

The woman's eyes narrowed. "You need to stop seeing Jesse Steele."

Tania could feel her temper flaring. "That isn't any business of yours."

"Oh, yes, it is," the woman answered in a steely voice that, any moment, sounded as if it would cross over into hysteria. "He's my husband."

For a split second, Tania felt her knees go weak. "What?"

A smug, cold smile took over the woman's pretty face. As she spoke, she moved about, as if there was unharnessed energy within her, energy that was liable to explode at any moment. But she made sure she didn't move away from the area of the front door.

"Didn't tell you that, did he? That he was married. That he vowed undying love to me such a short while ago. He's a charmer, that one," she allowed. "I don't blame you for having your head turned." She set her mouth hard. "But now you need to go."

The way she said it sent shivers down Tania's spine.

She refused to show any fear, sensing that the woman would only feel empowered.

"No," Tania declared, "you do." She made a lunge for the doorknob. Blocking her, the other woman pushed Tania aside so hard, she stumbled backward and nearly fell. She caught herself at the last minute, glaring at the intruder.

Just then, the phone began to ring. Tania's head jerked in the direction of the telephone.

"Leave it!" the woman ordered.

From where she stood, she could see the LED display. "It's Jesse," she said. Why was he calling? Why wasn't he here already?

"Let it ring," the woman snarled. Tania went for it anyway. The woman got to her before she could reach the phone and grabbed her by the hair. Tania yelped in pain. The next moment the woman shoved her down on the floor. "I said leave it!" she screamed.

Aching, Tania scrambled to her feet. "What the hell do you want?"

The woman's voice became singsong. "I want to do a good deed," she told her. "I came to warn you." And then her face clouded over, her expression malevolent. "Stay away from Jesse. He's bad news."

"Then why do you want him?" Tania challenged.

"Because he's *my* bad news," the woman all but screamed in her face.

Tania stood her ground, all the while desperately trying to think of a way to overpower the deranged woman and get the upper hand. She wasn't going to be a victim again.

"Look, 'your husband' is going to be here any minute," she retorted nastily. "Maybe you'd like to tell him all this yourself."

Tania was not prepared for the smug expression that came over the woman's face. "No, he's not." Her voice was low, dark. Mocking. "Jesse isn't coming to the rescue this time."

The uneasiness in her stomach began to spread. What had the woman done to Jesse? Had he just called her for help? Called and not gotten an answer because this witch was holding her hostage, threatening her?

"How do you know that?" she demanded.

"I know that because your 'hero' is having car trouble." Smug satisfaction fairly radiated from the woman. "Cars don't run without a distributor cap. It'll take him time to figure out. Time you and I can use well."

And then it suddenly all became clear to her. Why hadn't she thought of this before? "You're Ellen, aren't you?"

The mention of her name made the woman all but preen before her. "So he did tell you about me, after all."

She needed to get Ellen frustrated. To get her confused so that she let her guard down. "Just that you were some sick, twisted woman who'd been stalking him."

Fury entered Ellen's eyes. She looked really crazy, Tania thought. "I didn't stalk him! I'm his wife!" she insisted. "Wives are *supposed* to be around their husbands!" She held up her left hand, waving her ring finger in the air. "See? A wedding ring." She all but thrust it into Tania's face. "We're married, you bitch, and it's time that you stepped out of the picture once and for all. Now, let's go."

But Tania didn't make a move. Someone at the restaurant would realize she wasn't there and come back for her. All she had to do was hang on until then. "I'm not going anywhere with you."

"Oh, yes, you are."

She never even saw the taser until it was too late. One scream and Tania crumpled to the floor, unconscious.

"Oh, yes, you are," Ellen repeated triumphantly.

Chapter 15

Jesse admittedly knew very little about cars beyond keeping the gas tank filled and bringing it in for regular oil changes and maintenance. Other than adding oil once in a while and keeping jumper cables in the trunk, just in case his battery died, what went on beneath the hood was a complete mystery to him.

In exchange for regular maintenance, his present vehicle gave him no grief. So when he got in behind the wheel after stopping at his apartment to change, and heard absolutely nothing when he turned the key in the ignition, Jesse was caught entirely off guard.

Mystification swiftly became a hazy, uneasy feeling he couldn't quantify or put his finger on. Hoping it was some kind of fluke, Jesse turned the key again. Without success. The vehicle stubbornly maintained its silence.

Cursing the fact that his car should pick now of all

times to become uncooperative, he popped the hood release just to the left of the steering column and got out. Jesse lifted the hood and immediately found himself staring into no-man's-land.

He had no idea what he was searching for. He just knew he needed the car resurrected. And fast.

As Jesse tried to decide his next move, the stock broker who lived across the hall from him pulled into his parking spot several spaces down. Getting out of his own car, Evan, who'd been kidding him good-naturedly about his newfound fame as New York's current reigning hero, called out a greeting.

"Hi, Hero. Trouble?"

"You might say that." Jesse felt his frustration mounting. "I drove it here less than an hour ago and now it suddenly won't start."

Curious, Evan crossed over to him and looked over his shoulder into the Honda's yawning mouth.

"It sure as hell won't," he agreed. "Not without a distributor cap."

Jesse looked at him blankly. "A what?"

Evan pointed to where the distributor cap should have been in this car. "Little thing that the spark plugs take their orders from so that the engine fires correctly. You don't have one."

Jesse frowned. "Is that normal?"

"No, that most certainly isn't. Cars don't run without distributor caps." Evan came to his own conclusion. "Someone's playing a joke on you. Either that, or they have it in for you."

The uneasy feeling increased. Something was wrong, very wrong. He immediately thought of Tania.

"Evan, can I borrow your car?" he asked, turning to his neighbor. "I wouldn't ask, but I've got a feeling that it just might be a matter of life or death."

Evan dug into his pocket. "You heroes always this dramatic?" he asked with a laugh, taking his car key off his key ring. He held it out to Jesse.

"Only when the situation calls for it. Thanks." Key in hand, Jesse hurried over to Evan's sports car. Getting in, he put the key into the ignition and the engine purred to life. "I'll fill the tank up for you," he promised.

Jesse's restless irritation continued to grow as he drove. Despite weaving in and out of traffic in an attempt to gain headway, he wasn't making the kind of progress he wanted to. The minutes were moving as fast as the traffic was not. For a moment he even toyed with the idea of driving on the sidewalk, the way they did in the movies. But the sidewalks were even more crowded than the streets were.

Running a red light, Jesse actually hoped that there was a policeman around to pull him over. Sirens would clear the way for him once he explained why he was rushing. But he made it through the intersection without incident. The only thing he attracted was a barrage of curses from the other drivers.

Maybe he was overreacting. Flipping open his cell phone, he called Tania on the house line. If she answered, he'd tell her that he was running late. Hearing her voice would put this prickly uneasiness to rest.

The phone rang five times and then went to her answering machine.

Maybe she was already on her way to the restaurant. Hoping against hope, he tried her cell phone. With the same results. The knots in his stomach tightened.

This wasn't good.

When he finally arrived at her building, Jesse left the car parked right before the main entrance, an area clearly marked as a no parking zone.

With luck, they'd both be out before anyone had a chance to write him up. If she was home.

The elevator was elsewhere in the building. He wasn't about to wait. Jesse took the stairs. Adrenaline roared through his veins when he got to her door. Rather than ring her doorbell, he used the key Tania had given him just yesterday. It struck him as ironic that at the time he'd told her he didn't need a key because he wouldn't be coming over when she wasn't already there.

Please be here.

Unlocking the door, Jesse held his breath as he walked in. "Tania? Tania, are you home?"

He called her name over and over as he strode through the apartment, looking from one room to another. She was nowhere to be found.

Frustrated, he called her cell phone again. As it rang in his ear, he heard ringing coming from somewhere within the room. Tracking the sound, he found that it was coming from the hall closet.

Jesse threw the door open and discovered the ringing came from her purse. The purse was hanging from a hook inside the closet. Tania would have never left her purse behind.

Now it was official. Something was wrong.

His next call was to Tony. The moment he heard the phone being answered, he started talking. "Tony, this is Jesse. Don't repeat anything I say, just listen. I don't want to upset her family. Is Tania there?"

"No." Tony lowered his voice and could only hope that the detective had withdrawn from the others in order to talk more freely. "We left her at the apartment, waiting for you."

"She's not here." Jesse dragged his hand through his hair, trying to think. "Her purse is here, but she's not. Hold it," Jesse said, suddenly becoming aware of something.

Lowering the phone away from his ear, he took a deep breath. And then another one. There was a scent in the air, a very specific scent.

A scent he recognized.

Oh, God, how could he have been so stupid?

He quickly put the phone against his ear again. "Tony, I think Tania's been kidnapped and I know who has her."

"Palmer had an alibi," Tony reminded him. "But it wasn't airtight. I'm going to—"

"It's not Palmer," Jesse cut in. "It's not about Tania. This is about me." The admission alone made him almost physically ill.

"You? What are you talking about?" Tony wanted to know.

He didn't have time to go into detail, but he gave the other man just the bare bones. "About a year ago, I was being stalked by this woman from work. She had a few screws loose. Management fired her. I thought that it was all over six months ago."

There was no emotion in the voice on the other end. Tony required facts. "What makes you think it isn't?"

"The woman used to wear this one particular perfume. It had an almost sickeningly sweet scent. I'm catching a whiff of it in Tania's apartment."

"Give me the woman's name," Tony instructed. "I'm going to call this in and I'll be right there."

"Her name's Ellen Sederholm." To be on the safe side, Jesse spelled it out for him.

"Got it. Sit tight," Tony ordered. The line went dead.

He couldn't sit tight. He couldn't sit at all.

This was all his fault, Jesse thought, pacing restlessly. He'd been so focused on Tania's pain after she'd told him about the date rape, it never occurred to him that Ellen might have come out of the woodwork to stalk him again. The woman was crazy. If she'd seen him with Tania...

He didn't want to go there.

But he had to go somewhere, do something. Jesse clenched and unclenched his hands impotently at his sides. Every minute that went by was a minute Tania might not have to spare. But what could he—

Jesse stopped pacing. He saw Natalya's laptop on the coffee table. It was open. He sank onto the sofa. The laptop was still on.

Hitting a key, he watched the screensaver slowly vanish. A Web site came on. Natalya was still logged on to the Internet.

Bless you, Natalya.

Opening up a search engine he was familiar with, Jesse pulled up what served as the white pages. He typed in Ellen's name and then specified the city and state.

Three choices popped up. He vaguely remembered Ellen telling him that she'd been named after someone in her family. "I'm the new, improved Ellen Sederholm," she'd told him.

The first Ellen Sederholm lived in Staten Island. The

second was located all the way out in Wantagh. That was out on Long Island.

The third lived two blocks away.

That had to be the one.

Jesse scribbled down the address and phone number on a napkin that was on the coffee table. Shoving it into his pocket, Jesse left the apartment and ran down all five flights to the ground level.

He didn't bother getting into Evan's car. He could run the distance faster than he could drive. The fact that the vehicle stood a good chance of being ticketed and towed away was something he couldn't stop to deal with right now.

The only thing on his mind was Tania and this nagging feeling that he might already be too late.

Tania came to.

She was lying on something cool and hard. A roach skittered by inches from her face and she gasped.

Or tried to.

There was tape over her mouth. Her wrists were bound behind her, and she pulled so hard she thought her shoulder would pop. Her ankles were taped, as well.

Fear slithered through her.

"You woke up. Too bad," Ellen said. She knelt beside her, a roll of duct tape in her hands. "I was hoping that you'd stay unconscious until I finished gift-wrapping you." The laugh that followed was chilling. "It would have been better that way for both of us."

Tania began to buck and wriggle, trying to get free.

Ellen reached for the taser, her eyes malevolent. "Don't make me use this again," she warned.

Tania stopped moving.

* * *

Jesse ran all the way to Ellen's building. He took the six concrete steps leading to the front door two at a time. A small, elderly woman unlocked the wrought-iron door leading into the building. It was his way in.

"Let me get that for you," he offered.

The woman smiled her thanks and didn't challenge his presence. "Thank you, young man. Are you new here? I'm Margaret Gallagher. I like to meet the new people," she told him as she entered the foyer ahead of him. "Been here going on thirty years. Seen so many come and go."

Jesse was about to start hunting for Ellen's apartment number. There was a wall of mailboxes on the far side of the foyer, some with apartment numbers beside the names, some not.

He crossed his fingers mentally as he looked at the woman.

"Do you know an Ellen Sederholm?"

The woman instantly beamed, a squadron of wrinkles appearing at both sides of her mouth. "Yes, I do. Lovely girl. Talks about her husband all the time, although I've never met him. Jesse is his name. Always thought that was a girl's name," Margaret told him.

Ellen was fantasizing about him as her husband. He tried not to think about how far gone she had to be. Or how dangerous. He was positive now that she had to be the one behind the gas leak.

"Would you know her apartment number, Mrs. Gallagher?" In order to coax her, he added, "I'm an old friend of Ellen's from college."

"Oh, she'll like that. She lives in apartment 6-D." Jesse

started up the stairs. "But I don't think you'll find her there," she called after him. He stopped and turned around to look at her. "I saw her going down to the basement a little while ago. She had a friend with her. Poor thing was leaning all over her. Looked rather peaked."

That had to be Tania. He couldn't picture her submitting willingly. Had Ellen drugged her? "What's in the basement?" he asked Mr. Gallagher.

"Storage spaces." She sighed. "Mine's so full I'm going to have to go through it someday, start throwing things out. Hard to part with memories," she murmured. "Well, here's the elevator."

Jesse sailed down the stairs. He was at the elderly woman's side in an instant, just as the elevator door opened.

"Would you mind if I go down to the basement first?" Not waiting for Margaret's answer, he reached over to the row of buttons and pressed "B."

The woman scrutinized him. "Awfully anxious to see her, aren't you?"

He faced forward as the door closed again. "It's been a long time."

"Well, take my advice and don't let her husband get the wrong idea," she chuckled. "Ellen says he's very jealous of her."

They'd reached the basement. Jesse's blood ran cold. Getting out, he paused, his hand on the door, keeping it from closing again. "Are the storage spaces arranged in any order?"

"How clever of you," Margaret beamed. "First row, first floor, second row, second floor, and so on. I'm

3-C," she told him. "Come by and visit me sometime. I love to talk to young people."

Jesse drew back his hand. The door began to close. "I'll do that," he promised, already turning away.

The basement smelled musty and the artificial overhead illumination was of a low wattage, casting a mournful light about the area.

Remembering what Margaret had said, Jesse counted off five rows, then stopped at the sixth. There were ten compartments, all with their doors shut. The numbers on them meant nothing to him. He began to try the doors one by one.

The first five were locked. Approaching the sixth, he saw the light seeping out from beneath the door. Had someone left it on, or was there someone inside?

Holding his breath, he turned the knob, and it gave. Heart pounding, Jesse opened the door very slowly, praying it wouldn't creak and give him away.

The storage area was filled with boxes piled on top of each other, forming towers taller than he was. Jesse inched his way in, careful not to knock over any of the boxes. His eyes grew accustomed to the poor lighting.

And then he saw her.

Ellen.

Her back was to him. On her knees, she was busy ripping a length of silver duct tape from an all but depleted roll. She was wrapping something.

And then, to his horror, he realized it wasn't something, it was someone.

Tania.

Tania was bound with duct tape. Not just her mouth, hands and feet, but her chest, her stomach, her throat.

It looked as if Ellen was intent on wrapping *all* of her, including her face.

"Ellen," he said sharply, "get away from her."

Ellen wasn't startled. She didn't even turn around to look at him. Instead she continued pulling another length of tape from the roll.

"I knew you'd come back to me," she told him in a singsong voice. "Knew you'd realize that you missed me. That we belonged together. I made it easy for you to find me."

"Get away from her, Ellen," he retorted. When she went on tearing the length of tape off the roll, he pushed her aside. Dropping to his knees, he grabbed an end and began ripping away the duct tape. Tania winced, but there was relief in her eyes.

"She's evil," Ellen cried, her calmness shattering like a fragile spider's web. She tried to pull him away, but couldn't. "Don't you see?" she screamed. "She turned you against me. We belong together. You love *me*, not her. She cast some kind of a spell over you, that's why I have to get rid of her," she cried frantically. "To save you. Stop it!" Ellen beat on his back, trying to get him to stop removing the duct tape.

He didn't waste time looking at her. "Ellen, you need help. I promise I'll see that you get it, people who'll help you," he said as he quickly pulled off strip after strip. "I'm sorry, this is going to really hurt," he told Tania just before he yanked away the strip over her mouth.

"Jesse, look out," Tania cried.

Jesse turned just in time to see the taser coming at him. He ducked, then moving quickly, he grabbed Ellen's wrist and twisted it.

Ellen shrieked like a wounded animal as the taser hit her chest. And then she slid bonelessly to the concrete floor, unconscious.

Losing no time, Jesse tore off two strips of the remaining duct tape, using one to bind her hands, the other to bind her feet. Secure that Ellen no longer posed an immediate threat, he resumed removing the tape from Tania's body.

She sat up, working with him. "Look at the back wall," she told him.

Turning, Jesse looked and then his mouth dropped open. The wall was covered with photographs of him, some garnered from various newspapers, the rest digital photographs that Ellen had to have taken herself while stalking him.

"Damn," he muttered incredulously under his breath.

"That's one hell of a groupie you have there, Jesse," Tania said, pulling off the last of the tape. Throwing it aside, she took in a deep breath to calm herself. It was over, thank God. Over. "She was just going to leave me down here to die, like some giant caterpillar in a duct tape cocoon."

"I'm sorry, baby, I'm so sorry," he said over and over again.

Tania threw her arms around him. "Sorry? You saved me." She buried her face against his chest. "I knew you'd come for me, I just knew it." Lifting her head, she looked at him as she blinked back tears. A half smile played on her lips. "I knew you couldn't resist playing a hero again."

"Are you all right?" he asked her. His eyes swept over her face, her body, to assure himself that she was in one piece. "Did she hurt you?"

Tania tried to muster a smile. "Well, the taser was no picnic, but otherwise, I'm okay." She blew out a long, emotional breath. "Boy, loving you has some really heavy consequences, doesn't it?"

For the second time in as many minutes, his mouth dropped open. "Loving me?" he repeated, stunned. "You love me?"

She caught her lip between her teeth. Okay, she blew it. The man just had a stalker after him. A pushy woman was the last thing he'd welcome. "Wasn't supposed to say that, was I? Sorry, it was an emotional minute."

She continued talking, trying to backpedal. Jesse wasn't listening. Instead he framed her face with his hands and looked at her, looked at what he had almost lost. It made his head spin.

Cutting through the flow of her rhetoric, he said, "I love you."

Tania stopped talking. And then he saw a smile enter her eyes. "Really."

"Really." He said it as if it was an oath. Because it was. An oath and a pledge. He intended to love her as long as he lived. As long as *he* lived.

The rush of joy that surged through her almost made Tania dizzy. It took her a long moment to get her bearings.

"Okay," she said slowly, "I can live with that."

He grinned. "Can you live with being my wife?"

The brightness of her smile made up for the dim illumination in the storage area.

"Even better." And then her eyebrows rose a little as a grain of skepticism entered. "You're not just saying that because your groupie there almost turned me into a silver doorstop—"

"Shut up," Jesse told her, bringing his mouth down on hers.

"Just like a hero, throwing his weight around," she murmured.

Jesse tasted Tania's smile on his lips just before he deepened his kiss.

The sound of approaching sirens echoed in the background.

It looked like he was going to be paying Isaac Epstein a visit in the near future after all. As he recalled, the man had some beautiful diamonds. One would make a perfect engagement ring for the perfect woman, Jesse thought, just before he stopped thinking at all.

* * * * *

Enjoy a sneak preview of
MATCHMAKING WITH A MISSION
by B.J. Daniels,
part of the WHITEHORSE, MONTANA *miniseries.*
Available from Harlequin Intrigue
in April 2008.

Nate Dempsey has returned to Whitehorse to uncover the truth about his past…

Nate sensed someone watching the house and looked out in surprise to see a woman astride a paint horse just on the other side of the fence. He quickly stepped back from the filthy second-floor window, although he doubted she could have seen him. Only a little of the June sun pierced the dirty glass to glow on the dust-coated floor at his feet as he waited a few heartbeats before he looked out again.

The place was so isolated he hadn't expected to see another soul. Like the front yard, the dirt road was waist-high with weeds. When he'd broken the lock on the back door, he'd had to kick aside a pile of rotten leaves that had blown in from last fall.

As he sneaked a look, he saw that she was still there, staring at the house in a way that unnerved him. He shielded his eyes from the glare of the sun off the dirty window and studied her, taking in her head of long blond hair that feathered out in the breeze from under her Western straw hat.

She wore a tan canvas jacket, jeans and boots. But it was the way she sat astride the brown-and-white horse that nudged the memory.

He felt a chill as he realized he'd seen her before. In that very spot. She'd been just a kid then. A kid on a pretty paint horse. Not this one—the markings were different. Anyway, it couldn't have been the same horse, considering the last time he had seen her was more than twenty years ago. That horse would be dead by now.

His mind argued it probably wasn't even the same girl. But he knew better. It was the way she sat the horse, so at home in a saddle and secure in her world on the other side of that fence.

To the boy he'd been, she and her horse had represented freedom, a freedom he'd known he would never have—even after he escaped this house.

Nate saw her shift in the saddle, and for a moment he feared she planned to dismount and come toward the house. With Ellis Harper in his grave, there would be little to keep her away.

To his relief, she reined her horse around and rode back the way she'd come.

As he watched her ride away, he thought about the way she'd stared at the house—today and years ago. While the smartest thing she could do was to stay clear of this house, he had a feeling she'd be back.

Finding out her name should prove easy, since he figured she must live close by. As for her interest in Harper House... He would just have to make sure it didn't become a problem.

* * * * *

Be sure to look for
MATCHMAKING WITH A MISSION
and other suspenseful Harlequin Intrigue stories,
available in April
wherever books are sold.

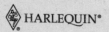

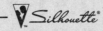

SPECIAL EDITION™

Introducing a brand-new miniseries

Men of Mercy Medical

Gabe Thorne moved to Las Vegas to open a new branch of his booming construction business—and escape from a recent tragedy. But when his teenage sister showed up pregnant on his doorstep, he really had his hands full. Luckily, in turning to Dr. Rebecca Hamilton for the medical care his sister needed, he found a cure for himself....

Starting with

THE MILLIONAIRE AND THE M.D.

by *TERESA SOUTHWICK,*

available in April wherever books are sold.

REQUEST YOUR FREE BOOKS!

2 FREE NOVELS PLUS 2 FREE GIFTS!

Silhouette® Romantic

SUSPENSE

Sparked by Danger, Fueled by Passion!

YES! Please send me 2 FREE Silhouette® Romantic Suspense novels and my 2 FREE gifts (gifts are worth about $10). After receiving them, if I don't wish to receive any more books, I can return the shipping statement marked "cancel." If I don't cancel, I will receive 4 brand-new novels every month and be billed just $4.24 per book in the U.S. or $4.99 per book in Canada, plus 25¢ shipping and handling per book plus applicable taxes, if any*. That's a savings of at least 15% off the cover price! I understand that accepting the 2 free books and gifts places me under no obligation to buy anything. I can always return a shipment and cancel at any time. Even if I never buy another book from Silhouette, the two free books and gifts are mine to keep forever.

240 SDN EEX6   340 SDN EEYJ

Name _____ (PLEASE PRINT) _____

Address _____ Apt. # _____

City _____ State/Prov. _____ Zip/Postal Code _____

Signature (if under 18, a parent or guardian must sign)

Mail to the Silhouette Reader Service:
IN U.S.A.: P.O. Box 1867, Buffalo, NY 14240-1867
IN CANADA: P.O. Box 609, Fort Erie, Ontario L2A 5X3

Not valid to current subscribers of Silhouette Romantic Suspense books.

Want to try two free books from another line?
Call 1-800-873-8635 or visit www.morefreebooks.com.

* Terms and prices subject to change without notice. N.Y. residents add applicable sales tax. Canadian residents will be charged applicable provincial taxes and GST. This offer is limited to one order per household. All orders subject to approval. Credit or debit balances in a customer's account(s) may be offset by any other outstanding balance owed by or to the customer. Please allow 4 to 6 weeks for delivery. Offer available while quantities last.

Your Privacy: Silhouette is committed to protecting your privacy. Our Privacy Policy is available online at www.eHarlequin.com or upon request from the Reader Service. From time to time we make our lists of customers available to reputable third parties who may have a product or service of interest to you. If you would prefer we not share your name and address, please check here. ☐

SRS08

nocturne™

The Bloodrunners
trilogy continues with book #2.

The hunt meant more to Jeremy Burns than dominance—
it meant facing the woman he left behind. Once
Jillian Murphy had belonged to Jeremy, but now she was
the Spirit Walker to the Silvercrest wolves. It would take
more than the rights of nature for Jeremy to renew his
claim on her—and she would not go easily once he had.

LAST WOLF
HUNTING

by RHYANNON BYRD

Available in April wherever books are sold.

Be sure to watch out for the last book,
Last Wolf Watching, available in May.

SN61785

Silhouette®
Romantic
SUSPENSE

COMING NEXT MONTH

SRSCNM0308

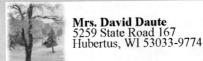

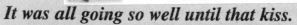

It was all going so well until that kiss.

But when he'd gotten his arms around Katie and her mouth under his…he'd lost it. Every shred of control.

The bald truth was that Justin had seriously underestimated the power of his own feelings for the shy librarian with the adopted family he despised. It was funny, really—though he wasn't laughing. A royal backfire of his basic intention: *he* was supposed to seduce *her*.

Not the other way around.

What the hell was his problem here, anyway? He was getting way too invested in her. She had nothing to do with the main plan, and if she never let him get near her again it wouldn't matter in the least. So why should he care if she smiled at him again or not?

He decided he'd be better off not thinking too deeply on that one.

Dear Reader,

Well, we hope your New Year's resolutions included reading some fabulous new books—because we can provide the reading material! We begin with *Stranded with the Groom* by Christine Rimmer, part of our new MONTANA MAVERICKS: GOLD RUSH GROOMS miniseries. When a staged wedding reenactment turns into the real thing, can the actual honeymoon be far behind? Tune in next month for the next installment in this exciting new continuity.

Victoria Pade concludes her NORTHBRIDGE NUPTIALS miniseries with *Having the Bachelor's Baby,* in which a woman trying to push aside memories of her one night of passion with the town's former bad boy finds herself left with one little reminder of that encounter—she's pregnant with his child. Judy Duarte begins her new miniseries, BAYSIDE BACHELORS, with *Hailey's Hero,* featuring a cautious woman who finds herself losing her heart to a rugged rebel who might break it…. THE HATHAWAYS OF MORGAN CREEK by Patricia Kay continues with *His Best Friend,* in which a woman is torn between two men—the one she really wants, and the one to whom he owes his life. Mary J. Forbes's sophomore Special Edition is *A Father, Again,* featuring a grown-up reunion between a single mother and her teenaged crush. And a disabled child, an exhausted mother and a down-but-not-out rodeo hero all come together in a big way, in Christine Wenger's debut novel, *The Cowboy Way.*

So enjoy, and come back next month for six compelling new novels, from Silhouette Special Edition.

Happy New Year!

Gail Chasan
Senior Editor
Silhouette Special Edition

Please address questions and book requests to:
Silhouette Reader Service
U.S.: 3010 Walden Ave., P.O. Box 1325, Buffalo, NY 14269
Canadian: P.O. Box 609, Fort Erie, Ont. L2A 5X3

Christine Rimmer

STRANDED WITH THE GROOM

Silhouette

SPECIAL EDITION

Published by Silhouette Books

America's Publisher of Contemporary Romance

Special thanks and acknowledgment are given
to Christine Rimmer for her contribution
to the MONTANA MAVERICKS:
GOLD RUSH GROOMS series.

For Montana Mavericks readers everywhere.
Welcome to Thunder Canyon, Montana.

 SILHOUETTE BOOKS

ISBN 0-373-24657-9

STRANDED WITH THE GROOM

Books by Christine Rimmer

CHRISTINE RIMMER

came to her profession the long way around. Before settling down to write about the magic of romance, she'd been everything from an actress to a phone sales representative to a playwright. Christine is grateful not only for the joy she finds in writing, but for what waits when the day's work is through: a man she loves, who loves her right back, and the privilege of watching their children grow and change day to day. She lives with her family in Oklahoma. Visit Christine at her new home on the Web at www.christinerimmer.com.

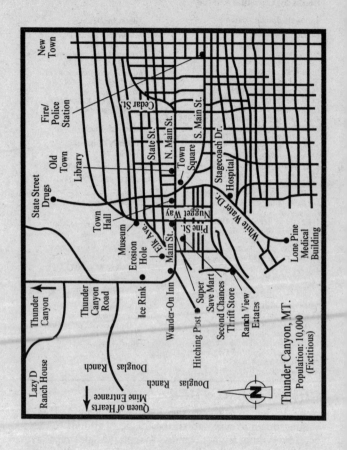

Thunder Canyon, MT.
Population: 10,000
(Fictitious)

Chapter One

"A mail-order bride," Katie Fenton muttered under her breath. "What were they *thinking*?"

In Thunder Canyon, Montana, it was the first Saturday after New Year's—and that meant it was Heritage Day.

The annual celebration, held in the big reception room of Thunder Canyon's sturdy stone-and-brick town hall, included rows of brightly decorated booths, some serving food and others displaying endless examples of local arts and crafts. There was always a pie auction and a quilt raffle and, as evening drew on, a potluck supper and dancing late into the night.

Also, this year, the Thunder Canyon Historical Society had decided to put on a series of historical re-enactments. In the morning, they'd presented the local legend of the great Thunder Bird, a mythical figure who took the form of a man every spring and met his mortal mate on sacred ground. According to Native American lore, their joyous reunion caused the spring rains to fall, the leaves and flowers to emerge and the grass to grow lush and green.

At two in the afternoon, there was the discovery of gold in 1862 at Grasshopper Creek—complete with rocks the size of baseballs, sprayed gold to look like huge nuggets.

And now, at four-thirty, it was time for the mail-order bride—played by Katie—arriving by train to meet and marry a man she'd never seen before.

Katie stood huddled on the narrow stage at the west end of the hall. Perched on a makeshift step behind a rickety cardboard mock-up of a steam engine and a red caboose, she kept her shoulders hunched and her head down so she couldn't be seen over the top of the fake train.

Utterly miserable—Katie hated, above all, to make a spectacle of herself—she stared at the door hole cut in the caboose. On cue, she was supposed to push it open and emerge to meet her ''groom.''

Outside, the wind howled. A storm was blowing in. Though the local weatherman had promised nothing much worse than a few flurries, most of the Heritage Day crowd had departed the hall during the past half hour or so and headed for the safety of their homes.

Katie herself was more than ready to call it a day.

But unfortunately, this year for the Heritage Day revels, a local merchant had come up with the bright idea of providing free beer on tap. The beer booth was a big hit. Certain of the citizenry had been knocking it back since eleven or so. They couldn't have cared less that the predicted flurries seemed to be shaping up into a full-blown blizzard. They were too busy having a grand old time.

Out on the main floor, someone let out a whistle. Katie heard the impatient stomping of heavy feet on the old, well-polished hardwood floorboards.

"C'mon, where's the bride?"

"Get on with it. We want the bride!"

"The bride!"

"The bride! Give us the bride!"

Katie cast a desperate glance to the tiny wing area at the edge of the stage where sweet old Emelda Ross, one of the few members of the Historical Society who'd yet to go home, hovered over an ancient reel-to-reel tape recorder.

"The bride, the bride!"

"Wahoo, let's see her!"

Katie gave Emelda a shaky nod. Emelda turned on the tape and two loud train whistles erupted: her cue.

Sucking in a big breath and letting it out slowly, Katie tugged on her 1880s-style merino wool frock, adjusted her bonnet and pushed open the cardboard door.

The beer drinkers erupted into a chorus of catcalls and stomping.

"The librarian!" one of them shouted. "Hey, the librarian is the mail-order bride!"

Another let out a whoop. "Hey, Katie! Welcome to Thunder Canyon!"

"We love you, Katie!"

"If your groom stands you up, I'll take you, Katie!"

Lovely.

With care, so as not to knock over the train, Katie emerged to face the crowd. She smoothed her dress again, her nervous hands shaking. How, she wondered miserably, had she let herself get roped into this one?

With great effort, she forced a wobbly smile and waved at the beer drinkers, who obligingly clapped and stomped all the louder. She stared out over the seventy or so grinning faces—many of them looking downright woozy by then—and longed to be anywhere but there.

It was all dear old Ben Saunders's fault. The high school history teacher had been the one to propose the mail-order bride reenactment. The Historical Society went wild for the idea—all except for Katie, who was lukewarm on the concept at best.

Since most of Katie's fellow society members were well into their forties at least and the other two younger ones were already slated to play the legendary Thunder Bird and his mortal love, it was decided that Katie should play the bride.

She had tried to say no, but who listened? *No one,* that's who. And now, here she was, alone in front of the cardboard train, a ludicrous spectacle for the Heritage Day beer drinkers to whistle and holler at.

Ben himself was supposed to be her groom. Unfortunately, the history teacher had awakened that morning with terrible stomach cramps. He'd been rushed to Thunder Canyon General for an emergency appendectomy. And then, when the sky darkened and the wind came up and the first snowflakes began to fall, pretty much everyone from the society except Emelda had decided to go home. *They* made the plans and now Katie stood on the stage alone, shaking with nerves and stuck with the follow-through.

Since her "groom" was in the hospital, she'd almost succeeded in canceling this ridiculous display. But then, a half hour ago, an out-of-towner named Justin Caldwell had agreed to step in and take Ben's part. Caldwell was a business associate of Caleb Douglas—Caleb being a local mover and shaker who owned half the property for miles around and also happened to be a second father to Katie. Caleb had ribbed the stranger into playing the groom. The poor guy resisted at first, but when Caleb kept after him, he couldn't refuse.

And speaking of Justin Caldwell...

Where was he?

Frantically, Katie scanned the noisy crowd for her impromptu pretend groom. Good gravy. In a moment, one of the drunken men down on the floor would be staggering up to take his place.

But no—there he was.

He stood off to the left, at the edge of the crowd, wearing the ill-fitting old-time garb—complete with silly red suspenders and clunky nineteenth-century-style boots—intended for the potbellied Ben Saunders. Katie met the stranger's piercing blue eyes and a crazy little thrill shivered through her. Even in the ridiculous outfit, the guy still somehow managed to look absolutely gorgeous. She felt the grateful smile as it quivered across her mouth. If she had to make a fool of herself, at least it would be with the best-looking man in the hall. And beyond being handsome, there was the added attraction that he appeared to be sober.

"The groom!" someone shouted. "Where's the damn groom?"

"Right here," Justin Caldwell answered easily in a deep, firm voice. He took off his floppy felt hat and waved it high for all of them to see.

"Get up there and claim your bride!"

"Yeah, man. Don't keep her waiting!"

Justin Caldwell obliged. He mounted the steps at the side of the stage and came toward Katie, his long strides purposeful and confident. When he reached her, he gallantly swept off the floppy hat a second time. Her overtaxed heart raced faster still.

And then, of all things, he reached for her hand. Before she could jerk it away, he brought it to his full-lipped mouth.

Katie stood stunned, staring into those gleaming blue eyes of his, every nerve in her body cracking and popping, as he placed a tender kiss on the back of her hand.

The crowd went wild.

"That's the way you do it!"

"Oh, yeah!"

"Way to go!"

His lips were so warm—and his hand firm and dry. Her hand, she knew, was clammy and shaking. Gulping, Katie carefully pulled her fingers free.

Caleb's business partner nodded and put his absurd hat back on. He looked so calm. As if he did this sort of thing every day. He leaned in closer, bringing with him the subtle scent of expensive aftershave. "Now, what?" he whispered in that velvety voice of his.

"Uh, well, I..." Katie gulped again. She just knew her face was flaming red.

"Kiss 'er!" someone shouted. "Lay a big, smackin' one right on 'er!"

Everyone applauded the idea, causing Katie to silently vow that next year, under no circumstances, would there be free beer.

"Yeah," someone else hollered. "A kiss!"

"A big, wet, juicy one! Grab 'er and give it to 'er!"

Justin Caldwell, bless him, did no such thing. He did lift a straight raven-black eyebrow. "The natives are becoming restless," he said low. "We'd better do *something....*"

Do something. His soft words echoed in her frazzled mind. "The, uh, ceremony..."

He smiled then, as if mildly amused. "Of course." He suggested, "And for that we would need..." He let his voice trail off, giving her an opportunity to fill in the blank.

She did. "The preacher." Her throat locked up. She coughed to clear it. "Uh. Right."

"Get on with it!" someone yelled.

"Yeah! Get a move on. Let's see the rest of the show!"

Outside, a particularly hard gust of wind struck the high up windows and made them rattle. Nobody seemed to notice. They kept laughing and clapping.

"So where is this preacher?" her "groom" inquired.

"Um, well..." Katie wildly scanned the crowd again. Where was Andy Rickenbautum? The balding, gray-haired retired accountant was supposed to step up and declare himself a circuit preacher and "marry" them, but Katie couldn't see him among the crowd. Evidently, like most of the Historical Society members, he'd headed home.

Maybe Caleb, who'd gotten such a kick out of the whole thing, could help out and play Andy's part....

But no. Caleb appeared to be gone, too. And Adele, his wife, who had taken in a teenaged Katie and raised her as her own, was nowhere to be seen, either. Now what?

At the Heritage Museum several blocks away, the society had set up a wedding "reception," complete with finger food and beverages and an opportunity for folks to see up-close the artifacts of the life the mail order bride and her groom would have lived. The idea was to lure everyone over there behind the "bride" and "groom," in the museum's prized refurbished buckboard carriage. They'd all enjoy the snacks, look around—hopefully make a donation—and then head on back to the hall for the potluck supper and dancing that would follow.

But without the fake wedding first, how could they hold a pretend reception?

A couple of the beer drinkers had figured that out. One of them yelled, "Hey! Where's the preacher?"

"Yeah! We need the dang preacher to get this thing moving!"

What a disaster, Katie thought. It was definitely time to give up and call the whole thing off.

Katie forced herself to face the crowd. "Ahem. Excuse me. I'm afraid there's no one to play the preacher and we're just going to have to—"

A resonant voice from the back of the crowd cut her off. "Allow me to do the honors." Every head in the room swiveled toward the sound. The source, an austere-looking bearded fellow, announced, "I'd be proud to unite such a handsome couple in the sacred bonds of matrimony."

Someone snickered. "And just who the hell are you?"

The tall fellow, all dressed in black, made his way to the front of the crowd. He mounted the steps and came to stand with Katie and her "groom." "The Reverend Josiah Green, at your service, miss," he intoned. He dipped his head at Katie, then turned to Justin. "Sir."

Someone broke into a laugh. "Oh, yeah. *Reverend.* That's a good one...."

"He's perfect," someone else declared. "He even looks like a real preacher."

Looking appropriately grave, the "reverend" bowed to the crowd. The usual whistles and catcalls followed. "Reverend" Green turned his gaze to the spindle-legged antique table a few feet from the cardboard train. "I see you have everything ready." On the table, courtesy of the Historical Society, waited a Bible, a valuable circa-1880 dip pen and matching inkwell and a copy of an authentic late-nineteenth-century marriage license.

Emelda, smiling sweetly, emerged from the wings. A smattering of applause greeted her as she got the Bible and handed it to the "reverend."

"Ahem," said the "reverend." "If you'll stand here. And you here..." Katie, Justin and Emelda moved into the positions Mr. Green indicated.

The man in black opened the old Bible. A hush fell over the crowd as he instructed, "Will the bride and groom join hands?" Caldwell removed his hat. He dropped it to the stage floor, took Katie's hand and gave her an encouraging smile. She made herself smile back and didn't jerk away, in spite of the way his touch caused a tingling all through her, a sensation both embarrassing and scarily exciting.

The fake preacher began, "We are gathered here together..."

It was so strange, standing there on the narrow wooden stage with the cardboard train behind them and the wind howling beyond the stone walls as the pretend reverend recited the well-known words of the marriage ceremony.

The rowdy crowd stayed quiet. And the words themselves were so beautiful. Green asked if there was anyone present who saw any reason that Justin and Katie should not be joined. No one made a sound. If not for the wind, you could have heard a feather whispering its way to the floor. Green said, "Then we shall proceed...."

And Katie and the stranger beside her exchanged their pretend vows. When the "reverend" said, "I now pronounce you husband and wife," Katie had to gulp back tears.

Really, this whole weird situation was making her way too emotional.

"You may kiss the bride."

Oh, God. The kiss...

It hadn't seemed so bad when it was only good old Ben. But Justin Caldwell was another story. He was just so good-looking, so exactly like the kind of man any woman would want to kiss.

Truth was, Katie wouldn't mind kissing him. Not at all. Under different circumstances.

Maybe. If they ever came to really know each other...

Oh, why was she obsessing over this? The final vow-sealing kiss was part of the program. It wouldn't be much of a pretend wedding without it.

Almost over, Katie silently promised herself as Caldwell turned to face her. With a small, tight sigh, she lifted her chin. Pressing her eyes shut and pursing up her mouth, she waited for her "groom" to lean down and give her a quick, polite peck.

The peck didn't happen. Warily, she opened her right eye to a slit. Caldwell was looking down at her, apparently waiting for her to look at him. When he saw she was peeking, one corner of that full mouth of his quirked up and he winked at her.

A ridiculous giggle forced its way up in her throat and almost got away from her. She gulped it back, straightened her head and opened both eyes. At the same time as she was controlling her silly urge to laugh, the man before her reached out his hand. He did it so slowly and carefully, she didn't even flinch.

He took the end of the bow that tied her bonnet under her chin. One little tug and the bow fell away.

Gently, he guided the bonnet from her head. Her brown curls, which she'd hastily shoved in beneath the hat, fell loose to her shoulders. Justin—all of a sudden, she found she was mentally calling him by his first name—tossed the hat to Emelda and then, with tender, careful fingers, he smoothed her hair.

Oh, God. Her throat had gone tight. She felt as if she would cry again. This pretending to get married was darned hard on her nerves—or maybe she had a little natural-born performer in her, after all. Maybe she was simply "getting into" her part.

Their formerly boisterous audience remained pin-drop quiet. How did people in the theater put it? The phrase came to her. She and Justin had the crowd *in the palms of their hands....*

Justin braced a finger under her chin and she took his cue, lifting her mouth for him.

His dark head descended and his lips—so gently—covered hers.

That did it. The Heritage Day revelers burst into wild applause, sharp whistles, heavy stomping and raucous catcalls.

Katie hardly even heard them. She was too wrapped up in Justin's kiss. It was a kiss that started out questioning and moved on to tender and from there to downright passionate.

Oh, my goodness! Did he know how to kiss or what? She grabbed onto his broad, hard shoulders and kissed him back for all she was worth.

When he finally pulled away, she stared up at him,

dazed. He had those blue, blue eyes. Mesmerizing eyes. She could drown in those eyes and never regret being lost....

"Ahem," said the "reverend," good and loud, gazing out over the audience with a look of stern disapproval until they quieted again. "There remains the documentation to attend to."

Katie blinked and collected herself, bringing a hand up and smoothing her hair. Justin turned to face Josiah Green, who had crossed to the spindle-legged table. He picked up the old pen and dipped it in the ink and expertly began filling out the fake marriage license. "That's Katie...?"

"Fenton."

"Speak up, young lady."

"Katherine Adele Fenton." She said her whole name that time, nice and clear, and then she spelled it for him.

"And Justin...?"

"Caldwell." He spelled his name, too.

They acted it all out as if it were the real thing, filling in all the blanks, signing their names. When the "reverend" called for another witness besides Emelda, one of the guys from down on the floor jumped right up onto the stage and signed where Josiah Green pointed.

When the last blank line had been filled in, Green expertly applied the sterling silver rocker blotter. Then he held up the license for all to see. "And so it is that yet another young and hopeful couple are happily joined in holy wedlock."

As the clapping and stomping started up again,

Emelda stepped forward. She waited, looking prim and yet indulgent, her wrinkled hands folded in front of her, until the noise died down. Then she announced that, weather permitting, there was to be a reception at the Heritage Museum over on Elk Avenue. "Everyone is welcome to attend. Help yourself to the goodies—and don't forget that donation box. We count on all of you to make the museum a success. Just follow the bride and groom in their authentic buckboard carriage."

Evidently, the crowd found that suggestion too exciting to take standing still. They surged up onto the stage and surrounded the small wedding party, jostling and jumping around, knocking over the cardboard train and almost upsetting the antique table with its precious load of vintage writing supplies. Laughing and shouting, they tugged and coaxed and herded Katie and Justin down the stage steps, across the main floor and out into the foyer.

Katie laughed and let herself be dragged along. By then, the crazy situation had somehow captured her. The day's events had begun to seem like some weird and yet magical dream. Her lips still tingled from the feel of Justin's mouth on hers. And she was pleased, she truly was, that her little reenactment, skirting so close to disaster, had ended up a great success.

In the foyer, the crowd surged straight for the double doors that opened directly onto the covered wooden sidewalk of Old Town's Main Street. They pushed the doors wide and a blinding gust of freezing wind and snow blew in, making everyone laugh all the louder.

"Brrrr. It's a cold one."

"Yep. She's really movin' in."

"Gonna be one wild night, and that's for certain."

The snow swirled so thick, the other side of Main Street was nothing more than a vague shadow through the whiteness. The horse, a palomino mare, and the buckboard were there, waiting, the reins thrown and wrapped around one of the nineteenth-century-style hitching posts that ran at intervals along Main at the edge of the sidewalk, bringing to mind an earlier time.

Katie herself had requested the horse, whose name was Buttercup. The mare belonged to Caleb. He kept a fine stable of horses out at the family ranch, the Lazy D. A sweet-natured, gentle animal, Buttercup was getting along in years—and, boy, did she look cold. Icicles hung from her mouth. She glanced toward the crowd and snorted good and loud, as if to say, *Get me out of this. Now...*

Really, maybe they ought to slow down here. The snow did look pretty bad.

"Um, I think that we ought to..." She let the sentence die. She'd always had a too-soft voice. And no one was listening, anyway.

The revelers herded her and Justin into the old open, two-seater carriage. It creaked and shifted as it took their weight.

"Use the outerwear and the blankets under the seat!" Emelda shouted from back in the doorway to the hall foyer. A frown had deepened the creases in her brow. Maybe she was having her doubts about this, too.

But then Emelda put on a brave smile and waved

and the wind died for a moment. Really, it was only two blocks west and then three more northeast to the museum. And, according to the weather reports, the storm *was* supposed to blow itself out quickly.

It should be okay.

Justin brushed the snow from a heavy ankle-length woolen coat—a tightly fitted one with jet buttons down the front and a curly woolen ruff at the neck. He helped her into it, then put on the rough gray man's coat himself. There was a Cossack-style hat for her that matched the ruff at her neck. No hat for Justin, and he'd left the silly, floppy one back in the hall. But he didn't seem to mind. There were heavy gloves for both of them.

They shook out the pile of wool blankets and wrapped up in them. Justin pulled on his gloves and Josiah Green handed him the reins.

"Bless you, my children," Green intoned, as if the marriage vows he'd just led them through had been for real.

"Thanks," Justin muttered dryly. "Looks like we'll need it." He glanced at Katie. "Okay…" He had a you-got-us-into-this kind of look on his handsome face. "Where to?"

"If you want, I'll be glad to take the reins."

"I can handle it. Where to?"

Even if he didn't know what he was doing, it should be all right, she thought. Buttercup was patient and docile as they come. "Straight ahead. Then you'll turn right on Elk, about three blocks down."

"What? I can't hear you."

She forced herself to raise her voice and repeated the instructions.

Justin shook the reins and clicked his tongue and Buttercup started walking. Her bridle, strung with bells, tinkled merrily as they set off, the beer-sodden townsfolk cheering them on.

The wind rose again, howling, and the snow came down harder.

A half block later, the thick, swirling flakes obscured the hall and the knot of cheering rowdies behind them. A minute or two after that, Katie couldn't hear their voices. All at once, she and this stranger she'd just pretended to marry were alone in a whirling vortex of white.

Katie glanced over her shoulder. She saw nothing but swirling snow and the shadows of the buildings and cars on either side of Main.

The snow fell all the harder. It beat at them, borne by the hard-blowing wind. Katie huddled into the blankets, her cheekbones aching with the cold.

Buttercup plodded on, the snow so thick that when Katie squinted into it, she could barely see the horse's sleek golden rump. She turned to the man beside her. He seemed to sense her gaze on him. He gave her a quick, forced kind of smile—his nose was Rudolph-red, along with his cheeks and chin and ears—and then swiftly put his focus back on the wall of white in front of them.

For a split second, she spied a spot of red to the side—the fire hydrant at the corner of Elk and Main. Wasn't it? "Turn right! Here!" Katie shouted it out good and loud that time. Justin tugged the reins and the horse turned the corner.

They passed close to the fire hydrant. Good. This was the right way. And as long as they were on Elk Avenue now, they'd literally run into the museum—a sprawling red clapboard building that had started out its existence as the Thunder Canyon School. It sat on a curve in the street, where Elk Avenue made a sharp turn due east.

The palomino mare slogged on into the white. By then, Katie couldn't see a thing beyond the side rails of the buckboard and Buttercup's behind.

Good Lord. Were they lost? It was beginning to look that way.

Hungry for reassurance, Katie shouted over the howling wind, "We *are* still on Elk Avenue, aren't we?"

Justin shouted back, "I'm from out of town, remember? Hate to tell you, but I haven't got a clue."

Chapter Two

Just as Katie began to fear they'd somehow veered off into the open field on the west side of Elk Avenue, the rambling red clapboard building with its wide front porch loomed up to the left.

"We're here!" she yelled, thrilled at the sight.

Justin tugged the reins and the horse turned into the parking lot. Ten or twelve feet from the front porch, the buckboard creaked to a stop—at which point it occurred to Katie that they couldn't leave poor Buttercup out in this. "Go around the side! There's a big shed out back."

He frowned at her.

She shouted, "The horse. We need to put her around back—to the left."

His frown deepened. She could see in those blue eyes that he thought Buttercup's comfort was the least of their problems right then. But he didn't argue. Shoulders hunched into his ugly old-fashioned coat, he flicked the reins and Buttercup started moving again.

When they got to the rear of the building, Katie signaled him on past a long, narrow breezeway and around to the far side of the tall, barnlike shed. "I'll open up," she yelled and pushed back the blankets to swing her legs over the side. She opened the gate that enclosed a small paddock northwest of the shed. Justin drove the buckboard through and she managed to shut the gate.

The snow was six or eight inches deep already. It dragged at her heavy skirts and instantly began soaking her delicate ankle-high lace-up shoes as she headed for the shed doors around back. How did women do it, way back when? She couldn't help but wonder. There were some situations—this one, for instance—when a woman really needed to be wearing a sturdy pair of trousers and waterproof boots.

There was a deep porchlike extension running the length of the shed at the rear, sheltering the doors. She ducked under the cover, stomping her shoes on the frozen ground and shaking the snow off her hem. Even with gloves on, her hands were so stiff with cold, it took forever to get the combination padlock to snap open. But eventually, about the time she started thinking her nose would freeze and fall off, the shackle popped from the case. She locked it onto the hasp.

And then, though the wind fought her every step of the way, she pulled back one door and then the other, latching them both to hooks on the outside wall, so they wouldn't blow shut again. She gestured Justin inside and he urged the old mare onward.

Katie followed the buckboard inside as Justin hooked the reins over the back of the seat and jumped to the hard-packed dirt floor. "Cold in here." He rubbed his arms and stomped his feet, looking around, puzzled, as Buttercup shook her head and the bells tinkled merrily. "What is this?"

"Kind of a combination garage and barn. The Historical Society is planning on setting it up as a model of a blacksmith's shop." She indicated the heavy, rusting iron equipment against the walls and on the plank floor. "For right now, it'll do to stable Buttercup 'til this mess blows over." There were several oblong bales of hay stacked under the window, waiting to be used for props in some of the museum displays. Buttercup whickered at them hopefully.

"Go on through there." Katie indicated the door straight across from the ones she'd left open. It led to the breezeway and the museum. "It's warm inside. And a couple of ladies from the Historical Society should be in there waiting, with the food and drinks."

He looked at her sideways. "What about you?"

She was already trudging over to unhook Buttercup from the buckboard. "I learned to ride on this horse, I'll have you know. I'm going to get her free of this rig and make her comfortable until someone from the ranch can come for her."

"The ranch?"

"She's Caleb's, from out at the Lazy D."

He stomped his feet some more, making a big show

of rubbing his arms. "Can't someone inside take care of the horse?"

"Anna Jacks and Tildy Matheson were supposed to set out the refreshments for the 'wedding reception.' They're both at least eighty."

"Maybe someone else has shown up by now."

Doubtful, she thought. And even if they had, they'd most likely be drunk. "I'd rather just do it myself before I go in."

He gave her an appraising kind of look and muttered, heavy on the irony, "And you seemed so shy, back there at the hall."

She stiffened. Yes, okay. As a rule, she *was* a reserved sort of person. But when something needed doing, Katie Fenton didn't shirk. She hitched up her chin and spoke in a carefully pleasant tone. "You can go on inside. I'll be there as soon as I'm through here."

He insisted on helping her. So she set him the task of searching for a box cutter in the drawers full of rusting tools on the west wall. When he found one, she had him cut the wire on a couple of the bales and spread the hay. Meanwhile, she unhitched Buttercup from the rig, cleaned off the icicles from around her muzzle and wiped her down with one of the blankets from the buckboard.

"Okay," she said when the job was done. "Let's go in."

He headed for the still-open doors to the pasture. "I'll just shut these."

"No. Leave them open. The walls cut most of the wind, so it won't be too cold in here. And Buttercup can move around a little, and have access to the snow when she gets thirsty.''

He shrugged and turned to follow her out—which was a problem as the door to the breezeway was locked from the outside. They ended up having to go out the big doors. Hunched into the wind, with the snow stinging their faces, they slogged through the deepening snow around the side of the shed and back through the gate that enclosed the paddock.

Once under the partial shelter of the breezeway, they raced for the back door, the wind biting at them, tearing at Katie's heavy skirts.

It was locked. Katie knocked good and hard. No one came.

Justin wore a bleak look. ''What now?''

''No problem.'' Katie took off her right glove and felt along the top of the door frame, producing the key from the niche there. She held it up for him to see before sticking it in the lock and pushing the door inward onto an enclosed back porch. He signaled her ahead of him and followed right after, pulling the door closed to seal out the wind and snow.

By then, it had to be after six. It was pretty dark. Katie flipped on the porch light and gestured at the hooks lining the wall next to the door that led inside. ''Hang up your coat,'' she suggested, as she set her gloves on a small table and began undoing the jet buttons down her front. The porch wasn't heated and she shivered as the coat fell open. ''Whew. Cold...''

''I hope it's warm in there.''

''It is,'' she promised as she shrugged out of the long gray coat and hung it on a hook. He hung his beside it. She swiped off her hat, shook out her hair and tossed the hat on a porch chair.

"This way." Katie unlocked the door and pushed it open into the museum's small, minimally equipped kitchen area. Lovely warm air flowed out and surrounded them.

"Much better," Justin said from behind her.

She led him in, hanging the key on the waiting hook by the door and turning on the light.

The long counter was spotless, and so was the table over by the side windows. A few cups dried on a mat at the sink. No sign of Tildy or Anna.

They moved on into the big central room, which a hundred years before had been the only schoolroom. The room was now the museum's main display area—and pitch-dark. Years ago, when rooms were added on around it, the windows had been closed up. Katie felt for the dimmer switch near the door, turning it up just enough that they could see where they were going.

The light revealed roped-off spaces containing nineteenth-century furniture arranged into living areas: a bedroom, a weaving room, a parlor, a one-room "house" with all the living areas combined, the furniture in that section rough-hewn, made by pioneer hands.

"No sign of your friends," Justin said.

"They probably got worried about the storm and went home."

A quick check of the two other display rooms confirmed their suspicions. They were alone.

"No cars out there," Justin said once they'd

reached the front reception area, where trays of sandwiches, cookies and coffee, tea and grape drink waited for the crowd that wasn't coming. "Remember? The parking lot in front of the building. It was empty." She did remember, now that he mentioned it. He asked, "What now?"

It was a good question; too bad she had no answer to it. "I guess we wait."

"For?"

She wished she knew. "For the storm to die down a little so we can leave?"

He gave her a humorless half smile. "Was that an answer—or just another question?"

Katie put up both hands, palms up. "Oh, really. I just don't know."

Justin studied her for a moment, wearing an expression she couldn't read. Then, out of nowhere, he plunked himself down into one of the reception chairs and started pulling off his boots.

The sight struck her as funny, for some crazy reason. She laughed—and then felt stupid for doing it when he glanced up from under the dark shelf of his brow, his full-lipped mouth a grim line. "These damn boots are at least a size too small."

Katie winced. "Sorry."

With a grunt, he tugged off a boot. "For what?"

She sank to a chair herself. "Oh, you know. Caleb shouldn't have roped you into this. And I should have spoken up and called the whole thing off."

He dropped the boot to the floor, pulled off the other one and set it down, too. "Are you capable of that?"

"Excuse me?"

That dry smile had gone devilish. "Speaking up."

She sat straighter and brushed a bit of lint off her skirt. "Now and then, absolutely."

His smile got wider. "Like with the horse."

She nodded. "That's right." Blowing out a weary breath, she let her shoulders slump again. "But back in the hall—oh, I just hate getting up in front of a lot of people. Especially a lot of people who've had too much beer."

"I hear you on that one." He looked down at his heavy wool socks—and wiggled his toes. "Now, that's more like it."

Her own feet were kind of pinched in the narrow lace-up shoes. What the heck? She hiked up her soggy skirts—which gave off the musty scent of wet wool— and set to work on the laces. When she had both shoes off, she set them neatly beside her chair, smoothed her skirt down and straightened to find him watching her. There was humor in his eyes and something else, something much too watchful. She found herself thinking, *What's he up to?* And then instantly chided herself for being suspicious.

What *could* he be up to? Except wishing he hadn't let Caleb talk him into this.

The watchful look had faded from his face as if it had never been. He asked softly, "Now, isn't that better?"

"What?"

"Without your shoes…"

She felt a smile tug at her mouth. Oh, really, he was much too good-looking for her peace of mind.

She answered briskly, "Yes, it is." And she picked up a tray of sandwich triangles from the reception desk. "Help yourself. It's probably the closest thing to dinner we're going to get."

He took one and bit into it. "Ham and American. With mayo. The best."

"Oh, I'll bet." She took one for herself and gestured at the big stainless steel coffee urn, the hot water for tea and the glass pitcher of grape drink. "And coffee. Or a cold drink…"

He got up. "You?"

"Coffee sounds good. With a little cream."

He poured them each a cup, splashed cream from a little stoneware pitcher into hers and handed it over with a courtly, "Mrs. Caldwell."

She played along. "*Mr.* Caldwell." Really, she was grateful he was taking this so calmly.

He sank into his chair again and sipped the hot brew. "Now we're married, I think you're going to have to call me Justin."

She had that silly, nervous urge to laugh again. She quelled it. "By all means. And please. Call me Katie. I firmly believe married people should be on a first-name basis with each other."

"I agree. Katie." He finished off the rest of his sandwich. She held out the tray and he took another. She took one, too. He asked, "So how was that train ride?"

She rolled her eyes. "I should have taken a club car."

About then, the false cheer they were both trying to keep up deserted them. They sat silent, like the strangers they really were, eating their sandwiches, listening to the wind whistling in the eaves outside.

Eventually, he turned to her, his expression grave. "Will anyone else show up?"

"In this?" She gestured at the six-over-six front windows. Beyond the golden glow of the porch light, there was only darkness and hard-blowing snow. "I don't think so."

He turned and looked at the round institutional-style clock on the wall above the desk. It was six thirty-five. "How long will we be stuck here?"

He *would* have to ask that. She cleared her throat. "Maybe, if we're lucky, the snow will stop soon."

"And if it doesn't?"

Katie sighed. "Good question. We'll just have to wait and see how bad it gets."

"Should we call someone, let them know we arrived here and we're safe?" He felt in his pockets. "Damn…"

"What?"

"I left my cell in my own clothes, back at the hall." He produced a handsome calfskin wallet and waved at her. "The good news is I've got plenty of cash."

Katie forced a grin. "Whew. I was worried. What if we wanted to do a little shopping?" He made a sound halfway between a grunt and a chuckle, and she added, on a more somber note, "And cell phones don't work all that well around these parts, anyway. Lots of mountains. Not many cell towers."

"I knew that," he said, his mouth twisting wryly.

She set her coffee cup on the edge of the reception

desk, reached for the phone and put it to her ear. "Dead." Carefully, she set it back in its cradle.

"Terrific."

"Count your blessings," she advised, trying to keep things positive. "At least we still have heat and electricity. And plenty of water, as long as the pipes don't freeze."

He didn't look too reassured, but he got the message. "Right. Might as well look on the bright side."

"Exactly."

Rising, he went to the trays of food and chose another sandwich.

The museum had propane heat throughout, but there was also the remains of a fire in the potbellied stove in the corner. Katie got up and put in another log. She jabbed it with the poker until it was well nestled in the bright coals. The red flames licked up.

She shut the stove door and turned—to find him watching her again. "Is something the matter?"

He frowned. "No. Of course not—well, except for the situation we're in here."

"You keep looking at me strangely."

His gaze remained far too watchful—for a moment. And then he shrugged. "Forgive me. I'm just... curious about you, I guess. Caleb Douglas told me you're the 'little girl he never had.' He raised you, I take it?"

She had no idea why she felt reluctant to answer him. What was there to hide? She said, "My mother and Adele were both from Philadelphia, best friends at Bryn Mawr—you did meet Addy, didn't you?"

"I did." He looked like he was waiting to hear more.

So she elaborated. "They had an instant connection, my mother and Addy, from the way Addy tells it. And their families were friends. When my parents died, I was fourteen. There was really no one left in my immediate family to take me. Addy came and got me." Katie smiled at the memory—Adele, with her suitcases at her feet in the foyer of the Center City brownstone near Rittenhouse Square that had belonged to Katie's grandparents and their parents before them. When Katie came down the stairs to meet her, Adele held out her arms, her blue eyes shining with tears....

Katie swallowed down the emotion the memory brought with it and Justin asked, "Adele brought you here, then—to Thunder Canyon?"

"That's right, to live with her and Caleb."

"And you loved it."

"Yes, I did. From the first."

"Because?"

She hesitated. Could he really want to hear all this? But he was looking at her expectantly. So she told him, "It was…just what I'd needed. A close-knit community, where people looked out for each other. I lived at the Lazy D through my teenage years, went to Thunder Canyon High and then on to college in Colorado. As Caleb told you, he and Addy never had a daughter, so it worked out beautifully. For all of us."

"All?"

"Caleb. Addy. And Riley. Have you met Riley?"

He nodded. "Their son. Caleb introduced me to him a few days ago—and I suppose he's like a big brother to you?"

She picked up her soggy skirt so it wouldn't drag on the floor and padded to one of the front windows, where she looked out at the porch, the darkness and the driving snow beyond. "Yes. I think of Riley like a brother...." She turned back to him. "They're fine people." Did she sound defensive? A little. She wasn't really sure why. Something hostile in the way he'd spoken of Riley, maybe.

But why in the world would Justin Caldwell be hostile toward Riley, whom he'd only just met? Clearly, the stress of their situation was getting to her, making her read things into his tone that weren't there.

She tried for a lighter note. "Caleb is so pleased that you've invested in his ski resort." Caleb had always been a wheeler-dealer. The resort was a long-time dream of his and it was finally coming true. He'd opened an office on Main Street for the project—complete with a model of the future resort in the waiting room—and hired a secretary. Thunder Canyon Ski Resort would be built on a ridge about twenty miles out of town on land the Douglases had owned for generations. Caleb had worked for months, hunting down investors. Everything had finally fallen into place in the past few weeks. Caleb had told her proudly that Justin's company, Red Rock Developers, was the main reason it was all working out.

"I think it's a solid investment," Justin said.

"Good for everyone, then."

"Yes. Absolutely."

Another silence descended. Oh, this was all so awkward. If she had to get herself stranded in a blizzard, you'd think it might have been with someone she knew. Or at least, maybe someone less...attractive.

He was almost too good-looking, really. And she felt a certain fluttery sensation in her midsection every time she glanced his way. Her excited response to him made her wary.

She wondered if he knew about her money. There *was* a lot of it. Katie mostly ignored it and let the estate managers handle everything. Her interests were in her family—and to her, that meant the Douglases—and in her town and in the Thunder Canyon Public Library, which she had generously endowed and where she was privileged to work at a job she truly loved.

But she could never completely forget that she was the sole heir to large fortunes on both her mother's and her father's side. Everybody in town knew it, of course. She'd even had a couple of boyfriends who'd turned out to be nothing more than fortune hunters in the end. From them she'd learned the hard truth: when it came to men, she had to be careful. If a man seemed interested, there was always a chance that his interest was more in her money than in Katie herself.

Sometimes she wished she could be like other women, and just go for it, when it came to guys. But she had a shy streak and she had too much money, and both made her more guarded than she would have liked to be.

She kept thinking of that kiss, back in the hall, kept remembering the feel of his mouth against hers....

But really, other than that kiss, which had only been for show, he'd made no moves on her. He wasn't even blaming her for the fact that they were stuck here for Lord knew how long.

She could have been stranded with worse, and she told herself firmly to remember that.

"Deep thoughts?" Justin asked softly.

"Not at all." She gestured at the trays of food. "If you've had all you want, I think we should go ahead and put this stuff away...."

He gave her a level look. She knew what he was thinking. They could very well end up enjoying those sandwiches for breakfast. "Let's do it." He rose and picked up a tray and the pitcher of grape drink.

She grabbed another tray and followed him through the main display room, to the kitchen at the back.

Twenty minutes later, they had everything put away. They returned to the reception room and sat down again. They made halting conversation. He told her a little about his company, said he'd started from nothing and had "come a long way."

"You're based in...?"

"Bozeman."

"Did you grow up in Montana?"

"No. I was born in California. We moved a lot. To Oregon for a while and later to Colorado, Nevada, Idaho..."

"Brothers and sisters?"

"Single mom—and she only had me. She died two years ago."

"It must have been tough for her...."

"Yeah. It was." He'd rested his dark head back against the knotty pine wall. He glanced her way. "We could use a television. Or at least a radio."

Boy, could they. "We can look around for one."

So they returned to the kitchen and went through the cabinets. Nothing but pots and pans and dishes and such. In the storage room off one of the side display rooms, where the society kept the donations they were collecting for their next rummage sale, they did find a battered old boom box.

Justin scanned the small room. "Any plugs in here?"

"Just the one in the light." They both looked up at the bare bulb above. The cord wouldn't stretch that far. "Why don't we take it with us out front?"

"Fine," he said, glancing around. "Lots of clothes in these bags..." They shared another look and she knew they were thinking along the same lines. If they didn't get out of here soon, they could always go through the bags, maybe find something more comfortable to wear.

The idea depressed her—that they might be stuck here long enough to need a change of clothes.

"Look at it this way," he advised gently. "We're safe and warm. And we've got plenty of sandwiches."

They took the radio out through the silent display rooms to the front. Justin plugged it in and turned the dial. Nothing but static.

Thoroughly discouraged, Katie went to the window

again. She wrapped her arms around herself and stared out for a while at the steadily falling snow.

Justin spoke from behind her. "Those old beds in the center display room…"

She faced him. They shared a grim look.

He asked, "Are you thinking what I'm thinking?"

Her nod was resigned. "It does begin to look as if they're going to get some use tonight."

Past midnight, Justin Caldwell lay wide-awake staring at the shadowed rafters in the museum's central room. He'd taken the narrow, hard little cot in the one-room pioneer cabin display and stretched out, fully clothed but for those damn too-small boots, under the star-patterned quilt. He'd had to pull out the sheet at the bottom of the bed. It was too short by a foot and his stocking feet hung out over the edge.

But at least the bedding was clean. Katie had told him it was all antique stuff donated by local families. The Historical Society took pains to keep it laundered and in good repair.

Katie…

He could hear her soft breathing from the "bedroom" on the opposite wall, where she lay in a wide four-poster with pineapple finials that some pioneer family had probably dragged across the plains in a covered wagon. He smiled to himself.

She was…a surprise. A quiet woman; self-contained. With those wide honey-brown eyes, that tender mouth and the shy way she had about her, she seemed, in some ways, so young—younger than her age, which he knew was twenty-four.

Yes. Very young. And yet, at the same time, she had that self-possessed quality that made her, somehow, seem older.

He knew much more than she'd told him so far. He'd paid and paid well to learn all about her—and about Caleb, Adele and Riley Douglas, as well.

Katherine Adele Fenton was the only child of the jet-setting Paris and Darrin Fenton. She'd been born in Venice, Italy—and immediately turned over to a nanny. Into her teens, Katie hardly saw her parents. She was fourteen and living a sheltered life with a governess in London when both Paris and Darrin died tragically; their private plane crashed on the way to a society wedding.

That was where the Douglases came in. As Katie's godmother, Adele had gone back east to claim the orphaned child of her dear college friend.

From what Justin had been able to learn, the Douglases considered Katie one of their own. She was, though not by blood, a full-fledged member of their family. She was the daughter Adele Douglas never had. Though he'd taken her into his home and treated her as family, Caleb had never made any effort to lay claim to a red cent of Katie's considerable inheritance. And from what Justin knew of Caleb Douglas—who loved nothing so much as making big deals involving large sums of money—that was saying something.

Justin pushed back the quilt. When he returned to the hard pallet laughingly called a bed, he'd leave off the blankets. The old building's heating system seemed to have one temperature: high. He sat and swung his legs soundlessly to the floor.

Rising, he ducked under the rope that was supposed to keep visitors away from the displays, and went to the door that led out to the reception area. It opened soundlessly and he shut it without letting the latch click.

In the men's room off the reception area, he flicked on the light and used the urinal. At the sink, he splashed cold water on his face and avoided meeting his own eyes in the mirror.

Back in the reception area, he stood by the window. The snow was still coming down. It lay, thick and white and sparkling, covering the steps up to porch level.

If it kept up like this, they could be stuck here for a day or two. Maybe longer. Who the hell knew?

Lots of time alone, just him and Katie...

Though he generally preferred a more outgoing, sophisticated type of woman, he *was* drawn to her. In the end, he supposed, there was no predicting sexual chemistry.

She felt attracted to him, too. He'd seen it in those big brown eyes of hers, known it in the way her body softened and melted into him during that kiss that had sealed their fake vows back there at the town hall.

Maybe he had something here. Maybe he ought to consider taking advantage of the way this sudden winter storm had thrown them together.

But he would have to watch himself. He couldn't let things get *too* hot and heavy. He had nothing with him to protect her from pregnancy and he'd have wagered half his assets that Katie Fenton wasn't on the pill.

No. He couldn't take the chance that she might become pregnant. He'd grown up without a father and he knew what that could do to a kid.

But he could certainly draw her out a little. No doubt she knew things about the Douglases—things that even his expert, high-priced sources couldn't have dug up. Knowledge *was* power and the more he had of it, the better his position would be in this special game he was playing.

And in spite of her wariness, Katie should be approachable if he took the right tact with her—if he were frank and friendly; helpful and easygoing…

It wouldn't have to go too far. Just enough for her to trust him, to tell him her secrets—and those of the Douglases. Just enough that she would *believe* in him as a man. Just enough that she'd come to…care for him.

In the end, if he worked it right, she'd be broken-hearted. He regretted that. But when it came time for payback, a man had to accept some degree of collateral damage. She would be hurt—and the people who cared most about her would hurt *for* her. It would add a certain…turn of the knife, you might say.

Justin flicked off the porch light. No need for it at this late hour. The window became a dark mirror. He saw his own reflection faintly, a lurking shadow in the glass.

Hell.

Maybe not.

He'd always been a man who did what needed doing. Still, he was having a little trouble getting around the fact that Katie Fenton was a good woman. An innocent in all this.

He should leave her out of it.

But then, if it worked out according to plan, he wouldn't be hurting her *that* bad. Just a little. Just enough to get to Caleb. She'd get over it in time.

And there was no saying that he could even fool her. She might be innocent, but she was also smart. It was just possible she'd see him coming and refuse to let him get close enough to make her care. They'd be locked in here for a day or two and she would merely tolerate him until their time of forced proximity had passed. She'd escape unscathed.

Maybe.

But then again, there *was* the real attraction between them. If he let himself go with that, he wouldn't be faking it. And he would tell her the truth—just not all of it.

Taking it forward from that angle…

Say it was all the same, except for the fact that she'd been raised by the Douglases. Say she was only the town librarian playing the mail-order bride and he'd been a stranger talked into taking the part of her groom. Say they ended up here, alone, snowed in at the museum, just as they had.

Take away her connection to the Douglases and he would still be intrigued with her, would still want to pursue her, to hear her secrets, to hold her in his arms and steal a kiss or two.

So in the end, he would only be doing what he

would have done, anyway: getting to know a woman who interested him.

Yes. He could look at it that way. He could take it from there and go with it. Be friendly and open and willing to talk about himself—to hear about her and her life and the people she cared for.

Maybe nothing would come of it.

Or maybe, in the end, he'd have found a second, more personal way to make Caleb Douglas pay for his sins.

Chapter Three

Katie woke to the smell of coffee brewing.

That was the good news.

Everything else? Not nearly so pleasant. Her mouth tasted like the bottom of someone's old shoe. Her wrinkled wool dress gave off a distinctly musty odor. And she had a crick in her neck from sleeping on a too-fat pillow.

She let out a loud, grumpy groan—and then snapped her mouth shut. After all, there was a virtual stranger in the bed across the way—or wait. Probably not. He must be the one who'd made the coffee.

Katie sat up. She'd left the dimmer set to low, so the light was minimal, but she could see that Justin Caldwell's narrow cot lay empty, the covers pulled up and neatly tucked in.

Anxious, suddenly, to know what time it was, to

find out if the storm had ended, if it might be possible that she could go home to her own comfy house on Cedar Street, Katie threw back the covers and jumped from the old bed. Ducking under the rope that marked off her "room," she pulled open the door to the reception area—and blinked at what she saw.

Beyond the windows, a wall of snow gleamed at her in the gray light of a cloud-thick Sunday morning. It was piled above the porch floor now. Though the wild winds of last night had died in the darkness, the snow itself continued to fall, a filmy white curtain, whispering its way down.

The clock on the wall read seven-fifteen. She picked up the phone. Silence. With a heavy sigh, she set it down again and headed for the ladies' room, where she used the facilities, rinsed her face and made a brave effort to comb her tangled hair with her fingers.

Snowed-in without even a hairbrush. Definitely not her idea of a good time.

In the kitchen, Katie found Justin sitting at the table by the window, wearing jeans and a cable-knit red and green sweater with reindeer leaping in a line across his broad chest. On his feet were a battered pair of black-and-white lace-up canvas All-Stars.

"It's true," he announced at her look. "I have raided the rummage sale bags and I feel no shame."

"Love the sweater," she muttered glumly. "Phone's still dead." Beyond him, out the window, the snow kept coming down. "They won't even be able to get the plow out in this."

"Relax," he advised with an easy shrug. "Have some coffee." He toasted her with his stoneware mug. "I even found a smaller pot, so we don't have to brew it up for a hundred every time we want a cup." He gestured at the plateful of sandwiches on the table. "And did I mention there are plenty of sandwiches?"

"Wonderful." She padded to the counter, poured herself some coffee, added cream from the carton in the fridge and plunked herself down in the chair opposite him.

"Better?" he asked after she'd taken a sip.

"A little. Though I'd give a good number of stale sandwiches for a toothbrush. And a comb." She put a hand to her tangled hair. "If we're stuck here much longer, I may consider raiding the museum displays for some long-gone pioneer lady's sterling silver dresser set."

He looked very pleased with himself—and, now she thought about it, he looked as if he'd shaved. And his hair was wet—was that shampoo she smelled?

She set down her cup. "You found a razor in the rummage sale bags—and you washed your hair."

He laughed. It was a low, velvety kind of sound and it played along her skin like a physical caress. "Was that an accusation?"

She sat back in her chair and regarded him with suspicion. "You're much too cheerful."

"And you are very cranky." He took another bite of his sandwich, chewed and swallowed. "If you don't be nice, I won't let you have what's in that bag over by the sink."

She glanced where he'd indicated. The bag sat near the edge: a plain brown paper bag. "What's in it?"

He pushed the plate of sandwiches toward her. "Eat first."

She reached for a sandwich, raised it to her lips—and lowered it without taking a bite. "Just tell me. Is there a hairbrush in there?"

He nodded. "More than one. And combs. And a few toothbrushes—still wrapped in cellophane. And travel-size toothpaste. And sample bottles of shampoo and lotion, boxed-up shower caps and miniature bars of soap—oh, and did I mention razors and travel-size shaving cream cans? Looks like someone held up a drugstore, raided a motel supply closet and gave what they stole to the Historical Society rummage sale."

"Shower caps," Katie repeated wistfully.

Justin grunted. "Yeah. No need for those."

"Since we don't have a shower."

"But remember. It could be worse. The heat could be out and there could be no wood for the stove. The ladies from the Historical Society could have failed to leave us these delicious sandwiches." He waved one at her.

"You have a surprisingly vivid imagination."

"Thank you. And what I meant is, we're doing okay here. And after you eat, you even get to brush your teeth."

She supposed he had a point. "You're right. I should take my own advice from yesterday and keep a more positive outlook on our situation."

He faked a stern expression. "See that you do."

Katie ate her sandwich and took a second, as well.

Her spirits had lifted. If she wasn't getting out of here today, at least she'd have clean teeth and combed hair.

Once she'd spent twenty minutes in the ladies' room using various items from the brown paper bag, Katie went to the storage area and chose a bulky sweater and a pair of worn corduroy pants. She even found thick gray socks and jogging shoes that were only a half size too big.

"Lookin' good," Justin remarked with a wink when she returned to the kitchen where he sat reading yesterday's newspaper.

"The fit leaves something to be desired—but I have to admit, I'm a lot more comfortable."

"And less cranky."

"Yes. That, too." She gave him a smile, thinking how even-tempered and helpful he'd been since she got them into this mess. Really, she could have been stranded with worse. She added, in an effort to show him her friendlier side, "While I was choosing my outfit, I found some old board games. Maybe we can haul them out later. I play a mean game of checkers."

"Sounds good." The paper rustled as he turned the page.

"Justin..."

He lowered the paper and gave her an easy smile.

"I just want you to know I appreciate how well you're taking all this."

He gestured toward the snow beyond the window. "This is nothing, believe me."

Really, this positive-attitude approach could be carried too far. "Oh. So you're telling me this kind of thing happens to you all the time?"

"Only once before."

"Oh. Well. Only once. That's nothing—and you're joking, aren't you?"

"No. I'm not. When I was thirteen, we lived in this vacation-home development in northern Nevada. I got snowed-in there alone for a week."

She couldn't have heard right. "Alone for a week—at thirteen?" He nodded. "But what about your mom?"

"She was supposed to be home, but she didn't make it. The situation was similar to yesterday's—a sudden storm that turned out much worse than predicted. It got bad fast and she couldn't get to me."

"But…where was she?"

His expression turned doubtful. "You sure you want to hear this? It's not that exciting. And as you can see by looking at me today, I got through it just fine."

She'd been planning to go check on Buttercup. But that could wait a minute or two. She pulled out a chair and slid into it. "I do want to hear. Honestly."

He studied her for a long moment, as if gauging the sincerity of her request. Finally, he folded the paper and set it aside. "At the time, we were living in this one-room cabin not far from Lake Tahoe."

"You and your mom?"

"That's right. The cabin was one of those ski chalet designs. On a two-acre lot. Intended as a vacation home. It had a single big, open room with lots of windows, the roof pitched high, a sleeping loft above?"

"Yes. I can picture it."

"My mother was in real estate at that point. She went off to show someone another cabin identical to ours. A bad storm blew in. She couldn't get back to me, so I was stuck on my own. It was...a learning experience, let me tell you."

"Yikes. I can't even imagine."

"Yeah. It *was* pretty grim, looking back on it. The phone line went dead the first day. Then, the next day, the power went out. But I had plenty of candles and a woodstove for heat. I kept the fire going and tucked into the canned goods when I got hungry."

"But what did you *do,* alone for all that time?"

One corner of his full mouth quirked up. "I got pretty damn bored, now you mention it. Bored enough that I taught myself solitaire with a dog-eared deck of cards I found in a kitchen drawer. When that got old, I started working my way through all my schoolbooks. For a thirteen-year-old boy to do every problem in his math book for recreation, *that's* desperation."

"But there was plenty of canned food, you said?"

He made a low sound in his throat. "For some reason, my mom had a case each of canned peaches and cream of mushroom soup. To this day, I can't stand the sight or smell of either."

"I'll bet—but what I can't imagine is how you made it through something like that." She scanned his face. "Thirteen," she said softly. "It's too horrible. You must have been scared to death."

He shrugged. "The wood lasted 'til the end of the sixth day. I got out the axe and chopped up my mother's oak-veneer kitchen table and chairs. Once I'd burned them, I kind of lost heart. The fire died and I piled every blanket in the place on my bed and burrowed in there for the duration. I have to admit, by that time I was getting pretty damn terrified."

"But then you were rescued."

"That's right. The snowplow arrived at noon the next day with my mother, in her Blazer, right behind it. She was seriously freaked, I can tell you."

Katie almost wished his mother could have been there, with them, right then. She'd have had a thing or two to say to her. "Your *mother* was freaked. What about you? *You* were the child, for heaven's sake. How could she leave you alone like that?"

He let out a low chuckle. "Katie. Settle down."

Easier said than done. His story had seriously hit home for her. She shifted in her chair, crossing her legs and then uncrossing them, feeling antsy and angry and definitely not *settled down.* "I'm sorry, but it just, well, it fries me, you know? Children are so vulnerable. Parents have to look out for them, take *care* of them, pay them some attention now and then...."

He sat back in his chair. "Why do I get the feeling you're talking about more than what happened to me when I was thirteen?"

She wrapped her arms around her middle and looked out the window at the falling snow, blinking against the glare of all that shimmery white.

"Katie?"

She faced him. "You're right," she confessed. "I was thinking about how things were for me, before Addy came and got me, when my parents were still alive."

"Rough?" Those blue eyes had a softness in them, as if he understood—and from what he'd just told her, she had a feeling he did.

She hugged herself harder. "I rarely saw them. They enjoyed traveling. They had a flat in London, the family brownstone in Philadelphia, villas in France and Italy. And where they didn't have a flat or a villa, they had *friends* who had one. You know the words. 'Globe-trotting.' 'Jet-setting.' My parents *were* the beautiful people. They came from fine families and the money was always there. They never had to work. So they didn't. They didn't even have to take care of their child. There were nannies and governesses, plenty of hired help for that."

"So you weren't left alone," Justin said, his eyes direct. Knowing.

"No, I wasn't."

"But you *were* lonely."

"Exactly." She looked down. Her arms were wrapped so tightly around her middle, they made her rib cage ache. With a slow, deep breath, she let go of herself and folded her hands on the tabletop. "I never knew a real family—'til Addy and Caleb." She smiled to herself. "And Riley. He was all grown up by the time I came to them, twenty-three, when I moved to the ranch. How many young guys in their twenties have time for a gawky fourteen-year-old girl? Not many. But Riley did. He was so good to me, you know?'' Justin made a sound of understanding low in his throat. "What the Douglases gave me was something so important. The two big things I'd never had. Their time. Their attention. Riley taught me to ride—''

"On Buttercup." He grinned.

"That's right." She glanced toward the door to the back porch, thinking she should get out there and check on the old mare. Soon.

But it was so…comfortable. Sitting here with Justin, talking about the things that had made them who they were. "So you don't blame your mother for leaving you alone in that cabin?''

He shook his head. "It's tough for a woman on her own, with a kid. She'd been left high and dry, pregnant with me by the no-good bastard who used her and then walked away from her when she told him she was having his baby. She was…a good mother and she took damn good care of me. But there was no getting around that she had to make a living and that meant when the storm blew in, I was at the cabin, and she wasn't. It's the kind of thing that can happen to anyone.''

"It's the kind of thing that could scar a child for life, that's what it is.''

He pressed a fist to his chest right over the row of reindeer prancing across the front of his sweater. "That's me. Deeply damaged.''

She tipped her head to the side, considering. "Well. I guess it's good that you can joke about it.''

He was quiet for a moment. Then he said, "It happened. I survived. And I've done just fine for myself, though I never had a father, never had much formal education and started, literally, from scratch.''

"In…development?'' She laughed. "What does that mean, exactly, to be a 'developer.'''

"Well, a developer 'develops.'''

"Sheesh. It's all clear to me now.''

He grinned. "Property, in my case. We start with several viable acres and we develop a project to build tract homes. Or say I got hold of just the right business-district lot. I'd start putting the people and financing together to build an office complex. A developer is someone who gets the money and the people and the plans—and most important, the right property—and puts it all together.''

He hadn't told her anything she couldn't have figured out herself, but she was discovering she enjoyed listening to him talk. She liked the way he looked at her. As if he never wanted to look away.

She said, "Like Caleb's ski resort? He's got the property and you'll work with him to 'develop' it.''

"That's right. But don't misunderstand. It's his project, his baby. He'll be in charge, though I'll be involved every step of the way.''

She looked down at her folded hands. She was just about to tell him how much the project meant to Caleb. Caleb *was* getting older and Katie knew that sometimes he worried he was losing his edge—but no.

Katie kept her mouth shut. Yes, she was finding she liked Justin. A lot. However, the last thing Caleb would want was for her to go blabbing his secret doubts to a business associate.

She glanced up and found Justin studying her again, his dark head tipped to the side. "Question."

"Ask."

"Yesterday. Didn't you mention that you went to college in Colorado?"

"That's right. CU."

"I'll bet you had straight A's in high school."

She gave him a pert little nod. "You would win that bet."

"High scores on the SAT?"

"Very."

"Then why not Bryn Mawr, like your mother, and Adele Douglas? You'd have been a legacy, right— pretty much guaranteed to get in—even if your grades and test scores hadn't been outstanding?"

"I liked CU. They have a fine curriculum. Plus, it was closer to home."

"Home being here, in Thunder Canyon."

"That's right and you? Where did you go to college?"

"I told you. No real formal education. I went to real estate school and then got my broker's license a couple of years later."

"You started in real estate because of your mother's connections?"

He chuckled at that, though there wasn't a lot of humor in the sound. "My mother had no connections. She'd been out of the real estate business for years when I started. It didn't work out for her. Like a lot of things…"

She might have asked, *What things?* But he wore a closed-in, private kind of look at that moment and she didn't want to pry. She coaxed, "So you started in real estate…"

He blinked and the brooding shadows left his eyes. "Yeah. By the time I was twenty-five, I'd branched into property development."

"A self-made man."

"Smile when you say that."

She *was* smiling. But to make sure he noticed, she smiled even wider. And then her conscience reminded her that she had Buttercup to think of. She stood.

He put on a hurt look. "Just like that. You're leaving. Was it something I said?"

"What you said was fascinating. Honestly. And I'll be back soon."

"The question is, where do you think you're going?" He tipped his head toward the window and the still-falling snow outside. "I hate to break it to you, but I doubt you could get beyond the front porch."

"I want to check on Buttercup."

He rose. "I'll come with you."

She started to argue—that it was cold out there and she could take care of the job herself and he didn't really need to go. But then again, it wasn't as if he had a full schedule or anything.

He ushered her out to the back porch, where they put on their antique outerwear. Then they pushed open the door to the breezeway.

The snow had piled four feet or so on either side, sloping to the icy ground, leaving a path maybe a foot wide. "After you," Justin said. "Watch your step. It looks pretty slick."

In the shed, Buttercup snorted in greeting and came

right to Katie. She stroked the old mare's forehead and blew in her nostrils. "How're you doing, sweetie? Kind of lonely out here?" The horse whickered in response. "And I'll bet you wish I had some oats. Sorry. That hay'll have to do you for a while." She patted Buttercup's smooth golden neck and pulled out one of the brushes she'd brought from inside. It was hardly a grooming brush, but nothing else was available.

She brushed the old mare's knotted mane and spoke to her in low whispers for a while. Then she and Justin broke open another bale of hay.

"Watch out," he warned when they were spreading it around a little. "It's damned amazing how much manure one horse can produce in a sixteen-hour period."

"It is at that."

"Just don't step backward without looking behind you first."

She found a shovel in the corner and took it to him. "Get to work."

"Shoveling horse manure?"

"That's right."

"But where am I going to put it?" The gleam in his eyes said he already had a pretty good idea.

"Just shovel it up, carry it out those open main doors there and toss it as far as you can into the snow."

"That snow's piling up pretty high out there. This could be dangerous."

"So pay attention when you throw it. Wouldn't want it to come flying right back at you."

He pretended to grumble, but he started right in. She looked around and found another shovel. With both of them scooping and tossing, they had the mess cleared away in no time at all.

As they went to put the shovels up, Justin remarked that if the snow got much higher, swamping out the shed was going to be a real challenge.

"We'll manage," she told him. "Somehow..." She set her shovel against the wall and turned so fast, she almost ran into him.

"Watch it." He laughed down low in his throat, the sound emerging on a cloud of mist.

She laughed, too.

And then, all at once, she wasn't laughing and neither was he. They were just looking at each other—staring, really. And the cold air seemed to shimmer between them.

Oh, my goodness. Those lips of his...

Too full, for a man's lips. Really. Too full and yet...

Exactly perfect.

If only she didn't already know how delicious those lips felt pressed against her own. Maybe, if she didn't know what a great kisser he was, she wouldn't be standing here, sighing out a big breath of misty air and lifting her mouth to him.

He said her name, on a fog of breath. "Katie..."

She was so busy imagining what it was going to feel like when his lips met hers, that she didn't register how close Buttercup was behind him—not until the mare let out a low whinny and head-butted Justin a good one.

"Hey!" He surged forward, right into Katie. She went over backward and down they went into the newly spread hay. He ended up on top of her.

Katie blinked up at him and he looked down at her and there was a lovely, strange, breath-held kind of moment. He was so…warm and solid, pressed all along the length of her—and heavy, too, but in a good way. He looked deep in her eyes and he said her name again and she held up her lips to welcome his kiss.

But Buttercup wasn't finished. She bent her head and started nipping the back of Justin's baggy old coat.

He rolled away from Katie to glare up at the mare. "Knock it off."

Buttercup whinnied again and clopped off toward the double doors. A moment later, she was outside beneath the overhang, lipping up snow.

Justin canted up on an elbow and looked down at Katie. "That animal has it in for me."

Katie was thinking that she really ought to sit up. Her hat had come off when Justin landed on top of her. She knew she had hay in her hair. But she felt kind of…lax. Lax and lazy and oh-so-comfortable, lying there in the hay on the frozen dirt floor.

"Hmm," she said, and the sound was every bit as low and lazy as she was feeling. "Maybe Buttercup thinks you're up to no good."

He leaned in closer. She gazed up at his thick black lashes and his red nose and that wonderful, soft, oh-so-kissable mouth. "I'm perfectly harmless."

"Perfect?" she heard herself answer, her tone as

husky and intimate as his. "Maybe. Harmless? Oh, I don't think so...."

There was a silence, a quiet so intense she could hear the soft sound of the snow falling outside and the faint rustling noises Buttercup made beyond the shed doors. Slowly, his mouth curved into a smile. And his eyes...

Oh, it was just like right before he kissed her, in front of everyone, back in the hall. His eyes kind of sucked on her. They drew her down.

"I don't think that mare wants me to kiss you."

And she probably *shouldn't* kiss him. "Well, Justin. Okay, then. Let me up and we'll—"

He cut her off by placing a gloved finger against her lips. "Not yet." She probably should have protested, told him firmly to let her up.

But she didn't. She watched, entranced, as he lifted his hand, took the tip of the glove's finger between his white teeth and pulled it off. He dropped the glove beside her and then he touched her lips again—skin to skin this time. That brush of a caress made her mouth tingle, made her whole body yearn.

He let his hand drift over until it lay against the side of her face. "Soft," he whispered. "So pretty and soft..." He lowered his mouth.

She expected a hot, soul-shattering kiss. But he only brushed his lips sweetly, one time, across hers— and then he lifted away again and she was looking in those haunting eyes once more. "What's another kiss? Between a man and his wife."

Now she felt truly torn. She longed to kiss him— yet she knew it was probably a bad idea. "We shouldn't…get anything started, you know? We hardly know each other and—''

"But that's just it. I *want* to know you better. What about you, Katie? Do you want to know me?''

She did! And that seemed…dangerous, somehow. That seemed foolish and scary and simply not right. "I—I don't really want to start anything *casual,* you know?'' She found her throat had gone desert-dry. She paused to swallow and then rushed to continue before he could do anything that would make her thoughts scatter and fly away. "I know it's probably every guy's fantasy to get stranded with a woman who, uh, knows what she wants and knows how to get it—not that I don't know what I want. It's just, well, I don't want…*that.*''

He only smiled. "*That,* huh?''

"Yes.''

"That…what?''

Oh, this wasn't going well. "Look. I just don't want to start anything I know I'm not going to finish. Okay?''

"Katie?''

She glared at him. "What?''

"It's only a kiss.''

"Oh, I just don't—''

"Katie. Do you *want* to kiss me?''

"We've just about talked this to death, don't you think?''

"But do you want to kiss me?''

"Oh, all right, damn it.'' Katie rarely swore. But right then, *damn it* seemed the only thing to say.

"But do you?''

"Yes." The word came out breathless-sounding. "I do."

"Good." He lowered his mouth to hers.

Katie sighed once and she sighed again.

Her hands slipped up to encircle his neck and she held on for dear life as he played with her mouth. With that clever tongue of his, he traced the seam where her lips met, teasingly at first and then with a more insistent pressure. She couldn't resist him— didn't *want* to resist him. Shyly, she let her lips relax and he swept that tongue of his inside.

It was a shocking, thrilling thing, the way Justin Caldwell could use that mouth of his. And it was a truly wonderful thing, the way his body felt, so warm and close, pressed against her side, the way he smelled of soap and shaving cream.

His cold nose touched hers and his hot breath burned her icy cheek. As he kissed her, he stroked her with his hands. That was wonderful, too. Each separate caress left a burning trail of longing in its wake. He wrapped his arms around her and rolled a little, so they were both on their sides, and his hand moved lower, to the small of her back. He rubbed there, a sweet, firm pressure, soothing muscles cramped from sleeping on that lumpy ancient mattress last night.

She moaned and pressed herself all the tighter against him. His hand swept lower. He cupped her bottom and tucked her up into him.

That was when she felt the hard ridge in his jeans.

Oh, my.

Time to stop.

Time to stop right *now.*

She braced her hands on his shoulders and tore her mouth away from his. "That's enough." She looked at his face and she feared...

What?

She realized she didn't know. Her fear was formless, and yet she did feel it.

Remember the others, she reminded herself. *They were after your money. They hurt you. He could so easily do the same....*

But even as she thought of that, she didn't believe it. Oh, he might hurt her, yes. But in her heart, she simply didn't believe it would be for her money.

Which probably made her the biggest fool in Montana.

He loosened his hold on her. With a deep sigh, he pressed his forehead to hers. "You're right," he said. "Enough."

She slid her hands down to his hard chest. Beneath her palms, she could feel his heat, and his heart racing. His breath came out in ragged puffs—just like hers.

She whispered, "We'd better go in."

He touched her hair. She thought that she'd never felt anything quite so lovely in her whole life as that—the tender caress of his hand on her hair. He threaded his chilled bare fingers up under the tangled strands and cupped the back of her neck. She took his cue and tipped her head up to look at him.

"Yeah," he said. His mouth was swollen from what he'd been doing to her, his eyes twin blue flames. "We'll go in. Now." He pressed one more quick, hard kiss on her lips—as if he realized he shouldn't, but couldn't resist. Her mouth burned at the contact.

Then he reached across her to grab his discarded glove. Rolling away from her, he rose. She scuttled to a sitting position.

"Here," he said.

She stared at his outstretched hand. It seemed...too dangerous to take it.

Her gaze tracked upward, to his face. She knew by the heated look in his eyes that if she reached out, he would only pull her close and start kissing her again—and the thrumming of her blood through her body left her no doubt that she would end up kissing him right back.

No. Not going to happen. She'd known this man less than twenty-four hours. And she refused to end up rolling around naked with him on a bed of hay in a freezing old shed.

"I can manage, thanks." She pulled off a glove and felt in her hair. It was just as she'd suspected: threaded through with bits of hay. "Oh, just look at me...."

Justin let his hand drop to his side. "I am." His voice was husky and low. And in his eyes she saw desire—*real* desire. For her.

And not only desire, but also something dark and lonely, something that might have been regret.

Katie's mouth went dust-dry. *This* was danger—a danger far beyond any threat a mere fortune hunter might pose. Peril to her tender heart, to her very soul.

No doubt about it. She wanted him—with a kind

of bone-melting yearning, with a merciless desire the like of which she'd never known before.

It was…a physical aching. A hunger in the blood.

Oh, she would have to watch herself with him. She would have to exercise a little caution, or she'd be in way over her head.

Somewhere far back in her mind, a taunting voice whispered, *Katie. Come on. You're already over your head. Over your head and falling fast.…*

Chapter Four

He shouldn't have kissed her.

It had been a major error in judgment and Justin damn well knew that it had.

He shouldn't have kissed her. Not so soon, anyway—and certainly not in a prickly bed of hay on the frozen dirt floor of the shed out back, with that irritating old mare looking on.

Getting hot and heavy so fast had spooked her. She had her guard up and now he couldn't get past it.

They spent the rest of the endless day playing checkers, watching the snow fall, stoking the fire in the stove out front and reading books and magazines they found stacked in the storage room. Whenever they spoke, she made sure it was in polite generalities.

The snow kept falling. The radio played only static. And the phone stayed dead.

Justin could have kicked himself with his rummage sale Converse All-Star. The big loss of ground with her was his own damn fault. He'd sucked her in beautifully, had her right in the palm of his hand once he'd told her the story of that lonely week in the cabin when he was thirteen. He'd hit the perfect common nerve: a lonely childhood; parents who weren't all they should have been.

It was going so well.

Until the kiss.

And even that could have been okay—could have been tender and sweet and worked beautifully to lure her closer.

But he'd gotten his arms around her and her mouth under his and that sweet body pressed close against him…

He'd lost it. Lost every last shred of control.

The bald truth was that he'd seriously underestimated the power of his own lust for the shy brown-eyed librarian with too much money and an adopted family he despised.

It was funny, really—though he wasn't laughing. A royal backfire of his basic intention: *he* was supposed to seduce *her*.

Not the other way around.

At six that evening, they sat at the kitchen table, reading—or at least, Katie was reading. He knew it because he kept sneaking glances at her and losing his place in the thriller that should have been holding him spellbound—or so it said in the cover notes. As ''taut'' and ''edge-of-your seat'' as the book was supposed to be, he kept having to go back and read the same paragraph over and over again.

Katie, though...

She seemed to have no trouble at all with her concentration. She'd laid the heavy volume she'd chosen open on the table, rested her forearms on the tabletop and bent her brown head to the page. She'd barely budged from that position for over an hour. He knew. He'd timed her. Occasionally, she'd catch her soft bottom lip between her teeth, worry it lightly and let it go. Sometimes she smiled—just the faintest hint of a smile. As if what she read amused her.

Justin scowled every time she smiled like that. He wanted her to look up and smile at *him,* damn it. But she didn't.

And he ought to be glad she didn't look up. If she caught him scowling at her, he'd only lose more ground than he already had.

And what the hell was his problem here, anyway? He was getting way too invested in this thing with her. She had nothing to do with the main plan and if she never let him get near her again it wouldn't matter in the least.

So why should he care if she smiled at him or not?

He decided he'd be better off not thinking too deeply on that one.

Luckily for him, he'd just looked down at his book again when she glanced up and announced, ''You know, when we went through the cupboards in here yesterday, I noticed some cans way in the back.''

There was something in her tone—something easier, a little more friendly.

His pulse ratcheted up a notch and he quelled a satisfied smile. *Better,* he thought. *Now, don't blow it....*

He shut the battered paperback without marking the page. Next time he picked it up, he'd have to start over, anyway. "Yeah," he said, sounding a hell of a lot more offhand than he felt. He gestured toward the cabinets on the far wall. "In the bottom, on the left." He started to rise.

"No. I'll look."

He sank back to his seat and she got up and went over there, leaving him debating whether to follow her. He decided against it. She *was* loosening up a little. Better let her get looser before he got too close.

She went to her knees, pulled open the cupboard and stuck her head in there. He looked at her backside. Great view. Even with the ugly baggy sweater and too-loose frayed corduroy pants.

"Yes," she said, her voice muffled by the cabinet. "Here they are." She pulled her head out and craned around to grin at him. "Lots of soup, but I see some canned fruit, too."

He got up, after all, and went to stand over her— just to be helpful. She passed him the dusty cans and he set them on the counter above the cabinet.

"That's it." She shut the cabinet doors and stood to read the labels. "Vegetable beef, chicken noodle, cream of asparagus, pears, applesauce..." She gave him a pert look. "Justin. Not a single can of cream of mushroom soup. And no peaches."

Absurdly pleased that she'd remembered the details of his childhood ordeal, he allowed himself to chuckle. "That's a relief. I admit I was getting worried."

"No need to." She brushed his arm—the lightest breath of a touch. Beneath the green sleeve of his sweater, his skin burned as if she'd set a match to it.

Their eyes met. *Zap.* His heart raced faster and the air seemed to shimmer around them. Damned amazing, her effect on him.

Katie smiled wider, a nervous kind of smile. Yes. She *was* trying. She wasn't cutting him out anymore. "So...soup with your sandwiches?"

He nodded. "Vegetable beef—unless that's your favorite?"

She admitted, "I have this thing for cream of asparagus."

"Well, then. Looks like we both get what we want."

Katie went to get ready for bed at ten. Justin said he wanted to read a little longer and then he'd be in.

She knew it was only a pretense. In the hours they'd sat reading, he'd hardly made it through the first few chapters in that book of his. No. He was being thoughtful, giving her a chance to get ready and go to bed in private.

In the ladies' room, she rinsed out her underwear and hung it over the stall door. She washed up and dressed for bed in a wrinkled old pair of red flannel pajamas—thanks, again, to the bags of clothing in the storage room.

She looked at herself in the mirror over the sink and scrunched up her nose at what she saw. Tomorrow, if they were still stuck here, she would have to wash her hair. Maybe she could find some bath towels in the rummage sale stuff—or if not, well, she'd work it out somehow. And really, Justin didn't need to be sitting in the kitchen pretending to read, respecting her need to keep her distance from him after the kiss that had gone too far out in the shed.

"Stupid," she muttered to her own reflection. "I'm being stupid about this and I need to stop." There was nothing alluring or lust-inspiring about the sight of her in flannel pajamas. They buttoned up to here and bagged around her ankles. If Justin saw her getting into bed in them he would not be the least tempted to make mad, passionate love to her.

Truly. In pajamas like these, she was safe from the potential to have sex of any kind.

She peered closer at herself, craned her head forward so her nose met the glass. The question was, why did that depress her?

Oh, come on. She knew why.

Because there had not been nearly enough sex—of any kind—in her life.

"I, Katherine Adele Fenton," she whispered, her breath fogging the glass, "am a cliché. I'm right out of *The Music Man*. I'm Marian the librarian—hiding in the stacks, waiting for some cocky con man to show up and let down my hair for me."

Really, it had to stop. She owed it to librarians everywhere, who, she knew, were a much more outgoing, ready-for-anything bunch than most people gave them credit for.

She pulled back from the mirror and then used her

flannel sleeve to wipe the steamed-up place her breath had left. She stood straight and proud. "I *wanted* him to kiss me and I'm *glad* he kissed me," she announced to the sink and the toilet stall and her soggy underwear hanging from the stall door. "I'm not afraid of my own feelings. I'm an adult and I run my own life and I do it very well, thank you." She *liked* Justin and he clearly liked her and she wasn't running away from that. Not anymore.

Yes, there was always danger—when you really liked someone, when you put your heart on the line. Things that mattered inevitably involved a certain amount of risk.

Her shoulders back and her head high, Katie marched to the ladies' room door and pulled it wide.

Justin looked up from his book when she entered the kitchen. The bewildered expression on his handsome face made her want to grab him and hug him and tell him it would be all right. She didn't, of course. There were a few things that needed saying before they got around to any hugging.

"Katie? Everything okay?"

She marched over, yanked out the chair opposite him and dropped into it. "It was very sweet of you, to sit in here with that book you're not really interested in and wait until I had time to put on these ugly old pajamas and get into bed. But it's not as if we had to share a bathroom or anything." She raised her arms and looked down at her baggy bedroom attire. "And as you can see, this outfit reveals absolutely nothing of my, er, feminine charms. We're both perfectly safe from any, um, dangerous temptation, don't you think?'' She lifted her head and met his eyes.

They were gleaming. ''Well, Katie. I don't know. You look pretty damn tempting to me.''

''Liar,'' she muttered, flattered in spite of herself.

He put up a hand, palm out, as if testifying in court. ''Sexiest woman I ever saw.''

''Oh, yeah, right.''

''Must be the color. You know what they say about red. The color of power. And sex.''

She sat up straighter. ''Power, huh? I kind of like that.''

In his eyes she could see what he almost said: *But what about sex?* He didn't, though.

Probably afraid she'd get spooked and shut him out again.

''Justin?'' Her heart pounded painfully inside her rib cage. She had things to say and she was going to say them, but that didn't make it easy.

''Yeah?''

''Justin, are you after my money?''

With zero hesitation, he replied, ''No.''

She peered at him through narrowed eyes. ''Are you *sure*?''

''Yeah. Money's not an issue for me. I have plenty of my own. Now, anyway. And I earned every damn penny of it.''

Her face felt as if it had turned as red as her pajamas and her heart beat even faster. She did believe him. If that made her a total fool, well, so be it.

He added, ''But don't take me wrong. I don't mind

that you're rich. Hey, I'm glad you are. It's always better, don't you think, to have money than not to?''

Katie thought about that. ''Sometimes I'm not so sure. Money can…isolate a person. It can make it so it's hard to believe that someone might like you, just for yourself.''

''Katie.''

She put her hand against her heart. Really, did it need to keep pounding so awfully fast? ''Yeah?''

''I do like you. For yourself.''

She realized she believed that, too, and her galloping heart slowed a little. But she wasn't finished yet. ''There's more.''

''Shoot.''

''Did you know that I was…?'' Oh, this was so awkward.

He helped her out. ''Rich?''

She gulped. ''Yes. Did you know I was a wealthy woman before you got up on that stage at the town hall and 'married' me?''

''I did.''

She blinked. ''Who told you?''

He chuckled. ''Some of those spectators were pretty damn drunk. When they heard I'd be playing your groom, I got a lot of ribbing. You know the kind. How you were not only a cute little thing, you were loaded, too. How, if I played my cards right, I might catch myself an heiress.''

Katie scrunched up her nose. ''A cute little thing?''

He shrugged. ''Drunk talk. You know how it goes. And you might like to know, I got more than one warning that I'd better be good to you. They were joking—but the look in every eye said I'd pay if I messed with their favorite librarian.''

That brought a smile. ''They did? They told you to be good to me?''

He nodded. ''So you've got backup, in case you were worried.''

She looked him directly in the eye. ''I guess I *was* worried. And scared. The truth is, in the past couple of years, I've had a tendency to let fear run my life. But I've had a little talk with myself. Fear is not going to rule me. Not anymore. I…well, I like you. And I think you like me.''

''I do. Very much.''

A sweet warmth spread through her. ''So then. I'd like to get to know you better.''

His gaze didn't waver. ''And I want to know you.''

Chapter Five

They talked for hours, lying in their separate beds in the central display room.

Katie told him about Ted Anders. She'd met Ted at CU. He was tall and tan and blond, a prelaw student. Interesting to talk to, with a good sense of humor—and charming, too. Extremely so. Ted had lavished attention on Katie. She'd started to believe she'd found the right guy for her—until she went to a party up on "the hill," where a lot of the students shared apartments. The place was packed, a real crowd scene. She got separated from Ted and when she found him again, he had his arm around a cute redhead.

"He was so busy putting a move on her, he didn't even see that I was watching," Katie said. "I heard him tell her how he'd like to, uh, 'jump her bones,' but he couldn't afford to. He had a 'rich one' on a string and he wasn't blowing that 'til he'd clipped at least a couple of her millions.''

''I hope you reamed him a new one right there and then.'' Justin sounded as if he wouldn't have minded doing that for her.

She laughed—and it felt so good. To think about something that had hurt so much at the time and realize it was just a memory now, one with no power to cause her pain. ''In case you didn't notice, I'm not big on public displays.''

He chuckled. ''Well, yeah. As a matter of fact, I did notice. So, what *did* you do?''

''I went home to my apartment. Eventually, Ted must have realized I'd left. He came knocking on my door. I confronted him then. He started laying on the sweet talk. But I wasn't buying. Once he saw he couldn't talk his way back into a relationship with me, he said a few rotten things, trying to hurt me a little worse than he already had. But he knew it was over.''

''And that made you sure every man you met would be after your money?''

''Well, there was another, er, incident.''

''At CU?''

''No. Right here in town, not long after I came home to stay and took the job as librarian. He was a local guy, Jackson Tully. He'd grown up here and gone to Thunder Canyon High ten years before I did. After high school, he'd moved away and then moved back and opened a souvenir shop on Main. He asked me out and he seemed nice enough. We had several dates and…oh, he was funny and sweet and I started to think—''

''That he was *the one*.''

She made a face at the shadowed rafters above. ''Oh, I don't know. I thought that we had something good, I guess. That it might really go somewhere.''

''As in wedding bells and happily ever after?''

''That's right.''

''So then…?''

''Well, he proposed.''

''Marriage?''

''What else?''

He made a low sound. ''I can think of a few other things, but I won't go into them. So the money-grubbing shop owner proposed and you said yes.''

She pushed the blankets down a little and rested her arms on top of them. ''Well, no. I didn't say yes. I did…care for him, but I wasn't sure. I said I wanted to think about it. And while I was thinking, his mom came to see me. She's a nice woman, Lucille Tully is. A member of the Historical Society, as a matter of fact.''

''Isn't everyone?''

''In Thunder Canyon?'' She considered. ''Well, just about everyone over forty or so is.''

''And Lucille Tully said…''

''That she loved her son, but I was a 'sweet girl' and she couldn't let me say yes to him without my knowing the truth.''

''Which was?''

''Jackson had had two bankruptcies. His souvenir shop—which Lucille had given him the money to open—wasn't doing well and he'd told his mother more than once that as soon as he married the librarian, she could have her money back. He'd close the store. Why slave all day long, catering to pushy tourists in some stupid shop when he'd be set for life and he could focus on enjoying himself.''

"Spending your money, I take it?"

Katie sighed. "Lucille cried when she told me. I felt terrible for her. It just broke her heart, the whole thing.''

"So you said no to the gold-digging Jackson Tully.''

"I did.''

"And where is he now?"

"Couldn't say. His shop went under and he left town. So far as I know, he hasn't been back.''

"And what about the mother?"

"What do you mean?"

"Come on, Katie. I've known you for two whole days and I can already guarantee that you took care of her.''

"Well, if you must know, I had Caleb buy the shop.''

"With *your* money.''

"That's right. Caleb made sure Jackson paid Lucille back. Then Caleb sold the shop for me. At a profit. Everybody came out all right—financially, at least. And by then, Jackson had moved on. Lucille doesn't talk about him much, not to me, anyway— and you know, now I look back on both Jackson and Ted Anders, I realize I was pretty darn lucky. At least I didn't marry them. At least I found out what kind of men they really were before I took any kind of irrevocable step.''

There was silence from the narrow cot on the other side of the room.

She grinned into the darkness. ''Justin? Have I put you to sleep?''

''I'm wide-awake.''

''You sound so serious…''

A pause, and then, ''Those two were a couple of prime-grade SOBs—and you're right, at least you didn't marry either of them.''

''No, I didn't. And Justin…''

''What?''

''I did have a *nice* boyfriend or two. Nothing that serious, but they were good guys. I actually enjoyed high school. How many people can say that?''

''Good point.'' The way he said that made her sure he was one of the ones who couldn't.

''And I went to both proms—junior and senior. For my senior prom I wore a—''

He made a loud snoring sound.

She sat up and the bed creaked in protest. ''I might have to unscrew one of these pineapple finials and throw it at you.''

He sat up, too. ''Please don't hurt me.''

They looked at each other through the darkness. For pajamas, he'd found a pair of cheap black sweats in the storage room. In the minimal light, he was hardly more than a broad-shouldered shadow. But then his white teeth flashed with his smile.

She flopped back down. ''I promise to let you go to sleep. Soon.''

His blankets rustled. "No hurry. As it happens, I don't have any early appointments tomorrow."

"Okay, then. But remember. I offered to shut up...."

"And I turned you down."

She raised her arms and slid her hands under her hair, lacing them on the too-fat pillow, cupping her head. "Sheesh. I'm starting to feel as if I know you so well. But I don't even know where you live—in Bozeman, right?" He made a noise in the affirmative. "Your house...what's it like?"

"Four thousand square feet. Vaulted ceilings. Lots of windows. Good views."

"And redwood decking, on a number of levels— with a huge hot tub, right?"

"How did you know that?"

"Oh, Justin. How else could it be? And come on. Fair's fair. Women?"

He let out a big, fake sigh. "Okay. What do you need to know?"

She thought of the way he'd kissed her out in the shed—and when they got "married." And she realized it had never occurred to her that there might be someone special in his life. A live-in girlfriend, or even...

A wife.

No. No, that couldn't be. He could never have kissed her like that if there already was a special woman in his life—not the way he had when they'd pretended to get married.

And certainly not the way he'd kissed her out in the shed.

And if he *could*...

Oh, God. Here she'd made such a big deal about asking him if he was after her money. And she hadn't bothered to find out if he had a wife.

"It's too damn quiet over there." His voice was deep and rough—and teasing.

"Justin, are you married?"

There was dead silence, and then, "What the hell made you think that?"

"Nothing. It's just that I never asked—and you never said."

He swore under his breath. "I've done one or two things I'm not...thrilled I had to do, I'll admit." She wondered what, exactly. But before she had time to ask, he said, "But I never will do that—play one woman when I'm married to another." He sounded totally disgusted with the very idea.

Which pleased her greatly. "Er...that would be a no?"

"Yeah. A no. A *definite* no—and let me guess your next question. Do I have a steady woman in my life?"

She was grinning again. "Yep. That would be it."

"That's a no, too."

"Well." She put her arms down on the blankets again. "Okay, then. Were you *ever* married?"

"Never. Too busy making something from nothing. Serious relationships just didn't fit into the equation."

"You're career-driven?"

"I guess one of these days I'll have to slow down and get a life. But I like what I do."

"What about...a high school sweetheart?"

A brief silence, then, "High school. Now, that was a long time ago."

She realized she didn't know his age. "You're how old?"

"Thirty-two. And as I think I told you, when I was growing up, we moved around a lot—no chance to fit in. I dated now and then. It never went anywhere."

"You make yourself sound like a lonely guy."

He grunted. "No need for a pity party. There have been women, just not anything too deep or especially meaningful."

There have been women…

Well, of course there had. He had those compelling good looks. That kind of dangerous, mysterious air about him. A lot of women really went for the dangerous type. And yet, he could be so charming, so open, about himself and his life. And then there was the way he could kiss….

Katie slipped her hand up, to touch her lips, remembering.

Oh, yes. A guy who could kiss like that would have had some practice.

But there was no special woman. No secret wife.

In spite of that aura of danger he could give off, Justin Caldwell was an honest guy—and Katie really did like that in a man.

The next day was Monday. They woke to find the snow still coming down, though not as thickly as the day before. On the ground, it reached halfway to the porch roof. After they'd dressed and had their fresh coffee and two-day old sandwiches, they both went out to the front porch, though the door could barely clear the spill of snow that sloped onto the boards of the porch floor.

"Shoveling our way out of here will be a hell of a challenge," Justin said.

She nodded. "If it would only stop coming down. Give us a chance to take a crack at it, give the snow-plow a break. It's piling up faster than anyone could hope to clear it."

Back inside, the phone was still out. And the boom box picked up the usual crackling static.

They made their way along the narrow covered path to the shed, where they spent a couple of hours cleaning up after Buttercup and keeping her company. Twice, the horse got feisty with Justin. She tried again to head-butt him into the hay. And once, in a deft move, she actually got the collar of his jacket between her teeth. She yanked it off him.

When he swore at her, she instantly dropped it. White tail swishing grandly, she turned for the doors that led out to a wall of snow.

"See?" he demanded. "That horse hates me."

"Could be affection," Katie suggested.

"Yeah, right." He picked up the old coat and brushed it off.

"Hey, at least it didn't land in a pile of manure."

He made a low sound, something halfway between a chuckle and a grunt, and slipped his arms into the sleeves. "Are we done here?"

She agreed that they were.

Back in the museum, Katie decided to get busy on the day's main project: clean hair.

Over her baggy tan pants, she put on a wrinkled white T-shirt with a boarded-up mine shaft and Stay Out, Stay Alive! emblazoned across the front. The rummage sale bags didn't come through with a bath towel. But hey. She had plenty of personal-size bottles of shampoo—in herbal scent and ''no tears.'' And there was a stack of dish towels in the kitchen cupboard. She'd make do with a few of them.

Then came the big internal debate—to use the bathroom sink: more private. Or the one in the kitchen: bigger.

Bigger won. Justin had seen her in her ugly sweater and saggy pants wearing zero makeup; he'd seen her in the distinctly unflattering flannel pajamas. He could certainly stand to get a look at her bending over a sink with her hair soaking wet.

Glamour just wasn't something a girl could maintain in a situation like this.

Justin sat at the table playing solitaire with a deck he'd found in the desk out front and tried not to sneak glances at Katie while she washed her hair.

The faint perfume from the shampoo filled the air, a moist, flowery scent. And the curve of her body as she bent over the sink, the shining coils of her wet hair, the creamy smoothness of her neck, bared with her hair tumbling into the sink, even the rushing sound of the water, the way it spilled over the vulnerable shape of her skull, turning her hair to a silken stream and dribbling over her satiny cheek and into her eyes....

He couldn't stop looking.

He had a problem. And he knew it.

There was something about her. Something soft and giving. Something tender and gentle and smart and funny…and sexy, too. All at the same time.

Something purely feminine.

Something that really got to him.

Every hour he spent with her, he wanted her more. It was starting to get damn tough—keeping it friendly. Not pushing too fast.

Too fast? He restrained a snort of heavy irony liberally laced with his own sexual frustration.

Too fast implied there would be satisfaction.

There wouldn't be. And he damn well had to keep that in mind.

Even if she said yes to him, there was no way he was taking her to bed while they were locked in here.

He couldn't afford that. Not without protection. And though the bags in the storage room seemed to have no end of useful items in them, what they didn't have were condoms.

He knew because he'd actually checked to see if they did.

And since he'd checked, he'd found himself thinking constantly of all the ways a man and a woman could enjoy each other sexually short of actual consummation.

He grabbed up a card to move it—and then couldn't resist stealing another look.

She'd rinsed away most of the flowery-scented shampoo, but there was a tiny froth of it left on her earlobe. She rinsed all around it, but somehow the water never quite reached it.

He gritted his teeth to keep from telling her to get that bit of lather on her ear. He ordered his body to stay in that chair. Every nerve seemed to sizzle.

Damned if he wasn't getting hard.

Ridiculous, he thought. *This has to stop....*

He looked down at the card in his hand—the jack of spades—and couldn't even remember what he'd meant to do with it.

This was bad. Real bad.

Some kind of dark justice?

Hell. Probably.

He meant to use her as another way to get to Caleb. Too bad he hadn't realized how powerfully—and swiftly—*she* would end up getting to *him.*

At last, she tipped her head enough that the water flowed over that spot on her ear. The little dab of lather rinsed away and down the drain.

Late that afternoon, Justin went out to the front of the museum to stoke the fire in the stove. Katie busied herself in the kitchen, putting away the few dishes that stood drying on the drain mat, wiping the table and the counters. The tasks were simple ones, easily accomplished.

After she rinsed the sponge and set it in the little tray by the sink, she found herself drawn to the window. She wandered over and stood there watching the snow falling through the graying light, wondering how long it would be until they could dig out, until the old mare in the shed got a little room to stretch her legs and a nice, big bucket of oats.

Justin returned from the front room. She glanced

over and gave him a smile and went back to gazing out at the white world beyond the glass.

He went to the sink. She heard the water running, was aware of his movements as he washed his hands and then reached for the towel. A moment later, she heard his approach, though she didn't turn to watch him come toward her.

It was so still out there. Snowy and silent. The museum sat at the corner, where Elk Avenue turned east. There was a full acre to either side, free of structures—what had, years ago, been part of the schoolyard. Katie could see the shadowy outline of the first house beyond the museum property. The Lockwoods lived there—a young couple with two children, a boy and a girl, eight and nine: Jeff and Kaylin, both nice kids. Kaylin loved to read. She and Jeff always attended the library's weekly children's story hour, run by Emelda Ross.

There was a light on in the Lockwood house, the gleam of it just visible, through the veil of falling snow. Katie hoped the Lockwoods were safe in there, with a cozy fire and plenty to eat.

"Katie…" Justin brushed a hand against her shoulder. The warm thrill his touch brought lightened her spirits—at least a little. "Watching it won't make it stop coming down."

She thought of the noisy beer drinkers back at the hall, of dear old Emelda, who'd stuck it out when all the other members of the Historical Society had left. "I was just thinking of everyone back at the hall. I hope they're all safe."

"They had food, didn't they?"

She looked from all that blinding white to the man beside her. "Yes. The potluck, remember? People brought all those casseroles."

"So they'll get by." He gave her a steady look, a look meant to reassure. "They have food. And rest-rooms. Water—and the sidewalks on Main are all covered. That's going to make it a lot easier for them to get out than it will be for us."

He was right. She added, "And the first place the snowplow will be working is up and down Main."

"See? They'll be okay."

But there were others—the ones who'd left the hall before Katie and Justin. "What about the people who left for home? We don't even know if they all made it."

He took her by the shoulders—firmly, but gently. His touch caused the usual reactions: butterflies in her stomach, a certain warmth lower down....

"Katie, you can't do anything about it. We just have to make the best of a tough situation. And so will everyone else."

In her mind's eye, she saw Addy's dear long, aris-tocratic face, her sparkling blue eyes and her prim little smile—and then she pictured Caleb, in that white Stetson he liked to wear, a corner of his mouth quirked up in his rascal's grin. "I don't even know where Addy and Caleb went. One minute they were there, in the hall, and then, when we were up there on the stage, just before the 'Reverend' Green stepped up, I looked out over the crowd and I didn't see either of them."

"They probably went home. Or maybe you just

didn't spot them and they're both still there. Either way, there's not a damn thing you can do about it. Just let yourself believe they're safe—which, most likely, they are.''

''But if—''

He didn't let her finish. ''Worrying about them won't help them. All it'll do is make *you* miserable.''

''But I only—''

''It'll be okay.'' He shook her, lightly. ''Got it?''

She made herself give him a nod.

He studied her for a long moment. Then he demanded, ''Why the hell do you still look so worried, then?''

She only shrugged. What was there to say? He was right. There was no point in worrying. But when she thought of Addy and Caleb—when she looked at the Lockwood's faint light across the snow-covered museum yard—she simply couldn't help it.

''Hey,'' Justin murmured. ''Hey, come on…'' He pulled her to him.

She didn't even consider resisting—why should she? Maybe she'd had her doubts about him at first. But gently and tenderly, he'd dispelled her reservations. She knew she could trust him now.

He wrapped those long, hard arms around her and she pressed herself close to him, tucking her head under his chin, laying her ear against the leaping reindeers on the front of his sweater, right over his heart, which beat steady and strong, if a little too fast. She smiled to herself—a woman's smile. His embrace brought more comfort than words could. And the sound of his heartbeat, racing in time to hers?

That wasn't comforting, not in the least. That sound thrilled her. It stole her breath.

She hoped—she *prayed*—that everyone else trapped by the storm was at least safe and warm with plenty to eat.

For herself, though, there was no place she would rather be than right here in the Thunder Canyon Historical Museum held close and safe in Justin's arms.

For herself, she was beginning to believe that getting snowed-in with Caleb's business associate was the best thing that had ever happened to her.

She felt his lips against her hair and snuggled closer. "Justin?"

"Hmm?"

She tipped her head up to find those blue eyes waiting.

And his lips…

It just seemed the most natural thing. To lift her mouth, to let her eyes drift shut.

His mouth touched hers—so lightly. Heat flared and flowed through her. Her lips burned. Her pulse raced.

Then he lifted away.

She didn't want that.

Oh, no. She wanted more. Much more.

"Justin?" She opened her eyes to look up at him again.

"Hmm?"

"Justin, do you like kissing me?"

He muttered something very low, probably a swear word. "I do. I like it too damn much."

"I like kissing you, too," she confessed. "I like it a lot."

His gaze scanned her face. "So...?"

She slid her hands up to encircle his neck. "Please. Kiss me some more."

"Katie," he whispered, and that was all. Then his mouth swooped down and covered hers.

Chapter Six

They kissed, standing there at the window, with the white hush of the snow drifting down outside, for the longest, sweetest time. When Justin finally lifted his head, he asked, husky and low, "Convinced?"

She blinked up at him. "Of what?"

"That I like kissing you?"

She pretended to consider that question—which, truthfully, required no consideration at all—and then at last, she said, "I think you should kiss me again—just to make sure."

"Ah. To make sure..."

"That's right."

He cupped her face—cradled it, really. His hands were warm and cherishing against her cheeks. And then he lowered his head again and his mouth touched hers and...

Oh, there was nothing like it. Kissing Justin.

Kissing Justin was everything kissing ought to be. His mouth played on hers and his arms slid around her to hold her close and she felt his heart beating, hard and steady, against her breasts, keeping pace with hers.

That time, when he lifted his head, she said in a voice gone husky with pleasure, "I'm getting it now. You like kissing me."

"Yeah. I do."

And to prove it, he kissed her again—a hard, deep, long one that melted her midsection and turned her knees to rubber.

She clutched his shoulders and sagged against him, feeling very aroused, totally shameless. She liked this feeling. She liked it a lot. There was so much she'd been missing. Not anymore, though. "I don't know. If you're going to *keep* kissing me, I might just have to sit down."

"Let me help you with that." He grabbed the nearest chair, spun it around and dropped into it—pulling her with him, onto his lap.

Her breath hitched as she landed.

"Better?" he asked.

"Oh, I think…"

He nuzzled her neck, pressed a burning kiss at the place where her pulse beat close to the skin. A lovely shiver went through her and she sighed.

"You think what?" He breathed the words against her throat—and then he caught her earlobe between his teeth. He worried it, lightly, as she clutched his shoulders and sighed some more.

"Oh, Justin…"

His tongue touched the place where his teeth had been, a velvety moist caress. He licked the tender hollow behind her earlobe. Briefly, with the very tip of that bold tongue, he dipped into her ear.

She let out a low moan. She was supposed to be telling him…something. The question was what. "I…well…"

He threaded his fingers up into her hair and he brushed a line of butterfly-light kisses along her jaw. "What you think…"

"Think?" The word sounded alien. Not surprising. At that moment, thinking was the last thing on her mind.

He cradled the back of her head, holding her still, bringing his mouth a breath's distance from hers. "You were telling me…what you think…"

"I…well…"

One corner of his mouth lifted in a knowing smile. "Well, what?"

"I forgot." And she had.

She'd forgotten everything. Nothing mattered, at that moment, but this man and the drugging pleasure of his hands on her body, his mouth so close to hers. "Kiss me. Again."

He obeyed. His mouth covered hers and she wrapped her arms around his neck and kissed him back with boundless enthusiasm.

This time when they came up for air, he took her by the waist and held her away from him. "We'd better stop." His voice was rough—almost curt.

She started to argue. She didn't want to stop. But

maybe he was right. Where could they go from here, except to the bed with the pineapple finials?

Was she ready for that yet?

As much as she liked kissing him and feeling his hands on her body…as much as she liked *him*…as much as she couldn't help but start to think that there was something very special going on here, between them…

That was a big, fat…maybe. Even given what she'd decided that morning—about the lack of sex of any kind in her life, about how she was going to stop being a cliché. Even given all that, well, they didn't need to rush this, did they? There was nothing that said they couldn't take their time. Though she was determined to get herself a sex life one of these days very soon—and with Justin—she *was* old-fashioned in some ways. She believed making love should be special. And it *shouldn't* be rushed.

He smoothed a wild curl of hair off her cheek. "Listen." His eyes teased—and burned, too. "I want you to get up. And I want you to do it very carefully."

She frowned, and then she understood. Oh, my. Yes. She could *feel* him and it was just like out in the shed the day before. He was very happy to be near her.

"Oh. Oh, well. You're, uh—"

"Katie."

"Uh. Yeah?"

"We don't need a lot of discussion here."

"Oh. Well, no. Of course, we don't." She put her feet on the floor and stood, backing off a little. Her gaze dropped to—oops. Blinking, she yanked her chin up and gave him a nervous smile. "Is that better?"

"Not really." The chair legs scraped the floor as he turned to face the table—a deft movement, in spite of the pained grunt that accompanied it. Now his lap, and the obvious bulge there, was hidden by the tabletop. "In a few minutes, I'll be fine."

"Well. Good."

He folded his hands on the tabletop. "It would help if you wouldn't stand there looking so damn... thoroughly kissed."

Her wobbly smile widened. "But Justin. I *am* thoroughly kissed."

He commanded sternly, "Think of an activity. One that doesn't involve kissing."

She pretended to give his request great thought. "Well, now...we could go out and visit Buttercup again."

He scowled. "Let me qualify. Something that doesn't involve kissing *or* that mean old mare."

"Hmm. It's a tough one."

He shifted in his chair, wincing. "Work with it."

An idea came to her. "I know. We could tour the museum."

"Why? I've seen it."

"Now, wait a minute. I'll admit, you've seen about all there is to see in the central room. But the two side rooms...why, Justin, you've hardly had a look. And you know, on second thought, you've only *slept* in the central room. That's not the same as a tour."

He let out a dry chuckle. "I've been up close and

personal with that dinky narrow cot of mine. Isn't that enough?"

"Oh, no. You have to see it all. I insist. The rich and varied history of Thunder Canyon is right here, only a few steps away. You owe it to yourself to explore it."

"I can't wait."

"Don't get so excited," she instructed, deadpan.

He tipped his head toward his lap. "I'm trying."

She couldn't help it, she burst into a laugh—and then she frowned. "You know, now I think about it, it's not really fair that I always get the big bed."

"Katie. I'm fine with the cot."

"But still, it's only right that we—"

"Stop. I *love* that cot of mine and you can't have it. Now, I want you to go on ahead of me, reconnoiter the display rooms, get your tour guide rap down pat. Let me, er, relax a little here."

She decided not to remark on what might need relaxing. "Hey, we could even take some rags in there, dust the display cases..."

He sent her a pained look. "The fun never ends."

She was dusting a case full of old gold-panning equipment in the south room when he joined her. She handed him a rag and one of the two bottles of spray cleaner she'd found in the storage room.

"I thought this was a tour," he groused. But he was grinning as he took the rag and bottle.

"The museum is a community effort," she told him tartly. "We all have to pitch in."

"Hey. I'm all for that." He saluted her with the spray bottle.

They set to work dusting the cases. As they sprayed and polished, she explained about the Montana gold rush that had begun in Idaho, with the Salmon River strike. "Gold fever came to Montana in 1862. John White and company, en route to the Salmon River mines, found gold on the way—at Grasshopper Creek." She paused to point out the exact location on the big laminated territorial map on the wall. "Bannack—" She pointed again. "—Montana's first boomtown, sprang up during that rush."

"Just like in the reenactment Saturday."

"That's right." She beamed at him. "For a man who didn't have the benefit of a Montana education, you're a very good student."

"Thank you. I try."

"Shall I continue?"

"By all means."

So she explained that the gold rush had lasted into the early 1890s, starting with placer mining and then, as the streams petered out, panning and sluicing gave way to hardrock mining. "There were a number of mines right here in the Thunder Canyon area. Caleb still owns one, as a matter of fact. It's called the Queen of Hearts."

"So I heard."

"From Caleb?"

"More or less." At her questioning look, he explained, "I'm in business with Caleb. My people have gone over his books, with Caleb's full knowledge and consent, of course. As a result, I know a lot about what his assets are, as well as which pies he's got his fingers in. I understand the gold mine's been shut down for years. 'Played out,' isn't that what they say in the trade?"

"That's exactly what they say—and I'll bet you didn't know that Caleb's great-grandfather, Amos Douglas, won the Queen in a card game." She sprayed and rubbed with her cloth. "Or so the legend goes."

"Fascinating."

She glanced his way, and found he was watching her. Her body went warm all over. "Less staring, more cleaning," she advised.

Once they'd finished in the mining display, she took him to the central room, where they dusted the tables and she told him the origins of the most interesting pieces.

She gestured grandly with her dusting rag in the direction of the big bed with the pineapple finials and the heavy, dark bureaus, vanity set, bed tables and chairs that surrounded it. "This bedroom suite was used at the Lazy D during Amos Douglas's time. It's of the finest mahogany."

"Only the best for the Douglases." There was something in his tone—something way too ironic, even cynical. She sent him a puzzled look, but he only shrugged and bent to dust a bedside table.

And she had to agree with him. "It's true. Only the best. For generations, the Douglases have been the wealthiest, most influential family in the area."

"Don't forget to dust those pineapples."

"That's right. If you don't watch it, I may still have

to throw one at you. I want it dust-free if I do.'' She reached up—but the intricately carved end-piece was too high. She couldn't get her rag around it.

Justin stepped closer. ''Allow me.''

Her pulse kicked up a notch, just to have him standing so near, eyes gleaming at her with humor and heat. ''Oh, by all means.'' She bowed and moved back and he did the honors.

Once every surface in the central room had been wiped clean of dust, they proceeded to the north addition, where the personal artifacts of life in Territorial and early-statehood Montana waited to be admired—and the cases that protected them, dusted.

Justin went straight to the tall case containing a mannequin in a faded red satin dress. Cinched tight at the wasp-thin waste, the dress had a deep neckline and lots of black lace trim. The mannequin wore several ropes of fake pearls around her neck, a thick bracelet of glittering jet stones and an ostrich feather in her pinned-up hair. In one hand, she carried a black fan edged with lace. The other hand held the red skirt high, revealing a froth of red and black petticoats—and a fancy black silk garter.

Justin wolf-whistled. ''Love that red dress.''

Katie grinned. ''That dress belonged to one of Thunder Canyon's most memorable early citizens. The Shady Lady, Lily Divine.''

''Is this the part where I say, 'Ooh-la-la'?''

''That would be appropriate, yes. Back in, oh, 1890 or so, Lily owned the Shady Lady Sporting House and Saloon. The building still stands at the corner of Main and Thunder Canyon Road, though the place is now a restaurant and bar called the Hitching Post. The original bar from the Shady Lady is still there, in the building. And a very risqué painting of Lily hangs above it.''

''Risqué, how?''

''In it she wears nothing but a few wisps of strategically draped semitransparent cloth.''

''I have to see that.''

''And if it ever stops snowing, you just might.''

He tipped his head toward the low case beside the mannequin in the red dress. ''A few of Lily Divine's things, I take it?''

''That's right.'' Katie moved in beside him. They looked down at the tortoise shell dresser set in a gold floral design studded with rhinestones, at the black lace gloves and the faded filmy undergarments. There was even a corset—a black one, dripping with red silk ribbons.

''It looks to me like the Shady Lady was a very fun gal.''

Katie shrugged. ''So they say. And not only fun, but a suffragist, as well. Or so some accounts claim.'' He looked up from the case and when their eyes met, she realized she never wanted to look away.

Back to the Shady Lady, some wiser voice in the distant recesses of her mind instructed.

She tuned out that wiser voice. ''Oh, Justin…'' The two words escaped her lips, full of hope and longing, and having nothing at all to do with either the notorious Lily Divine, or with getting the dusting done.

He whispered her name.

Her heart seemed to expand in the prison of her chest.

And at that moment, *not* to kiss him…

Well, that was impossible. It just wouldn't do.

She set down her rag and her spray bottle on the glass case beside her. He did the same.

"Justin," she whispered, thinking she should really try a little harder to resist the overwhelming urge to feel his lips on hers.

"Katie…"

A long moment elapsed. She looked at him and he looked back at her and—

"Oh, Justin, I think we're in trouble here."

He only nodded. His eyes said he knew exactly what kind of trouble she meant.

"We shouldn't," she whispered. "We told ourselves we wouldn't."

"That's right," he agreed, his voice rough and low. "No more kissing."

"It's not a good idea."

"Things could…get out of control."

"Easily."

"It's crazy."

"Wild…"

"Dangerous…"

"Oh, I know," she said.

And then he reached for her.

With a glad cry, she reached back. His arms went around her and all doubt fled.

Eager and oh-so-willing, she lifted her mouth to receive his kiss.

Chapter Seven

"We...have to...be careful..." He whispered the words between quick, hungry kisses.

She nodded. "Oh. Yes. Careful. You're so right."

His mouth closed on hers again, drugging. Magical. She slid her hands up his broad chest to wrap them around his neck, and he caught her wrists. He guided them down, so her arms were straight at her sides.

His fingers slipped over the backs of her hands and he wove them between hers, lightly rubbing—in and out and in again, never quite clasping, flesh brushing flesh, little tingles of excitement zipping through her with every featherlight caress. All the while, as his fingers teased hers, he kissed her, his tongue sweeping her mouth, his lips hot and soft and oh-so-tender.

She moaned as he finally twined his fingers with hers, tightening, curling his hands to fists, so her hands were cradled in his palms, her fingers captured between his. A thoroughly willing captive, she smiled against his lips as he guided her hands around behind her.

Their joined fists resting at the small of her back, he kissed her some more. She sighed at the wonder of it, and gave her mouth up to his.

After forever of the two of them kissing and kissing as if they would never stop, he began walking her backward.

She stumbled at first, surprised. A giddy laugh escaped her; he chuckled in response.

Quickly, she regained her balance, and, as he guided her, she backed up toward the open door to the central room. It was like a dance, a beautiful, slow, erotic dance.

He waltzed her through the open doorway, his mouth locked to hers. On they went, slow, delicious step by slow step, to the turn in the roped-off walkway, and then down toward the wide, high bed that had once graced a guest room at the Lazy D.

There, with only a stretch of rope keeping them from the waiting bed, he paused. She swayed in his hold, her mouth fused to his.

A small cry of loss escaped her when he lifted his head. He eased his strong fingers free of hers and stepped back.

"We should stop now."

For a suspended moment, she gazed up into his gleaming eyes. And then, with a sigh, she rested her head on his shoulder. "You know, you keep saying that."

His arms closed around her, tight and warm. She felt the sweet brush of his lips in her hair as she breathed in the scent of him: of the motel-issue shampoo they'd both used, of his clean skin and a faint hint of the inexpensive aftershave he'd found in the brown bag. "I know I keep saying it," he muttered against her hair. "I just don't seem to be *listening* to myself when I say it."

She lifted her head and captured his blue, blue gaze again. Boldly, she suggested, "We could just go ahead and slip under the rope. We could kick off our shoes, stretch out on the bed...."

His arms dropped away. "And then what?"

She swallowed. "Well, and then, we could...take it from there."

"Take it from there," he repeated, gruffly. "I'd like that. Way too much. But we can't lose our heads here. We've got to be sensible."

Now she was the one repeating after *him.* "Sensible."

"That's what I said."

"I have to admit, I don't feel all that sensible recently. Not since I met you."

That brought a smile to his beautiful mouth. "All my fault, then."

She tipped her chin higher. "No. This thing between us, it's fifty-fifty. You're not leading me anywhere I don't want to go."

He studied her face for a long moment—long enough that she felt a blush begin to burn her cheeks. And then he said flatly, "I've got no condoms. I don't suppose you do?"

"Uh. No. Sorry." She looked down, not embarrassed, exactly, but definitely feeling in over her head.

He put a finger under her chin and made her look at him again. "It's something that has to be considered."

"Oh, I know. You're right. I just…well, we could be careful, couldn't we?"

He swore under his breath. "I keep telling myself the same thing. But I don't feel all that damn careful, and that's the hard truth. Once I get my arms around you, caution flies right out the door."

"I could…be cautious for us." Even as she suggested it, she knew that wouldn't work. When he kissed her, words like *careful* and *caution* vanished from her vocabulary.

He gave her a rueful smile. "No doubt about it. Time to go out and check on that mean mare."

The snow stopped around seven. They were sitting at the table eating applesauce and more of the never-ending sandwiches, when Katie looked across at the light in the Lockwood's window and realized there was no curtain of white obscuring it.

Justin noticed, too. "Tomorrow we can probably start digging out."

"Hey, the phone may even be working soon." She'd checked it just a half an hour before. "And if the snow doesn't start in heavy again, the plow should get to us by tomorrow sometime."

"And we'll be free."

They stared at each other across the expanse of the

tabletop. ''Free...'' She repeated the word softly. And somehow, she couldn't keep from sounding forlorn.

She looked out the window again, at that golden light from the house across the museum yard.

No question that stale sandwiches, wearing other people's ill-fitting cast-off clothes, and sponge baths at the sink in the ladies' room got old very fast. She'd be grateful for a shower, something different to eat, her own clothes to wear. And more than any of those minor inconveniences, it would be a huge relief to know that everyone she ·cared about had come through the unexpected blizzard safe and sound.

But still. They *had* made themselves a private little world here, in the center of the storm. She would miss it—miss just the two of them, all alone. Talking through the night. Kissing. Laughing together. And kissing some more....

She would miss it a lot.

Would she see Justin again, once they were out of here?

She frowned. Well, of course she would. Really, she didn't need to even ask herself the question.

They had a...connection, something special going on between them. She felt it in her bones. This was different from anything she'd known before. Even after what had happened with Ted Anders and Jackson Tully, she had no doubts about Justin.

None at all.

He spoke then. ''For someone who's probably going to be out of this place tomorrow, you're looking pretty glum.''

She turned from the golden light across the way to

meet his waiting eyes. "I want to see you again, when this is over. Do you want to see me?" She was proud, of the steadiness of her voice, that she'd put her own intention right out there, hadn't waited for him to make the first move, handing him all the power and then hoping he'd give her a call.

Oh, yes. Katie Fenton, a cliché no more.

"I do want to see you again. I want that very much."

Her heart leaped—and then something in his eyes spoke to her. Something...not right. "But?"

He blinked. "No buts. I want to see you when we get out of here."

And I will. She thought the words he didn't say.

The silence stretched out. Painful. Empty. She wanted to demand, *And will you?* But somehow, that seemed one step too far. He should say it of his own accord, or not at all.

She wanted him. She *cared* for him. She had no doubt that he wanted and cared for her.

Would it go any further than that?

That secret something behind his eyes was telling her no. "Justin?"

"Yeah?"

"Is there...something else you want to say to me?"

Justin looked at the incredible woman across from him and never wanted to look away.

His chest felt tight—as if something strong and relentless was squeezing it. His gut twisted.

The urge was there, in his clenched gut and his tight chest—an urge almost too powerful to deny.

To tell her everything. To throw over his carefully constructed plans.

To lay it all out for her: what Caleb really was to him and how he meant to make the older man pay for the cruel things he'd done.

To hit her with the whole truth: how from the first night fate threw them together, he'd felt the heat between them and decided to make use of it, to toss her into the mix. How he'd purposely set out to take advantage of the situation, and of her.

It was crazy, even to think he might open his mouth and…

No.

He wasn't going to blow it. He'd waited too long to get to the man who'd ruined his mother's hope and happiness. He had to remember.…

All of it. The times she didn't come home until he was sick with fear and worry. The nights she *was* home, when he'd wake and have that strange, lost feeling and come out of his room to find her at the kitchen table or curled up on the couch, her eyes swollen and red from crying, the end of her cigarette glowing like a burning eye in the dark.

He had to remember.…

The suicide attempts. The never-ending new starts that always went wrong. Caleb's name on her lips like an unanswered prayer the day that she died.…

Of lung cancer. She never would give up those damn cigarettes until the last few months of her life. And by then it was too late. Lung cancer got her—

but Caleb Douglas killed her as sure as if he'd put a gun to her head and pulled the trigger.

Caleb Douglas broke her heart and she never did find a way to mend it again. Justin, just a kid, had been powerless to help her.

He wasn't powerless anymore.

And damned if he was giving up now.

He was set on a course and it was a just course. What he would do was perfectly legal; he had the power now—power Caleb himself had put in his hands—and he would use it.

In the end, if all went according to plan, there would be big profits for everyone. Including Caleb.

That was the beauty of it. Everybody would win.

At least in terms of the bottom line.

He only wished...

Wished.

It was a word for fools, for helpless little boys who spent too much time alone, for boys with no fathers, whose mothers too seldom came home....

He wasn't a little boy anymore.

And he wasn't going to spew his guts to anyone—not even to sweet Katie Fenton who was turning out to be a hell of a lot more woman than he'd ever bargained for.

Those amber eyes were still waiting.

He couldn't stand the disappointment he saw in them. "I *want* to see you when we get out of here, Katie. I want to see you and I *will.*"

And I will.

Now, where the hell had that come from?

He'd been so careful. He'd never actually lied to her.

Not until now.

But then again, he *did* want to see her again.

Though he knew damn well he shouldn't, he wanted to keep on seeing her. He wanted...

A whole hell of a lot more with her than he was ever going to get.

He shouldn't have lied. But the words were out now. No calling them back. In future, he'd just have to keep a closer watch on his tongue.

He silently vowed he would do just that as she watched him with worried eyes.

Chapter Eight

Katie opened her eyes to the sight of the shadowed rafters overhead.

For a second or two, with the soft mist of sleep still fogging her mind, she wondered where she was.

And then she placed herself: the four-poster bed in the Historical Museum. With no windows to let in the light from outside, she couldn't begin to guess what time it was. There *was* one clock. An intricate gold leaf ormolu piece with Cupid strumming a lyre perched on top. It sat on the mantel in the "parlor" area.

She couldn't see the face of it from the bed. Plus, it wasn't wound and always read ten-fifteen.

And what did it matter, anyway, what time it was? She and Justin weren't going anywhere until the snowplow finally showed up. They could sleep all day and stay up all night. There was no schedule, just whatever suited them.

Justin...

What was going on with him?

There had been a certain...reserve—a new distance between them, since dinnertime, when she told him she wanted to see him after they got out of here and asked him if *he* wanted to see her.

He'd definitely withdrawn from her after that. From then on, when she spoke, he gave her single-sentence replies. When she looked at him, his gaze would slide away. Also, it had seemed to her that he was careful to avoid touching her. He kept his distance emotionally—and physically, too.

All evening she'd told herself to let it be. The guy didn't have to be hanging on her every word every minute of the day. Maybe he just wanted a little time to himself. In such close quarters, there was no easy way for him to claim some private space.

But in her heart, she knew it wasn't about lack of privacy. It was about them seeing each other after they got out of here.

It hurt a lot, to admit it to herself, but she was beginning to think she'd gotten things all wrong. She'd read more into this thing between them than was actually there.

Oh, not in terms of herself. She knew how she felt. It was real and strong and...maybe it was love.

Or something very close to it—something that *could be* love, given the time and space to grow.

But just because she was feeling something didn't automatically mean he had to feel it in return.

She'd gone to bed, however long ago that had been, ahead of him. And she'd lain here waiting for him.

He'd yet to come in when she finally fell asleep.

Was he even here now?

She sat up.

Across the room, the too-short, too-narrow cot lay empty, the star quilt smooth and undisturbed, the flat little pillow without a wrinkle.

He hadn't even come to bed.

Quietly, carefully—as if there was someone in the empty room she might disturb should she make a sound—she lay back down.

And popped right back up again.

No. This was wrong. If he didn't want to get anything going with her, well, that was his prerogative and she would learn to accept it.

But she wasn't going to just lie here, worrying. And what about tomorrow? What about whatever time they had left here until the plow came? If she spent that time tiptoeing around him, keeping her head down and her mouth shut, well, wouldn't that be just like the woman she'd told herself she wasn't going to be anymore? Wouldn't that be like Katie, the cliché?

She needed to clear the air between them.

How, exactly, to do that, she wasn't quite sure. But it certainly wouldn't get done with her lying here in bed agonizing over what had gone wrong and him off somewhere in another room doing whatever the heck he was doing.

She shoved the covers back and slid her stocking feet to the floor.

* * *

"Justin."

He turned from his own dark reflection in the window to find Katie standing in the doorway to the central room, wearing her wrinkled red pajamas and a pair of fat wool socks, blinking against the bright overhead kitchen light.

A slow warmth spread through him, just to see her standing there. It was that feeling of well-being and contented relief a man gets when he comes in from the cold and finds a cheery fire waiting—that feeling multiplied about a thousand times.

Damn, she looked good, all squinty-eyed with a sleep mark on her soft cheek and her dark hair a tangled halo all around her sweet face. Had there ever been a woman so outright adorable? Not in his experience, and that had been varied, if not especially meaningful.

She stuck out a hand in the direction of the book that lay open on the table in front of him. "Still on chapter three, I'll bet."

He glanced down at the book in question, then back up at her, an ironic smile twisting his lips. "Page sixty-seven, to be exact."

She wrapped her arms around herself. Her soft mouth was pursed tight. "Look. Mind if I sit down?"

The set of her mouth, the determined look in her eyes, her defensive posture—they all told him more than he wanted to know.

No doubt about it. Katie had questions.

Which meant he would have to try to answer them honestly, but without ever telling her the whole truth.

Things got ugly when a man had too much to hide. He probably should have known that when he started this whole charade. Hell. He *had* known it. And he'd been willing to live with the ugliness.

Then.

He gave her an elaborately casual shrug and closed the book. "Sure. Take a seat."

She marched over, yanked out the chair opposite him, and plunked herself down into it, unwrapping her arms from around herself and folding her hands in her lap.

"Okay…" He drew the word out, eyeing her sideways. "What's up?"

She craned around to get a look at the kitchen clock. When she faced him again, she replied, "Well, *you* are. It's three-fifteen in the morning and you're just sitting here, staring out the window."

He lounged back in his chair, displaying an ease he didn't feel. "And this is a problem for you?"

"No No, of course not." She huffed out a frustrated-sounding breath. "You can sit here all night if you want. What's bothering me is…" She ran out of steam, sucked in another big breath, and started again. "Look. I spent most of last night staying out of your way, and *you* spent most of it avoiding looking, talking or getting too close to me. I just, well, I'd like that to stop and I came out here to ask you what I could do to make that happen."

Her distress was palpable. He hated to see her so miserable, and he hated worst of all that he was the cause of her unhappiness.

But what the hell did he have to tell her?

Half-truths.

And when half-truths failed him, outright lies.

He wanted out of this—out of this damned museum, away from the reality that he was using her.

He didn't want to use her anymore. It had been a bad idea from the first and he wanted to walk away from it.

But there was no walking away now. The damage was done. She cared for him. When it all went down, she would be hurt, and hurt bad. There was no getting away from that now.

Even if he gave up his original plan to see that Caleb Douglas paid—which he wasn't about to do— he would still end up hurting her. It was simply too late to walk away and leave her untouched.

Untouched.

An interesting word choice given the plain fact that all he wanted to do was reach out.

And touch…

"Justin," she prompted, when he went too long without answering her. "Did you hear one thing I said to you?" A deep frown creased her brow.

He resisted the powerful urge to rise, to go to her, to smooth that frown away. "I heard you. Every word. Go on."

"Ahem. Well. The truth is I know very well why I stayed out of your way—because it seemed to me that you were avoiding me. *Were* you?"

"Yeah." What else was there to say? "I was."

"Why?"

Why? He should have known that one was coming. What to say now? How to weasel out of this one…

And then, out of nowhere, the exact right words seemed to well up of their own accord. "Because I want you. Because I want to *be* with you. And because it scares the hell out of me, that I do—and how much I do."

The words took form and he let them out and…

Damned if they weren't the absolute truth. More truth than he wanted to face himself, let alone share with her.

But he *had* shared them.

What did that mean?

Where was he headed with this?

Hell if he even knew.

Her soft face had gone softer still, all the worried tension melting out of it. Her eyes shone and her pursed-up mouth had relaxed to its usual sweet fullness. "Oh, Justin…" She lifted a hand from her lap and stretched it across the table to him. "Come on. Take a chance. Take a chance on me."

And before he could think twice, he was leaning toward her, reaching right back. Their hands met and heat shot up his arm, broke into a million swift, burning arrows that splintered off in all directions, hitting every nerve in his body at once.

All he could say was one word: her name. "Katie."

And then, as one, they stood. They stepped around the barrier of the table and there was a moment—painful and electric—when he almost managed to make himself let go, almost stepped back, almost told her, *Katie, I can't. Can't touch you, can't hold you…*

But the pull was too strong. It wouldn't be denied. He gathered her in and she landed against him, soft and warm and so willing, smelling of shampoo and sweetness, naked beneath the fuzzy red flannel.

"Katie." He buried his face in her fragrant hair. "Katie."

She nuzzled his chest, pressed her lips there, sent a warm, thrilling breath through the wool of the old sweater. The warmth spread, borne on that breath, a caress of hope and life itself. He held her tighter.

And she turned her head, pressing her mouth to his neck, a velvety pressure. Her lips opened slightly. He felt the wet brush of her tongue.

He groaned deep in his throat and an answering sound came from her, a soft, heated, purring sound. It vibrated through him, that sound, right down to the core of him.

He felt himself harden in an instant, and he did what he had to do, what he longed to do, sliding his hands down, over the tempting swell of her hips and under, tucking her into him, making her feel him, feel his need and his hunger.

She gasped, the sound purely female, speaking better than any words could of her eagerness, of her complete surrender.

Mine. The word exploded in his brain, bright as a shooting star in a dark winter world. *Mine.*

She gasped again and she tipped her head back, offering her mouth.

He took it, his blood roaring in his ears, his body burning, on fire.

All his lies, all his scheming, his lifelong quest for justice—all that was nothing. There was only Katie, the promise of Katie, the *truth* of Katie, held close in his hungry arms.

As he plunged his tongue into her eager mouth and cupped her bottom in his hands, pressing her harder into him, as his blood pounded through his veins and his heart beat so hard it was like thunder in his ears, he knew....

This...*this* was what mattered. This woman's tender heart, her lips, her breath, her yearning, willing body.

This was his truth. His real justice.

The truth that could save him.

The truth he could never claim.

He knew he had to stop this, that he owed it to her.

Somehow, from some deep hidden resource of rightness within him, he managed to break the never-ending kiss.

He tore his mouth from hers, groaning at the effort. "Katie."

But she only reached up, touched his mouth and whispered, "Shh, it's okay."

He bit the soft pad of her finger. She cried out—not in pain; it had been a gentle bite—but in hunger, with a fire that answered his own.

Her cry of need broke him. His last resistance shattered into a thousand tiny shards. He surrendered to the pounding of his own blood, the yearning like fire spreading through his veins.

She pulled her hand from his mouth and he cupped her head and claimed her lips again.

He kissed her and she kissed him back and he took a step and she moved with him.

No stumbling, not this time. Backward she went, knowing where he guided her, through the open door to the central room, down the roped-off walkway to...

The big, old bed with the pineapple finials, the bed that had once stood in a Douglas bedroom over a hundred years ago.

Was that irony?

Probably.

Did it matter? Did he care?

Not right then. Right then, there was nothing and no one but Katie in the world.

Nothing mattered, nothing even existed, but her tender lips and the wetness beyond, her soft, willing body, her eager sighs, the light and heat that seemed to radiate from her, warming him down to a place that, until she had found him, had lain forever cold, forever shadowed.

A place unknown even to him.

He held her close, his willing prisoner, with one arm. With the other he reached back, found the hook that held the thick rope to the pole and released it.

He let it drop. With a heavy, final thumping sound, it hit the hardwood floor.

She clasped his shoulders.

And then *she* was the one waltzing *him* backward, around the carved trunk at the end of the bed, to the knotted rag rug that waited beside it.

She pushed him onto the tangled blankets. The bed was high; he had to lift himself up to it, and he did, with little effort, bringing her with him, so she rested on top of him, a tempting pressure all along the length of him.

Until he rolled and captured her beneath him.

"Oh!" Her lids fluttered open and he looked for the briefest, sweetest moment into those honey-brown eyes. "Oh…" And her lashes settled, feather-soft, against her cheeks.

He shut his own eyes and lost himself in the sensation.

Of kissing her. Of touching her.

He slid to the side a little and put his weight on one arm, bringing the other up, laying his hand between her small, soft breasts, feeling the heat of her and beneath that, the strong, hungry beating of her heart.

The buttonholes on the old pajamas were worn and loose. The red plastic buttons slipped free with no difficulty at all. He undid them, one by one, only pausing when he once again got so lost in her kiss he could do nothing but press his mouth tighter to hers.

When all the buttons were undone, he eased the sides of the top open to reveal her beautiful white breasts. He took one in his hand.

"Oh," she cried, and "Oh!" again, as he positioned the hard, pink little nipple for his mouth.

He took it, closing his lips around it, and she moaned as he caught it lightly in his teeth and flicked his tongue across it, felt the puckered nub of flesh tighten all the more. She arched her back and clutched his head, her fingers threaded in his hair. He drew on her sweetness and more cries escaped her. The pleading, hungry sounds enflamed him, driving him on.

To know her.

In spite of everything, in spite of the lies he'd told

and the harm he would do her. To know her, anyway, in the deepest, most complete way.

To find the truth in spite of himself, here, in this moment, in the dark windowless quiet, with the artifacts of other, long-lost lives all around them.

Here among the ghosts of the past.

His body on fire with her, her scent all around him, her yielding flesh under his hands, his heart pounding out her name, it seemed to him he could sense them, those long-lost souls, that he could *feel* them.

The pioneers who came before. The hopeful families seeking a brighter future, the miners struck hard by gold fever, scouring streams, digging into mountainsides, after a fortune destined to elude all but a fortunate few. The merchants, the cattle barons, the Shady Lady in her red dress, lounging provocatively against the bar in her sporting house saloon.

They came to Thunder Canyon with desperate ambition, a grasping, undaunted will to match his own. How many found the dreams they sought?

It was too long ago. He would never know.

He only knew that, for this night, in this moment, he held the happiness he'd never understood he was seeking. *She* was his happiness.

He couldn't hold her past this night. Cold, hard reality *would* intrude. He knew that, too.

But for now, for this brief time in this old bed with Katie in his arms, he was someone else.

He was...

Her groom. And she was his sweet mail-order bride, come in on the train intending to marry a stranger—himself—and start a new life with him out here in the raw, untamed West.

They had said their vows before a drunken crowd of well-wishers and the buckboard pulled by the mean old palomino mare had brought them here.

A sudden blizzard had snowed them in, forcing them, with astonishing swiftness, to know each other.

To want each other.

And now, it was finally time. To seal their vows in the age-old way.

Yes, in some cynical corner of his mind, Justin was more than aware that such wild flights of imagination, such absurd leaps of logic, were ridiculous in the extreme.

But right then, with Katie soft and willing in his arms, he believed them, anyway.

And that was the greatest miracle of all: that right then, Justin Caldwell *believed*.

He captured her other breast in his mouth and she groaned low in her throat, her body arching, offering him more. He moaned in answer, his fingers skimming the creamy flesh of her belly, dipping lower…

"Oh! Oh, yes…"

He murmured soothing, ardent sounds against her breast and he continued to explore the warm, soft curves and hollows of her body.

The pajamas tied at the waist.

Easily dispensed with. He pulled on the tail of the little bow she'd made and the bow gave way. It was a simple matter then to slip his hand beneath the worn flannel…

She gasped and clutched his head tighter against

her breast. He drew on her nipple more strongly and her hips began to rock against the lumpy mattress. She moaned, her fingers loosening in his hair. He lifted his head enough to glance up at her sweet face as she tossed her head on the blankets, her dark hair, alive with static, clinging where it rubbed.

He stroked the inward curve of her smooth belly, dipping a finger into her navel.

Her breath caught. She made small, hungry mewing sounds. He wanted to kiss those sounds from her lips.

And he did, letting go of her breast and taking her mouth once more, as his hand slid upward, to caress the sleek flesh high on her stomach, to clasp the side of her slim waist, to trace the lower curve of her ribs where they arched above her midsection.

By then, the sounds from her throat were pleading ones.

He dared to ease his fingers beneath the flannel again, to stroke the silky curls at the place where her soft thighs joined. She stiffened, but only for a moment.

Soon enough, her hips began rocking again.

He dipped farther down, parting the soft curls, easing a finger into her moist cleft. She bucked hard against his hand and he cupped her, steadying her as he kissed her deeply, his own body aching with the need to be buried within her.

No.

Not yet. This part was for her—and, yes, for him, too.

He wanted to feel her give herself over; he wanted to give her satisfaction first, before he took his own.

Right then, as he stroked her, as her body moved in rhythm to his intimate touch, it came to him. Like a blinding, painful light switching on in velvet darkness, he realized...

It wasn't going to happen.

Ridiculous fantasies of past lives aside, crazy dreams of a mail-order marriage come true to the contrary, he wasn't going to have her fully.

Even tonight she couldn't be really his.

He had no condoms and she didn't, either.

This. Right now. Her body moving in hungry yearning under his hand, her mouth eager and soft against his own, this was all he could have.

All he would ever have.

He groaned in agony at the thought and pressed himself, hard and aching, against the side of her thigh.

She clung to him, whimpering, as he slipped that finger inside again, even daring to ease in another, stretching her a little. She was tight and very wet.

So good, so right.

He realized he was whispering the words against her parted lips. "So good, so right..."

"Yes," she answered, soft and sweet and oh-so-willing. "Oh, Justin, yes...."

Her hips moved faster. He followed the cues her body gave him, finding the nub of her greatest pleasure, rubbing it, stroking it....

She said his name again against his mouth, on a low breath of yearning and building excitement.

And then he felt it. The soft pulsing beneath his stroking finger, the silky spurt of wetness as she came...

She cried out and he caught that cry, kissing her deeply, as below the tiny, hot, wet pulsing continued.

In the end, her body went loose and boneless. She gave a final, gentle sigh.

His body *hurt.* He ached for more, and yet...

It was good. Better than good, just to be here, in this old bed with her, to know she'd hit the peak and loved every minute of it, that he had done that for her.

She lifted a lazy hand to stroke the side of his face and he raised his head to look down into her shining eyes.

"Oh, Justin..." Her sweet mouth trembled on a smile.

He kissed the tip of her nose. And then, slowly, reluctantly, he took his hand from that wet, hot secret place between her sleek thighs and smoothed her pajama bottoms to cover her to the waist. He took the sides of her top, one and then the other, bringing them together, proceeding to slip the buttons back into their too-loose holes.

She caught his hand. "Oh, don't..."

He gave her a dark look. "Katie. We've got to be careful. You have to know. That was as far as we can go."

She only looked at him, eyes dazed, mouth swollen from his kisses, cheeks flushed: a woman more than willing to go on from here.

Willing? Hell. Eager.

Ready.

For him.

With a low groan, he fell back on the bed, throwing his arm across his eyes, ordering the bulge in his jeans to subside.

Now.

It didn't happen—which hardly surprised him.

The bed shifted as she sat up. He dared to steal a peek at her from under the shadow of his arm.

She was taking off her pajama top.

"What the hell are you doing?"

Her high, cute breasts bounced as she tossed that top aside. "Getting undressed." It flew over and hooked on the vanity mirror. "And so should you. Now."

He shouldn't be peeking. He should cover his eyes again.

But somehow, he couldn't. The bulge in his pants only got bigger as she slithered out of the pajama bottoms and tossed them over to land with the top.

Now, all she had left were those thick, gray socks of hers. Her skin seemed to glow in the dimness, rich as vanilla ice cream, but with a pearly kind of luster, too. The sable hair between her soft thighs was shiny with moisture.

And the scent of her...ripe. Purely sexual. The scent of a woman aroused and satisfied. It clung to his hand.

Exercising every last shred of will he possessed, he held back a groan.

This was not going well.

She got rid of the socks, ripping them off, one and then the other, and tossing them to the rag rug beside the bed. "Okay, Justin. I'm naked."

As if he didn't know. As if every inch of him wasn't painfully aware.

He pressed his arm hard against his eyes. He was not going to look. Not again. No matter what.

She spoke again. "Justin. I want to get into bed. But you're on the blankets..."

"Uh. Right. Sorry." He shut his eyes tight and jumped from the bed, letting out another groan as his jeans dug in at the crucial spot.

He stood there, eyes shut, body rigid and burning, facing away from her. Behind him, he heard the covers rustling.

"Safe to look now," she said at last, her tone just slightly teasing. "I'm all covered up."

He yanked his sweater down low over his jeans, to mask the clear evidence that his body refused to be ruled by his mind. And then, with a deep breath and a silent vow that he would not climb onto that bed with her again, he turned to face her.

She sat against the pillows, shining dark hair soft and wild on her satiny shoulders, the blankets pulled up to cover those tempting breasts, looking achingly sweet, and not quite as confident as a moment ago. "I...well, I can't help it. It's crazy, but I almost feel as if we *are* married, you know? As if making love with you is the most natural, *right* thing for us to be doing."

It was exactly what he'd been thinking not long before.

But so what? his cynical side reminded him. *So damn what?* They *weren't* married. They would never be married. In a week she would hate him and know him for the enemy he was and had always been.

And, all sentimental talk of "feeling" married aside, they had no protection. They shouldn't have gone as far as they had.

And they damn well weren't going to go any further. "Katie." His voice was rough. Pained. Pushed out through his clutching throat, threaded with his own frustration. "We can't. You know we can't."

She picked at a thread on the velvet patchwork spread, eyes cast down, lashes wisps of silk against her cheeks. "You're right. I know…" She looked up. Those honey-brown eyes captured him, held him—a prisoner of his own burning need for her. "But couldn't we just…" She paused to swallow, convulsively—and then didn't seem to be able to go on.

"Couldn't we, *what?*" he demanded way too gruffly.

She swallowed again and licked those soft lips with a nervous pink tongue—an unintentionally provocative action that inflicted yet another blow to his barely held self-control.

"Well," she suggested, all wide eyes and innocence, "you could put on those black sweats you sleep in. I'll put my pajamas back on, too. You can…come to bed with me."

"Come to bed with you." There was nothing—*nothing*—he'd rather do. And it was exactly what he was *not* going do. "Katie—"

She cut him off before he could tell her no. "Oh, listen. Please…"

"We can't—"

"No, see. Just listen. We won't do anything more. I promise…to be good."

They shared a look—hot and hungry, crackling with need.

And then, out of nowhere, she laughed, a happy, startled, captivating trill of sound.

That laugh was infectious. He laughed, too—and then he stopped himself and glared at her. "What the hell are we laughing at?"

"Well, Justin, it's only…me, sitting here naked. Promising not to try anymore to seduce *you*. Who would have guessed *that* would happen?"

He only looked at her, making no attempt to smile. He was thinking that she'd been seducing him since the first moment he saw her, when Caleb introduced them and he got his first look into those wide, soft brown eyes.

There was just something about her. She got to him in ways he'd never been gotten to before.

"Please," she said, so sweetly.

"Hell," he replied.

"Please," she said, once more.

And once again, there was no stopping the wrong words from escaping his mouth.

"Put on those damn pajamas," he growled. "I'll be right back."

Chapter Nine

"Spooning," Katie whispered.

They lay on their sides, her slim back tucked into him, her legs cradled on his, his arm across her waist. He nuzzled her hair, cuddled her closer, in spite of the fact that holding her tighter only aroused him more.

"Yes," she said. "Spooning."

"What in hell are you talking about?"

She chuckled. The sweet sound vibrated through him. "What we're doing, tucked in this bed together, fully clothed, with you curved all around me. We're spooning."

He grunted, smoothed a wild coil of fragrant hair away from his mouth, and muttered, "We're driving me crazy, that's what we're doing."

"Hmm," she said, and wiggled her bottom against him.

He took a slow breath. "That was completely uncalled for."

"Sorry."

"Liar."

"But seriously, courting couples used to do this, in the old days...lie down together, with their clothes on, tucked up nice and cozy, like spoons in a drawer. Thus, spooning."

"Spooning." He laid his hand over hers, stroking the back of it, until she opened her fingers and he slid his between. She tucked their joined fists against her soft, flannel-covered breasts. He growled in her ear. "Frankly, I'd rather be shtupping."

She giggled. "I don't believe you said that."

"The truth hurts. Let me tell you, it really, *really* hurts."

She elbowed him lightly. "I'll distract you."

"Don't worry, you already are."

"I mean, from your, er, pain."

"Oh. That. Good luck."

"Back to spooning... Soldiers have done it, far back in history, spooning in the trenches to ward off the cold on a freezing night before a big battle. They'd keep warm using each other's body heat."

"Speaking of which, it's too damn hot in here." He pulled his hand from hers and readjusted the covers, pushing them down on his side.

"Umm." She wiggled in against him again. "Better?"

It was agony, but at the same time... "Yeah."

"Give me your hand back, please." He obliged. She tucked it under her soft chin. "Yes," she said on a gentle sigh. "This is nice…"

Nice wasn't exactly the word for it.

Spooning.

Never in a million and a half years would he have pictured himself, lying here, *spooning* Katie Fenton.

But he *was* lying here, with her sweet-scented softness plastered all along the front of him, holding her tight, both of them covered in clothing from neck to ankle. He *was* lying here, never wanting to let her go.

He knew he'd never get any sleep like this. But he closed his eyes, anyway.

He woke abruptly as Katie threw back the covers and jumped from the bed.

He sat up. She was already past the rope he'd dropped last night, racing for the door to the front reception room.

He raked the hair back from his forehead. "Huh, wha –?"

She sent him a dazzling smile and hauled open the door. "The phone's ringing."

It rang again as she slipped through the doorway.

Katie picked up the phone in midring. "Hello?" No one spoke. She asked again, more urgently, "Hello?"

"Katie, darling? Oh, thank goodness."

She felt the huge smile burst across her face. "Addy."

"You're there…you're safe?"

"Oh, Addy. Yes. I'm fine. Justin and I got stuck here, at the museum. But we're okay. We're safe. Buttercup's even okay—though she's getting pretty cranky, trapped in the shed out back with only hay to eat."

"You're safe." The relief in Addy's dear voice was achingly clear. "We've been so worried...."

"I'm fine. Really. And so is Justin. Don't worry anymore. Everything's great, but what about you? And Caleb? And Riley?"

"Safe. We're all safe." A gentle chuckle followed. "Riley made it home from the hall before the snow got too bad. Caleb and I and Mr. Sy Goodwin got stuck in that office in town."

"The ski resort office?"

"You know Caleb. Sy's visiting from Billings. He expressed interest in the project and Caleb wanted to take him right over there to show him what a good investment he'd be making. I tagged along. By the time we realized we needed to get home, it was too late. But we all three made it back to the hall, and spent Sunday and Monday and three endless, uncomfortable nights there, with the others who didn't make it home. It was an adventure, I'll tell you."

"Where are you now?"

"The snowplows started working last evening. Thunder Canyon Road was cleared by seven this morning."

Katie looked at the clock on the wall—ten thirty-five. "So you're at the Lazy D?"

"That's right. Home safe and sound."

Katie clutched the phone tighter. "Oh, I'm so relieved. I was worried about everyone."

"Nothing to worry about. We're all safe, and Caleb wants to talk to you."

"Okay, I—"

Before she finished her sentence, Caleb's deep voice was blustering in her ear. "Katie. Honey, you're all right?"

Katie smiled all the wider. "I'm fine. Really. Safe and warm, and we had food to eat, sandwiches left by the Historical Society ladies. We're pretty tired of ham and cheese, but it all worked out. Truly."

"Justin Caldwell?"

The sound of his name on Caleb's lips made her blush, for some silly reason—or maybe it was the memory of last night. "He's here, with me. Safe. I promise."

"All right, then. Katie, honey, you'll be out of there in no time. I'm making a few calls to see that plow gets to you right away."

"Caleb, that's really not necessary. We're perfectly safe and we can wait."

Caleb wouldn't hear of that. "I'm getting you out of there, and I'm doing it quick. Just sit tight now and hold on." He spoke to someone—Addy, no doubt—on his end of the line. "Addy wants you to come on out to the ranch for dinner tonight. We'll celebrate how we all got through the worst blizzard of the century—so far, anyway—safe and sound. She says to invite Caldwell, too. Can't have an out-of-towner thinking we don't know how to treat a guest."

He chuckled again. "Especially one who happens to be my business partner."

Nice idea, she thought. *Lovely* idea. "I'll ask him."

"Good. I'm going to let you go now. I want you to call me if that plow doesn't show up in the next hour."

She wouldn't, of course. She and Justin could wait as long as it took. But Caleb always enjoyed pulling strings for the people who mattered to him. "Thanks, Caleb. I love you—Addy, too."

He made the usual, gruff, blustering sounds. "Well, now, who's my girl?"

"*I* am. Always. Bye now."

She hung up and turned to find Justin leaning in the doorway to the central room, one bare foot crossed lazily over the other. Her heart set to pounding and her breath caught at the sight of him—at the memory of last night that seemed to shimmer in the air between them.

"That was Caleb and Addy." She sounded breathless. Probably because she *was*. "They were worried. I told them we were fine. And they said everyone else is safe, too."

"Good." He straightened from his easy slouch and came toward her, the predatory gleam in his eyes causing her knees to go weak and something low in her belly to go soft as melting butter.

She suffered dual urges—to back away from him; and to throw herself against him and lift up her mouth. In the end, she did neither. She held her ground, waiting, as he stalked toward her.

He reached her, his eyes still burning into hers.

A nervous laugh escaped her. "Justin, you look so…" The sentence trailed off. She didn't know quite how to finish it.

He lifted a hand. With a light finger, he guided a stray coil of hair behind her ear. A little shiver went through her. "Cold?"

"No. No, not at all. Justin, are you okay?"

His hand dropped to his side and he stepped back. "So, today we're really getting out of here."

She nodded. "If we're lucky, the plow should be here in the next few hours."

He turned from her, abruptly. "Let's get the coffee going."

She caught his arm. "Justin…"

He swung back, his eyes dark. Turbulent. His bicep was rock-hard with tension beneath her hand. "What?"

She let go, fast. "I…well, you almost seem angry. I just don't get it."

He kept staring at her, giving her that strange, hot, dark *devouring* look, for an endless, tense moment and then…

His eyes changed. Softened. His wonderful, sensual mouth went soft, too. "Hell." And he reached out and pulled her into his strong arms, squeezing the breath right out of her.

"Justin, what—?"

"I don't want to lose you." The rough, whispered words seemed dredged up from the deepest part of him.

"Oh, Justin." She held on, tight as he was holding her. "You won't. Of course, you won't."

A low, pained sound came from him and he crushed her so close, as if he would push himself right into her, meld their separate bodies into one undividable whole.

An image flashed into her mind: of the boy he once was, a boy all alone when he shouldn't have been, standing at a wide window, watching the snow come down, wondering what was going to happen to him.

"You can count on me," she whispered, meaning it with every fiber of her being. "You can hold on to me. I'll always be here."

He held her close for an endless moment more and then, with a shuddering sigh, his arms relaxed. She raised her head to meet his eyes and a rueful half smile lifted a corner of his mouth.

"Damned if I wasn't kind of getting to like it here."

She surged up, pressed a kiss on his beard-shadowed jaw. "Me, too. Oh, Justin…me, too."

Over morning coffee and the inevitable sandwiches, she relayed Addy's dinner invitation.

His eyes shifted away for a split second, and then he shook his head. "Wish I could. But I need to get back to Bozeman, ASAP. In my business, there are a hundred issues to deal with on a daily basis. I've been away since Saturday morning and that's three days too long."

She set down her stale sandwich and resisted the urge to work on him to stay. The guy had a demanding job and if they were going to get anywhere together, she'd have to learn to live with that—and on second thought, there were no *ifs* about it. The way he'd held her, as if he'd never let her go, out in the reception room a while ago, had banished all doubts on that score.

"I'm disappointed," she said, matter-of-factly. "But I do understand."

"Will you thank Adele for the invitation—and express my regrets?"

"You know I will—and it could be tough to get home at this point. You realize that?" Well, okay, she couldn't help hoping that maybe bad road conditions would keep him in town tonight, after all. He could stay at her place.

They could catch up on their spooning.

She might even make a quick trip to the drugstore, take care of the contraception problem. She'd never bought a condom in her life and old Mr. Dodson, the pharmacist, might give her the lifted eyebrow when she plunked the box down at the cash register counter. But it would definitely be worth the slight embarrassment, to make tonight extra special, a night to remember.

Always…

But then Justin said, "It's not even twenty miles. And by later today, at least, I'm sure they'll have the highway cleared."

He was probably right. Darn it.

The plow came within the hour. By then, Caleb had called a second time to tell her not to worry about Buttercup. A couple of hands would be over a little later with the snowblower and other necessary equipment to free the mare from the shed out back. Emelda

Ross had called, as well, just to check and see that Katie was all right.

Katie and Justin, still dressed in their rummage sale clothes, bundled in the coats and gloves they'd arrived in, shovels in hand, waited on the porch as the plow lumbered up the street. It turned into the museum parking lot and kept on coming, right up to the steps. Katie waved at the driver, a local man whose wife and kids paid frequent visits to the library, and shouted, ''Thanks!''

The driver gave her a wave in return and then backed to the street again. The plow, which had already made the Elk Avenue curve, headed east at a crawl, toward what was known as New Town, clearing the high white drifts into yet higher piles at the sides of the street as it went.

Justin turned to her. ''Well. What next?''

A dragging feeling of sadness engulfed her: for all they had shared in the dim rooms behind them, for the uncertain future—which, she told herself firmly, wasn't uncertain at all.

She and the man beside her had found something special. Nothing could change that. ''Where's your car parked?'' she asked with a cheery smile.

''In the lot behind the town hall.''

''It's not far, and mine's there, too. Let's get the steps cleared off and put the shovels away and then we'll start walking.''

All along Main Street, folks were out with their shovels. The roar of snowblowers filled the icy air.

People called out and waved as Katie and Justin walked by.

"Katie, how you doin'?"

"Some storm, eh?"

"Talk about your New Year's surprise!"

"Come on. This is nothin'. Five or six feet. Piece a cake."

"And they say it's turning warm right away. In the fifties by Friday. What do you think of that?"

They waved back and called greetings and when they reached the hall, they found the front steps already cleared and the driveway to the back parking lot passable, as well.

They went in the front to ask after the things they'd left behind the night of the storm. Rhonda Culpepper, well past sixty with a white streak in her improbably black hair, waited at her usual post behind the reception desk.

Rhonda greeted Katie and nodded at Justin and announced with a wink, "I'll bet I know what you two are after." She bent down behind the desk and came up with Katie's purse and Justin's briefcase, phone and keys, along with a big bag for each of them filled with their own clothes and shoes. "Have I got everything?"

"Looks like it. Thanks, Rhonda."

"Always glad to help."

They went down a side hall and out a door at the back. A couple of guys were at work there, clearing the snow between the vehicles so people could get them out. Katie exchanged greetings with the men and then Justin asked which car was hers.

She pointed at the silver-gray Suburban, near where the men were working. "In a few minutes they'll have me dug out."

"Let's get the snow off the roof and the windshield cleared, then," he suggested.

She caught his hand. Even through their heavy gloves, she felt his warmth. Her pulse quickened. "It's okay. Doug and Cam will help me." She gestured at the two busily shoveling men.

"You're sure?"

"Absolutely. Where are you parked?"

His black Escalade was near the edge of the lot, not far from the drive that led around to the front. The snow had already been shoveled away around it.

She helped him knock some of the snow off the roof and the hood and he got inside and turned the vehicle on, ducking back out with a scraper. He set to work. She went on tiptoe and pushed more snow off the Escalade's roof as he cleared the windshield.

It wasn't all that long before he had the wipers going and he was ready to head out.

He cast a glance toward Cam and Doug, still shoveling away between the snow-covered cars and pickups. "Come here." He grabbed her hand and towed her to the back of the Escalade, where they were out of sight of the working men. She went eagerly into the warm circle of his arms.

"Time to get out of here." His breath came out on a cloud.

"Drive safely. I want you back soon. Very, very soon…"

By way of answer, he bent and pressed his lips—cold on the outside, so warm within—to hers.

The icy day, the growls of snowblowers on Main Street, the scraping of shovels on the frozen blacktop a few feet away—all of that faded to nothing. There was only Justin, his arms tight and cherishing around her, his mouth claiming hers in a bone-melting kiss.

With a regretful growl low in his throat, he lifted his head. "I'll call you."

She let out a laugh. "Good luck with that. You don't even have my number."

"Katie, you're the town librarian and you're like a daughter to Caleb Douglas, who happens to be a colleague of mine. I don't think you'll be that hard to track down. Plus, I'd bet the last strip mall I built that you've got a listed number."

"Now, how did you know that?"

"You're the listed-number type."

She gave him a frown. "That's good, right?"

He kissed her nose, her cheeks and even her chin, his lips warm now against her cold skin. Then he pulled away enough to look at her, a deep look, a look she couldn't quite read. "I have to go." His arms fell away and he turned toward the driver's door.

She followed, already missing him, feeling bereft. He climbed up into the seat and shut the door. She went around the front of the vehicle to the other side, getting out of his way.

He saluted her—a gloved hand to his forehead. She mimicked the gesture. And then he was backing out, turning to get the right angle, and rolling forward. She watched as the big, black SUV disappeared around the side of the town hall, her heart pounding hard and heavy as lead beneath her breastbone.

She knew he would call her. Hadn't he just told her he would? Still, she had the strangest, scariest feeling right then that she would never see him again.

Chapter Ten

Dinner at the Lazy D was a festive affair. Adele had the cook prepare a juicy prime rib and Tess Little-hawk, the ranch's longtime housekeeper, set the long table in the formal dining room with the best china and crystal.

Riley, who'd been out earlier checking the stock, came in from his own place a half a mile from the main house to join them, his dark hair slicked back, wet from the shower he must have just taken.

"I was the lucky one," he said, smoothing his linen napkin on his lap and sparing a wink of greeting for Katie. "Safe and sound at my place before things got too rough."

Sy Goodwin, a feed-store owner and family man who'd decided to stay the night before heading back to his wife and four kids in Billings, laughed with

Caleb and Adele over their shared "ordeal" in the hall—especially Sunday morning, when most of the others were suffering from an excess of beer the day before.

"A number of extremely discouraging words were exchanged," Goodwin reported, his expression jokingly solemn, a definite gleam in his eye.

The creases in Caleb's nut-brown face etched all the deeper as he let out his big, boisterous laugh. "I tell you, Katie, a bottle of aspirin that first day was worth its weight in gold."

Sy laughed, too. "And anyone with a box of Alka-Seltzer could have gotten a fortune for it."

Adele and Caleb agreed that Sy wasn't exaggerating.

Caleb asked, a little too meaningfully as far as Katie was concerned, "And what about you and Justin? Stuck there in that musty old museum with nothing but mining equipment and Indian artifacts for company."

Adele was shaking her head. "What *did* you do for all that time?"

We kissed, Katie thought. *Forever. We spooned. All night. And I dropped in at State Street Drugs this afternoon and bought myself a box of condoms.* Mr. Dodson hadn't even batted an eye when she plunked it down on the counter.

She said, offhand as she could make it, "Oh, we found some books and board games in the storage room. We managed to occupy ourselves."

Addy clucked her tongue and sent Katie a sly look. "A handsome guy, that Justin."

Katie put on her sweetest smile. "Yes. He is. Very."

Adele added, "I do wish he'd been able to stay and join us tonight."

"He had to get back," Katie said. "Business, you know."

"Yeah," Caleb agreed. "That man's a real go-getter. Started from nothing and now he's the biggest developer in western Montana—and not even thirty-five yet." Those devilish green eyes of his were twinkling. "And our Katie's gone and married him."

Addy and Riley shared a glance and Sy Goodwin looked confused.

Adele had to explain to him about the mail-order bride reenactment they'd missed when they went down to the ski resort office.

"We heard after we got back to the hall that it was quite an event, that marriage of yours," said Caleb. "Heard some old character named Green stepped up to play the preacher. Got right into the part. Even called himself 'Reverend.'"

"Yep," Katie agreed, keeping it light, but thinking of Justin. Of his low, teasing voice through the darkness that night they'd talked and talked. Of his kiss. Of his hands on her body. She should have gotten his number. But no. He'd said he'd call. And of course he would. "That 'wedding' was…really something."

Maybe tonight, she thought. At least by tomorrow…

The talk moved on to other subjects. After coffee and dessert, Caleb and Addy urged her to stay. They didn't want her driving home on the icy roads in the dark.

She said she really had to get back. The roads to town had been cleared and salted and the snow hadn't started up again. She'd be just fine.

It was after eleven when she let herself into her two-story farmhouse-style Victorian on Cedar Street.

She'd been home earlier, after Justin left her in the town hall parking lot, and she'd turned up the thermostat then, so the house was cozy-warm and welcoming. Switching on lamps as she went, she headed for the phone in the kitchen in back, where she found the message light on her machine glowing a steady red.

No one had called.

He didn't call Wednesday morning, either. Katie went to the library at nine and jumped every time the phone rang, though there was really no reason he'd call her at work when all he had to do was look up her home number in the book.

Still, whenever the phone rang, her heart would race and the clerk would answer.

And it wouldn't be him.

Emelda, who put in a lot of volunteer hours at the library, arrived at two. "It's going to be fifty degrees today, can you believe it?" she marveled as she peeled off her muffler and hung up her heavy coat. "Snow's already melting. It'll be gone in no time if this keeps up." She clucked her tongue and got to work shelving some new novels Katie had waiting.

At three, Emelda took over the check-out desk so

the clerk, Lindy Peters, could have a break. The phone rang just as Lindy left the desk. Katie raced over and grabbed it on the second ring, though Emelda was moving down the counter toward it.

"Thunder Canyon Public Library," Katie answered, absurdly breathless. "May I help you?"

It was only someone wanting the library hours for the week. Katie repeated them and said goodbye.

Emelda shook her silver-gray head. "I swear you are jumpy as a frog on a hot rock today. I would have gotten that."

Katie hardly heard her. Her mind was full of Justin. What was he doing now? Had he gotten back to Bozeman safely? Well, of course he had. And it had barely been twenty-four hours since he left her at the town hall—well, okay, twenty-six hours, thirty-plus minutes, to be more exact. Not that long, not really. No doubt he had a mountain of work to catch up on. He probably wouldn't be able to get away to see her until the weekend. He'd be calling—soon—to set something up.

"Katie? Did you hear a single word I said?"

"Oh. Emelda. Sorry, I…" She was saved from having to make some lame excuse for her distracted behavior when a little girl with a towering stack of picture books, her mother right behind her, stepped up to the counter.

After that, Katie managed to keep herself from rushing to grab the phone every time it rang.

Besides, by then she was feeling more and more certain that Justin would be calling her house, not the library. There was probably a message waiting for her at home right now.

When she got home at five-fifteen there were two messages, but neither was from Justin.

She simply had to stop obsessing over this. He'd said he'd call and he would. Justin was an honest man.

That night she hosted the Historical Society meeting at her house. As she served up the coffee and cookies and listened to everyone bemoan the storm that had ruined their museum reception, and trade news on Ben Saunders's rapidly improving health, she couldn't help expecting the phone to ring.

It didn't. Not that night, not Thursday morning, not during her prelunch hours at the library, either.

She met Addy for their usual Thursday lunch date at the Hitching Post. Addy mentioned that she thought Katie seemed distracted.

Katie met Addy's eyes across the table and longed to tell her everything—of the magic time she'd known with Justin when they were marooned in the museum, of the shattering beauty of the one night she'd spent in his arms.

Of how she couldn't stop longing, every second of the day, for his call.

But no. It was all too new. She didn't want to share what she was feeling with anyone. Not yet. Not until…

Well, soon. But not now.

She reassured Addy that she was fine.

And then Justin didn't call the rest of the day, or in the evening, either.

By Friday morning she was beginning to wonder if something really might have happened to him, if he'd had some kind of accident on the way home to Bozeman. Whatever had kept him from calling her, she prayed he was all right.

She pored over the special edition of the *Thunder Canyon Nugget* that had come out Wednesday. It was chock-full of great stories of how folks had weathered the big storm. Two storm-related accidents were reported. One had occurred after the roads were cleared, when a pickup going too fast rolled on Thunder Canyon Road. The other concerned a high-schooler who'd driven his snowmobile into a tree while the snow was still falling on Sunday afternoon. Injuries were surprisingly minor in both cases. She found no mention of any accident on the road to Bozeman, nothing about a black Escalade or an out-of-towner named Caldwell.

Before she left for the library, she called Bozeman information. His home phone wasn't listed. But they did have a number for Red Rock Developers. She dialed it and a service picked up. The offices opened at nine. She could leave her number and Mr. Caldwell's secretary would get back to her during business hours.

"Uh, no thanks. I'll call later."

She hung up and considered calling Caleb, asking him if maybe he had Justin's home number. But she found herself hesitating to do that. Caleb would be curious. He'd tease her about her "groom," and ask her why she thought she needed his number. And then Caleb would tell Adele that Katie was trying to get ahold of Justin—and Addy would tell Caleb how distracted Katie had been at lunch the day before…

Oh, not right now, she thought. She wanted to find out how Justin was, wanted to *talk* to him, wanted to be reassured that everything was all right, with him and between the two of them, before she said anything to Caleb or Addy.

She went to work and tried to keep her mind on her job, a difficult task when every thought kept tracking right back around to Justin. Where was he? Was he okay? Why hadn't he called?

By lunchtime, after Lindy had asked her twice what was wrong with her and Emelda had expressed concern over whether she might be coming down with something, Katie realized she had to snap out of it.

Worrying about Justin wasn't going to do anybody any good. She'd track him down that evening, one way or another. Until then, she was keeping her thoughts strictly on her work.

At four-fifteen, the kids started arriving for Emelda's story hour, which started at four-thirty. They all gathered around the low round table in the center of the children's section, where Emelda would keep them spellbound with fairy tales and stories by the best contemporary children's authors—and sometimes true-life accounts from Montana history.

Cameron Stevenson, one of the two men Katie and Justin had found shoveling out the town hall parking lot on Tuesday, brought his seven-year-old, Erik, as always. Often the parents would leave their kids and come back at five-thirty to collect them.

Not Cam. The tall, athletic auburn-haired teacher

was a single dad and he took fatherhood seriously. He stuck around, even though he coached at the high school and would have to rush back there the minute the story hour ended to get his team ready for the evening's home game. As he waited, he read sports magazines from the periodicals section and browsed the fiction stacks.

After five, as Katie was wrapping things up for the day, Cam wandered over to her workstation at the central reference counter and he and Katie chatted about nothing in particular: how good the varsity basketball team was looking this year and how Cam and Erik had barely made it home Saturday before the snow shut them in.

Cam joked that he'd heard how she and her "groom" had been stuck at the museum alone for the duration. "Some honeymoon, huh?" he asked with an easy grin.

"It was...quite an experience," she replied in a library-level whisper, mentally congratulating herself on how offhand she sounded. "Poor Buttercup."

"That old mare of Caleb's, you mean?"

She nodded. "The old sweetheart was stuck out in the shed all that time, no exercise and nothing but hay to..." She didn't finish.

How could she? Her throat had clamped tight. Joy and relief went exploding through her.

Justin!

He must have just come in. He stood over by the check-out counter, wearing a sweater that matched his eyes and a gorgeous coffee-brown suede jacket. He was scanning the room.

He spotted her. Her heart froze in midbeat and then started galloping. Somehow, she managed to lift a hand and wave.

He headed toward her, long strides eating up the all-weather gray carpet under his boots. She was vaguely aware that Cam had turned to see what—or who—had stolen the words right out of her mouth.

"I had a feeling I might find you here," Justin said.

Good gravy, he really was the best-looking man in the whole of Montana! She had to swallow to make her throat relax before she could speak. "Uh. Good guess. And, um, great to see you."

It was the understatement of the decade.

She collected her scattered wits enough to introduce him to Cam. The two men exchanged greetings and then Cam left them alone.

The second the coach was out of earshot, Justin asked low, "When do you finish here?"

She ordered her crazy heart to stop racing. "Give me a minute. I'm almost ready to go."

As they passed the check-out desk, Lindy called out, "Have a nice night." Plump and pretty and very curious, the clerk gave them a big grin and wiggled her eyebrows at Katie.

Katie, getting the message, stopped to introduce them.

"Terrific to meet you!" Lindy enthused. Sheesh. She was practically drooling.

Then again, who could blame her?

Justin made a few cordial noises and at last they were out of there.

They walked down the library steps into a winter sunset. The cloudless sky was shades of salmon above the white-topped mountains and the melting snow at their feet sent rivulets trickling, down the steps, along the parking lot. A hundred miniature streams gleamed in the gathering dark.

She sent a quick glance toward the silent man at her side. He hadn't touched her—hadn't taken her arm. She longed to take his, but didn't feel comfortable enough with him at that moment, with the way he'd popped up out of nowhere, with the strange, shadowed look in his eyes and the hard set to his square jaw.

"Where's your car?" he asked flatly when they reached the big, black Escalade.

"I walked. It's only a few blocks and it was nice to get out." She almost said more. Meaningless chatter. About the warming trend. About how she liked to walk whenever the weather permitted. But she didn't. His eyes didn't invite chitchat. "Justin, what—?"

He cut in before she finished. "Who was that guy you were talking to inside?"

Her heart warmed. So that was the problem. He was *jealous*. "Cam? He's only a friend. Honestly. A friend…"

His mouth twisted into something meant to look like a smile. "Not that I had any damn right to ask."

She looked at him levelly. "If you were wondering, then I'm *glad* you asked. It's important that we both feel we can say whatever's on our minds."

"Is it?" He lifted a dark brow at her.

She blinked. "Now what is *that* supposed to mean?"

He shrugged. "Nothing."

Untrue and she knew it. It was very much *something*. She could see it in his eyes.

But before she could open her mouth to pursue the issue, he spoke again. "Will you have dinner with me?"

There was only one answer to that one. "I'd love to."

"Where would you like to go?"

He sounded so...formal. As if she was some stranger.

It came to her that she didn't want to go and sit in a restaurant with him. Surrounded by other people, she wouldn't feel she could really talk to him. And she needed that, to feel free to talk. This new distance between them scared her a little. She wanted, with all her heart, to bridge it.

And then again, was this feeling of distance really all that surprising? They'd found a rare and thrilling intimacy, just the two of them, in the museum. But she had to remember that they'd known each other less than a week. The attraction had been immediate and the forced proximity had made it possible for them to grow close very fast.

And then he'd returned to his life and she'd gone back to hers.

No. She had to expect that things would be a little awkward, now they found themselves face-to-face again at last.

She intended to eliminate the awkwardness, to

break down any and all barriers between them. That would be easier if they were alone.

"Tell you what? Let's just go to my place. How about fried chicken and oven-browned red potatoes, would that be all right?"

He frowned. "You're sure?"

She stepped back, a half laugh escaping her. "Justin. What's not to be sure of?"

He hesitated a moment longer. But finally, he agreed. "Well, all right, then. Let's go."

Chapter Eleven

"Big place," Justin said, when Katie ushered him into a high-ceilinged foyer, where a walnut staircase rose gracefully from the far end, curving upward toward the second floor.

She set her purse on the long marble table by the door and turned to knock the breath out of him with a glowing smile. "It was in bad shape when I bought it, but I've had a lot of work done. It was built in 1910, by the owner of the town dry goods store. Cedar Street used to be where all the town merchants lived. A lot of them were well-to-do."

"Clearly." Beneath his boots, the fine, old wood of the parquet floor gave off a polished shine in the glow from the antique light fixture overhead. Carved walnut moldings crowned the walls.

She teased, "Take a good look around. Just in case

you're thinking of making me an offer.'' He met those brown eyes again and a shock of sensual awareness ricocheted through him.

He wanted to grab her and carry her up the curving staircase, to find a nice, big bed up there and never let her out of it. "I'm tempted," he muttered, and they both knew damn well he wasn't talking about her house.

He ached. All over. His damn skin felt too tight. He had only himself to blame for the state he was in. Not only for starting up with her in the first place, but for not taking care of his physical needs since he'd left her on Tuesday.

There were a couple of women he knew: willing, bright, beautiful women, who didn't expect—or even want—anything beyond a nice evening and a good time in bed. But he hadn't been able to make himself pick up the phone and call one of them.

His body burned for the satisfaction he hadn't allowed himself to take four nights ago in that big, old bed in the museum. But he'd done nothing to ease the ache. The thought of touching some other woman for the sake of a much-needed release...

It made him feel vaguely ill.

His mistake. To add to all the others. He should have at least taken a few minutes in the shower to get the edge off, but he hadn't even had sense enough to do that.

Somehow, he couldn't. He wanted Katie. His *body* wanted Katie. Only Katie.

Though he knew damn well he was never going to have her.

"Oh, Justin…" Her voice was so soft, like the rest of her. His arms itched to hold her. With monumental effort, he kept his hands at his sides. She seemed to shake herself and then, shyly, she offered, "May I take your jacket?"

He shrugged out of it and handed it over. She hung it on the antique claw-footed rack by the door, along with her heavy coat. Then she turned to him again, those amber eyes alight, her smile so bright it could chase away the darkness of the blackest night.

Damn. He was gone. Gone, gone, gone. He kept trying to remember why he'd come here, what he needed to say to her. He should say it.

And go.

But he said nothing as she gestured toward a door at the back, past the foot of that impressive staircase. "This way…" He fell in behind her and she led him to a big kitchen with acres of granite-topped counters and cherrywood cabinets fronted in beveled glass. "Have a seat." She nodded toward the cherry table in the breakfast area. "I'll get the dinner started."

He didn't want to sit there at the table while she bustled around across a jut of counter fifteen feet away. "Let me help."

"Well, sure." She was already at the sink, washing her hands. "If you want to…"

He followed her lead at the sink and then turned to watch her as she tied on an apron, set the oven and began assembling the stuff she needed. He scrubbed the potatoes for her. She cut them into quarters and shook spices on them, then drizzled them with olive oil and stirred them with a wooden spoon.

In spite of the constant, burning ache to grab her and hold her, to kiss her and feel her body go soft and warm and achingly willing against his, in spite of the nagging awareness that he had a grim purpose here and once he accomplished it, he'd have to walk out the door.

And never see her again.

In spite of all of it, a strange sort of peace settled on him, just to be there, with her, in the big, well-appointed kitchen, handing her a spoon or an oven mitt when she asked for it, watching as she prepared their meal.

She battered the chicken, her soft mouth curved in a happy smile. "So. What have you been up to since we broke out of the museum Tuesday?"

He told her how busy he'd been, catching up, getting back on top of the job again. As he talked, she put the chicken on to fry and checked the potatoes.

As she shut the oven door, she asked, "How about some wine?"

"Sounds good."

She went to the chef-quality fridge and brought out a bottle of Pinot Grigio. "Do the honors?"

He opened the wine and poured them each a glass. Then she started on the salad, keeping an eye on the chicken as she worked, and chattering away about the happenings at the library, about the Historical Society meeting she'd held on Wednesday.

"There was much concern over how the storm had ruined our 'wedding reception.' The society members were hoping the event would generate a few generous donations."

"Understandable. Did you tell them how grateful we were that they left all those sandwiches—and what they're collecting for a rummage sale?"

"I didn't," she confessed. "But I guess I should have."

He knocked back a big slug of the excellent wine to keep himself from flinging the glass to the hard-wood floor and hauling her into his arms. "Speaking of the rummage sale, I should have brought back that reindeer sweater—not to mention the ugly coat, the jeans and those beat-up sneakers. Sorry. I completely forgot." His mind had been filled with her, with the shining central fact that he'd see her face again. One more time.

Before the end.

"No one's even going to notice that stuff is missing, believe me." She sipped from her own glass—much more daintily than he had. "But if you're feeling *really* guilty, you could make a donation."

"I'll do that."

"It doesn't have to be much. And you'll have the society's undying gratitude."

"Never hurts to build goodwill." He knew he should have choked on those words. After next Tuesday, he'd be the lowest of the low in her eyes. No amount of goodwill would help him then.

She nodded. "Never hurts."

Never.

The word got stuck in his mind.

Never to hold her again...

Never to see her smile at him...

Never to look into those wide brown eyes...

He set his wineglass on the counter—a stupid move, and he knew it. With both hands empty, the urge to fill them with her softness was nearly overpowering.

She watched him, her eyes tracking from his face, to his glass and back to his face again. After an endless few seconds of that, she set down her glass, too.

Behind her at the stove, the chicken sizzled in the pan, giving off a mouthwatering, savory smell. The salad sat, half-made, beside her glass.

And he couldn't stop himself from thinking…

If she were someone different, or if he was.

If those vows they'd exchanged Saturday in the town hall had been the real thing.

If she were truly his wife.

This would be their life, here, in this graceful old house, her in her apron, the chicken on the stove, the salad on the counter and the potatoes in the oven.

The two of them, talking about what had happened at work, sharing the little details of their separate days, before they sat down to dinner.

Together.

And later, he'd take her to bed—*their* bed.

He'd hold her and kiss her—kiss every last inch of her. Until she was pliant and heated and ready to have him. He'd enter her slowly, by aching degrees….

"Oh," she said quietly, the word like a yearning sigh between them. "Oh, I did miss you."

It was too much. More than he could bear. His need to touch her took over. He reached out.

With a cry, she swayed toward him. And he wrapped his arms around a miracle.

Katie. Right here. In his hungry arms.

He rained kisses on her soft, flushed cheeks. "I missed you, too. So damn much."

"Oh, me, too. I missed *you*." She let out a giggle and a sweet blush stained her cheeks. "But I already said that, I know I did. I— Oh, Justin. You should kiss me." She tipped up that plump mouth. "You should kiss me right now."

"You're right."

He took her lifted mouth. And she gave it, eagerly, sending a blast of heat exploding through him. She opened for him, so he could plunge his tongue inside and taste her—so sweet, so eager, flavored with wine.

She wore a kitten-soft sweater over a skinny wool skirt. It wasn't enough, to feel her through that fluffy sweater. He eased it up—just a little. He wasn't going to go too far.

He put his hands on the velvety, warm flesh at the small of her back. She moaned into his mouth. He sucked in the sound, breathing in her breath, letting it back out so she could take breath from him.

He muttered her name, between deep kisses on her open lips. "Katie, Katie, Katie…" And his hands…

He couldn't stop them. They wandered up her back, found the place where her bra hooked and eased those tiny hooks apart.

Yes! He brought his hands around, both of them, between them, and he cradled her small, round breasts, groaning at the feel of them, the soft, slight weight against his palms. He scraped her nipples with his thumbs and then caught them, each one, between thumb and forefinger, rolling, pinching a little, just enough to make her push her hips against him, just enough to make her moan.

More.

He had to have more of her.

He had to have *all* of her. Stark need pounded through him as his blood spurted, thick and hot and hungry, through his veins.

He raked that sweater up, losing her mouth so he could kiss her chin, scrape his teeth along her throat, nipping and licking as he went. He nuzzled the fluffy sweater, but only briefly. And then he found her breast.

He latched on and she cried out, clutching his head. He drew on the sweet peak, working his teeth against it, making her cry out again.

As he suckled her, he let his hands slide downward, over the glorious inward curve of her waist and out, along the warm shape of her hips beneath the nubby wool of her skirt.

The skirt was in his way and he wanted it gone.

He grabbed two handfuls of it and eased it upward, over those warm, slim, waiting thighs.

Her panty hose stopped him. His fingers brushed them, and sheer as they were, the slight barrier of nylon reminded him.

He shouldn't be doing this.

He had no damn right to do this.

It took every last ounce of determination he possessed, but he lifted his head. She tried, at first— raising her body to his, pleading sounds rising from her throat—to pull him back to her.

But no.

He couldn't. He had no right to give in to her tender urging.

He lifted his head and her soft hands fell away.

Gently, he smoothed down her skirt as she looked at him, dazed, flushed and dreamy-eyed. "Justin?" She whispered his name on a yearning, slow breath.

He didn't answer. *Couldn't* answer. He took her by the waist and carefully turned her around, taking the loose ends of her bra straps and hooking them together again.

He smoothed the sweater back down.

Only then, when those tempting bare inches of skin were safely covered, did he guide her back around.

Lazily, she raised her arms and rested them on his shoulders. "Oh, my." She let out a long, sweet sigh. "I think the chicken's burning."

He gritted his teeth to keep from taking her kiss-swollen mouth again. "Better see to it."

"Yes." She looked adorably regretful. "I suppose I'd better."

He let go of her—yet another impossible task somehow accomplished—and she turned for the stove.

The wine was right there and his glass was empty. He needed more. A river of it, to wash the tempting taste of her from his mouth—to numb the reality of what he was here to do. He filled his glass and topped off hers, too.

I could...just drop the whole thing with Caleb, he found himself thinking as he stood a few feet behind her, sipping more wine, his gaze tracking the length of her. From her gleaming, thick brown hair that curled sweetly at her shoulders, down to her trim waist, and lower still, over the smooth swell of her hips, along the shape of her thighs outlined beneath the slim skirt, and lower, to the backs of her slim calves. She sent him a smile over her shoulder as she moved from the stove to the oven again. From there, she came closer and set to work finishing the salad.

He watched her hands, narrow and smooth, clear polish on her short-trimmed nails.

I could just never make my move, he thought. *Let it all go ahead as Caleb believes it will. Give it up. At this point, no one would even have to know what I had meant to do.*

But then what?

Try to make his dream of a life with Katie come true?

And if he tried for that—what? Tell her the truth about himself? That basic fact that he'd lied—a whopping lie—in the first place, could ruin it between them.

So if not the truth, then what?

To hold forever within himself the central lie of his very existence? Seeing Caleb and his wife and their son all the time, becoming, in a sense, a part of the family?

No.

It was impossible.

He had to remember his mother. Remember Ramona Lovett, who called herself Ramona Caldwell. Remember the life they'd had. Barely holding on too much of the time. He had to remember, all of it.

Like that night when he was twelve. The night

she'd locked herself in the bathroom. Remember breaking down the door to find her limp in the bathtub, her forearms slit, bleeding out on the white tiles of the bathroom floor.

He'd slipped in her blood as he plowed through the medicine cabinet looking for something to staunch the flow.

After that, the Child Protective Services people had come sniffing around, so they'd moved. Again.

And then, always, he would have to live with the night she died.

She'd come to find him in Bozeman when she learned she wouldn't make it, come and let him take care of her for those final months. Once or twice, in the last weeks, she'd remarked that it was strange— maybe even meant to be. That he'd ended up here, in Western Montana, when she'd never once so much as brought him here the whole time he was growing up.

"I thought I raised you to live anywhere *but* here. And look. Here you are. Must be fate. Oh, yeah. Must be fate. When I'm gone you'll get your chance to make it all right."

He would ask her what she was getting at. What did Montana have to do with anything? And she would turn her head away.

Until the last. Until the night she died in the hospital, where he'd taken her once she couldn't get along without round-the-clock care.

"I know I never told you, who he was...your father. Maybe I should have." Her skeletal hand, tubes running from the back of it, weakly clutched his fingers. "Caleb. That's his name. Caleb Douglas. Wife,

Adele. They had one son. All they *could* have. Riley. In Thunder Canyon.''

"Thunder Canyon. That's right here. In Montana.''

She'd swallowed, sucked in another breath that wheezed like she was dragging it in through a flattened straw. Even the oxygen didn't help her by then. Nothing helped. "Yes. Twenty miles from here. In Montana. Caleb…'' she'd whispered, her eyes closing on a final sigh. "Caleb…''

And with that name on her lips, she was gone.

"Justin? Are you in there?'' Katie laughed, a light, happy sound. A sound from another world, a world of possibilities he couldn't let himself explore. "You should see your face. A million miles away.''

He shook himself. "Sorry.''

"Nothing to apologize for.'' She handed him the big wooden salad bowl. "Put this on the table? We'll just eat right here, in the breakfast nook, if that's okay?'' She handed him the salad tongs.

"Sounds good.'' He carried the bowl and tongs to the table, then helped her set it for two.

A few minutes later, she took out the potatoes, spooned them into a bowl, and transferred the chicken to a serving platter.

They sat down to eat. He looked at the food, and wondered if he'd be able to get anything down, though the chicken was crispy-brown and the potatoes perfectly cooked. The salad was crisp and green.

No. It wasn't the food.

It was the wrongness of being here, of holding her, of touching her soft body, kissing her lips, of drinking her wine and letting her cook for him.

Yeah. It was all wrong, to steal these last perfect moments with her, when in the end he could do nothing but continue on the course he'd set two years ago, on the day of his mother's death. In the end, his choice wouldn't change. He would get his payback—for Ramona Lovett Caldwell's sake, above all.

And that meant he had no right to sit here with Katie, in her house, at her table, pretending that there was some hope for the two of them.

There wasn't.

There never could be.

Katie set down her fork with a bite of potato still on the end of it. Justin had been much too quiet for several minutes now—ever since that kiss, as a matter of fact, a kiss that had almost ended with the two of them rushing to the bedroom.

But he had stopped it.

And ever since then...

"Justin, what is it?" She forced a joking laugh. "The food can't be that bad."

He pushed his plate away. "It's not the food." He really didn't look right.

Alarm skittered through her. His face was set. Kind of...closed against her. Why? "Was it something I said?" She tried to make the question light and playful, but didn't fully succeed. There was an edge to her voice. She couldn't help it.

She had the most powerful feeling that something had gone wrong.

Something major.

Something she had a sinking feeling she wasn't going to be able to make right.

Which was crazy. What could have gone wrong in the space of a few minutes? Hardly anything had been said.

"Justin, was it that you kissed me? But no. I don't see how it could be that." She raised both hands, palms up. "Did I do something to upset you? I just don't get it. I don't underst—"

He grabbed her hand. "Listen." He stood, pulling her up with him.

"Justin, I don't—"

"No. Hear me out. It's nothing you did." His eyes gleamed at her with a strange, wild kind of light.

"But if you—"

"No." He squeezed her fingers. Hard. "Wait. Listen."

She pulled her hand free of his, dread moving through her, dragging at her body, like an awful gravity from within. "All right." She folded her hands in front of herself, twining them together to keep from reaching out for him. He wouldn't like it if she tried to touch him now, she knew it, knew it in a deep and undeniable way.

Oh, what was up with him? How could something so right suddenly veer off into something so strange and wrong? It made no sense. And he still wasn't talking, in spite of telling her twice to listen. How could she listen if he had nothing to say?

"Justin, you're acting so strangely. Is something wrong? I'd appreciate it if you'd just tell me what's bothering—"

He interrupted. ''Nothing.'' The single word was far too curt. Not to mention a whopping lie.

''But if you'd only—''

''Listen.'' He reached out as if he would grab her, then jerked his hand back as though he'd been burned.

''But I've *been* listening. You're not talking.''

''It's only…I couldn't stay away. I missed you. I missed you like hell.''

She would have smiled in relief and delight, if only he hadn't sounded so angry about it. She made another feeble attempt at lightness. ''And this is a problem?''

He stared at her for a long, sizzling moment. She had the sense that he was going to spin on his heel and slam out the door. Why?

The word screamed in her mind.

Why, why, why?

''I shouldn't have come here. It was wrong.''

This was making no sense. No sense at all. ''Wrong? I don't see how. I invited you here. I wanted to make our dinner. I wanted to…be with you. I'm so glad you came.''

He stepped back abruptly, knocking over his chair, catching it at the last minute, righting it—and then turning, backing away from her, toward the door to the foyer. ''I should never have come. I only…''

She waited for him to finish, to say something that made sense. When he didn't, she prodded, ''You only, what?''

''I couldn't stay away.'' He hung his dark head. He looked so lost. So alone.

Her yearning heart went out to him. But when she

took a step toward him, he put up both hands, palms out, to keep her at bay. "No," he said, and, "No," again.

She stepped back, to show him she wouldn't come closer.

Oh, what was happening here? "It doesn't make sense. You say you couldn't stay away, that you missed me so much." It was like a sharp knife, turning in her belly, in her heart, in the very center of her, to admit it. But it had to be said. "I just don't see it. The way you're acting now, well, what am I supposed to think but that I've had it all wrong, about you and me?"

"No," he said flatly, his mouth twisting. "No. You weren't wrong. Not about that. Never about that."

"Then what?"

"Listen." He said that word again and he reached for her—again. Every atom in her body cried out to move toward him. But she made herself stay right where she was.

And, as before, his hands dropped to his sides. "I came here to tell you something." His voice was infinitely weary. "To tell you, and leave. I thought I'd do it over dinner, in a restaurant, where I wouldn't be tempted to…" The words trailed off. They both knew what he meant.

Tempted to kiss her.

Tempted to hold her.

Tempted to make sweet, passionate love with her.

They stared at each other across a short distance that felt like a million miles.

Finally, she made herself speak. "Do you still plan to say it, whatever it is?"

There was a slight hesitation, but then he nodded. "Yeah. I do."

She felt weary, too, now. Weary and sick at heart. Still, she straightened her spine and lifted her chin. "Then I guess you'd better say it, don't you think?"

He drew in a long breath and let it out hard. And, at last, he came out with it. "You're going to hate me, soon enough. But when you do, remember. None of it was about you. You shouldn't have been involved. It was one rotten step too far, what I did with you. A gross error in judgment on my part. You are exactly the woman a man like me never finds."

"But then I don't see why—"

"It's simple. I'm not who you think I am."

Her legs felt achy and rubbery. And her heart was a big lump of lead in her chest. She felt for the chair behind her. Slowly, with great care, she lowered herself into it. "I don't understand you. *What* wasn't about me? And if you're not who I think you are, well, who are you, then?"

There was a long, ugly silence. Finally, he muttered, "I can't say any more. Goodbye, Katie."

And that was it.

That was all.

Without another word, he turned and went out through the door to the foyer. She didn't follow him. She knew, in an awful, final kind of way that there was no point. A moment or two later, she heard the front door open—and close.

Chapter Twelve

He had said she would hate him.

But she didn't.

She felt numb, as if she were floating, as if none of this was real.

The meal still waited, his plate untouched, hers almost the same, right there beside her on the table. She probably ought to go ahead and eat.

Through the numbness, she felt a touch of nausea.

No. No food. Not now.

She rose, very slowly, her legs wobbly and uncertain. Once she was on her feet, she leaned on the table for a moment or two, getting her bearings.

When she felt more certain her legs would hold her up, she calmly cleared the table and put the food away. She rinsed the dishes and put them in the dishwasher, washed the frying pan and hung it back on the overhead rack.

Once everything was cleaned up, all evidence of the meal they should have shared out of sight, once the sink was empty and the counters wiped down, she went through the door to the foyer, the same way he had gone. There, she locked the front door.

That taken care of, she turned for the stairs. As she climbed, she felt like someone very old and stiff, doggedly dragging herself up to bed. She held on to the polished railing, taking one careful step at a time.

What had happened, the things he'd said to her—none of it made any sense.

She only knew that it was over between them. Over before it had even really gotten started.

Beneath the ugly numbness, she knew she was going to have to get over him, get over a man who'd managed to fill up her world, to change everything, in the space of six days.

She hoped the numbness lasted awhile, bleakly aware that when it faded, she would have to deal with the pain of losing him, have to somehow learn to mend her shattered heart.

At eleven-thirty the next morning, Addy showed up at her door. "I came into town to pick up a few things and I thought we might go out and grab a bite of…" She peered at Katie closer. "Darling, what's happened? What's the matter with you?"

Squinting against the bright morning sun, Katie put her hand up to her tangled hair. "I…" She looked down at the pajamas she was still wearing. "I…well, I slept a little late."

Addy wasn't buying. She stepped over the threshold and closed the door firmly behind her. Quickly, she slipped out of her coat and hung it on the rack, then turned to face Katie again. "Something bad has happened. I can see it in your eyes." She grabbed Katie's hand and towed her into the living room, where she sat on the sofa and pulled Katie down beside her. "Now…" She seemed unsure of how to continue. "Oh, my dear. Please. Tell me what's happened."

Katie hadn't the faintest idea how to answer. She looked at the woman who'd been the mother she'd needed so much, the woman who'd come for her when she had no one else, the woman who'd been there, ever since, whenever Katie needed a listening ear or loving arms to hold her.

Katie realized she needed that now—Addy's loving arms around her. "Oh, Addy…"

Addy reached for her with a worried cry. "Now, now. Oh, honey."

Katie sagged into Addy's embrace, breathing in the faint scent of Addy's subtle perfume, feeling at least a little less numb.

Which maybe, on second thought, wasn't such a great thing. Something loosened in her chest. Without the numbness to keep them down, she felt the sudden tears rising. "Oh, Addy…"

"It's okay. It will be okay."

It wouldn't, and Katie knew it. Not for a long time. And that seemed so awful, so infinitely sad, that the tears rose high enough to burn her throat, to fill her eyes with scalding wetness. "Oh, I don't think so…oh, Addy, it won't. Not for a long time."

Her shoulders started shaking as the sobs took over, deep, wrenching ones. The tears dribbled down her cheeks and kept on coming, a river of them. Addy held her, not caring the least that Katie was soaking the front of her angora sweater. She whispered comforting words as Katie sobbed for the love—for the future with Justin—that was never going to be.

Finally, Katie spoke against Addy's warm, willing shoulder, the words fractured, broken—just like her heart. "It was…oh, Addy, I don't know how it happened, that I ended up caring so much. It shouldn't hurt like this, should it? It was only a few short days."

Addy stroked her hair. "Now, now…"

With another shuddering sob, Katie pulled free so she could meet Addy's eyes. "I—I think I love him," she said in terrified wonder. In complete disbelief. "But that can't be, can it? Not after so short a time, not after what happened last night—"

Addy asked the pertinent question. "Who, darling? Who do you love?"

Katie bit her lip. Suddenly she remembered: Caleb's ski resort project. It was so important to him. And this…what had happened, well, this was strictly personal. Between her and Justin. It had nothing to do with Caleb's business. But somehow, at that moment, she feared…

If Caleb found out how deeply Justin had wounded her, how she'd sobbed out her hurt and bewilderment in Addy's arms, he might confront Justin. He might even decide he couldn't allow Justin to be involved in his project.

She hadn't any idea what would happen then—maybe nothing. Or maybe Justin would back out and everything would have to be put on hold.

She didn't want that.

This wasn't about that.

"Addy, you have to promise me that you won't say a word to Caleb. I don't want him upset over this."

"Honey. Say a word about what?"

"You just have to promise me."

Addy's mouth pinched up tight. "It's that Justin Caldwell, isn't it?" When Katie only stared at her, she asked, outraged, "Well, who else could it be?"

Katie looked away.

Addy didn't allow that. "Look at me." Reluctantly, Katie did. Addy said, "It *is* Caldwell, isn't it?"

Katie only shut her eyes and wilted into Addy's arms again.

Addy held on tight. "There, there. Whatever he's done, I can see you're better off without him. You know that, don't you?"

The really awful, hopeless thing was that she didn't know it. She *still* didn't know it—oh, maybe in her head, she did. But not in her shattered heart, where it mattered. Even after he'd made it perfectly clear that she'd better learn to live without him, that he wouldn't be back, her hungry heart refused to believe it.

Somehow, though, she made herself nod against

Addy's shoulder. "Yes. I'm better off. I really am."
She pulled free of Addy's hold again and took the
tissue Addy handed her. She dried her tears and blew
her nose and drew herself up straight. "He broke it
off last night."

"You grew close in the museum?"

"Oh, Addy. It was a beautiful time. I felt as if I
knew him so well. It's so hard to explain. I felt this
powerful connection to him. I was so sure I'd found
the right guy."

"And then, out of nowhere last night, he told you
he wouldn't be seeing you anymore?"

"That's right."

"But why?"

It was the million-dollar question and Katie still
had no answer to it. "He didn't explain."

Addy grunted in pure disgust. "Some other
woman, no doubt."

"No. I really don't think so."

"Then what?"

"He just said it was over."

"But it makes no sense."

"That's what I've been thinking—*all* I've been
thinking. I've been trying to accept the fact that I'll
probably never know why he broke it off. I don't feel
very accepting, though. I really don't." She forced a
wobbly smile. "But, Addy. You're right. I'll be okay.
Eventually. I know I will."

Addy gave her a game grin. "That's the spirit."
Her grin became an angry frown. "And as for that
Caldwell fellow—"

Katie interrupted. "No. Listen. What happened was

strictly personal, between him and me. I shouldn't even have told you.''

"Of course you should have,'' Addy huffed. "What affects you affects the people who love you. Never forget that.'' Addy sighed and took Katie's hand again, enclosing it between the two of hers. "Sometimes, when you're suffering terribly, it's hard to keep from cutting yourself off from the people who matter. Promise me you won't do that now.''

There was something in Addy's voice, in her eyes. Something sad. And heavy with regret. Katie had to ask. "Have you done that? Cut yourself off from the ones who love you? Is that what you're saying?''

Addy patted her hand. "Am I so obvious?''

"Oh, no. Not at all. But I know you and love you. How you feel doesn't have to be obvious, for me to pick up on it—and it did seem to me as if you were talking about yourself just now.''

There was a moment of silence. Then Addy admitted, "Well, yes. Maybe I was. I…well, I had a tough time when Riley was born. I almost didn't make it. And then they told me there would be no more children. I came from a big family and I always wanted, oh, ten or twelve or so of my own. I was cut to the heart by the news. I couldn't eat. Couldn't…love my husband. Or my new baby. The doctors said it was a serious case of postpartum depression.''

"But…?''

"I don't know. I think maybe it was the death of my most cherished dream. To have a big family, to someday be surrounded by an adorable crowd of happy grandchildren. It hurt so much to lose that dream, I lost sight of all the wonderful things I *did* have. It was a terrible time. I almost drove Caleb away."

"Impossible. He loves you so much."

"I know. But he's a man who needs a lot of attention. You know him, full of life and energy. Always on to the next big plan. He needs a wife to help him live his dreams, a woman who's there, right beside him, while he makes those dreams come true. After Riley was born, I was like a shadow of myself, for much too long. And a man like Caleb can't live with a shadow for a wife. And certainly it wasn't any good for Riley, either. He was an innocent baby, then, a baby who needed his mother's love."

"But you worked through it."

"Yes. Barely. I should have reached out. But instead, I disengaged from the two people who needed me the most." Addy smoothed a wild strand of Katie's uncombed hair, guiding it back behind her ear. "Don't make the same mistake yourself. Please."

"I won't," Katie promised. "But I do need a little time, you know? Addy, I really cared for him. It was sudden, yes. But somehow, being sudden and short-lived doesn't make it any less powerful."

"I understand. I truly do. Just don't hold it all in. Just remember that we're here, Caleb and Riley and I, any time you need us."

Addy stayed for lunch. As the two of them fixed sandwiches and heated up some soup, Addy asked more questions. She pressed for specifics about Justin, about what had gone wrong.

But Katie only shook her head. "It's over, that's all. All the little details don't matter." *Except to me.*

She couldn't get Addy to promise not to say anything about Justin to Caleb. "Business is business," Addy said. "But Caleb certainly has a right to know the kind of man he's dealing with."

Katie tried to argue that Addy didn't really know what kind of man Justin was. "You've just been complaining that I haven't told you anything. Remember that. I haven't. I didn't say anything against Justin, and I won't. All you know is there was…something. And now it's over."

"I know that he hurt you, and that's enough for me. Unless you're ready to tell me a little more about what happened?"

It was too much. "Let's just let it go for now. Please."

Addy looked slightly put out, but she did drop the subject. They ate lunch and Addy hung around for an extra cup of hot tea and then said she had to get back to the ranch. "Come for dinner tonight. Let us cheer you up."

"I can't. Not tonight. I need a few days. A little time to myself, to…lick my wounds, I guess. Maybe that's self-indulgent, but—"

"Oh, of course it's not," Addy cut in tartly. "You get through this however you need to. Just remember what I said before. Don't shut us out for *too* long."

"I won't. I promise you."

After Addy left, Katie wandered back upstairs to

her bedroom. She climbed into bed and closed her eyes. Sleep wouldn't come, so she simply lay there, wishing the numbness would return, feeling broken and much, much too sad.

Eventually, she dragged herself from bed, took a shower and forced herself to go out for a walk through Old Town. The snow lay in patches on the wet ground by then. It was hard to believe that it had been a deep, unbroken blanket of white just four days before. She waved at friends and neighbors she saw on the street and even stopped to chat with Emelda, who emerged from Super Savers Mart, the grocery store that had once been known as the Thunder Canyon Mercantile and had been owned and run by the Douglas family for generations.

"Will you look at this weather?" Emelda shifted her bag of groceries to one arm and stuck out the other in a gesture intended to include the wide, sunny sky and the melting patches of snow just beyond the covered sidewalk. "Amazing, isn't it? Snow past my eyeballs one day, dirty patches on the bare ground in no time at all—are you all right, dear? You do look a tad under the weather, and I know you didn't feel all that well last week." She leaned closer to Katie and kept on talking, saving Katie the discomfort of having to answer the question about how she was feeling. "One thing I did like about that nice, deep snow pack. Kept trespassers away from that erosion hole behind my back fence."

The hole in question was a caved-in section of tunnel from Caleb's played out mine, the Queen of Hearts. Riley had seen to boarding it over, but someone kept pushing the boards aside. Probably adventurous kids, Katie thought, kids wanting to holler down the hole and pitch rocks into the dark puddles of stagnant water at the bottom. Emelda worried constantly that someone was going to fall in. She'd called the Thunder Canyon police department more than once to report that she'd spotted trespassers around the hole.

"Those boards were moved again this morning," Emelda reported with a fretful cluck of her tongue. "I hope you'll speak to Riley about it. I worry, I do."

What else could she say? "I'll call Riley today."

"Thank you, dear. It's just that it's so dangerous."

Katie made a few more reassuring noises and then, at last, Emelda toddled off, headed up Pine, toward her tidy little house at the west end of State Street.

Katie walked on, trying to remember to smile and wave when folks said hi, though her mind kept tracking back to last night, to the way Justin had kissed her, so hungrily, as if he would never let her go, the way he had unhooked her bra and cupped her breasts, putting his hot mouth to them, the way his hands had stroked her, the way he'd gathered up her skirt, as if he had to touch her all over or die.

And then, not twenty minutes later, for no reason she could see, he was saying goodbye forever and walking out the door.

None of it was about you. You shouldn't have been involved. What did that *mean?*

You are exactly the woman a man like me never finds....

If she was so special, then *why* had he left her?

I'm not who you think I am....

It made no sense. None of it.

It made no sense and it hurt.

A lot.

When she got home, she resisted the temptation to put on her pj's again and climb back in bed. She went to the kitchen, thinking she'd try focusing on what to have for dinner.

Easily handled. She had plenty of leftovers.

But when she pulled open the refrigerator door and looked at the covered dish full of chicken, at the plastic containers with the salad and potatoes inside, the bittersweet memory of last night overwhelmed her.

She saw him at the sink, scrubbing the potatoes; at the counter, handing her the slotted spoon. She could almost hear their voices, talking of everyday things, could see his smile and the warmth and admiration in his eyes.

Swiftly, before she could feel guilty for wasting good food, she took out the covered dish and the plastic containers and emptied them into the trash.

There. Now didn't that help a lot?

Hardly. Still, she would never eat that food and she was glad it was gone.

And there was still Riley. She'd promised Emelda she'd give him a call, though she didn't really feel like talking to anyone right at that moment. Reluctantly, she dialed his number. His machine picked up and relief flowed through her. She left a quick message about the problem at the erosion hole and hung up. There. She'd kept her word to Emelda and she hadn't had to listen to Riley's dear deep voice, hadn't been faced with the possibility he might pick up on her misery and want to know if something was bothering her.

She went upstairs early and lay in bed forever, pretending to sleep.

Sunday, Addy called after church. "We missed you at the service."

"I just felt like staying home today."

"Honey, now remember what we talked about. You can't let yourself—"

"Addy. It's only been two days."

"I know, I know. I guess I just, well, I want to make things all better."

Katie suppressed a sigh. "You can't. Not right now. I'm okay. Really." As okay as could be expected, anyway, given the circumstances.

"You're right. Of course you're right. I couldn't possibly talk you into coming on out to the ranch for dinner, now could I?"

"Next Friday. How's that?"

"And our usual lunch on Thursday."

"Of course."

"You call me. I mean it. If you need anything."

"Oh, Addy. You make it sound as if I've got some terrible disease."

"Sorry. Remember. I'm here."

Katie almost chuckled. "As if I could forget."

Addy clucked over her and urged her to take care of herself and finally said goodbye.

Katie spent a peaceful day, reading, taking a long

walk, watching television in the evening. She told herself she was feeling better, and she was.

Maybe. In a way.

Monday she went to work at nine, as usual.

Lindy was waiting for her, an avid gleam in her eyes. "Katie. Wow. That Justin Caldwell...total hunk. So did you have a great time Friday night, or what?"

It hurt—that cruel knife, twisting—just to hear his name. "Yes," she said flatly. "Great." And it had been, until the end. "And don't you have work to do?"

Lindy stepped back. "Well, excuse me for breathing."

Katie knew she'd skirted the borderline of rudeness, but somehow, right then, she didn't have it in her to smooth things over. She turned for her workstation in the center of the room.

The whole day, she did her very best to keep her mind on task. Neither Lindy nor Emelda asked if there was anything wrong with her. But she caught both of them looking at her, sideways looks of confusion and concern.

That night, at home, she tried to read, but it was no good. She didn't have the concentration for it, not right then. So she turned on the television and stared at the changing images, hardly aware of what she was watching.

Her mind kept circling back to the central question, kept worrying at it, trying to make sense of it....

Not for another woman. She would have bet every cent she had on that. And not for her money, either.

If it had been about her money, he'd still be there, he wouldn't have left. He'd be busy sweeping her off her feet, getting ready to propose marriage for real, paving the way at a chance for a big payoff when it came time for a divorce.

And if not for another woman, or for the money, then *why?*

She simply could not understand.

Why?

Chapter Thirteen

The meeting of the Thunder Canyon Ski Resort Investor Group was scheduled for ten on Tuesday morning, in the conference room at the back of the project offices on Main Street.

It was to be a strictly routine proceeding. As project manager, Caleb would sit at the head of the table and run the meeting, explaining the current status of the project to any investors who happened to show up. He would list the contractors who would supervise construction and assure everyone that the financing was in order and building would be ready to begin in May, right after the gala groundbreaking ceremonies.

Justin arrived at fifteen before the hour—which was fifteen minutes too early. When it came to dropping bombs, it was always advisable not to hang around the water cooler making casual chitchat beforehand.

The wrong subject might come up. He'd have to evade or lie outright and that could lead to questions he didn't want to answer—at least not before the crucial moment.

No. Better to be right on time, go straight to the conference room, ready to blow them all—Caleb most especially—out of their fat leather chairs.

In the lot behind the town hall, Justin parked and turned off the engine and sat behind the wheel, ready to dig into his briefcase and look busy if anyone noticed him just sitting there.

As he waited, he tried to keep his thoughts where they belonged: on the final stroke ahead. On his payback, at last.

Instead, his mind kept wandering to the one subject he had sworn to himself he would avoid.

Katie.

He stared out the windshield and saw nothing but her face: those wide amber eyes, that soft mouth, the shining brown hair.

She'd be at the library now, wouldn't she? Standing behind that central counter, ready to help any reader who needed to know where to find a certain book. She'd be—

A tapping sound on the driver's door window cut into his self-indulgent reverie. He turned his head.

Caleb. Damn it.

The older man swept off his big white Stetson and signaled with a jerk of his head.

No way to fake being busy now. Justin grabbed his briefcase and got out of the SUV.

"We've got a minute or two before the meeting,"

Caleb said, without any of the back-slapping how-you-been-and-good-to-see-you routine that was his usual style. "I want a word with you."

"What's up?" Alarm bells jangling along every nerve, Justin tried to keep it casual, despite the cold look on Caleb's tanned, creased face.

But even if the silver-haired wheeler-dealer had somehow found out what was up, there wasn't a thing he could do about it now. It was, in the truest sense, a done deal. Justin had the needed proxies in his briefcase and he *would* make his move.

Caleb didn't answer his question. "Let's go inside, to my office."

They went in the back way, Caleb ushering Justin ahead. The door to Caleb's private office stood open and Justin led the way in.

"Have a seat." Caleb shut the door.

Justin stayed on his feet. "Is there a problem?"

Caleb sent the white Stetson flying. It landed on a sofa in the small sitting area. He strode around Justin and pulled out the studded leather chair behind his wide inlaid desk. But he didn't sit down. He moved in front of the chair, pressed his knuckles to the desktop and loomed toward Justin. "What's this I hear about you breaking my little girl's heart?"

Katie.

Damn it to hell. He should have known. "She… went to you?"

Caleb snorted. It was not a friendly sound. "Hell, no. Adele got it out of her. But it doesn't make a damn how I know. The point is, whatever you thought you were up to with her, you've messed her over and I want to know why.''

Justin stared at the stranger who had fathered him. This was exactly the way it was supposed to go.

So why didn't he feel the least bit triumphant? Why didn't he feel righteous and eager to deal the final blow instead of fed up with this whole thing, fed up and sick at heart, an ashy taste in his mouth?

''I asked you a question.'' Caleb craned farther across the big desk.

The words came to Justin, the ones he'd once imagined himself saying. He went ahead and spoke them. He had nothing else to say. ''It's interesting how concerned you are for the tender feelings of your wife's goddaughter, when you never spared a thought for the woman who did nothing wrong but to love you—and bear your son.''

Caleb blinked. ''Never spared a thought. For Addy? I don't know what the hell you're blathering about.''

''You'll understand everything. I promise you. Soon enough.''

''I don't know what you think is going on here. But I'll tell you this. You hurt my Katie—for no damn reason that anyone can see. And I'm not going to forget it.''

Justin glanced at his Rolex. ''Time for the meeting. I think we should go in.''

Prior to the formal start of the meeting, the investors milled around, exchanging greetings, while Caleb's secretary bustled up and down the big table, carrying coffee to anyone who asked for it and bringing extra water glasses. A thick blue file imprinted with the ski resort logo of a downhill racer crouched and flying along a snowy slope waited at every seat.

Eventually, Caleb cleared his throat and suggested that everyone sit down. He settled into his seat at the head of the long table and glanced around at the investors. ''Well. We have a pretty nice turnout.'' There were a few empty seats, including the ones that should have been filled by Verlin Parks and Josh Levitt. Verlin and Josh had thirteen and fifteen percent of the project, respectively. With Justin's twenty-six percent, that made a total of fifty-four. Three percent more than he needed, as a matter of fact. Caleb added, ''Let's begin.''

Up and down the table there were murmurs of agreement.

And so they began.

Caleb led them through the file. He was pleased—though he sent a hard look Justin's way as he said it—to announce that the project was a definite go. The financing was taken care of, and the contractors lined up. Justin sat and pretended to listen. He was only waiting for the proper moment.

Waiting and wishing that he even gave a damn anymore. Longing to get up and walk out and let Caleb have his damn project.

But he didn't get up. He would do what he'd come to do. He would make Caleb Douglas pay in the way that mattered most to him: Justin would take away control.

And *wishing* was an activity for fools, anyway.

He kept having to remind himself of that.

Ever since he'd met a certain amber-eyed brunette who'd made him start *wishing* for what he was never going to have.

Finally, it was time. Caleb asked, "Well, gentlemen. Is there any other business we need to discuss?"

And Justin said, "Yes, as a matter of fact, there is. There's the question of who's going to manage the project."

The room went dead silent—until Caleb boomed out, "What the hell are you talking about? I'm project manager. We're all in agreement on that. I'm listed as manager on the limited partnership contract that everyone here has signed."

There were murmurs and nods down the table.

Justin spoke again. "I have another man in mind. He's got the experience. Much more so than you, Caleb."

Beneath his deep tan, a hot flush rushed up the older man's neck. "I *have* the experience. And I have everyone's support but yours." There were more nods and whispers of agreement. Caleb blustered on, "It's been a given from the first that this was my baby and I would be in charge. The financing was arranged with that understanding. If anyone tries to change horses in midstream, the money could fall through."

Justin didn't waver. "If the current financing becomes a problem, I'll see that we find another lender. It's not going to be a problem. As you just spent an hour telling us, the project is in excellent shape. And as to your holding majority support…" He reached in his briefcase and pulled out the two proxies. He tossed them down on the table. "Joshua Levitt and Verlin Parks are in support of any decision I make. Here are their proxies to prove it."

The flush had left Caleb's face. Now he looked a little green. Justin could see in his eyes that until that moment, he hadn't guessed that Verlin and Josh were longtime business associates of Justin's—or that Justin had sent them in ahead to buy in for specific amounts. Caleb spoke low and furiously. "All right, Caldwell. What the hell is going on?"

Justin only shrugged. "As I said, Verlin and Josh have given me their proxies. I now speak for them. Look the proxies over. Please. You'll see they're in order. Between Parks, Levitt and me, we hold fifty-four percent. More than enough to choose a new project manager—according to the terms of the partnership."

Again, the room was pin-drop silent.

Then Darrell Smart spoke up. "Let's have a look." Darrell was one of Caleb's good buddies, and legal counsel for the project. Justin shoved the proxies toward the lawyer. Smart picked them up and studied them in a silence so total, the crackling of the papers as he handled them sounded loud as gunshots.

Finally, the attorney glanced over the top of his reading glasses at Caleb. "Sorry. Looks in order to me."

Caleb barely seemed to hear him. He was too busy glaring at Justin. Justin could read what he was thinking as if the older man had spoken aloud. *Why are you doing this? What the hell does it prove?*

Justin dealt the telling blow. "All right, then. I

move that we put in my man as manager. Since I hold control of fifty-four percent of this partnership, what I move, goes." He granted Caleb a frosty smile. "And since these offices are part of the project, I'll expect you to turn them over. My man will be here next Monday, ready to get to work."

There was some discussion—heated, but pointless. In the end, everyone conceded that Justin had the power to bring in his own manager. Caleb was finished as project head.

Finally, after sending Justin lethal looks and offering regrets to the by-then silent Caleb for the dirty trick that had been played on him, the others filed out.

Caleb remained in his chair, his gray head lowered, as the others took their leave. His left arm lay lax on the tabletop, his thick gold wedding ring gleaming in the shaft of winter sunlight that slanted in the room's one tall, narrow window.

Finally, it was just the older man, slumped in his big chair, Justin, still seated in his, and the secretary.

"Alice, you can go now," Caleb said quietly, not bothering to glance up. The secretary, looking wide-eyed behind her thick glasses, rose. "Shut the door on the way out, will you?"

Alice did as she was told, pulling the door quietly closed as she left.

There was a long moment where Caleb simply sat there, head lowered as before, arm still outstretched on the table, wedding ring catching the light, giving back that eerie gleam

Eventually, he rested his other arm beside the first, folded his beefy hands together and lifted his head. His green eyes had a lost look in them, one of shock and dazed confusion. He said one word. "Why?"

The question echoed in the silent room.

And Justin had his answer ready. "Because being the big dog, running everything in sight—that's what matters to you the most. I wanted to take away something you'd miss. And I have, haven't I?"

Caleb still wasn't satisfied. "Why?" he asked again. "Why would you want that? What the hell have I ever done to you?"

Justin reached in his briefcase again and brought out an envelope. From the envelope, he removed two snapshots. He pushed his chair back, rose to walk down the table and stood over the other man.

Shoving the ski resort file aside, he laid the pictures down, one beside the other, in front of Caleb. He pointed. "That's my mother, thirty-five years ago, before she met you."

Caleb stared down at the old, dog-eared snapshot. "Ramona..." It came out a bare husk of sound.

Relentless now, determined to finish this and get out, Justin pointed at the other picture. "That one was taken a month before she died. She came to me, returned to Montana at the end, so I could take care of her, when it was too late for anything else—too late for you to do anything to her that cancer wasn't going to do, anyway. She doesn't look much like the woman you knew, does she?"

Caleb raised his eyes then. He'd moved beyond dazed confusion. Now he looked like a man who'd seen a ghost—which, in a way, Justin supposed, he had. His face had a gray cast beneath the tan. "But…her last name was Lovett."

"That's right. But after you told her you wanted nothing more to do with her—or the baby you'd made with her—she left the state, just the way you wanted her to. She left Montana and she never returned until she knew she was dying. When she left, she took the name Caldwell. She went by that name for the rest of her life. She put it on my birth certificate. So that's who I am."

Caleb shut his eyes and slowly opened them. "You're…my son." He said it in a kind of horrified understanding. "My son…"

"By blood, yes. By blood only. You broke her, do you know that? She never could make a real life for herself, after what you did to her, after you threatened to do her serious damage if she ever came near you again, if she ever dared to let anyone know whose child she was carrying."

Caleb jerked back as if Justin had struck him. "No. You've got it—"

Justin cut the air with an arm, a brutal, final gesture. "I don't want to hear it."

"But you have to listen for a moment. You have to let me—"

"That's where you're wrong. I don't have to listen to you. Who are you to me, besides the man who destroyed the woman who gave me life, the woman who raised me the best she knew how?" He scooped up the two snapshots and turned for the door, stopping before he went out to deliver one last command.

"Clear out your office. My man will be in Monday morning, nine sharp."

Chapter Fourteen

Katie's phone rang at nine Tuesday night. She picked up the remote extension and checked the display before she answered it: Addy.

"No, thanks. Not right now," she muttered, and let her machine get it. She settled back in her favorite chair, and heard the sound of Addy's voice coming from the kitchen, as she recorded her message.

Katie couldn't make out the words, but there was something in the tone, something agitated. Something not right.

With a sigh, she picked it up. "Addy? Are you okay?"

"Oh, thank God."

Whatever it was, it wasn't good. Grim images invaded Katie's mind: Riley, in an accident. Caleb having a heart attack. "What? What's the matter?"

"Darling, it's Caleb."

She felt a hollowness below her ribs. "Has he been hurt?"

"Not physically. No. It's nothing like that. He... Well, he's locked himself in his study. He's been in there since noon. Nine hours. He won't come out and he won't let anyone else in."

"But why?"

"Sweetheart, if I only knew. I called Riley over here a couple of hours ago, when I couldn't get Caleb to open the door myself. Riley's tried. Caleb wouldn't let him in, either. Honey, it's just not like him. He came home from that meeting and he walked right by me. He looked so awful. Not sick, exactly. But sick at heart. Kind of beaten down and gray in the face, his shoulders slumped and sagging. I asked him what was wrong, but he only shook his head and headed for his study."

"Addy, what meeting?"

"The one for the ski resort project."

"Something bad happened at the meeting?"

"Well, if it did, he's just not acting his usual self over it. You know how he is. When things don't go his way, he paces. He gets loud and he lays down the law. But he never locks himself in a room somewhere and refuses to come out. Plus, I'm sure he's drinking. The times he barked at me through the door to go away, he was slurring his words."

"Have Riley call someone who was at the meeting and ask them what went on there."

"Oh, honey. Yes. Good idea," Katie heard her

speaking to Riley. Then she came back on the line. "All right. Riley's taking care of that."

"I'll be over as soon as I can get there."

"Darling, would you? I'm so worried. And you know how he adores you. Maybe he'll open that door for you."

Addy greeted her at the front door, her face drawn, eyes grim with worry. She helped Katie out of her coat and hung it in the front closet of the huge two-story foyer as she blurted out what she knew. "Riley got through to Darrell Smart. At the meeting, Justin Caldwell took the job of project manager away from Caleb."

Katie's heart lurched. "Justin...but how?"

"Oh, it was something about proxies. And percentages of the partnership. Somehow, that Caldwell fellow got control over enough of the investors to be able to kick Caleb out. Caleb has until Monday to vacate the offices so the new man can take over."

Could this really be happening? Justin. Breaking her heart, then stealing Caleb's dream.

The question was there again, echoing through her mind. She said it out loud that time. "Why would he do such a thing?"

"I haven't the foggiest. But if that man were in this room right now, I'd go get Caleb's best hunting rifle and shoot him straight through his evil heart. What did Caleb ever do to him, that he would treat my husband so shabbily—and for that matter, what did *you* ever do to him?" Addy answered her own questions. "Nothing. Absolutely nothing, that's what.

And now Riley's in a fury over it. He's insisting he's going to Bozeman to confront Caldwell. Oh, I don't know where we're headed, I don't know what to do.''

Katie took the older woman by the upper arms, to steady her. ''Slow down. We're going to get to the bottom of this, I promise you.''

''Oh, Katie. I'm sorry to drag you into this, but I must admit, I'm so relieved you're here. I'm…well, I'm just a wreck.''

Katie pulled her close and hugged her hard, then she took her arms again and met her eyes. ''First, I'll talk to Riley, get him to slow down a little. And then we'll see if I can get Caleb to let me in.''

Katie found Riley in Caleb's den, off the study, pacing back and forth. He was hot under the collar and far from willing to slow down.

''Good. You're here,'' he said at the sight of her. ''Look after Mom, will you? I'm heading for Bozeman.''

Katie grabbed one of his big, tanned hands and wouldn't let go. ''Please. Let me try to talk to Caleb first. Let me see if I can find out what's really happened here.''

Riley's green eyes shone hard as emeralds. ''I know what's happened. That bastard worked you over, and now he's done this. If there's a reason he's decided to come after my family, I want to find out what it is.''

So, Katie thought glumly. Riley knew about her and Justin, too. She supposed she shouldn't be surprised. Adele had never agreed not to tell Caleb. And once Caleb knew, Riley was bound to hear. "We all want answers." She squeezed Riley's hand between both of hers. "I beg you. Give me a chance to get to the bottom of this first. Then, if you still think you have to, you can go deal with Justin."

Riley made a low, angry sound. "Face it. Dad's not letting you through that door."

"Just give me a chance. Please."

Riley swore low. "All right. But if he won't let you in, I'm out of here."

"Thank you."

"No reason to thank me. He's not letting you in."

She gave his hand one more reassuring squeeze and then relinquished it.

Riley gestured at the shut door to the study. "Go for it." He stood back and folded his muscular arms over his broad chest, his mouth set in a grim line.

Riley was probably right. If Caleb wouldn't open the door for his wife or his son, there was no reason to believe he'd let Katie in, either. But she had to try. She didn't like the look in Riley's eyes. If Riley took off after Justin now, who could say what might happen when the two met up. One of them—or both— could get hurt. She didn't want that. Not for Riley. And, God help her, not for Justin, either.

She marched over, raised her hand and rapped sharply on the door.

Nothing. Complete silence from the room beyond. She glanced back at Riley. He still had his arms folded over his chest—and an I-told-you-so look in his eyes. She tried the door: locked.

Riley muttered, "See, I told—"

Katie put up a hand to silence him and called to the man on the other side of the door. "Caleb. It's me, Katie. Won't you let me in, please?"

Dead silence from beyond the door. Riley uncrossed his arms. "That does it. I'm—"

"Wait." She pressed her ear to the door, heard heavy footsteps on the other side. She put up her hand again, for Riley to be still.

The footsteps stopped. Caleb spoke from right beyond the door. "Katie? That you?"

"Yes. Oh, yes. It's me."

"Katie, I don—" He didn't seem to know how to go on. And Adele had been right. It sounded as if he'd been drinking. His words came slow and slurred-sounding.

"Oh, Caleb. Won't you let me in?"

Another pause, then Caleb growled, "Riley still out there?"

She glanced at Riley again. He looked as if he wanted to break something, to pick up one of the bronze cowboy sculptures that decorated the den and hurl it at the wood-paneled wall. "Yes. He's here."

"Tell him to go 'way. Can't talk to 'im now. Only you, Katie. Jus' you, 'kay?"

Riley muttered more swear words. Katie only looked at him, pleading with her eyes.

With another low, furious oath, Riley strode from the room.

"Katie?" Caleb asked again.

"It's all right. Riley's left. Now, won't you please let me in?"

Almost before she finished asking the question, the door swung inward.

She gasped at the sight of the man on the other side. "Oh, Caleb..." His green eyes were droopy and bloodshot. His mouth hung lax. He looked a decade older than the last time she'd seen him. And the smell of too much Tennessee whisky came off him in waves.

He gave her the saddest, most hangdog sort of look, and then he turned and trudged to his wide burled walnut desk and around to the back of it. With a heavy grunt, he dropped into his studded buckskin swivel chair and stared down at the papers spread on the desktop in front of him. A telltale half-empty bottle of whisky stood uncapped at his elbow. "I been...busy. Thinkin'. Thinkin' and drinkin'..." He looked up, let out a low, rough bark of humorless laughter, and then leaned back in the chair. His chin drooped on his chest. He gazed mournfully at the scatter of papers in front of him. "How, I keep askin' mysel'...how did it all go so wrong...?" Behind him, a picture hung askew on the wood-paneled wall, revealing his private safe, the door to which stood open. All the blinds were drawn and the only light came from the lamp on Caleb's desk.

Katie hovered before him, a million dismayed questions spinning through her mind. She pressed her mouth shut and kept quiet. She knew, in the end, he would tell her what she needed to know. There was no other reason for him to have let her in here when he refused to open the door to Adele or to Riley.

He *wanted* to talk. And he'd chosen her to do his

talking to. It was only a matter of waiting and listening—and applying gentle pressure at the right moment.

Gingerly, she lowered herself to one of the two carved, leather-seated guest chairs that faced the big desk. Once she was in the chair, she realized she'd been holding her breath. She let it out with great care.

Caleb shook his head. "Katie, Katie, Katie. Where the hell did it all go so wrong?" He raised his hanging head enough that she could look into those bleary eyes.

"Tell me," she said softly. "Just tell me. Everything. And then we can talk about what to do next."

He kept shaking his head. "Bad idea. To tell you. Yeah. Pro'ly a bad idea…"

"Just tell me. We can't work this out until you do."

"Hell. I don't know…"

"Oh, yes, you do. You know. It's time to talk about it—whatever it is."

"Maybe."

"Uh-uh. No maybes. It's time. You know it is."

He regarded her woozily. She looked back at him, waiting.

At last, haltingly, he began to speak. "I was…a true husban'. I swear it to you. Never looked at another woman…"

Suddenly she was recalling what Addy had told her a few days before and prompted gently, "But then Riley was born…"

He grunted. "Tha's right. Riley. Af'er Riley was born, they tol' Adele she couldn't have any more chil'ren. It broke her heart. Lo's o' kids. She always wanted that. For the longes' time, she was…like a stranger in our house…in our bed. She jus' ignored me. An' Riley, too. Poor little fella. He was cryin' all the time. I couldn'…take it. It got so I, well, I jus' needed someone."

He said he'd met Ramona one night when he went out to a roadhouse to get his mind off his vacant-eyed wife and their poor, screaming baby. "Ramona was a waitress. A tall, black-haired beauty." He heaved a heavy sigh. "Ramona. Damn my soul. Ramona."

For over an hour, his voice low and whisky-rough, the words sometimes slurring together, he told her the sad story of his own folly and betrayal. When the tale was told, Katie sat silent, hardly able to believe what she'd just heard.

Justin was Caleb's son. His *son*.

Suddenly, everything was making sense. A hideous, awful, ugly kind of sense, but sense nonetheless.

Caleb threw out a hand—missing the whisky bottle by an inch. In a sweeping, unsteady gesture, he indicated the papers scattered on his desk. "I's all here. Righ' here…you jus' see for yourself."

Katie stood and bent over the desk.

"See. Look here." He waved a snapshot. "Ramona an' me." He dropped the picture and picked up what looked like a letter. "Her love letters. She wro'e me a hundred of 'em. Sen' 'em here, to the house. Addy never knew. She wasn' up for checkin' the mail. She jus' stayed in our room, then. Alone. I hardly saw her. Ramona wro'e me, love letters first.

And then there were the ones that came later, the ones with the threats.'' He scanned the desk and snatched up a small scrap of paper. "An' this. The check I gave 'er. Jus' like I tol' you, cancelled. See?''

Katie took it from his fingers. "Yes. I see." It came to her, right then, as she stared at all those zeroes. She knew what she had to do.

"I—I did care for her, for Ramona," Caleb muttered. "But...she wasn' Addy. Addy is...my love, my life. Never should have started up with Ramona. I know it, I do. And then, well, after Ramona disappeared, Addy got better. The years went by an'...I started thinkin' it was maybe for the bes', jus' to let it be, not go stirrin' up ol' trouble.''

A large yellow envelope lay at the edge of the desk. Katie took it and dropped the cancelled check into it. Then she gathered up the letters and the photographs and put them in the envelope, too.

"What d'you think you're doin'?" Caleb demanded.

She hooked the envelope's metal clasp. "I'm taking these to Justin."

He regarded her blearily. "Wha' for?"

"Because he doesn't know the whole truth, and it's time he did."

Caleb rubbed his eyes. "Hell. What good's that gonna do now?" He was shaking his head again. "No point. Too late."

"Caleb," she said softly. "It's never too late to do the right thing." Turning, she set the envelope on her chair, then she went around the desk and put her hand on Caleb's sagging shoulder.

He looked up at her, a lost look. ''I...don' know what to do.''

She squeezed his shoulder. ''First, and foremost, you have to remember that Adele loves you. And, though I know you've had your rough patches, Riley loves you, too.''

''They'll hate me. After this.''

''No,'' she said firmly. ''They love you. I'm not saying it will be easy, getting past this. You've done wrong. Very wrong. Not only because you betrayed your wife, but also because of the way you handled it when Ramona told you she was having your baby. But now you've got to clean up the mess you made, as best you can. You've got to tell Adele everything. You've got to take the first steps toward making things right.''

''Oh, no. I can't.'' His head hung down again.

''Look at me,'' she commanded. Slowly, he raised his bloodshot eyes. ''Caleb, you can't let this break you, can't let the bad things you did once destroy your family now.''

''But I—''

''No buts. It's the only way.''

He tried to bluster. ''I didn' let you in here so you could tell me what to do.''

''Yes, you did. That's exactly why you let me in here.''

He let out a hard breath that reeked of too much whisky. ''Oh, no...''

''Oh, yes. You need to do the right thing and you know it. You let me in here so I could help you to do it.'' She touched his silver hair, pressed his shoulder again. "I'm going to go get Addy now. And you're going to tell her. Everything."

He said nothing and she figured that was acceptance enough. She turned for the door.

"Katie?"

She glanced back at his hangdog face, his haunted eyes. "You're a good girl, my bes' girl."

"I love you, too. Put the cap on that bottle. I'll be right back."

A half an hour later, Riley walked her to her Suburban. She had the envelope in hand, Justin's home address and phone number scrawled across the front of it.

"Thanks," Riley said, and gave her a hug.

"Any time." She hugged him back, good and hard.

When he pulled away, he looked doubtful. "You sure you don't want me to go with you, to see Caldwell?"

"Nope. I'll be fine."

"Damn." He raked a hand back through his dark hair. "What a mess, huh? And I've got a half brother…"

"Yes. You do."

"That'll be something to get used to—after I get through telling Dad just what I think of him."

She suggested gently, "Wait 'til he's sober. For tonight, Addy's going to need your strong shoulder to lean on once she's through dealing with Caleb."

Riley swore. "At least what Caldwell did to Dad is more understandable now. If I were in his position, I might have done a lot worse." He scowled. "But there's still no excuse for what he did to you. I could bust his face in for that.''

She put her hand on his arm. "No need to go hitting anyone. I can handle this. You watch me.''

He almost grinned. "You know, I believe that you can.'' He chucked her under the chin. "You're a tough little tenderfoot.''

"That's me. Tough as they come.''

He grew more serious. "When will you go?''

She looked up into his face and for the first time, she saw the resemblance to Justin. In the shape of his brow and the strong, aggressively masculine jut of his jaw. So strange. Why hadn't she noticed before?

Riley was frowning. "Katie. You okay?''

She drew herself up. "I'm fine. And I'm going to go see Justin right now. It'll be near midnight when I get there. I'm figuring that's late enough on a weeknight he'll probably be at his house.'' Plus, if she went right away, there was less of a chance she'd lose her nerve.

Riley gave her a sideways look. "You sure about this?''

"Riley, he needs to know and, given the circumstances, I think I'm the best one to tell him.''

Justin was sitting in his study at the front of the house when the doorbell rang.

His laptop waited, open and ignored, on the desk before him. His mind was far away from the spreadsheet on the screen, stuck on a brown-haired woman and a silver-haired man and why he didn't feel the sense of triumph and vindication he'd always expected to feel after finally making his move.

The doorbell chimed and Justin ignored it.

He wasn't expecting anyone; he didn't want to see anyone—and anybody who came ringing his bell at midnight could damn well go away and come back at a decent hour.

But then, a minute later, the doorbell rang again. "Get lost," he muttered, and stared blindly at the computer screen in which he had no interest at all.

But then it rang a third time.

That did it. He swore, low and crudely, and pushed himself to his feet. Whoever was out there was going to get an earful.

He strode, fast, through the door to his study and across the hardwood floor of the entry hall. When he got to the door, he flung it wide.

"Hello, Justin."

The breath fled his lungs. He felt as if an iron hand had just punched him a good one square in the solar plexus. He blinked and stepped back. "Katie."

"May I come in?"

"What—?"

She cut him off, sweetly but firmly. "I said, may I come in?"

He fell back another step. He just wasn't getting this. What reason could she possibly have to seek him out now?

It made no sense. Katie, here. At his door.

And still, though it gained him nothing but more pain, he couldn't help drinking in the sight of her, of her shining hair and angel's face, of the grim set to her soft mouth and the strange, determined gleam in those beautiful brown eyes. The scent of her taunted him—warm and temptingly sweet.

Katie. All his senses seemed to call out her name.

"I'll take that as a yes." She stepped over the threshold. She had a big envelope in one hand. She waved it at him. "I have a few things I need to say to you. Is there somewhere we can talk?"

Quelling the urge to sputter out more exclamations of disbelief that she was standing right there, in front of him, he muttered, "Yeah. All right."

She slipped out of her coat, switching the envelope from hand to hand as she shrugged free of the sleeves.

"Here." He reached for it.

But she held on. "No. I'll keep it. This shouldn't take long."

The more he looked at her, the more certain he was that he didn't like the strange gleam in her eyes.

But why should he like it? No way she'd come here to tell him she loved him and couldn't live without him.

Any chance he'd had for that, he'd blown Friday night—and doubly, at the meeting fourteen hours before. Which meant it was going to be something he didn't want to hear.

Might as well get it over with. "Suit yourself." He turned on his heel. "This way."

He led her to the great room at the back of the house, where the ceiling soared up two stories high and two walls of windows looked out on the night. She perched on a chair in one of the sitting areas and folded her coat in her lap. He hovered a few feet from her.

"Please," she said. "Sit down."

He wanted to refuse, felt he'd be better off to stay on his feet. But she looked up at him, mouth set, amber eyes afire with a steely sort of purpose. He gave in and dropped into the chair across from her.

She bit her lip. "I...hardly know where to begin."

He said nothing. It was her damn show, after all.

She sat up straighter and cleared her throat. "Okay. To start, I know about what you did to Caleb this— or rather yesterday—morning. I also know why, at last. I know that you're his son, that he had an affair with your mother when Addy suffered a serious bout of depression after Riley was born. Caleb couldn't take it, watching Addy suffer—her continued rejection of him. He met your mother and they had an affair."

Impatience curled through Justin, coiling like a spring. He wanted her out of there. Every moment in her presence brought it more clearly home to him that he had lost her.

Hell, lost her? He'd never *had* her.

And he never would.

He demanded, "Is there some reason you imagined I needed—much less, *wanted*—to hear all this?"

Her sweet mouth got a pinched look about it. "Be a little patient. Please. I'm getting to the part you need to know."

"Speed it up."

She outright glared at him "Fine," she said. "It went like this. Caleb and your mother had an affair.

When your mother got pregnant, Caleb told her he did care for her, but he still loved Adele. He wouldn't marry your mother, but he offered to give her a half million dollars. For you."

He couldn't stay in his seat. He shot to a standing position. "That's ridiculous. It never happened."

A hot flush flowed up her neck and over her soft cheeks. "Will you let me finish?"

He turned from her, stared at his own shadowed reflection in the dark window opposite where she sat. "Make it fast."

She picked up the pace, each word emerging clipped and cold. "Caleb offered your mother five hundred thousand dollars if she'd give you up, if she'd give you to him—so he and Adele could raise you. Somehow, he hoped to make Adele understand and accept you into their family. It might even have worked. Addy wanted more children so badly."

He whirled on her. "So what? It doesn't matter. My mother turned him down and then he started threatening her. She had to run away."

"No. She didn't turn him down. And she was the one who made the threats."

He refused to believe that. "No."

"Yes. She threatened all sorts of wild things—to kill Adele, to kill Riley. To tell the world that she was carrying Caleb's child and what a rotten bastard he was. But then, in the end, she agreed to Caleb's terms. She took the check." He was shaking his head, but Katie just went on talking. "She took the check when she was eight months along. But instead of sticking around to give you to Caleb when you were born, she ran off. She cashed that check. And she raised you on her own—just as you told me she did, always moving from one place to another, keeping ahead of any chance that Caleb might find her—and you.''

"No."

She threw the envelope on the table between them. "It's all in there. Her threatening letters, what Caleb offered, what she refused—and then eventually accepted. There's even the cancelled check for a half million dollars, complete with her endorsement on the back.''

"No. I don't believe you.'' He glared down at her.

And her face softened, suddenly, with something that might have been pity. "It's all there. Look it over. Come to grips with the truth.'' She stood. "We can all use a little more truth around here, and that's a plain fact. And the truth is, your mother took Caleb's money and she ran off. Where do you think she got the start-up funds for those businesses you mentioned to me once—you know, the ones that failed?''

"No,'' he said. Again. He couldn't say it enough. "No, no…''

Katie refused to back down. "I'm sorry, Justin. I truly am. Sorry for you, for what you've become. I think, if there's ever going to be any hope for you, you're going to have face what your mother did. And accept it. You're going to have to admit how angry you are at her. Because I know, just from the few things you said to me about her, that she made your childhood a living hell.''

It wasn't her fault, he thought, as he'd been thinking for his whole life. *She did the best she could....*

Too bad his old excuses for the woman who'd raised him rang so hollow now.

And Katie wasn't finished. "What Caleb did was wrong. All wrong. Using your mother, and then trying to buy her off, to cut her out of your life, to take you away from her. He was so wrong. And now he's paying for it. But don't imagine he didn't want you. Don't even try to tell yourself he walked away from *you.* He would have claimed you, would have possibly lost Adele for your sake, would have taken the chance of putting Riley's childhood in jeopardy, if your mother had kept her end of their bargain."

Justin couldn't stay upright. He sank to a chair, muttered, one last time, "No. It can't be...."

"Justin. It *is.*"

He stared up at her—at the matchless woman he'd lost to his own blindness and pride. Right then, as he began to fully understand the depths to which he'd sunk, his mother's words came to him.

When I'm gone, you'll get your chance to make it all right.

He saw it all then, in a blinding burst of terrible clarity that had his stomach churning, and acid rising to his throat: the truth Katie spoke of.

He'd made nothing right. He'd only made a bad situation worse.

Yes. Katie was right. His anger with his mother went deeper than he'd ever realized.

But that anger was nothing against how much he was finding he despised himself.

"Go," he said. "Please. Go now."

Katie looked uncertain. A miracle, that woman. *His* miracle, lost forever to him now. He saw in her sweet face that, in spite of everything, she was afraid. For him.

He sat up straighter. "I'm not going to do anything...drastic. I'm going to sit here and read over the stuff in this envelope. I'm going to think about what you've said to me. I need to do that alone."

She swallowed. "All right, then. You may not believe this. But I do wish you well. And I hope that, somehow, you'll find a way to make peace. With Caleb. And with your mother's memory."

He forced a twisted smile. "Goodbye, Katie."

A shudder went through her. But she lifted her head high. "Yes. All right. Goodbye."

Chapter Fifteen

The next day, Justin Caldwell did something he'd never before done in his adult life. He called his office and said he had personal business to see to and he wouldn't be in.

Strange, now he thought of it. He really didn't have a personal life to speak of. He could think of only one other time when he might have needed a personal day and that was when his mother died.

But as it turned out, Ramona had died on a Saturday afternoon, so Justin had his "personal" days on the weekend and showed up at the office at nine Monday morning.

This time, the personal business in question consisted mostly of wandering around in his bathrobe, reading and rereading the letters in the envelope Katie had left with him—reading the letters and staring at the photographs of his father and mother, together.

And occasionally, picking up that cancelled check with his mother's signature on the back of it and wondering…

At his blind, thoughtless and pigheaded father.

At the selfish vengefulness of his mother.

Really, when it came down to it, blood did tell. Hadn't their son turned out to be all those things?

Blind, thoughtless, pigheaded, selfish—and vengeful.

Justin Caldwell. Biggest SOB on the planet, bar none.

The question now was: what the hell could he do about that?

All day long, wandering around his gorgeous, empty house in his bathrobe, he pondered that question. All day long, and into the evening.

It was a little after seven and he was starting to think that maybe he should make himself go into the kitchen and microwave something to put in his stomach, when the doorbell rang.

Katie…

His pulse started racing and his heart did something acrobatic inside his chest.

But the thrill quickly faded. It wouldn't be her. It *couldn't* be her. It was over between them. He knew it. At least in his mind. Over time, he hoped the rest of him—body, heart, soul—would learn to accept it.

Shaking his head at his own foolish yearning, he got up and went to the door.

"Mr. Caldwell. How are you?" Josiah Green stuck out a hand.

Baffled, Justin took it. They shook. "Er. What can I do for you?"

Green took in Justin's unshaved face and the bathrobe he'd never gotten around to changing out of. "Oh, my. I see I've come at an inopportune time."

It was the perfect excuse—but for some weird reason, Justin didn't take it. "Come on in."

After a moment's hesitation, Green came through the door and Justin shut it behind him. The tall, somber fellow wore a long black coat over what appeared to be the same ministerial black getup he'd worn the day Justin and Katie exchanged their fake vows. "Well. Can I take your coat?"

"Thank you." He had an envelope in his hand— an envelope like the one Katie had brought the night before. Bizarre. "Hold this, please."

Justin took the envelope and Green removed his coat and laid it over one of the two entrance hall chairs. When Justin tried to hand the envelope back, Green put up a lean, long-fingered hand. "No. That's yours."

"I don't understand."

"Ahem. Well. We shall get to it." Weirder by the minute. Green said, "Right now, I'd so enjoy a cup of nice, hot coffee."

Justin blinked. "Coffee."

"Yes. Please." Green gave him a tight little smile.

"Uh. Well, okay. This way."

They proceeded to the kitchen, where Justin set the envelope on the table and Green took a seat.

"I'll just get the coffee going."

"Bless you."

While the coffee dripped, they spoke of the weather—the warming trend had ended; snow was predicted for tomorrow—and of how Green admired Justin's lovely home.

"And, may I ask," the older man inquired with some delicacy, "where is your charming bride?"

Katie.

Didn't he have it bad enough, trying not to think of her, without some crazy old guy showing up at his door and asking where she was? He peered more closely at the old guy in question. "I have one question."

"Certainly. Ask away."

"What's going on here?"

Green did a little throat-clearing. "Well. Sadly, I must inform you that, while you and your bride are married in the eyes of Our Lord, the state of Montana has its own rules."

"Rules?" Justin repeated, for lack of anything better to say. He sincerely was not following.

Green tapped the envelope. "I've brought you your marriage license. I'm afraid I was somewhat remiss when I stepped forward to lead you through your vows a week ago last Saturday."

"Uh. Remiss?"

Green chided, "It appears the two of you never applied for this license. When I attempted to file it, I was told they had no record of your application. Nowadays, I regret to inform you, the blessing of a man of God is simply not enough."

Without a doubt. Weirder by the minute. "You mean you actually are…a minister?"

Green snapped his thin shoulders back. "Well, of course I'm a minister."

Justin put up a hand. "Look. Sorry."

"Ahem. Well. All right, then. Your apology is graciously accepted."

"Thanks. But I thought you understood. That 'wedding' was a reenactment. It wasn't—"

"There are no reenactments in the eyes of heaven," Green cut in reprovingly before Justin could finish. "One does. Or one doesn't. You did. So don't mistake me, young man, Katherine *is* your wife in the eyes of the Lord, and those eyes, as you should very well know, are the ones that truly matter. Ahem." He frowned. "Now, where was I?"

As if Justin had a clue. "Something about applying for a license, I think.…"

"Yes. Well, and that is the crux of it. You and Katherine must go immediately to the county clerk's office and apply for a valid license, then the marriage can be resolemnified and all will be well. I will be pleased to perform the ceremony for you, if you would like me to do so. But any ordained minister will certainly suffice. Legally, you can simply say your vows at the courthouse, if that's your bent." Green put a dark emphasis on the word, *bent,* making it crystal clear that he felt all marriages should be *solemnified* by a man of God.

And Justin hadn't the faintest idea what to say to all this. It seemed to him that the old guy might be a little off in the head—in a harmless sort of way. So he simply announced, "Coffee's ready."

"Wonderful. Two sugars. No cream."

Fifteen minutes later, after handing Justin a card, "In case you should wish to request my services for the ceremony," Green put on his big, black coat and went out the door.

He left the envelope on the kitchen table.

Justin tried to ignore it. But it was like his mother's letters, like the photographs of her and Caleb, like that damn cancelled check.

The envelope on the kitchen table would not be ignored.

He microwaved some canned spaghetti and sat at the table to eat it, his gaze tracking to the waiting envelope after every bite.

Finally, muttering a string of very bad words, he pushed his plate away and grabbed the damn thing.

He pulled out the license and stared down at it. "Katie…" he whispered to the empty room. With a shaking finger, he traced the letters in her name. "I love you."

He said the three impossible words and he knew they were true.

Out of all the lies, all the dirty tricks, out of everything he'd done so very wrong.

This one truth remained.

He loved Katie Fenton.

He loved her.

It was all wrong and it was too late.

But that didn't change the basic truth.

He loved Katie.

And now it was up to him do what he could—though it would never be enough—to make the wrongs he'd done right.

Chapter Sixteen

At eight-thirty on Monday morning, Justin entered the Thunder Canyon Ski Resort Project offices through the front door.

He found Caleb's secretary standing behind her desk in the reception area, packing a large cardboard box. She glanced up and gasped.

He tried a friendly smile. "Alice, isn't it?"

Alice didn't smile back. Instead, in a clear attempt to show the evil man before her exactly how she felt about the current situation, she adjusted her thick-lensed glasses more firmly on the bridge of her pointed nose and dropped a bronze paperweight into the box—hard. "We have until nine," she announced loftily. "Certainly you can wait until then."

He spoke gently. "Alice. You were never asked to leave."

"I prefer *Ms.* Pockstead—and I'm Mr. Douglas's assistant. He goes, I go."

Justin nodded. "Ms. Pockstead, I completely understand." He waited while she threw a stapler and a red coffee mug with dancing white hearts on it into the box. Then he cautiously cleared his throat. She sent him a hot glare. "What *is* it?"

"I wonder, is Caleb in?"

For that, he got another gasp of outrage and a tightly muttered, "The unmitigated nerve of some people…" She tossed some pencils and a ruler in the box, simmering where she stood.

Justin moved a step closer and injected a note of command into his next question. "I asked you, is he in?"

Ms. Pockstead picked up a letter opener and stabbed the air in the direction of the hallway that led to Caleb's private office. "See for yourself."

"Thank you."

She muttered something. It wasn't, *You're welcome.*

The door to Caleb's office stood slightly ajar. Justin hesitated in front of it. There was silence from inside the room beyond.

But he couldn't stand there forever. With some reluctance, he lifted a hand and tapped lightly.

"What the hell now?" grumbled the gruff voice from the other side. "It's open."

Justin flattened his palm against the door and pushed it inward.

Caleb sat at his desk surrounded by open, half-packed boxes. He appeared, at the moment, to be doing nothing about filling them.

He glanced up. Something sparked in his eyes—and then went cold. "Justin."

"Hello, Caleb."

They regarded each other. Justin had no idea what, exactly, he should say. He got the impression Caleb was having the same problem.

Finally, Caleb put out a hand at the guest chairs facing the desk. "Sit. If you've a mind to."

It seemed like as good a suggestion as any. Justin strode over, moved a box to the floor, and took one of the chairs.

They looked at each other some more. Eventually, Caleb inclined his head at the boxes surrounding him. "Sitting down on the job, I'm afraid. But I'm working on it."

How to begin, Justin was thinking.

Hell. *Where* to begin...

Caleb must have been pondering the same questions, because, again, he spoke first. "Katie said she told you...everything."

Justin found the best he could manage right then was a nod.

Caleb nodded, too. A lot of nodding going on. Oh, yeah. They were a couple of nodding fools.

Caleb said, "Well, then. It's all out in the open." He grunted. "I have to keep reminding myself how that's good. I..." He paused, seeming to seek the right words. Evidently he found them, or close enough. He said, "I understand now, why you did what you did at the meeting last week. Given the

circumstances, I've got no damn problem with it."
He raised both hands, indicating the office—the
whole ski resort project. "In a half an hour or so, it's
all yours." Justin started to speak, but Caleb cut him
off before he got a word out. "What you did to Katie,
though. No damn excuse for that."

"I know," Justin said.

Caleb stared at him, narrowed-eyed. And then he
grunted again. "Hope you do. You threw away a
good one. The very best, as a matter of fact."

"You don't have to tell me."

"Hell. I guess I don't. I can see it in your eyes."
He sat back. "You love my girl, don't you?"

Justin reminded himself that he was through with
lies. He gave Caleb the painful truth. "Yes. I do. I
love her."

Caleb pondered that for a moment, then he
shrugged. "Well. Evidently you're not as big of a fool
as I'd been thinking—and don't go imagining you're
the only one who's trifled with a good and loving
heart. I've done the same thing, as you damn well
know."

Justin said nothing. He was realizing that here was
another way he was like this man who'd fathered him.

"Your mother," Caleb said softly. "She was a
good woman. A good woman done wrong. She
couldn't…get past that, what I did to her, that's all."

Justin waved a hand. "She's gone now."

"Don't judge her."

"I'm working on it. Your…wife?"

It took Caleb a moment to answer that one. "Addy
and me, we've been together too long to give up now.

She's not happy with me. But I've got hopes that someday…'' He let that sentence finish itself. "Riley, though. I don't know. He's not in a mood for forgiving.''

"Give him time.''

"Time.'' Caleb chuckled, a dry sound with no real laughter in it. "Well.'' He stood. "Better get this junk packed up.''

Justin stood, too. "Put it back where it came from.'' Caleb blinked. And Justin continued, "I put my man on something else. This is your project and you're fully capable of seeing it through to a successful conclusion. I'm leaving it to you, where it always belonged. And I'll be pulling out completely, as soon as I find some other solid investors to step in and fill the gap.''

Caleb sank to his chair again. "You don't have to do this.''

"Yeah. Yeah, I do—and don't even think of trying to turn me down. I'm out. And you're going to be needed here.''

Caleb looked up at him. "Don't pull out. Stay in.''

Justin frowned. "That's probably a bad idea.''

"No. It's a good one. An excellent one. Stay in. We'll make a little money together. We'll give a shot in the arm to the local economy and we'll…start getting to know each other.''

"You want that?''

"Yeah, I do. I want that a lot.''

"Let me think about it.''

"Take as long as you need. Just be sure the answer's yes.''

* * *

Caleb called him at home at seven that night. Skipping right over anything resembling hello, he said, "So. You made up your mind yet?"

Justin couldn't hold back a chuckle. "I thought I was supposed to take all the time I needed."

"You've had time enough. Say yes."

He'd already decided, anyway. "All right. I'm in."

"Good. You have a nice night, now." And the line went dead.

Justin took the phone away from his ear and stared at it, shaking his head. Then, gently, he set it down.

He turned for the table where the remains of his solitary dinner waited to be cleared off. The job only took a few minutes.

Then he went out to his study, where he booted up his laptop and settled in for a few hours of work on a new project he was putting together.

The doorbell rang at five to eight. He hit the save key and got up to answer.

The last person in the world he'd ever expected to see was waiting beyond the front door.

"Katie." Damned if his heart didn't do a forward roll.

She looked up at him, brown eyes gleaming, soft cheeks flushed. There was snow on her shoulders, sparkling in her chestnut hair. She brushed at it. "Caleb said you wanted to see me."

His mind was a fog of hope and yearning. "Caleb…"

Her sweet face fell. "He…was wrong?"

"No," he said—so forcefully that she jumped back.

He tried again, more gently. "No. Caleb was absolutely right."

"Well. So, then?" She managed a hopeful smile. "Do you think maybe I might come in?"

He gaped at her, and then, at last, he remembered to speak. "Yeah. Absolutely. Come in."

Chapter Seventeen

He took her coat, his heart racing like a runaway train at the mere fact that she'd handed it over.

Because, after all, if she let him take her coat, that meant she would stay, didn't it? At least for a little while.

He shook the remaining snow off it, set it on the entry hall chair and led her through to the great room. "Sit down. Please."

She perched on a long sofa. "I…" She seemed to be doing a lot of swallowing. He understood. His throat kept locking up, too. She tried again. "Emelda tells me you made a generous donation to the Historical Society—very generous, is what she said."

He looked down at her, astounded. Amazed. Was there ever a woman so damned, incredibly beautiful?

No. He was sure of it. She was one of a kind.

"Justin?"

"Yeah?"

"You're staring."

He gulped again. "Uh. Sorry. Listen, want some coffee? I made it an hour ago, but it should still be okay."

Her gaze scanned his face, sweetly. Hungrily.

Or was that just him seeing what he wanted to see?

"Coffee," she repeated.

"Yeah. You think?"

"Yes. Okay. I'll have some."

"Stay right there."

She let out a nervous little giggle. "Well, Justin. Where would I go?"

He raced for the kitchen, poured the damn coffee—two mugfuls, since it seemed a little rude to let her drink hers alone. He remembered she liked cream and splashed some into hers. Then he rushed back to the great room, coffee sloshing across the Kelim area rugs as he went.

When he got back to her, she was standing at a narrow section of wall between two wide windows, looking at...

Damn. She was never supposed to see that.

He'd never dared to imagine she'd set foot in his house again, or he wouldn't have put the thing up.

She turned to him. "Justin? That's the fake license. From that day at the town hall."

"Uh..." He scooted over and plunked the mugs down on a low table. Coffee, still sloshing, dribbled down the sides.

"It is, isn't it?"

He rubbed his hands together, brushing off the coffee he'd spilled on them. "Well, yeah. That's what it is."

She came toward him. He watched her as she moved, devouring her with his eyes. When she stood about a foot from him, she asked, "Where did you get it?"

Her scent swam around him. His fingers itched to grab for her. To keep them busy, he gestured at the table. "Coffee. There you go."

"Justin." Her voice was so soft. And the tiniest, most radiant smile had begun at the corners of that mouth he wanted so badly to kiss. She touched his arm. He felt that touch all the way down to the center of his soul. "Where did you get it?"

"Josiah Green."

"Our fake minister?"

"Turns out he wasn't a fake. A little eccentric maybe, but not a fake."

"You're kidding. The real thing?"

He managed a nod.

"He gave you the license?"

"He did."

"But why?"

His throat loosened a little and he told her about Green's visit, about the things the old guy had said.

She hadn't removed her hand from his arm. Her touch burned him. He was going up in flames.

She said, "Caleb says you love me. Is that true?"

Struck mute again, he could only nod.

"Oh, Justin…"

He knew she needed more than that. Hell, *he* needed more than that. "I... Katie, I know the things I did were wrong. Unforgivable, even. I know I blew it. Lost you. Lost the best thing that ever happened to me. That's why I had that fake license framed. I hung it on the wall, where I'd see it all the time. Where I'd remember, what might have been. If only I hadn't—"

"Justin."

"What, damn it?"

"Close your eyes."

"I don't—"

"Just do it. Close your eyes."

"Hell." But he did what she asked.

And as he stood there, blind before her, he felt her warm breath against his neck, felt the living, sweet-scented heat of her.

She whispered, "Personally, I *believe*. In forgiveness. I believe in hope. And faith. And..."

"Wishes," he whispered. He didn't know where that word came from. Or maybe he did.

"Yes." It came out on a gentle breath. "Yes." That *yes* shivered through him. He felt it echo, in the beating of his heart. "Wishes," she said. "Wishes that can come true. If you..."

"Make them."

"If you're—"

"Done with lying. With dirty tricks."

"Oh, yes. That's right. Wishes and hope and faith. And forgiveness. I do believe in them, Justin. I believe in *you*."

It was too much.

It was everything.

Every wish he never dared to make.

Every dream he'd never known how to believe in.

All of it. Right here.

Everything. Katie.

She put her hands on his shoulders. A shudder went through him. And he felt her lift up, on tiptoe, to place a kiss on each of his lowered eyelids, one and then the other.

And that did it. He couldn't keep still one second longer.

He opened his eyes and he reached for her.

With a happy, willing cry, she came into his arms.

He lifted her high against his chest and, holding her close, knowing he'd never, ever let her go, he carried her out of the high-ceilinged room, away from all those dark windows, down a long hallway to his bedroom.

They undressed each other, quickly, hands shaking, sharing kisses and nervous, eager glances—soft whispers, and yet more kisses.

At last she stood before him, slim and proud, her body gleaming, pale and pearly, in the dimness.

''Katie…''

She held her head high, and she looked right back at him. ''Justin.''

He swept her up again, carried her to the bed and laid her down on it.

And he kissed her. Kissed every fragrant, smooth,

beautiful inch of her, lingering at her breasts, her belly, her thighs.

He kissed his way up them, and then he parted her and he kissed her some more, there, at the wet, hot feminine heart of her, as she called out his name, her soft fingers tangled in his hair.

When she came, he drank her, taking her release inside of him. So sweet. So exactly what he'd never dared, till now, to dream of.

She touched his shoulders, reaching, urging him up over her. He settled—so carefully, his body aching for her—between her open thighs.

He looked down at her, met those shining eyes. "Your first time?"

She pressed her lips together and nodded. "It's what I want, though. You. You're what I want."

He didn't want to leave her. Not even for a moment. But there was protection to consider. "I should…" Her sweet heat was all around him, her body pliant, ready. "We need to…"

She caught his face between her hands. "What Reverend Green said…we're married. Right? How did you say he said it?"

He groaned. "In the eyes of heaven."

"Oh, yes. I…well, don't say I'm crazy. But I like that. I *believe* in that. And if there was a baby…"

A baby. Incredible.

She asked, so softly, "Would that be all right with you?"

It *was* crazy. Absolutely insane. But he found that it would. He swallowed. Hard. And he managed to croak out, "Yeah."

And she wrapped her satiny legs around him. "Then it's okay...it's all right."

He made himself go slowly, pushing in just a little, holding still...waiting.

It was the sweetest kind of agony—the pleasure, within the pain. He held still and he kissed her—eyes, cheeks, nose, chin. He whispered, "Slowly...slowly..."

She moaned and held him, her sleek body moving, then going still. He pushed in farther—felt resistance and then, at last, the slow, gentle opening.

Welcoming.

It took forever. An eternity of slow, controlled degrees.

Until at last, he felt himself fully within her. "Don't...move..." he pleaded on a ragged sigh.

But she had other ideas. "I...I have to. Oh, Justin. I need..." And her hips began to rock him. "I need...you. You. Only."

He kissed the words from her lips and gave them back to her. "Only you."

The pleasure took over, all the words flew away. They rode an endless, swirling river of it, of pleasure. It sucked him into a whirlpool. He went spinning...

Spinning.

And then it centered down.

Down into Katie. Into the soft pulsing of her heat and wetness all around him.

He let out a cry, tossing his head back. And she cried out in answer.

The rest was soft sighs, tender caresses.

"I love you," she whispered.

And he could only smile.

* * *

It was an hour later when he dared to suggest, "Marry me. Again."

She looked up at him from under the sable fringe of her lashes. "Yes. I will."

"Soon," he demanded.

"Oh, absolutely. And in the town hall. With everyone in Thunder Canyon invited. And the Reverend Green presiding. What do you think?"

"I think, yes. Beyond a shadow of a doubt. No conditions. Yes."

"Just one thing."

"Anything. Everything."

She laughed then, and the sound banished all darkness. It filled up the world with golden light.

"Promise me," she said. "No free beer."

So he promised, sealing it—and all the other, more important promises—with a tender kiss.

Epilogue

On the first Saturday in February, Katie and Justin said their vows for the second time, in the town hall. In spite of the blizzard gathering force outside, the old hall was packed. The bride, radiant in white satin, had asked Caleb to give her away. Riley stood up as Justin's best man. The eccentric Reverend Green, looking pleased with himself *and* the proceedings, officiated.

When the reverend asked Katie if she would take Justin to be her lawfully wedded husband—to love him, to honor and to cherish him for as long as they both should live—Katie, so often soft-spoken, especially in crowds, answered loud and clear.

"I will." Her brown eyes shone. Her face was suffused with a glow of pure joy.

After the vow-sealing kiss, the party began, right

there in the hall. Montana Gold, a band of local boys, took the stage and a generous buffet, laid out on long tables, eased the appetites of the assembled guests. Beer was limited, as per the bride's instructions.

But there was champagne, and it flowed freely. When the band took its first break, the toasting began. Caleb was delivering a long speech about true love and happiness and getting through the tough times, when Cameron Stevenson's seven-year-old, Erik, sneaked up on the stage and started banging on the keyboards. Caleb sent a quelling look over his shoulder at the boy, who quickly moved on to the drums. With a crashing sound, the high hat tumbled to the stage.

Cam went after Erik, then, and led him off, but everyone laughed and burst into raucous clapping and catcalls.

After the toasts and speeches, Katie and Justin cut the enormous cake. As Adele supervised the cake distribution, the band took over again for a second set.

Several men pitched in to push the tables back against the wall and Caleb led Katie out on the floor. They danced, but not for long. Justin cut in.

As the citizens of Thunder Canyon applauded the bride and groom's first dance, Justin whispered, "Happy?"

Katie looked up at him, all her love shining in her eyes. "Happy doesn't even begin to describe it."

He pulled her closer. She settled her head against his shoulder. Other couples joined them, filling the floor.

When that dance ended, the band swung into another number. Katie stayed where she wanted to be: held close in Justin's loving arms. The band played on. They danced every dance.

It was no time at all until Montana Gold announced their second break. Justin took Katie's hand and led her to the sidelines, where a special table had been set up specifically for the bride and groom and family.

Adele was just serving them each a piece of cake, when Cam Stevenson edged his way toward them through the milling crowd.

One look at Cam's too-pale face, and Katie knew there was trouble.

Cam bent down to ask her, "Have you seen Erik?"

She shook her head. "But he's probably out in the foyer. I saw a bunch of the kids heading that way."

"No. He's not there. I looked."

"Did you look—?"

"Everywhere, damn it. I've been all through the building."

Justin was already on his feet. "Come on. Let's look again. He can't have gone far...."

* * * * *

*Don't miss the second book in the
exciting new Special Edition continuity,*

MONTANA MAVERICKS:
GOLD RUSH GROOMS

*When Erik Stevenson goes missing, his
father teams up with a beautiful
rescue worker to find him in*
ALL HE EVER WANTED
by
reader favorite
Allison Leigh

*Coming February 2005
Available wherever
Silhouette Books are sold.*

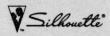

™ SPECIAL EDITION™

**This month, Silhouette Special Edition
brings you the newest
Montana Mavericks story**

ALL HE EVER WANTED

(SE #1664)

by reader favorite

Allison Leigh

When young Erik Stevenson fell down an abandoned
mine shaft, he was lucky to be saved by a brave—and
beautiful—rescue worker, Faith Taylor. She was struck by
the feelings that Erik's handsome father, Cameron, awoke
in her scarred heart and soul. But Cameron's heart had
barely recovered from the shock of losing his wife some
time ago. Would he be able to put the past aside—and
find happiness with Faith in his future?

GOLD RUSH GROOMS

Lucky in love—and striking it rich—
beneath the big skies of Montana!

**Don't miss this emotional story—
only from Silhouette Books.**

Available at your favorite retail outlet.

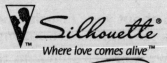

Where love comes alive™

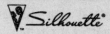

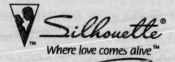

If you enjoyed what you just read,
then we've got an offer you can't resist!

Take 2 bestselling love stories FREE!
Plus get a FREE surprise gift!

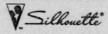